D0403583

WESTWARD DREAMS SERIES

WESTWARD DREAMS SERIES

Runaway Heart

JANE PEART

BOOK I

ZondervanPublishingHouse

Grand Rapids, Michigan

A Division of HarperCollins*Publishers*

Runaway Heart
Copyright © 1994 by Jane Peart

Zondervan Books is an imprint of:
The Zondervan Publishing House
Grand Rapids, Michigan 49530

ISBN 1-56865-149-X

Printed in the United States of America

PART 1

To travel hopefully is better than to arrive.

R. S. Stevenson

Perhaps one day this, too, will be pleasant to remember.

Virgil

Chapter 1

*J*ust before sundown a stagecoach, rattling and swaying precariously, lurched down the rutted road into the small Oregon town, sending up cartwheels of dust in its wake.

Inside, its only remaining passenger, Holly Lambeth, clinging desperately to the hand strap, slid from side to side on the tattered leather seat, terrified that the vehicle might pitch over at any minute.

At last with a bone-jarring jolt it came to a stop. Drawing a deep sigh of relief, Holly wiped the small mud-spattered window and peered out hopefully. Before she could get a good look, the coach door was yanked open by the grizzle-bearded driver who stuck his head inside and, displaying tobacco-stained teeth, announced, "This here's Riverbend, lady. This is where you get off. End of the line."

Ignoring her qualms of the probable truth of his statement, she gathered the tiered skirt of her peacock-blue traveling suit, crisp and smart three days ago but now quite the worse for wear, and prepared to get out. Lifting it carefully over two layers of ruffled petticoats, she stepped gingerly down the rickety steps onto the wooden sidewalk.

It felt good to stretch her stiff muscles after the long, cramped journey over rough winding roads. For a moment she stood straightening her snug braid-trimmed jacket, then slowly pivoted to look about her. Just then a gust of wind caught her tiny feathered bonnet, tugging the pins that held it, loosening strands of her russet-brown hair from its coil, and blowing dust and grit into her face. Grabbing her hat brim with one kid-gloved hand, she fumbled into her purse for a handkerchief, then lifted her veil to dab her eyes.

Since it was close to six o'clock and therefore supper hour for most of Riverbend's citizens, there were only a few people on hand as the stage arrived; otherwise, the appearance of a fashionably dressed young woman might have received more than one or two curious glances.

Holly Lambeth was used to drawing admiring looks. In spite of having a peach-bloom complexion, long-lashed hazel eyes, and a dimpled smile, Holly would never be considered beautiful. What made her so attractive was her vivacity and sparkle.

That sparkle, however, was sadly missing now. As she gazed around with mounting dismay, Holly's conviction grew that she had made the *second* worst mistake of her twenty-three years. The first and worst, of course, was to have kept Jim Mercer dangling for over a year in an "on-again, off-again" engagement.

The sun began slowly slipping behind a rim of purple hills. Overhead dark clouds gathered.

This must be the center of town. Holly glanced down the long unpaved road where the signpost read "Main Street." It was lined with an odd assortment of buildings. Some were old weather-beaten wooden ones with sagging balconies, others of raw brick, some uncompleted. Wheelbarrows of bricks stood abandoned as if left by workers.

So *this* was Riverbend, Oregon.

Numb with fatigue, Holly bit her lower lip and fought back the tears that threatened, tightening her throat. There was no use telling herself it was her own fault she was here. Her family and friends had all been quick to tell her that.

But at the time, "*any* port in a storm" had seemed the answer to her problem, the "storm" being the gossip whirling around her when the fact that she had been jilted became known. Anything had seemed better than facing the curious looks, the whispers, the pitying glances that had followed her. Even harder to bear were the smugly spiteful looks of those who made it no secret that they thought it was high time Holly Lambeth got her "come-uppance."

Now that it was too late, she realized she had been vain and foolish in recklessly risking Jim's love and patience with all her silly flirtations, her careless disregard for his pride. If only . . .

But it was too late for "if only." She had nobody to blame but herself that she was here in a forsaken Oregon frontier town instead of planning a fairy-tale wedding, with a white lace gown and veil, walking arm-in-arm with her army-lieutenant husband beneath an arch of crossed sabers held by his West Point classmates.

As if it had just happened, Holly felt the shock of that morning when she had read in the local paper, along with the rest of Willow Springs, the announcement of Lt. Jim Mercer's marriage to the daughter of his commanding officer at his first army post.

"This all yours, miss?" The whiskey voice of the driver cut through her remorseful memory. With a start, Holly turned to follow his dirty index finger pointing to his helper on top of the stagecoach, straddling her trunk and unstrapping it.

"Yes, and please be careful—," she began, but her voice was lost in the noise of the tumbling luggage. Holly was forced to jump back as her trunk catapulted down and landed at her feet. She gasped and was about to reprimand the fellow sharply when he hollered down, "Anything else?"

"Yes, my valise and hatbox, and please—," she started to caution again when the valise and hatbox, containing her very best bonnet, came hurtling down in the same manner as her trunk.

"Well!" she gasped indignantly. But whatever else she might have said was checked by the surly expression on the driver's face. She realized he was expecting a gratuity, highly undeserved in her opinion. Under his glare she dug into her purse and handed him a coin. Acknowledging it with only a pull on the soiled brim of his battered felt hat, the man turned and shuffled down the street.

It came as no surprise to Holly to see him push his way through the doors of the nearby saloon, the Nugget. She had observed that this was his custom at every stagecoach station en route, a practice that had not done much to lessen her anxiety, traveling the treacherous mountain roads on the way to Riverbend.

The one he now entered was one of several other such establishments along Main Street with names like Last Chance and the Doggoned Best. Most of Holly's information about the far West had been gained from the covers on the pulp magazines confiscated by her cousin Willy's mother from his hidden horde. These depicted lurid scenes of cowboy shoot-outs, Indian attacks, and barroom brawls. Looking down the unpaved street lined with saloons, she felt as if she might have stepped right into the pages of one.

Before being hit by her next attack of second thoughts on her fateful decision to come West, she heard a familiar male voice behind her say, "Cousin Holly?" Holly whirled around to find herself face-to-face with Ned Thornton.

"Oh, Ned! It's so wonderful to see you!" she exclaimed holding out both hands to him.

When his kind, homely face turned crimson, Holly realized she may have greeted him too effusively. Belatedly she remembered that Ned had been one of the many young men flocking around her at Willow Springs parties, hoping to add his name to her dance card. He'd had quite a case on her then—now, of course, he was married to her cousin Hetty Granville. The same Hetty who was providing her "a port in the storm."

"Welcome to Riverbend, Holly," Ned stammered.

Trying to allay any embarrassment Ned's own memories might be causing him, Holly rushed on, "Is Hetty with you? Where are the children? I can't wait to see them."

"They're all at home. They're so excited about their cousin's coming all the way from Kentucky that they've run Hetty crazy with questions all day. Hetty's fixed a real special supper so we best get along home or else she'll be might—" Ned stopped abruptly and pointed to her three pieces of luggage. "Are these yours?"

"Yes, but I can carry my hatbox and valise," Holly said.

Shouldering Holly's small trunk, Ned told her, "It's not very far. It's only a short walk. We live just at the end of town so I

10

can be near the store. You knew, didn't you, I have the General Store? That's it right over there." There was a note of pride in Ned's voice as he nodded his head to a neat-looking building across the street.

"Yes, I do know, Ned. I've heard you've done very well. Of course Hetty has written to her folks, Aunt Dolly and Uncle Sid. We all think it's fine you and Hetty have made such a good life for yourselves. Although it does seem awfully far from home." How far, Holly was just beginning to realize.

"It's a good place and it's growing. The railroad's going to be coming in here before long—branch line through here between Portland and Sacramento. That's going to bring a lot more people and more business here. Everyone's counting on that. Thirty years ago this was just a raw gold-mining camp, but the vein ran out within a few years. Then homesteaders came here and brought their families. Farmers came and prospered. This is fine orchard country; Riverbend's becoming famous for its pear crop. Yes, indeed, Riverbend's turned into a solid township. One day folks think it will become the county seat," Ned said with conviction. "It's home now to me—to us."

Good for Ned, Holly thought as they walked along. Ned had been wise to leave Willow Springs, move out from under the shadow of his critical father, a prominent judge, and his older brother, a brilliant lawyer. Evidently here Ned had become his own man, made a place for himself. And, Holly reminded herself a bit ruefully, Hetty had been smart enough to see his potential and marry him.

Holly doubted her cousin's welcome would be as genuine as Ned's. The truth was she and Hetty had never been friends. In spite of the facts their mothers were sisters and throughout childhood the girls were constantly thrown together at family gatherings of the Lambeth and Granville clans, they had always clashed. Holly considered Hetty a prig, a tattle-tale, a goodie-goodie, and Hetty accused her of being a showoff, a tomboy, and a tease. Both of them were right.

As they grew up it was worse, and the differences between them became more pronounced. Holly developed into a young lady of natural charm and gaiety that was enormously appealing. Unfortunately Hetty inherited her father's plain looks and prickly personality instead of her pretty mother's sociability. While Holly's fun-loving vivaciousness attracted many beaux, Hetty became a typical wallflower. Of course, now the shoe was on the other foot. Hetty was married to a prosperous man, had children and a home, while Holly remained unmarried and possibly on the brink of becoming an old maid!

Well, whatever their past differences, Holly determined to try to get along with Hetty. Surely they were beyond all their old squabbles. She would do her best to make herself useful, helpful, and be cheerful, making sure Hetty wasn't sorry she'd offered her cousin a temporary haven.

These mental resolutions were interrupted when a tall man stepped out of the door of one of the buildings in front of them. "Evenin' Ned."

"Evenin', Adam," Ned replied. Putting down Holly's trunk on the wooden sidewalk, he turned to her saying, "Holly, this is Adam Corcoran, the editor of our local newspaper, the *Riverbend Monitor*. Adam, I'd like you to meet Hetty's cousin, Miss Hollis Lambeth."

Holly set down her valise, gratefully. It was heavier than she thought, jammed with last-minute things she'd forgotten to put in her trunk.

At Ned's introduction Adam Corcoran removed his broad-brimmed hat, bowed slightly. "Delighted, Miss Lambeth." The fast-fading light cast shadows upon an angular face. Although the high-bridged nose gave a look of arrogance, that was offset by the humor in his eyes and his mouth under the well-trimmed mustache. "I take it you have just arrived? Then you have not yet had a chance to get much of an impression of Riverbend." He smiled. "And just how long to you plan to stay in *our fair city?*"

Holly thought she detected a hint of irony in his tone and had the feeling he might be baiting her. It made her uncomfortable, and she replied coolly, "I've not any definite plans as yet, but I'm sure I'll enjoy my visit however long."

"Ad, here, runs the newspaper practically single-handed. Besides writing all the articles and doing all the reporting, he helps Tom Simmons set type and gives young Mike Flannery a hand with the press."

"You didn't mention my editorials, Ned, and the fact that they are often controversial and not always well received. We also print some pretty outraged letters to the editor and have had a few smashed windows—mainly on Saturday night!" Looking directly at Holly, Adam said, "What Ned's too polite to tell you, Miss Lambeth, is that I'm not the most popular man in town."

"I wouldn't say that." Ned shook his head. "You give folks a lot to talk about. Debate never hurt anything."

Adam threw back his head and laughed a rich, full laugh. "Ned, you should have been a diplomat instead of a storekeeper. Or maybe, better still, a politician. Let me know if you ever want to run for mayor or—"

"Not me, not ever." Ned joined in the laughter, then said, "Well, we best be getting on home. Hetty'll be wondering what's keeping us. I'm sure she probably saw the stage arrive, and the children will be driving her crazy. Even when I went home at noon for dinner, they were already asking if it was time yet and running to the window to see if their cousin Holly had arrived."

"I wish you a very pleasant stay in Riverbend, Miss Lambeth, and I'm sure we'll meet again."

Adam Corcoran's voice held a confidence that annoyed Holly, so she merely nodded, then picked up her valise again, and moved on with Ned.

They had gone only a few more steps along the uneven boardwalk when a small, shabby, black buggy pulled to a stop on the road beside them. A man called out, "Howdy, Ned! Did my box of medical supplies come in on the stage?"

The man leaned farther out, took off his hat, ran his hand through a shock of thick hair, and greeted Holly.

"Howdy, Doc!" Ned responded. "Not unless it was on this last one. I haven't had a chance to check the freight yet. I had to meet my wife's cousin from Kentucky who came in this evening." Ned indicated Holly, saying, "Miss Hollis Lambeth."

13

To her he said, "Holly, I'd like you to meet the most important man in town, our doctor, Blaine Stevens."

The man in the buggy took off his hat, leaned farther out, and greeted Holly, "Good evening, Miss Lambeth, welcome to Riverbend. I hope you had a pleasant journey."

While Holly hesitated between truth and exaggeration, Ned answered for her. "Well, that kind of depends what you mean by pleasant, I guess." He chuckled. "It was Joe Rossiter's run—"

"Oh, no! Not *Joe Rossiter!*" the doctor affected a look of horror. Even as he shook his head, he laughed. "What an introduction to Riverbend! I've ridden with Joe a time or two myself. It's like being with one of those circus stunt riders! I sure hope it didn't ruin your impression of Oregon!"

"Well, not completely," Holly retorted, dimples appearing at his accurate description, adding saucily, "—*but* my fondness for stagecoach travel has been severely impaired!"

A boyish grin showed that he appreciated her humor. For the next few minutes they conducted a lively exchange on the dangers of stagecoach travel and tipsy drivers while Ned looked on with indulgent amusement. Then, almost mid-sentence, Holly checked herself. This was just the sort of unconscious flirtatiousness Jim had resented in her. He had accused her of flirting with any man in sight. It was just this kind of behavior that had landed her in her present situation, she reminded herself. Hadn't she promised herself she was cured of it forever? No matter how attractive the man was—and she had to admit Dr. Blaine Stevens certainly was—

Abruptly Holly suppressed a jesting remark, the dimples vanished, and she tried compressing her mouth into a prim line. Her sudden withdrawal from the conversation seemed to puzzle both men, and an awkward pause followed. Finally Blaine said, "Well, at least you made it here safely. I'm sure Hetty's delighted that she'll have someone from her hometown for a visit."

Holly, who was not at all sure of that, made no comment. But Ned did. "And speaking of Hetty, if we don't get home, she'll be sending out a posse to find us. The stage being late won't be enough excuse if supper's spoiled—"

"You *married* men have it rough all right, having to hurry

home to a good, hot, home-cooked meal after a hard day's work!" the doctor scoffed jovially.

"And you *bachelors* don't have to worry about a tongue-lashing if you're late!" was Ned's good-natured retort.

"Well, so long," Blaine said. "My regards to Hetty, and I hope to see you again, Miss Lambeth."

As they started walking again, Holly couldn't help wondering if all that emphasis on who was married and who was a bachelor in that joking exchange had been for *her* benefit. Was Ned setting her up with his good friend the doctor? But Holly dismissed the idea. She had other more immediate things on her mind. The closer they got to her cousin's home the more anxious she began to feel about her meeting with Hetty. After all it had been almost six years since they had seen each other.

"This is it, home sweet home," Ned declared, opening the gate of a picket fence in front of a neat board-and-batten house. They went up the path edged with familiar flowers that Holly guessed Hetty must have grown from seeds Aunt Dolly sent her. Just as they reached the porch steps, the front door was flung open and there stood Hetty.

The light from an oil lamp she was holding in one upraised hand fell on her face, making harsh shadows on her high cheekbones and strong jawline. Her hair was pulled straight back, and her narrowed eyes, glittering like jet beads, moved over Holly—not missing a single button, bow, or feather. She could not see the accumulated dust and stain of travel, only the stylish outfit her cousin was wearing, and Holly saw the expression on Hetty's face—a mixture of envy and dislike.

A chilling wave of certainty froze Holly. On Hetty's face she read the truth, the confirmation of all her doubts—that her cousin resented her coming—and that she was unwelcome.

Chapter 2

*Y*ou're late," Hetty said tersely to Ned before Holly even had a chance to speak.

"The stage was late, and then I had to close up the store and walk over to the hotel—," Ned began apologizing.

Holly chimed in, trying to smooth things over, "And then we met some friends of Ned's and stopped to chat—" When Hetty's face did not lose its stony expression, Holly attempted a quick change of subject and greeted her cousin cheerfully, "Well, Hetty! Hello! It was so nice of you to have me come."

Hetty's glacial gaze came back to rest on Holly. "It's the least I could do for kin," she replied stiffly.

More than a little taken aback by this "uncousinly" reception—a far cry from the kind the word "kin" she had used would ordinarily imply, at least in Willow Springs—Holly glanced at Ned as if seeking some explanation of Hetty's attitude, but Ned couldn't seem to meet Holly's eyes.

"Well, come in, don't stand there letting all the night air in," Hetty said sharply to Ned, then turned her back on both of them.

"You first, Holly," Ned murmured in a low voice.

Holly stepped inside while he followed with her trunk. She looked around at the large room and got a fleeting impression of starched calico curtains, a round table and chairs in the middle, and at the other end a big, shiny black stove.

"The parlor is in there," Hetty said, gesturing to a closed door to the right.

"We don't use it except on Sundays or when company's comin'," piped up a clear high voice.

"Mind your tongue, Aurelia."

When Hetty spoke, Holly turned to see a little girl wearing a starched pinafore, her coppery brown hair in tight braids bristling with bows, staring at her.

"Why, hello there!" Holly exclaimed.

"I'm Aurelia." The little girl took a step forward, smiling, then pointed a chubby finger at a small boy who was peering from behind one of the chairs drawn up to the table. "And that's Teddy."

"Well, Aurelia, come and give me a kiss! What a pretty name!" With her plump rosy cheeks, tiny turned-up nose, cornflower blue eyes sparkling with curiosity, the child seemed to Holly more like a miniature Aunt Dolly than like her mother. "And how pretty you are, too!"

"Don't talk nonsense," Hetty cut in sharply. "I don't want her getting silly notions about herself, her looks, or anything else."

Surprised to be chastised for such a spontaneous remark, Holly looked at her cousin. What she saw in Hetty's eyes was unveiled hostility. In a moment, Holly realized Hetty did not like her, never had, and nothing had changed. What she could do about *that*, at the moment, Holly had no idea.

Seemingly undaunted by her mother's curtness, Aurelia held up her hand, spreading her fingers, and announced, "I'm five. And Teddy's nearly four."

"Stop chattering, Aurelia," her mother reprimanded, then she turned to Holly, and pointedly eyeing the quantity of Holly's luggage, said, "I don't have a spare room. When we built this house we didn't count on having house guests, so you'll have to sleep in with the children." Her mouth pursed.

"Oh, don't worry about it, Hetty. I'll be just fine." Holly assured her quickly, stung by Hetty's use of the words "house guests." In Willow Springs *family* were never considered *guests*. Relatives were always welcomed warmly whether for one night or a week and

17

were usually urged to stay longer. Hetty was making it no secret that she considered having Holly here an imposition.

Hetty's chin jutted out defensively as if she knew how she had sounded. "Come along, I'll show you where to put your things."

"Let *me* show her, Mama!" begged Aurelia, coming over to Holly's side and slipping a tiny hand into hers.

Holly squeezed it gratefully. "Yes, *do* let Aurelia."

Frowning, Hetty looked at Aurelia then back to Holly, and then said, "Well, all right, go on. But don't be all day back there. Supper's ready to serve if it hasn't been ruined what with Ned's dawdling with his men friends—"

"I'll carry something," Aurelia offered, and Holly let her take the hatbox.

As they went hand in hand down the short hall, Holly could hear Hetty haranguing Ned about something.

"Here we are," Aurelia announced, pulling a little ahead of Holly and opening the door to the bedroom they were to share.

Holly entered, set down her valise, and looked around. There was a pine chest of drawers, a large bed with low posters, covered with a sunburst quilt in indigo-and-orange colors. Pushed against the wall on the other side of the room was a smaller cot.

"That's Teddy's," Aurelia told her. "He hid under the table when he heard you and Pa coming. He's shy."

Obviously *she* wasn't. Holly had the feeling that she and Aurelia would get along just fine.

While Holly took off her bonnet and rummaged through her valise for her hairbrush to remedy the havoc the long trip and the wind had done to her hair, Aurelia climbed up on the bed ready to chat. There was a narrow mirror hanging over the chest, and Holly went over to it and began taking out her hairpins. Watching her from her vantage point on the bed, Aurelia said, "When we knowed you was comin', Mama had Pa order that looking glass special to hang up there. Mama said we better have one because you liked to primp."

Holly was half-amused, half-annoyed at the remark. Of course, she realized the little girl spoke with the sublime innocence of childhood, just repeating what she'd heard. She won-

18

dered what else Hetty had said about her, and she asked casually, "Did your mama talk a lot about me before I came?"

"Oh, yes, after Grammum's letter came, she and Pa talked about it all the time. Then Pa said, 'That's enough, Hetty, she's comin', and that's all there is to it," Aurelia gave a little bounce after quoting her father.

Holly's cheeks flamed with humiliation at the thought that she had been discussed and almost refused the haven her aunt and mother had sought for her. In the aftershock of Jim's surprise engagement to another girl, Holly had been dazed and vulnerable to suggestion. She should never have succumbed to Aunt Dolly's persuasion to get out of town for awhile, away from all the gossip, to go on a long visit to her cousin in Oregon. *I should have known better.* Holly fumed inwardly, thinking of Hetty's cold greeting. *Well what did I expect? Hetty's still the sour little girl she always was. I should have remembered.*

Holly shook out her hair and brushed it vigorously until it made a crackling sound.

"Your hair is just *be-yootiful!*" Aurelia sighed. "You are *so* pretty! You're about the prettiest lady I've ever seen. Prettier than any of the ladies in this town, I think." She paused and for a long moment regarded Holly, her brow wrinkled, her curly head to one side, then asked, "So why aren't you married? Mama says you're an old maid, but you don't look old to me. And she said you were jilted. What's jilted, Holly?"

Resentment flared up in Holly. Hetty had certainly not hesitated to detail her private story even to her children! Was it just to Ned? Or did unknown listening "little pitchers have big ears"? And if Hetty had told her friends, how many other people in Riverbend knew Holly's personal disaster? Maybe the whole town knew! Maybe Adam Corcoran would feel it was newsworthy enough to print in the *Riverbend Monitor*. Holly flung down her brush in irritation.

Then realizing Aurelia was still observing her, waiting for an answer to her question, Holly went over to her, took the puzzled little face in both her hands, and kissed her cheeks. "Actually, Aurelia, being an 'old maid' means you just haven't been lucky enough yet to find a man to make happy."

"Oh, I see." Aurelia grinned, the answer seeming to satisfy her.

"Now, Aurelia, could you tell me—is there a—?"

Aurelia jumped off the bed. "Yes, I'll show you." She ran and opened the bedroom door saying over her shoulder, "I'd go with you, but I don't like going out there when it's dark."

Holly followed the little girl through the hall, out through a back door, and onto a porch. "That's it," Aurelia told her, pointing to a shedlike structure at the end of a large garden.

"I'll wait 'till you're done and walk back with you," Aurelia offered as Holly hurried along the flagstone path. When she rejoined the little girl, Holly said, "Thank you, Aurelia. Now I'll just wash up a bit and tidy myself then we'll go in for supper, all right?"

"Oh, yes. We're having roast chicken and dumplings, and peach pie for dessert. Do you like peach pie? Umhmm. I do! I think it's my favorite kind, 'less it's rhubarb and strawberry, but we only have that in the summertime—"

Aurelia went right on talking, not waiting for Holly to comment or make any reply. This gave Holly a chance to think while she poured water from the ironstone pitcher into the washbowl, getting ready to scrub some of the gritty grime of stagecoach travel from her face and hands. Taking her toilette case from the valise, she got out her small cake of rose-scented glycerin soap from its shell box. She wished she had time to wash all over and put on a fresh chemise, but she was afraid to delay too long and keep Hetty's supper waiting. Causing Hetty any more upset than she had caused by her arrival was something Holly did not relish.

The image of herself she saw in the mirror revealed that she was more tired than she realized. She looked pale, and there were purple smudges under her eyes. She hadn't had a really good night's sleep in weeks! Not on the transcontinental train coming cross country nor in any of the places that passed for hotels in which she had spent a night or two as she made connections to California then Oregon!

Holly made quick work of her wash-up and redid her hair. Then whirling around, she held out her hand to Aurelia and with an effort at gaiety, asked, "So, shall we go in to supper?"

When they came out into the big kitchen, Hetty was standing at the stove, stirring something and did not turn around at their entrance. Ned was sitting in the big Boston rocker reading a newspaper, but when he saw Holly, he got to his feet and stood there uncertainly. The table was spread with a crisp white cloth and set with the Blue Delft dinnerware, which Holly recognized as Aunt Dolly's second-best, probably given to Hetty to bring west with her.

"Everything looks so nice, Hetty," Holly remarked to Hetty's back.

Hetty turned, and Holly was shocked to see she she still wore the same "mad-at-the-world" expression she had often seen on her in childhood. Hetty said with a shrug, "It's not as fancy as you're used to, I'm sure. But I like to do things proper even if this isn't Kentucky!"

At this Holly nearly choked. As if Hetty had not been brought up in the very same environment as Holly! They had the same grandparents, and their mothers were sisters, for goodness' sake! What was Hetty trying to prove? And how could *she* not have remembered what Hetty was like? Hetty had sat glum-faced through too many family celebrations for Holly to have forgotten.

Holly sat down without another word. Aurelia wiggled up into the chair beside Holly. Teddy, still with his head burrowed almost to his chin, climbed up into the chair opposite. Ned took his seat at the end of the table.

Hetty brought a large tureen over from the stove, set it down before Ned's place at the table, nodded brusquely to Ned, and said, "We'll have the blessing now, Ned."

All heads bowed reverently while Ned mumbled something in so low a voice Holly had to strain to hear. *Poor Ned,* was her reaction. Had he escaped from under the shadow of his father, the pontifical judge, and his brother only to be brought under Hetty's less benevolent domination? She certainly hoped not. She had caught a glimpse of the "new" Ned in his encounters with Adam Corcoran and Dr. Stevens, and she liked what she saw.

For all Holly's valiant efforts, supper was a strain. Even though Ned did his best by asking her about mutual friends in Willow Springs and Holly cooperated by bringing up news of events and people they all knew and might be interested in hearing about, Hetty's determined nonparticipation hung over the table like a pall. She spent most of the time correcting the children's table manners and once in awhile giving a sniff of disdain at some of Holly's remarks.

Teddy held Holly in a steady stare throughout the meal, but everytime she tried to make eye contact with him, he would duck his head into his plate. If it had not been for Aurelia, who alternately gazed at Holly adoringly or smiled at whatever she said, the meal would have been intolerable. As it was, Holly found she could hardly eat a bite. By the time it ended, she felt as if her neck were in a brace from stress and her face stretched from maintaining as pleasant an expression as possible.

Finally it was over. Hetty ignored Holly's compliments on the delicious supper and turned down her offer to help clear away or do the dishes. So, in desperation, using weariness from the long trip as an excuse, Holly said she believed she would retire early.

"I'll fix your lamp then, Holly," Ned said. While he trimmed the wick, lighted it, adjusted the flame, and replaced the glass globe, Hetty banged pots and pans. Holly darted a quick look at her cousin. Did Hetty even resent Ned's attending to her needs?

As he handed her the lamp, Holly said, "Thank you, Ned—," then added hesitantly, "Well, good night, Hetty—good night, everyone." Hetty acknowledged her with a brief nod; Aurelia waved and smiled. Teddy had disappeared again under the table.

Holly left the kitchen and went down the hall to the bedroom. The discomfort she felt during this first evening was unbelievable. With a sense of relief she closed the door, leaned against it, and shut her eyes for a full minute. Placing the lamp on the bureau, she sat down on the edge of the bed. She would have loved nothing better than to take a hot bath, but she hadn't dared risk asking Hetty to boil water or for the use of the copper tub she had seen hanging on the porch when she went out back.

She felt exhausted not only from the long day of travel but from the emotional stress. What weighed her down most heavily was the knowledge that she had done the wrong thing by coming. Hetty's feelings were plain. She hadn't wanted her to come, didn't want her here. But at the time, taking her aunt's and mother's advice had seemed reasonable enough. She herself had been anxious to escape, so it was easy enough to believe that by the time she came back to Willow Springs some other topic of gossip would have replaced the one that everyone was enjoying about her and Jim Mercer.

Back home it wouldn't have mattered. Holly hadn't cared about Hetty's opinion of her. Although, to her credit, Holly *had* tried to include Hetty in the parties and picnics and fun she herself was enjoying. Even though it *was* at her mother's prompting, to be sure, Holly *had* tried to encourage some of the young men who had clustered around *her* to dance with her cousin. Truthfully, Holly had to admit, for the most part she had lived in her own world, surrounded by admirers, basking in the sunshine of doting parents and dazzled beaux.

Now that the tables were turned, *Holly* was the needy one, Hetty had the upper hand. Their roles were going to be reversed. Now that it was too late, she deeply regretted having come. How could she possibly put up with Hetty's insufferable attitude until it was safe to go home? Or would it ever be safe? What if Jim decided finally to do what he had often promised to do when *they* were "courting"? Many times he had talked of resigning his Army commission and going into business with his father. What if Jim brought his bride home to Willow Springs?

I can't think about all that now, Holly told herself firmly. *I've got to make the best of it, even if it was a mistake to come.*

She started undressing, undoing the tiny satin-covered buttons of her Basque jacket, unfastening the tiered skirt, loosening the strings of her petticoats, and letting them drop to the floor. She unlaced the stays of her little corset, and took off her stockings and high-heeled bronze boots.

From her purse she got out the key to her trunk and unlocked it. As she lifted the lid, the faint fragrance of roses recalled the day she was packing to come to Oregon. A picture of her mother tucking the little net sachet bags of crushed, dried rose petals from their garden in among her freshly washed and ironed chemises and nighties floated into her mind, and she was overcome with a wave of homesickness.

Quickly she checked the urge to cry and determinedly took out a white cambric nightgown, frilled and edged with tatting. For a moment she held it to her breast, closing her eyes, relishing its scent. Then she put it on, slipped into her pink-flowered flannel wrapper, took the lamp, and went down the hall and outside to the "necessary."

The summer darkness was velvety; a starless, dense blue sky enveloped her; the grass between the flagstone path was wet with evening dew; the air spicy with the smell of cedar and evergreens. In a breath, Holly was swept back thousands of miles to where a soft Kentucky twilight lingered and fireflies darted among the wisteria—suddenly, although it wasn't cold, Holly shivered.

When Holly went back inside, Aurelia was in her nightie sitting up in the big bed. "If I crowd you, Holly, just give me a shove, all right?" she said. Stifling a yawn, she slid down into the covers. Holly blew out the lamp and got in beside the little girl. She smiled in the darkness.

In spite of Hetty's attitude, *at least* she had *one* ally in this house. Of course, Ned was kindness itself, but he had to be cautious for fear of provoking Hetty. Holly was sure she could soon win over little Teddy. She had always loved children, and they loved her.

But what was she to do about Hetty? Hetty was the real challenge. She yawned, sighed; tomorrow she'd figure out some way to win over Hetty, she decided drowsily. She had always been able to make friends easily, hadn't she?

She turned, spoon-fashion, around Aurelia's small warm body. Immediately Aurelia cuddled close.

Holly began drifting off to sleep when suddenly something jerked her awake again—it was the memory of the stage driver's voice shouting "end of the line"—

Chapter 3

*H*olly opened her eyes slowly, then snuggled deeper into the quilts, delaying until the last possible minute getting up and facing another day of Hetty's questionable hospitality.

From the kitchen she could hear movement, voices. She knew Hetty was already bustling about, frying bacon, whisking a pan of biscuits out of the oven, while at the same time fussing at the children and nagging Ned about something or other. In the two weeks Holly had been here, she'd been appalled at Hetty's constant picking at Ned. She should be grateful she had such a kind, patient, caring husband. Ned was also a wonderful father. Hetty was luckier than she seemed to realize. But, of course, there was no way she could tell her cousin that.

Holly lay there a little longer, dreading the moment when she would have to toss the covers aside, knowing, since there was no stove in the bedroom, how cold it would be. She would have loved a cup of coffee and dreamily remembered how her mother sometimes brought her one in the morning—especially if she had been out at a party or dance the night before. Holly sighed; those days were certainly gone forever.

She also knew if she went out to the kitchen now, Hetty would make her feel she was just in the way. Her offers to help were usually turned down, brushed aside curtly, making her feel generally useless and inadequate. If it hadn't seemed so deliberate, it would be almost funny. Whenever Holly had insisted that there *must* be *something* she could do to help, Hetty always seemed to pick the worst and most menial of tasks.

Like the day Hetty handed her the wire brush and said she could beat the rugs. With the best of intentions Holly had gone outside where the rugs were hung on a clothes line stretched between two poles in the backyard and started beating them. Dust flew out at once, enveloping her and causing her to sneeze and cough. Teddy, who had slipped out of the house and was sitting on the steps of the back porch watching her, started to giggle. Catching him, Holly began to play "peek-a-boo" with her shy little cousin behind the flapping rugs. It ended up in riotous hilarity. When Aurelia heard the laughter she, too, came outside to join the fun. Of course, Hetty quickly followed and put a stop to the game. Marching over to Holly, she snatched the beater out of her hand, saying curtly, "If you can't do it right, don't bother doing it at all."

Covered with dust, Holly stood aghast watching her stiff-shouldered cousin go back inside the house, holding on to the protesting Teddy with one hand and pushing Aurelia in front of her.

There was just no pleasing Hetty! Smothering a groan, Holly burrowed her head into the pillow, remembering another unpleasant incident that had happened the very same day.

Not having thought to cover her head while in the process of rug-beating, Holly had decided to wash her hair to get rid of the dust. While Hetty had gone to the store, Holly heated her own water and got out her shampoo. Aurelia, as usual, was her interested audience.

Impulsively Holly had asked the little girl if she wanted her hair done, too. Of course Aurelia did. She also wanted it put up in curling rags. They were in the process of doing that, sitting out in the warm September sunshine, when Hetty returned. With one look she took in the scene and halted it.

"I thought I told you I don't want Aurelia growing up vain and silly. Her hair's worn in plaits, and that's that."

"Oh, just this once, Hetty? Just for fun?" Holly persisted, not believing Hetty really meant to prevent the little girl's pleasure.

"I wish you would *just for once* realize that *I'm* in charge here, not *you*, Holly." Hetty's voice was edged with sarcasm. "Come along, Aurelia, I'll braid your hair proper," she said, brushing past Holly and marching into the house.

Holly had repressed a natural urge to argue with her. It was so stupid of Hetty to get into a tug of wills over something so harmless. She also kept herself from doing the spontaneous thing of hugging Aurelia, who was struggling not to burst into tears at her mother's dictum.

That night when they were in bed together, Holly cuddled Aurelia and told her a long story to make up for her disappointment of no curls.

Shortly after that, another incident occurred that put Holly even more at her wit's end. Again she had asked Hetty how she could help, and Hetty had pointed to the stove and said shortly, "It needs blacking." Then she added sarcastically, "But of course, you wouldn't want to get your hands dirty."

At this, Holly had simply smiled. "Where's the polish?"

Hetty looked startled but got out some rags and a jar of Queen's Mirror-black and set them down on the kitchen table before leaving for her Sewing Circle.

Holly had never in her life before cleaned or shined a stove, but she was stubborn enough not to give Hetty the satisfaction of a job not well done. She was down on her knees, having already skinned two knuckles, when the children woke up from their naps and came out to the kitchen.

"Your face is all smudge, Holly!" gasped Aurelia.

"Just call me 'Cinderella'!" Holly laughed at the two stunned little faces as she blew some strands of hair that had fallen over her eyes. While she finished up on the stove, she regaled them with a fine dramatic version of the fairy tale while they sat cross-legged on the floor beside her. When Hetty got home, she was not only astonished, but Holly could see she even resented the fact that the stove shone with new brilliance.

Recalling the uncomfortable moment, Holly thumped her pillow behind her head and stared gloomily out the window. She wished desperately she had never come to Oregon. If it weren't for the children—

At least the children accepted and loved her. It had taken some time for Teddy to get over his first shyness, but now he followed her around like a puppy. Aurelia would have become her shadow if Hetty allowed it. However, Hetty seemed to resent the little girl's uninhibited affection for Holly and restricted it as much as possible.

Holly found this hard. One would think any busy mother would be grateful to someone who could entertain children. Both children were entranced by Holly's talent for storytelling. Aurelia would ask her questions like, "What did you do when you were a little girl?" and Holly would spin out stories from her vivid childhood memories. Although always within hearing during these times, Hetty kept a stony silence.

But one day when Holly was holding them spellbound about her Shetland pony and describing her tree house in the big oak in the backyard, where her friends climbed up the little ladder to have tea parties, Hetty had cut in crossly, "I don't want you filling up my children with all those make-believe stories."

Astonished, Holly exclaimed. "*Make-believe!* What do you mean, Hetty? Surely you remember the tree house Papa built— and Rags, the pony? Why, we all used to take turns riding him."

Hetty's expression tightened. "It was a make-believe life. Not like life is out here in the West. My children have to learn to live in the real world; they aren't being reared pampered and sheltered and no good to anyone," she snapped. "Out here folks don't set much stock on silly birthday parties and making a fuss about things." To the children she said, "Come on, you two, instead of listening to a bunch of silly stories, you can help me get in the laundry." With that she picked up the oak-chip clothes basket and started toward the back door.

Holly was too startled by Hetty's outburst to say anything. Was Hetty trying to erase everything about the life they both had lived in Willow Springs? And if so, why?

With a sorrowful glance at Holly, Aurelia obeyed. Teddy started to howl saying he wanted to hear more about the pony, and Hetty gave him a smack on his bottom.

Holly longed to give Hetty a piece of her mind. But, of course, she didn't. After all Aurelia and Teddy *were* Hetty's children, and

28

she had no right to argue about any rules Hetty laid down for them.

After that incident, Holly confined her storytelling to when she and Aurelia were in bed at night or other times when they happened to be alone—which wasn't often. Hetty kept both children busily occupied with little chores most of the day, so there wasn't much time for Holly to invent games or tell them stories.

Holly could not help wondering if such enforced "busyness" was all that good. Shouldn't there be time for playing? Even for dreaming? Aurelia was bright and creative, loved pretending and make-believe. She loved it when Holly would leave off a story midway and let her finish it. Holly just hoped that when *she* left to go back to Willow Springs, Aurelia's active imagination wouldn't be stunted.

Holly bunched up the pillow, flipped over onto her back, and stared moodily at the ceiling. She knew she should get up. She thought she knew exactly how the French aristocrats must have felt mounting to the guillotine, or even the early Christians going into the lions' den. Of course, that was an exaggeration, but Hetty *was* a formidable adversary. Nothing Holly did or said met with Hetty's approval.

Hetty maintained a constant distance. She never initiated a conversation. Often she did not even reply to Holly's comments or concerted efforts to be companionable. But there was still another way Hetty made Holly feel unwelcome. She consistently excluded Holly from any of the social life that *she* had made for herself in Riverbend. Hetty had never invited any of her friends to meet her cousin, nor had she asked Holly to accompany *her* when she went to visit any of them.

On several occasions after Ned returned to the store following the noon dinner, without a word to Holly, Hetty would simply gather up her sewing basket, put on her bonnet and shawl, button Aurelia and Teddy into their outdoor garments, and start to the front door. Then, as if an afterthought, she would call over her shoulder the brief announcement, "I'm going over to Selma Peterson's. She's got a pattern I want to trace," or "I'm going to my quilting group, something I know you wouldn't be interested in since you never enjoyed handiwork."

Sometimes Aurelia would plead, "Can't Holly come with us?" but Hetty would ignore her and, without a backward look, leave.

After the door closed behind them, Holly vented her indignation. True, she never *had* enjoyed needlework nor embroidery, but she might have enjoyed meeting some of the young women in town even if she did not share their interest in *handiwork!* Who knows, she might even enjoy learning how to quilt. What in the world did Hetty expect her to do with her time?

Holly would have to be blind not to see. Hetty did not care if Holly was happy here or not. She was not going to lift a finger to introduce her to anyone, or try to make her life in Riverbend interesting. This was such a contrast to the way newcomers were treated in Willow Springs that Holly could not believe it.

I must have been out of my mind to come here! In self-disgust Holly threw back the covers and got up. The day ahead held nothing but gloomy prospects. Back in Willow Springs she might be going shopping, making visits with her mother, having "gentlemen callers," or looking forward to an afternoon party. In the evening there may have been a play or a concert to attend or perhaps a buffet supper and dance. Well, thinking about all those things was like Alice's following the Red Queen's instructions and "imagining six impossible things before breakfast!" Holly thought with a sigh, *I can't go back. Not now. Not until spring at least. I have to somehow make the best of things here.*

Holly had started taking long walks. Within days after her arrival in Riverbend she had discovered that the slightest thing seemed to cause Hetty to fly off the handle. Holly began watching her every word, remark, and gesture. Sometimes the only alternative to avoid an argument with her cousin was to get out of the house. On these walks Holly found that Riverbend was a pleasant enough little town with a wealth of natural beauty. Now in early September the weather was sunny, and along the roadside a profusion of wildflowers, golden poppies, and delicate purple-blue wild asters delighted the eye. Beautiful trees, tall firs, sweeping-boughed hemlocks, dark green cedars grew right to the edge of town. One day she had found a path that led right down to the river, and this became a favorite place for her to go when tension with Hetty became unbearable.

In the town itself quite a lot of building was going on in anticipation, she supposed, of the coming of the new branch line of the railroad, which was to catapult Riverbend into unprecedented prosperity. There was a fine brick courthouse being constructed at one end of Main Street, and on some of the new roads fanning out from the center of town some houses were being built. Somewhat to her surprise, she saw several churches as well as saloons; the saloons, however, were winning about three to one.

There were more settled areas of town; tree-lined streets forming small neighborhoods, nicely painted frame houses with neat fences, deep yards, and flower and vegetable gardens around the side. Wistfully she wondered if there might be people in those houses who could be acquaintances, perhaps even friends.

One house she passed often and found particularly appealing was nestled under large trees at the end of a winding lane. It was a doll-sized yellow clapboard with a slanting roof and lacy white fretwork on the little porch. There was a painted sign on the gatepost, V. DODD, DRESSMAKING, FINE NEEDLEWORK.

Often Holly had stood at the gate of that house, half-tempted to go up and knock on the blue-painted door, perhaps on the pretext of asking about alterations or to look at patterns or to discuss a new outfit?—to see for herself if "V. Dodd" matched the charm of the exterior. But, of course, she couldn't do that. Holly had always had girlfriends to go shopping with or simply to visit—she sadly missed the companionship, the camaraderie and fun. Of all her many Lambeth and Granville cousins, Hetty was the only one with whom she was not congenial.

Holly got dressed slowly, unconsciously steeling herself for another prickly encounter with Hetty. *No matter what, I must try to be cheerful and pleasant,* Holly lectured her reflection in the mirror sternly. *Maybe, today will be different. Maybe Hetty will be in a better mood. Maybe . . .*

But, of course, Hetty wasn't. Ned had already departed for the

31

store when Holly came out to the kitchen. Hetty, who was stirring something in a big pot on the stove, turned her head and gave Holly a swift glance, then turned her back again. Holly gritted her teeth. Why couldn't Hetty at least be civil? With determined brightness Holly said, "Good morning."

Aurelia, sitting at one end of the table cutting out little squares of calico from a huge pile of scraps beside her, looked up and smiled, "Morning, Holly. See what I'm doing? I'm cutting out patches for Mama." She held one up with pride.

"That's wonderful," Holly nodded encouragingly.

Teddy was sitting on the floor, struggling to get his high-topped shoes buttoned, his small pink tongue moving from one side of his mouth to the other as he concentrated, his chubby little hands fumbling at the task.

On impulse, Holly asked him, "Want some help?" and dropped to her knees beside him.

The words were hardly out of her mouth when Hetty swung around from the stove ordering, "No! You're not to help him. He's got to learn to do it himself. He's a big boy. I won't have you babying him!"

Startled at the harsh command, Holly stared at Hetty whose face had turned red and mottled. Ugly. Slowly, Holly rose from the floor, but not before she saw tears well up in Teddy's eyes. She didn't say anything, just looked at Hetty speechlessly. Hetty's face got redder, but she didn't apologize. She turned back to the stove and started stirring again.

"There's coffee still in the pot if you want some," she said in a muffled voice, "and biscuits."

But Holly was too shaken by the anger bristling through her. Aurelia looked up at the sudden stillness in the room, a deadly quiet tingling with tension. Her eyes widened as she looked anxiously from Holly to her mother.

Holly knew she had to control her fury for the children's sake. She managed a reassuring smile for Aurelia, then said in a tight voice, "No, thank you, I'm not hungry. I think I'll go for a walk. I need some fresh air." That was all she allowed herself to say to indicate her reaction to Hetty.

Back in the bedroom, Holly put on her bonnet, carefully

32

anchoring it with two long hatpins, trying to calm herself. Her hands were actually shaking.

"If it were possible, I'd take the first stagecoach out of here!" she declared to her reflection. But where could she go? She was trapped. "I must get hold of myself. I must not lose my temper. Whatever happens I won't let her break me." Maybe she could walk off her seething anger. Whatever, Holly was determined not to stoop to Hetty's level.

Returning to the kitchen, she halted at the door and, in the most even tone she could muster, asked Hetty if she needed her to stop at the store for anything.

Still at the stove, her back to Holly, Hetty merely shook her head. But as Holly turned the doorknob and started out, Hetty's voice followed her, warning, "Don't bother Ned at the store, Holly. He's got customers to look out for; he don't have time to waste gabbing."

"I had no intention of doing that, Hetty," Holly could not resist calling back. It was all she could do not to slam the door after her.

She went down the porch steps and out of the yard, so angry she had no idea in what direction she headed.

Chapter 4

*H*olly's heart was beating like a metronome; her pulses raced. She was angrier than she could ever remember being. She walked so fast that before long she was quite warm and breathless.

Without realizing it, she took the path off the road onto the trail leading down to the river. She had come quite a way before she calmed down enough to notice what a beautiful day it was. Under the ponderosa pines and the red-barked manzanita, clusters of wildflowers sprinkled with early morning frost, glistened like gems in the sunlight streaming down between the trees. Through the heavy brush she caught a glimpse of the sparkling water below.

She found a sun-warmed rock to sit upon. This close to the river, the sound of water rushing over the rocks was loud but in a way rhythmically soothing. A few leaves from the aspens and birch trees on the bank had fallen and drifted onto the shining surface. She watched them dancing and drifting with the rippling flow.

As the silence of the woods settled around her like a peaceful cloak, from high up in one tree came the fluting sound of a bird. But the peace of it all—instead of soothing her—only seemed to accentuate her sense of isolation and loneliness. Eventually, she began to think about the dilemma of her situation. Her walks had become a palliative but no solution. Yes, the woods *were* beautiful and the weather lovely and these walks *did* help, but what was she to do when the legendary Oregon winter rains began? What would she do then to escape? Her every attempt with Hetty met with resistance. She was at the end of her rope.

It wasn't only the problem with her cousin, it was everything else! Losing Jim had been a dreadful blow. Nothing like that had ever happened to her before. Life had always been so easy and pleasant for her that she had never dreamed it wouldn't go on being that way forever. It was even more painful to know she had brought the whole terrible thing on herself!

Holly had never been introspective, never explored her feelings nor thought much about her life; she had been too busy living it. Rarely had she thought beyond the next dance or party, what she should wear, or which invitation to accept. Life in Willow Springs, in the large white clapboard house with its deep porch and green shutters had been, in retrospect, serene and blissful!

Before Jim's "betrayal" nothing really bad had ever happened to her. It had left her dazed and bewildered. In that state, she had let others make up her mind for her, suggest to her what was the "best thing" for her to do. Now she realized the "*best*" thing may not have been the "*right*" thing for her to do at all!

Suddenly Holly felt very young and sad and childishly like crying. She put her head in her hands and let the pent-up tears come. After awhile, she lifted her head and sniffled. What good would crying do? She couldn't sit here moping all day. She wasn't ready yet to go back to the house. She still had things to sort out, to think about. She was now hungry and could have used a cup of coffee and something to eat.

She would go by the store, which she had not had a chance to see yet, being careful not to "bother Ned" as Hetty had cautioned her. Perhaps she could amuse herself looking around.

Wiping her eyes, she dug into her reticule for a hanky to blow her nose. As she drew out one of the fine lawn, lace-edged ones that her great-aunt Ancilla had made and given her at Christmas, a small, rectangular, printed paper fell from it onto the ground. Curious, Holly picked it up. As soon as she saw

35

what it was, she started to smile. *Of all things!* she thought. Great-Aunt Ancilla up to her usual "tricks." A tract!

Her mother's aunt was known in the family as "the Evangelist." Passing along tracts was the dear old soul's "ministry," as she told everyone. She was forever giving them out to family, friends, and perfect strangers. She slipped them into books, put them under dinner plates, folded them into freshly ironed laundry, tucked them under bed pillows.

Even as the tears dried on her cheeks, Holly laughed. She had been asking for help with her problem, and here like a message from home came one of her fey little auntie's tracts.

Great-Aunt Ancilla held staunchly to the belief that no matter what your problem, whenever you need guidance of any kind, go to the Word. To her mind, the Bible had all the answers. Well, if ever Holly needed guidance it was *now*. She read the bold line of type at the top of the little booklet: "WHATSOEVER YOUR HAND FINDS TO DO, DO IT WITH ALL YOUR MIGHT" ECC. 9:10. On down the page there were further exhortations to be cheerful, patient whatever your path in life happened to be, to trust in God and He would make "straight your path."

Oh, if I could only believe that is true, Holly sighed, and her shoulders drooped a little. But as she continued reading, oddly enough, some of the anger, some of the lostness she had felt began to fade. There *was* "comfort in the Word" as Great-Auntie Ancilla declared so positively.

The wind off the river had risen, and the sun shifted and moved up behind the towering trees. Involuntarily Holly shivered and, feeling chilly, got to her feet and started walking down toward the edge of the river where it was warmer. But as she did, a stone caught in the tiny heel of one of her dainty boots causing her to twist her ankle. As she did, the heel broke off.

Drat it! Holly picked up the narrow little heel and held it in the palm of her hand frowning. The fragile nails were bent and loose. She could not possibly reattach it. It would have to be fixed by a shoemaker—if there were such a thing in Riverbend!

Stepping on the toe of one foot, she hobbled awkwardly back toward the road and turned in the direction of Hetty's. In her anger after leaving the house, she had walked very fast and

36

come much farther than she realized. Now, thus handicapped, she would have to retrace her steps. *This is a fine kettle of fish!* she complained glumly to herself as she limped along.

She had to stop to rest every few minutes, and her lopsided gait made her very tired. Holly wasn't sure how long she had hobbled, although it seemed like forever when she heard the clopping sound of horses' hooves approaching. She halted and turned to see a small, black-hooded buggy rounding the curve of the road. As it came nearer, it slowed then pulled alongside her. With a mixture of embarrassment and relief she saw that it was Riverbend's doctor, Blaine Stevens.

"Miss Lambeth!" he tipped his hat and leaned toward her. "You're limping! Have you injured yourself?"

"Well, no, not exactly—I've—" She held out her hand, opening the palm and showed him the dainty broken heel.

"Well, thank goodness, it's nothing serious. You don't need a doctor; you need a ride, right?" He smiled and in a flash jumped down and helped her into the buggy.

"Would you like me to take you back to the Thorntons' or to town, where you can get your shoe fixed?"

"I guess to town, if it wouldn't be too much trouble."

"Right! And it's not any trouble at all. Luckily, I'm on my way from a house call, not on my way *to* one." He looked over at her and smiled.

Once settled in, Holly glanced over at the doctor. "I can't thank you enough for rescuing me! I don't know how much longer I'd have lasted, hobbling like that."

"That's my role in life!" he laughed. "Rescuing people."

"Lucky for me!" she joined in his laughter. At close range, Dr. Stevens did not appear as young as she had thought at their first meeting. Of course, that had been in the evening, when it was fast growing dark. Now she guessed him to be in his early thirties. His was a face that was both young and old, the skin of his cheeks was taut and tan, his eyes remarkably clear and blue, but there were fine lines around them. There were deeper lines around his mouth, etched there, perhaps, by the suffering and pain he had witnessed in his profession. It was a face that Holly instinctively felt that one could trust.

As he looked over at her, smiling, his eyes held both laughter and interest. "So, other than today's mishap, I hope you've been enjoying your stay in Riverbend. I'm sure you and Hetty have had lots of things to catch up on—I know how most folks enjoy hearing about things back home. It must be even better to have a visitor."

Holly was at a loss as to how to reply. Blaine's natural assumption about her and her cousin was one that anyone would make. But nothing could be further from the truth. He was looking at her expectantly, so she hedged her answer carefully. "Well, of course, it's been six years since I've seen Hetty or Ned, and—to be honest, we never were very close. I mean our lives were—*are* quite different. I mean, she's busy with her home and children and I—"

Holly halted. Why on earth was she rattling on like this, and to a perfect stranger? She felt her cheeks get hot.

"Of course. I understand. Life in the East is much different—takes some adjustments and getting used to the West isn't all that easy, either—" Blaine stopped, then tactfully switched the subject, saying, "Here we are, and I'll take you right by Hedrick's, the shoesmith; he'll have your heel back on in a jiffy."

"Thank you, Dr. Stevens, you've been very kind."

Blaine drew up in front of a small storefront, secured the buggy brake, and got out. He came around the other side and helped Holly down.

"I'd be happy to wait for you, then drive you home, Miss Lambeth."

"Oh, that won't be necessary, but thank you," Holly said. "I'm very grateful you came along when you did."

"It's no trouble at all. I'd be delighted, in fact. I have a house call to make out in the direction of the Thorntons' and can drop you off there on my way."

Holly hesitated, then seeing no reason to refuse the offer, smiled and said, "Very well, thank you."

Blaine spun the hat he held in his hand for a second before saying shyly, "I'd suggest you ask Jake about some sturdier boots if you're going to do much more walking, Miss Lambeth." He

38

smiled shyly. "There's some awfully pretty country around here, but some of it's kind of rugged."

"As I have just found out!" Holly laughed. "Thank you for the advice. I'll do that."

When the heel was replaced, Blaine was waiting outside. He helped her back into his buggy for the short distance back to the Thorntons' house.

Blaine assisted her from the buggy and escorted her to the gate. Before opening it for her, he said, "There's some very nice country around Riverbend, not all within walking distance. If you'd like, Miss Lambeth, I'd like to show you some of it. Maybe some Sunday? After church? That's my day off—well, at least—I cannot always be certain of attending the service. A doctor's life is not exactly his own, Miss Lambeth. Sometimes there are emergencies—so far, I'm reasonably sure of next Sunday." Little lines crinkled around his intensely blue eyes as he smiled.

He went on to quickly to explain that he could not always be certain of attending the service. "A doctor's life is not exactly his own, Miss Lambeth. Sometimes there are emergencies—I do like to try to make church. But I'm reasonably sure of next Sunday." He smiled; little lines crinkled around his intensely blue eyes as they looked down at her.

For a moment Holly debated whether it was wise to accept the young doctor's invitation, then she became conscious of the movement of the curtain at one of the windows and realized Hetty must be watching. She felt a flare of indignation. Somehow she knew it would irritate Hetty if she made plans to drive out with Blaine Stevens. Defiantly, she thought, *Why not?* "Why, yes, Dr. Stevens, that sounds very nice indeed. I would enjoy that." Here was a chance to break the awful monotony of Sunday at Hetty's.

Smiling demurely, she put out her hand and said sweetly, "and thank you again for rescuing me."

The following Sunday, Holly came out of her room, ready for church, dressed in a bronze poplin "promenade" dress. Her bonnet beribboned with brown grosgrain sported a cluster of golden daisies, and she carried a silk, flounced parasol. Aurelia, seated on a high stool while Hetty finished braiding her hair, saw

39

her and exclaimed, "Oooh, Holly, you look so-o pretty!" Hetty turned to look at her cousin, and her expression made Holly draw in her breath. What she saw on Hetty's face was ugly. For a minute, Holly was stunned. It was devastating to be the target of such raw dislike. Nervously she drew on her gloves, trying to think of something to say to ease the tension. But none came. Then Hetty said to Aurelia, "You're done now. Go out to the wagon. Your pa's waiting."

Holly stood there uncertainly. Hetty had turned away, presenting only her back, with its rigidly held shoulders, shutting out any possibility for any words. Silently Holly went out the door, feeling sad that she had caused her cousin such distress. But what could she do? A few minutes later, Hetty came out wearing a Quaker plain shovel bonnet and gray bombazine. Without saying anything, she got up into the driver's seat of the wagon beside Ned.

Seated with the children, Holly sought for something she might do to scale the barrier between her and her cousin. If somehow Hetty envied her outfits, the way she dressed or looked, why didn't she do something about her *own* appearance? There was much she could do! A less severe hairstyle would soften her sharp-featured face. She could certainly wear brighter colors. Surely she had the pick of the yards of fabric at Ned's store, many colors to choose from and more becoming patterns from which to make her clothes. Holly would have easily made such suggestions to any of her other cousins—but not to Hetty! Never Hetty. By this time they had reached the church, and without a word, Hetty marched the children off to the Sunday school rooms, leaving Holly to walk into church with Ned.

The Thorntons' pew was at the front of the church. It took all of Holly's willpower not to look around to check the congregation for Dr. Stevens. She hoped he had not forgotten or that there had not been an unexpected emergency this morning. That possibility kept her preoccupied during what turned out to be a rather dull sermon. After the service she stood with Ned outside on the church steps, searching for him. But there was still no sign of Dr. Stevens. Holly began to get worried. What if he didn't show up?

Holly had intended to tell Hetty about Blaine's invitation, but after the scene in the kitchen that morning there had been no chance. Now it was awkward. It would appear that she had purposely withheld the information. Which is exactly the reaction she got when Hetty returned with the children.

Ned was in conversation with some of the men when Hetty said, "Come along, Holly, we'll wait for Ned in the wagon." Hetty's voice had its perpetual impatience.

"I'll not be going home with you, Hetty," Holly replied coolly. "Dr. Stevens is meeting me here; he has asked me to go for a drive."

Hetty's eyes popped wide then squinted suspiciously. "Oh?" she said, then pointedly glanced around the quickly emptying churchyard. Neither Blaine nor his small black buggy were anywhere to be seen. A sly smile twisted her mouth, and she asked "You sure about that? Maybe you misunderstood Dr. Stevens' intentions?"

Because she was having her own misgivings, the snideness in Hetty's voice brought Holly's own anxiety into sharp focus. *Could* she have been mistaken? Unwilling to give Hetty a chance to gloat, Holly lifted her chin, saying with more assurance than she felt, "He's possibly delayed by a patient's sudden illness or—he told me this was always a possibility—"

Ned finished his conversation with the man he'd been talking with and joined them. "Ready?" he asked innocent of the building tension between the cousins.

"Holly isn't going home with us, Ned. She has an appointment with a gentleman," Hetty told him with a toss of her head. "Come on, children." Hetty grabbed Aurelia and Teddy by the hand and marched down the church steps without a backward glance. Ned stood for a minute looking after his wife, then doubtfully at Holly.

"You go ahead, Ned. Blaine Stevens invited me to go driving. I'll be home later," Holly said with all the poise she could gather.

"Oh, Blaine? Well, that's nice, Holly. He's a prince of a fellow." Ned looked both ways down the road then back at Holly. "You sure? He could have been called out, you know—"

41

"Yes, I know, he said there's always that chance." Holly nodded her head wishing Ned would go. If Blaine *didn't* show up for some reason, she didn't want any witnesses to her embarrassment.

Ned hesitated. He looked up at the sky where some shadowy clouds moved ominously. "It looks like it might rain—I don't like to leave you here by yourself in case—," he halted, flushing, and amended, "what I mean to say is, you know how it is with doctors—Blaine may have got called out on an emergency—"

"I understand that, Ned. He told me he might be late. Please go on, don't keep Hetty and the children waiting. Something must have delayed Dr. Stevens, he'll be along soon," she assured him.

Reluctantly Ned left. The children waved as the wagon went by; Hetty looked straight ahead.

Now, I've done it again, Holly thought grimly. *Oh, well, it wouldn't have mattered what I said or did, Hetty just doesn't want to be friends with me, no matter what! It probably riles her that someone as attractive as Blaine Stevens has asked me out.*

As the minutes passed and there was still no sign of Blaine, Holly experienced a whole gamut of emotions, reciting to herself all the reasons why he hadn't come. The grayness of the day was disheartening as well. Then to her dismay a few drops of rain began to fall. Startled, she stepped back under the eaves of the narrow church porch. But soon they increased in rapidity and force, and before long it was raining hard.

Well! What now! The church doors had been locked; there was not a soul in sight. Should she wait here any longer or, horror of horrors, walk back to Hetty's house and face her derisive scorn?

Resolutely, Holly decided that would probably be easier than being stranded here indefinitely. She had a dainty parasol with her, which was no bigger than an upside-down thimble and was only carried as a fashion accessory. For some reason she had brought it with her this morning, thinking it would shield her from the sun as the day had promised to be fair. With a sigh of resignation she slipped it from her wrist, where it hung by a wide ribbon, unfurled it, and, picking up her skirt, went down the church steps, out of the churchyard, and started along the road toward the Thorntons'.

Immediately the skies opened up, and a strong wind sent leaves scuttling from the trees and the rain tugging her tiny umbrella. Holly could feel it spattering the back of her jacket and moaned at the damage it must be doing to her best velour bonnet.

Over the insidious patter of the rain on the small circle of silk she was barely managing to hold over her head, Holly heard her name shouted, "Miss Lambeth!"

A moment of indecision. Having recognized Dr. Stevens' voice, should she walk haughtily on, soundly snubbing him in order to show him that one didn't stand up Holly Lambeth and get away with it, or should expediency take precedence here and avoid ruining her best outfit and shoes?

She whirled around and saw the little buggy weaving and wobbling down the lane with a red-faced doctor driving it with one hand and wildly waving the other. He reined up beside her, jumped out, and, thrusting a huge black umbrella over her, stammered out a profuse apology. "Tom Haskins' boy jumped on a haystack and onto a pitchfork, Miss Lambeth, and sparing you the details—I had to rush out to their farm, take care of him. I hope you'll forgive me and I'm sorry about the rain—"

At his evident genuine distress, Holly couldn't help melting. At the same time the rain seemed suddenly to diminish and turn into a gentle patter. As they stood there, unexpected sunshine seemed to push through the clouds and envelope the abject doctor in a beatific light.

"Am I forgiven?" he asked.

The alternative being an ignominious return to Hetty's house, Holly chose to be magnanimous.

"Well, of course, you're not responsible for the rain, Dr. Stevens, and certainly such an emergency has to be met, so, yes, of course."

"We could still take a drive, if you like," he suggested tentatively.

The rest of the afternoon proved fair enough with pale sunshine alternating with sporadic showers. But Holly hardly minded. It turned out to be the pleasantest afternoon she had yet spent in Riverbend.

She found Blaine Stevens to be charming and intelligent and also blessed with a lively sense of humor. He was not only interesting but easy to talk to as well. They found that, although they were from different regions of the country, both had come from small towns, close families. They shared common interests in books and music and enjoyed the beauties of nature.

It was late afternoon when they started back toward town and, without warning, Blaine reined up sharply in the middle of the road. Pointing, he said in an awed voice, "Look, Miss Lambeth, a rainbow!"

Before them a delicate arch of yellow, lavender, green, blue, and orange formed a bridge in the pale blue sky against the purple hills.

"How beautiful!" Holly sighed.

They both sat motionless for a long while until the glorious vision faded away. Without a word, Blaine gave the reins a flick and they drove on silently, still caught in the beauty of the moment they had shared.

"I would say a day that ends with a rainbow has to be a good omen for a friendship, wouldn't you, Miss Lambeth?" he asked her as they reached town and turned down the road to the Thorntons' house.

"I agree, Dr. Stevens, it would certainly seem so," replied Holly thinking that seeing Blaine again presented a very pleasant prospect.

By the time they reached the Thorntons' it had started raining again. Blaine said, "Although there's a chance we still might have some good weather, this is what I'm afraid you've got to expect, Miss Lambeth, as we head into an Oregon winter."

"That's what I've heard."

"I hope you're not easily depressed by weather?"

"Oh, I don't think so," Holly assured him as he walked with her up to the door under the shelter of his big umbrella.

But Holly was wrong. That Sunday began a week of incessant rain.

"Doesn't it ever stop?" Holly asked the third morning as she stood at the kitchen window staring out at the steady drizzle.

Confined to the house where she was either ignored by Hetty or annoyed by her, Holly spent most of her time in the bedroom she shared with the children. She decided to finish taking her things out of her trunk, which for some reason she had left partially packed.

As she brushed and hung up her clothes with clove-studded orange balls to prevent the chance of mildew from all the dampness Hetty had warned her about, Aurelia crept in and deposited herself on the bed to watch.

"What's this, Holly?" the little girl asked smoothing the thick, velvet cover of Holly's photograph album.

"Would you like to see?" Holly asked and sat down beside her and opened it for the child to look through the pages of pictures.

"That's my house in Willow Springs," Holly told her with a tiny lump in her throat as she placed her finger on a photo of the Lambeth homestead. "And there's my Grandma Vinny and Grampa Granville sitting on the porch, and there's my mama and papa, and that's our collie, Tamas, lying on the steps . . . ," and Holly began to turn the pages slowly pointing out each picture and telling Aurelia who was in it.

Then they came upon the page with Jim Mercer's picture, his handsome face trying to look brave and stalwart in his West Point cadet uniform, the cape folded back, the glittering double row of brass buttons, the epaulets and shoulder cord, the gauntleted hand on the saber hilt.

"Ohhhh-ummm," breathed Aurelia, "Is this a prince?"

In spite of the sudden clutch in her heart, Holly had to laugh.

"No, honey, not a prince—but he *is* a soldier, a lieutenant in the United States Army." She went on, "His name is Jim Mercer, and I was supposed to marry him."

"You *were?*" Aurelia sounded awed.

"Yes."

"Then why didn't you?"

"Because I was a very vain and foolish young lady," Holly told her. "He married someone else instead."

"Oh, Holly, I'm sorry!" Aurelia looked at her with sorrowful eyes.

Holly gave her a hug. "Oh, honey, that's sweet of you, but it was my own fault."

"Did he marry a princess?" Aurelia was still interested in the story, sad as it was.

"Not exactly. She was a colonel's daughter, and I guess a sort of princess," Holly said. "Let's turn the page."

On the next page there was a full-length picture of Holly in the lovely ball gown she had worn at her coming out party. She had camellias in her hair and was holding a bouquet in a frilled lace ruff.

"Oh, Holly, that's *you*, isn't it? And *you do* look like a princess. Tell me about the dress—," Aurelia begged.

"Well—," began Holly, "it was sky blue and had a tulle over-skirt caught up with tiny blue velvet bows and—"

They were both so occupied that they didn't hear the short knock, if there was one. Suddenly the bedroom door burst open. She stood on the threshold; her voice was shrill. "Aurelia, get down off that bed this instant. You know I don't like you lolling around wasting time."

Startled and still holding the album, Holly stared at her cousin.

"But Mama, Holly's showing me pictures of the town you both grew up in and pictures of Great-Gramma and your mama and Holly's party and—"

"That's enough, Aurelia, go on out to the kitchen. You've got chores to do."

As the little girl slid obediently down from the bed, her eyes glistened as she bit her lower lip to keep back the unshed tears.

Holly rushed to defend her. "Hetty, it was *my* fault, I was just showing her pictures of Willow Springs and—"

Hetty went white. "I said I don't want you filling my child's head with a lot of nonsense—"

"Hetty, I was showing her pictures of *our* grandparents, *your* parents—surely you shouldn't mind—"

"Since when did you give a fig what anyone minds?" demanded Hetty. Then she went out and shut the door.

After Hetty left, Holly sat rigidly on the edge of the bed. Outside, the rain drummed relentlessly. Appalled by Hetty's reaction, Holly asked herself why Hetty should object to this harmless pastime?

Staring out the window, where the rain beat monotonously

46

against the panes, Holly felt trapped. A prisoner! She must find a means of escape. But how?

She looked down at the album she was still holding in her lap, turned the rest of the pages stiffly, the images of the people, the events, the places that had made up her life before, reminding her of what she had left. Willow Springs and all the gaiety and sunny memories it evoked had disappeared in the rain and fog of Oregon. To tell herself it would be only a year didn't help. A year could seem like forever.

At the end of the week the heavy rain had slowed to a steady drizzle. For days Holly's sense of desperation had deepened. Finally, she felt she could not possibly stand being cooped up in the house with Hetty's punishing coldness and intractable hostility any longer.

The children were both napping, and Hetty, tight-lipped, was mending. Without explaining, Holly flung on her warm cape and, defying the weather, went out for a walk.

By the time she reached town, it had stopped raining. Wet leaves plastered the board walkways, and puddles were everywhere, making navigating the streets hazardous. But Holly didn't care. It was so good to be out, with the cool wind in her face, the feeling of being free surging through her.

At the *Riverbend Monitor* Adam Corcoran sat with his long legs and booted feet up on the editor's desk. Leaning back in the swivel oak chair, he stared gloomily out the window onto Main Street. He was alone in the office. It was Friday, and the weekly edition of the paper had been "put to bed" yesterday. Old Tom was probably parting with most of his paycheck over at the Nugget, and young Mike had gone squirrel hunting.

Ad squinted his eyes and surveyed the street scene in front of him. Not much going on this noon. Not that there ever was in this isolated "neck of the woods." It was a far cry from San Francisco with its busy streets crowded with all sorts of colorfully dressed people on the go, filled with purpose and activity. Only a few short months ago, he had been part of it. Blazes, he missed it!

My own blasted fault, Ad thought grimly. Maybe he should

have curbed his instinct about O'Herir, reined in that powerful reportorial drive, but it was too much a part of him. He had caught the scent, and the hunt had been on, and Ad had had to follow it. His dogged probing and investigative reporting of the shenanigans of a popular and powerful politician had landed him here. A series of articles delineating the number of payoffs and kickbacks had cost him his job.

With a rush of adrenaline, Ad remembered the intense excitement of working on the big-city daily newspaper from which he'd been fired. The firing came from the top, the ownership, management. It had been final. There had been no recourse. Privately his editor, sorry to lose one of his best men, told him to "lie low" for a couple of months, maybe only until the next election, and he'd see if he could get him his job back.

Ad hadn't wanted to leave San Francisco; he loved the city, the life he lived there. His job was one he enjoyed, had worked hard to get, but after he was fired, no other newspaper would hire him. At least until the flurry his series had caused died down.

So Ad had been forced to leave the city and seek employment elsewhere. Eventually he landed the editorship of this small weekly, off the beaten track, in this remote part of Oregon, a town only a few years past its "gold rush" days, now settling in as a community of farm families, timber fellers, small lumber mills, a twenty-minute stop on the stagecoach line.

A temporary "stop-gap," he reassured himself when he came nearly seven months ago. But the dreary exile had dragged on, and from what he heard from friends in San Francisco, the situation there was still chancy. The politician he had been investigating was reelected and it looked as if it would be a long time before Ad could safely return and expect to be reinstated.

He keenly missed the camaraderie of his fellow reporters; he missed San Francisco, the theaters and fine restaurants, the amusing conversation of attractive women, and the sophisticated pleasures a city offered.

In Riverbend there wasn't much for a man like Ad, little to stimulate him intellectually, few people well-read enough to argue or debate with him on many subjects he liked to explore,

48

little to do for a man who had never enjoyed hunting or fishing. Nights were spent reading until, bored with himself, he flung the book aside and sauntered over to the Golden Slipper in search of company, only to stay too long and drink too much. He'd had no feminine companionship for months, unless you counted the poor, painted saloon girls with whom the miners in from the hills and the ranch hands in from nearby spreads drank, danced, and had a few laughs. But it wasn't Ad's style and he often left feeling depressed and deeply lonely. Something he'd never experienced before.

He had made no close friends here. At first he'd received a few Sunday dinner invitations from some of the families, but he soon found if you didn't attend church regularly or fit neatly into the category of prospective husband for marriageable daughters, the invitations stopped coming.

After he'd written a few editorials that were considered "downright radical," Ad was thought too controversial for most of the town folk. But since there was no one else to print the weather reports, the cattle stock prices, the church socials and bake sales, announce the births, accept the eulogies to go along with the obituaries, publish the preacher's weekly sermons or the times of the Town Council meetings, Ad was tolerated as a "necessary evil" for Riverbend.

He liked Blaine Stevens, but as the only doctor in the vicinity the man was so conscientious about his patients, he rarely had any time to call his own. There was always a baby to deliver, a child with colic, or an old woman, alone and ill, he had to ride out to see. Ad also liked Ned Thornton, but he was totally henpecked, and that kind of nonsense disgusted Ad. A confirmed bachelor, Ad was thankful he had escaped a similar fate, having survived several near-lapses and thus far successfully dodged matrimony.

But thinking of Ned brought instantly to mind the young woman Ned had introduced as his cousin. Hollis Lambeth. Unconsciously, Ad shook his head. How such a lovely creature had appeared so unexpectedly in Riverbend, of all places, went beyond Ad's powers of imagination. It was as if she had been dropped from Mt. Olympus.

Ad closed his eyes for a moment, willing her image back onto the screen of his mind. Tall, slender, with creamy skin and wide, heavily lashed eyes. Dressed simply in a peacock-blue suit, everything about her was neat and trim. She looked unrumpled, without too many flounces and furbelows that can make a woman traveler look frumpy. She wore little jewelry, no dangling earrings, only a small fob watch pinned to her jacket lapel. She wore dark-blue kid gloves, and a tiny, pert bonnet with a veil barely covering the cinnamon-brown hair. A veil and gloves were two things you didn't often see on Riverbend ladies. There was a coolness about her, a reserve, that Ad immediately admired.

What was she doing here visiting a couple like Ned and Hetty? And why had she come to a place with so little to offer in the way of social life a young lady of her apparent grace should enjoy? Ad's investigative reporter instincts stirred. There was some mystery about this new arrival. What it was triggered his curiosity.

As if he had willed his thoughts into reality, he looked out the window and saw Holly coming up on the other side of the street opposite the *Monitor* building. Ad swung his feet down and leaned forward to watch her. Unconsciously he smiled. She had such a graceful walk, erect yet natural, not mincing nor stiff. Still there was something purposeful in her stride. Where was she going? Where was she headed?

He saw her pause at the corner, close her umbrella, look for a long time down either side of the street. Would it be too obvious if he strolled out and met her apparently by chance?

But Ad was a man who figured one should always take whatever opportunity Fate graciously presented. This seemed to be one that had landed happily right in his lap. Ad decided to seize the moment. He swiveled his chair around, slipped on his jacket coat, grabbed his hat, and made it out the door just as Holly came directly across the road.

Chapter 5

*I*n a few long strides Ad crossed the road and approached Holly casually as if he had been leisurely sauntering down the street and had come upon her quite accidentally. Giving no hint of the mad dash he had made from his office into the street, he swept off his hat. "Good afternoon, Miss Lambeth."

Holly stopped short. She had been so engrossed in her own troubling thoughts that hearing her name startled her. Adam Corcoran's greeting took her quite by surprise and brought color like twin blushing roses into her cheeks.

"Good day, Mr. Corcoran," she replied, acknowledging with a nod that they had been previously introduced, then started to move on.

But Adam was standing right in front of her, making that impossible. To sweep past him would have been rude, and, after all, he *was* a friend of Ned's. Besides, it seemed clear he intended to exchange more than merely a polite greeting as he asked, "I hope you're having a pleasant stay in Riverbend, Miss Lambeth?"

Innate honesty tempted Holly to blurt out a truthful "No!" But her ingrained good manners and social grace compelled her to give the obligatory although somewhat ambiguous response. "Indeed, thank you, Mr. Corcoran. I am finding it most interesting."

Almost as if he had discerned the subtle evasion in her answer, looking amused, he pursued the subject. "However, I assume you find it a great deal different from the East?"

"Oh, well, yes. Very," Holly countered and again attempted to pass him. But all six feet and at least three inches of him were blocking her way.

"Especially this weather, I presume," Adam said as if determined to continue the conversation he had initiated. "It will take some time to get used to; I can tell you that from my own experience." Ad paused, then seeing he had aroused her curiosity, he went on, "I must admit I had a few qualms when I arrived here a few months ago from San Francisco."

He let the name "San Francisco" sink in for a minute, watching what her reaction might be. Ad knew that Eastern periodicals gave their readers rhapsodic descriptions of San Francisco, calling it the "Paris of the West Coast." Such padded verbiage attributed more ambiance than it really had—or deserved, for that matter. But it tended to lend a certain aura to anyone lucky enough to be able to say he knew the city.

Holly looked at Adam Corcoran with a new interest. Obviously he was a gentleman, well-dressed. The gray broadcloth coat, spotless linen, and silk cravat spoke of good taste and certainly not the kind she had seen worn by other Riverbend men. He was certainly well-groomed, clean-shaven except for his mustache; his olive skin was smooth and clear; his eyes held both intelligence and humor. His speech was that of an educated man with a southern courtliness of manner that made her feel a bit homesick and prone to be friendly.

While Holly was making this calculated survey of him, Adam's practiced eye was reaffirming his first impression of her. Miss Hollis Lambeth, he decided, was the most attractive young woman he had seen in a very long time, especially in Riverbend. The cool air had brought the bloom of roses to her skin, several strands of hair loosened by the moisture clung in fetching tendrils to the side of her cheek, and there was surely a suspicion of dimples around her very tempting mouth.

Holly was as curious about Adam Corcoran as he was about her. What might have brought such a man to this remote

Oregon border town? Why had he buried himself here? Was he running away from something, someone? Did he have a past he was trying to forget? Even that possibility did not frighten her; rather, it intrigued her. It made her think that maybe she had more in common with Adam Corcoran than anyone else in Riverbend.

All this went through Holly's mind in a second. Now she listened with a new spark of interest as Adam said, "However, in case you may be a bit concerned by the exterior of the town—" Ad made a sweeping gesture to encompass the "down and out" look of Main Street "—I hasten to assure you, it is not completely without some of the cultural amenities one hopes to find in a new place. There are traveling theatrical troupes who come up from San Francisco regularly, with a good repertoire of plays, ones that have received good reviews in the East. Often the players are well-known in Europe and are making American tours. Some are even stars of Shakespearean drama and comedy."

Ad saw he had hit the mark. Holly's eyes suddenly sparkled. He played his advantage quickly. "I would consider it a real pleasure if, on one of these occasions, you would do me the honor of accompanying me to such a production should one happen while you are here."

Holly loved going to plays, and the possibility of such a diversion gave her the needed "light at the end of the tunnel" she had not thought to find in Riverbend. She gave Ad a delighted smile. "Why, thank you, Mr. Corcoran, I surely would."

Gratified by his success in achieving her acceptance, Adam was about to suggest he walk on with her wherever she was going, when Ned Thornton came out onto the porch of the General Store, waved, and called, "Holly! Your box came on the morning stage!"

Holly returned the wave and called back, "Oh, good! I'll be right over, Ned, thank you." To Ad she explained, "I've been expecting a package from my mother, and it's come. So, if you'll excuse me—"

"What a coincidence! I was going over to check on the very same thing myself."

53

"A package from your mother?" Holly's eyebrows arched in surprise.

Ad chuckled, "No, not a package from my mother, but a friend in San Francisco sends me a bundle of the daily newspapers each week. Of course, the news is a week late, but it's a feast I look forward to, I can tell you. So may I escort you?" he offered.

With only a split-second's hesitation, Holly took his arm, and they crossed the street together, Ad skillfully manipulating them around the potholes and mud puddles.

A bell over the door jangled as they entered the store. Ned, in his shirtsleeves and wearing a blue cotton storekeeper's apron, greeted them both. "Holly, I was going to bring your box with me when I came home for supper."

"Well, I'm here now, so I can carry it myself."

Ned shook his head, "'Fraid not, Holly. It's real heavy. Don't know what your mother must have put in it! Bricks?"

Holly laughed while Ad quickly offered, "I'll be happy to carry Miss Lambeth's box for her and see her home."

Ned looked from one to the other; a smile played around the corner of his mouth. He glanced at Holly as if to say, "Another male admirer, ready to do your bidding, eh, Holly, just like in Willow Springs?" But there was no maliciousness in Ned's eyes, just an indulgent twinkle. "Why don't I just open up the box for you, Holly? It's over there in the corner, and you can take your time looking through it, decide what you want now, and I can bring the rest later."

"Good idea," Holly agreed, and she and Ad followed him to the back of the store.

Ned cut the cords binding the sturdy box; then, taking the pronged end of a hammer, he pried out the nails and with a wrenching sound pulled up the lid. Pushing aside some layers of excelsior, they all peered inside.

"Books!" they said in unison.

"*That* should keep you busy all winter, Holly," Ad remarked dryly.

"Oh, I hoped it was books," Holly sighed happily. "Mama promised to send me some."

Just then the bell over the door jangled, and a woman came into the store. "I better go wait on my customer," Ned told them in a low voice and left Holly and Ad bending over the box of books.

"So you like to read, Miss Lambeth? Better watch out, you'll ruin your 'Southern belle' image. Unless you're not afraid of being considered a 'blue stocking'!"

"I despise labels!" she retorted icily. "Educated women—*even in the South*—enjoy good literature. I grew up on Lamb's *Tales of Shakespeare.*"

"You consider *these* books *literature*, do you?" Ad asked, picking a book up at random and reading the title out loud, "*Wherever the True Heart Leads* by Marcella Valencourt?" He looked at her with an amused expression.

Holly had the grace to blush and half-indignantly snatched it out of his hands. One special thing she shared with her mother was a love of romantic novels. She was glad some were mixed in with other favorites, Dickens' novels and George Eliot's, too. They had both wept over *The Mill on the Floss.* She was ready to defend her mother's choices when Ad apologized. "I didn't mean to offend, Miss Lambeth. Variety, as they say, is the spice of life, in reading material as in everything else."

"Books?" a woman's voice behind them asked. "I didn't know you carried books, Mr. Thornton."

Holly turned around to see a woman. She was dressed in a beautifully cut buff poplin walking suit, trimmed with brown cording, standing with Ned at the counter but peering in their direction.

"I didn't order them, Mrs. Dodd; they belong to Hetty's cousin. They just arrived for her by stage," Ned explained. "Come over, I'd like you to meet her. Holly, I'd like you to meet Viola Dodd, Riverbend's finest seamstress. Hollis Lambeth." *Viola Dodd, Seamstress!* The resident of the charming little yellow house she had wondered about and now at last had the chance to meet.

The woman was very small, slight with a delicate almost fragile appearance. Under a tastefully trimmed bonnet, her face was a pale oval. Her features were refined; her mouth was rather compressed; her nose was delicate and aristocratic. Holly always particularly noticed noses probably because her own was short and tended to tilt at the tip.

"I'm pleased to meet you," Holly said. Knowing that Mrs. Dodd was a seamstress, Holly realized that she must have made the stylish outfit herself. Holly was duly impressed.

"And I you," Mrs. Dodd murmured politely at the introduction, then her eyes wandered back to the pile of books.

Recognizing the longing in Viola Dodd's eyes, impulsively Holly offered, "Would you like to borrow one?"

A look of surprise broke through the woman's composed expression. Flushed with pleasure, she exclaimed, "Oh, may I? How very generous of you. I do enjoy relaxing with a good book after sewing all day!"

"Of course," Holly said. "Do choose any one you like," and she stepped back to make room for Mrs. Dodd at the edge of the box.

With one gloved hand she reached into the neatly packed contents of the box, slowly examining the books one by one. Her deliberateness in making her selection made Holly aware that Viola Dodd would be careful about any choice. She also had the instant longing to know her better.

"I believe this one will do nicely," Mrs. Dodd said as she picked up *Silas Marner*. "I hope this wasn't one you were planning to read yourself, Miss Lambeth?"

"No, not at all, not at the moment," Holly assured her.

"I will take very good care of it and return it promptly. I suppose here at the store with Mr. Thornton?"

Holly hesitated, wishing she could invite Viola Dodd to bring it to the house, stay for a visit, but of course, she knew that was out of the question. As if reading her thoughts, Viola spoke softly, rather shyly, "Unless," a slight hesitation, "—unless you might care to come to my house some afternoon for tea? Perhaps then we could discuss our shared interest in books?"

Holly nodded eagerly, and Mrs. Dodd continued, "Very well, then, thank you again." Mrs. Dodd slipped the small volume into a large reticule. "I shall send you a note when I finish the book, and we can set a time and day."

"Oh, yes, that would be lovely. Thank you very much."

Suddenly Holly felt lighthearted. At last something to look forward to, the promise of an invitation, the prospect of a friendship!

Chapter 6

*H*olly's mother had thoughtfully packed some children's books along with the novels. There was a large book of fairy tales that Holly could read to Aurelia and a book illustrated with pictures of all kinds of carriages any little boy would love. Holly knew Teddy would be thrilled. Ned gave them a smaller box, and Ad helped her put those in along with a number of the novels, including one she thought Hetty might like to read.

"I guess that's enough for now since Ned will bring the rest home later," Holly said.

"I hope you don't intend to read during your entire time here, Miss Lambeth," Ad commented.

Holly responded with pretended shock. "Certainly not, Mr. Corcoran. Besides books, I intend to read the editorials in the *Riverbend Monitor* as well. I understand they are educational as well as entertaining!"

"Well put and well taken." Adam smiled. Bending to pick up the box, he gave a mock groan. "Are you sure you don't want to take one or two *more*?"

Amused at his clowning, Holly laughed and shook her head.

On their way out, they stopped to speak to Ned who was busily stocking shelves. "We're going now, Ned," Holly said; then seeing glass jars of peppermint sticks, molasses chunks, and licorice twists, she asked, "Would it be all right if I took the children some candy?"

For a minute Ned seemed about to say no; then giving Holly a conspiratorial wink and leaning toward her, he said in a stage whisper, "Why not? As long as we keep it a secret," and filled two small paper bags with a mixture of the candies.

"I'll bring the rest of the books home with me this evening," Ned promised as she left.

Outside the store they turned in the direction of the Thorntons' house. Holly was feeling a great deal better than earlier when she had rushed out in anger. Being with Adam Corcoran had restored some of her natural good humor. The frank admiration in his eyes and his light, teasing manner had been beneficial as well.

She was even feeling optimistic about Hetty. Maybe Hetty would be so pleased with the books, especially those for the children, she would get over whatever was making her so unreasonable. Holly's mind was filled with possible ways she could soften up her cousin and reach some kind of amicable relationship. After all, they weren't children anymore but two grown-up women who should be able to get along. Otherwise—well, otherwise, Holly still didn't know what to do.

Suddenly Ad put out a warning hand on her arm to hold her back. "Let's cross the street," he suggested.

"Why?" asked Holly, puzzled.

"Because—" Ad never got to finish the sentence because the sound of loud voices shouting, punctuated with swear words, made hearing anything momentarily impossible. A moment later the double doors of the Doggone Best saloon swung open, and a figure lunged out.

"Uh-oh, too late. I wanted to avoid this—," Ad said and drew Holly quickly off the sidewalk onto the street. "That's poor Cliff Larkin," he told her, adding, "I only hope nobody on the Town Council sees him."

"Who is he?" asked Holly. As Ad steered her to the other side of the street, she looked back over her shoulder at the man staggering down the opposite sidewalk, weaving from post to post, hanging on each trying to get his balance.

"Believe it or not, he's the town schoolteacher. School's due to start in another week, and he's probably having a last fling before having to face all those bright little faces early every morning."

"*He* teaches *school?*" Holly's tone matched the look of astonishment on her face. All she could think of was her own schoolteachers—prim Miss Rebecca Burns who had taught her in grammar school; Louisa McGill, the severe headmistress at the Blue Ridge Female Academy she had attended after sixth grade. And Mr. Bradley, the principal at Willow Springs Secondary, had also been a church elder and taught Sunday school. All the teachers she had ever known were a far cry from this poor wretch stumbling down the street.

"Shouldn't someone help him?" she asked anxiously, twisting her head around to watch the man's unsteady progress.

"Someone will," Ad assured her. "Yes, see, there he comes now. The town's good Samaritan. The doctor."

Holly saw Blaine emerge from the door of one of the buildings along the path the drunk was taking. With a few steps he caught Larkin in time to keep him from falling.

"That's Blaine Stevens, better known as Doc," Ad said, unaware that Holly knew him. "He'll take care of him, take him upstairs to his own place above his office, let him sleep it off, then sober him up."

"What a shame!"

"He'll be all right. That is, until the next time. Blaine tells me the man has a brilliant mind—or did before it got soaked with alcohol. Comes from a good family back east, too. Although they've disowned him now," Ad said; then he placed Holly's hand on his arm. "Don't worry your pretty little head about it. Doc knows what to do, and Larkin will be at his blackboard with his pointer, teaching all those eager little scholars when the schoolhouse bell rings come next Monday."

Holly watched the two men entering the door over which was a neatly lettered sign: "Blaine Stevens, Physician and Surgeon." Blaine had not seen either Holly or Ad; he had seemed totally concerned with helping that sadly in-need human being.

"Doc's an enigma." Adam shook his head. "I'll never understand why someone of his caliber has buried himself here. I've seen his diploma. He graduated from one of the best medical colleges in the country and studied in Scotland and Germany. He could probably get a post in any hospital in America or teach in a university. He's a fine doctor and—" Ad halted "—well, it's none of my business, I guess, everyone who comes to Riverbend has his own reasons." He glanced at Holly as if daring her to tell him why *she* had come.

By this time they had reached the Thorntons'. Ad opened the gate for Holly to pass through. As they walked up onto the porch, the front door flew open and Hetty stood there glaring at them both.

Ad whipped off his hat, held it to his chest, and bowed slightly. "Good day, Mrs. Thornton. I'm bringing your cousin home safely after piloting her through some hazardous obstacles."

His speech was designed to be amusing, but Hetty didn't smile. Indeed she was looking very unamused. Quickly Holly explained, "My box from Mama arrived by stage and was at the store, Hetty, but it was too heavy for me, so Mr. Corcoran kindly offered to carry it here for me."

"Ned could have brought it home," Hetty replied shortly.

Holly felt embarrassed at Hetty's unfriendliness. What on earth could Mr. Corcoran think? However, Ad seemed not at all disturbed by Hetty's lack of cordiality. He simply smiled and suggested courteously, "Shall I put it inside?"

Hetty was forced to step back and hold the door open for him to place the box inside by the door.

He then tipped his hat to her. "Nice to see you again, Mrs. Thornton; have a pleasant day." Turning to Holly, he bowed over the hand she extended, saying, "Good day, Miss Lambeth, and I hope I may have the pleasure of calling on you soon."

Conscious of Hetty's eyes boring into her like two sharp knives, Holly murmured. "Thank you for your help, Mr. Corcoran."

With an enigmatic smile Ad went down the porch steps, nonchalantly strolled down the path, went out the gate, and turned back toward town.

Holly stepped inside the house. The door had barely closed behind her when Hetty confronted her, demanding, "What are you trying to do, Holly? Have every available man in Riverbend dancing to your tune? Don't you know how it looks? Flirting and flitting all over town, attracting attention? This isn't Willow Springs, you know. It doesn't take much here in this town to give a woman the tag of 'fast.' Ned and I have a good name here, and I don't appreciate your damaging it by being seen with anyone you can find to fetch and carry for you. Especially someone like Adam Corcoran whose reputation in this community is questionable, to say the least!".

Stunned at the vicious attack, Holly stared back at her. Anger welled up hotly, then seeing Hetty's flushed face, bulging eyes, the heat turned to ice.

"Are you quite finished, Hetty?" she asked coldly. "If you are, I have something to say. I doubt that you care about *my* reputation. And for your information, Mr. Corcoran is as perfect a gentleman as I have ever met here or anywhere else. Furthermore, I like to make up my own mind about people, not be told whom I should speak or walk with. It was *your* husband who introduced me to Mr. Corcoran in the first place, and *Ned* seems to have high regard for him. Now if you'll excuse me, I'm going to take off my bonnet and open my box from my mother!"

Holly brushed past Hetty, biting her lip to avoid saying anything more she might regret. Without another glance in her cousin's direction, Holly shoved the heavy box with her foot across the floor, down the hall. She went into the bedroom, letting the door bang behind her.

She was angry. Angry for losing her temper. Even angrier that Hetty could make her *this* upset. Worse still, it spoiled what Holly had hoped would be a happy, conciliatory occasion. Hetty's outburst had prevented her from sharing the books her mother had sent for all of them to enjoy, to perhaps bridge the gap that separated them.

The longer she was here, the more impossible it got. Was there no solution? Was there no escape?

Chapter 7

$\mathcal{H}$olly had no sooner reached the haven of the bedroom when there was a sharp rat-a-tat-tat on the door. Whirling around, she yanked it open to face a flushed Hetty.

"I don't want you to start giving Aurelia the notion that she can loll around looking at books all day. I'm trying to teach her to do her fair share of chores, and there's plenty for her to do to help around here, so I'd suggest you put those books out of sight."

Holly stared at her cousin in disbelief. "You don't want Aurelia to enjoy books?" she gasped.

"People out here have more to do than daydream and live make-believe lives. Things out here don't come easy. People work hard and don't have time for nonsense."

"But Hetty, our family always loved to read. You and I both were given books when we were little girls," Holly protested, and leaning into the box, she pulled an *Alice* volume out to show her. "Look, see what Mama sent? Don't you remember how we loved *Alice in Wonderland?*"

Hetty's expression just got grimmer. "I guess you didn't hear what I said—I want Aurelia to fit in; I don't want my daughter to grow up any different, with high-falutin' ideas, thinking she's better than anybody else," and she turned around to leave.

Still, Holly made one last try. "Can't I even give this to the children as a gift from my mother, Hetty?"

"I've said what I meant and I meant what I said," was Hetty's rejoinder as she marched back down the hall to the kitchen.

Totally bewildered, Holly shut the door again and sat down on the edge of the bed, Hetty's words echoing in her head. They brought back the hilarious discussion that Alice had had with the Duchess that, as children, they had repeated endlessly, always dissolving into helpless laughter afterward. Holly, now recalling that ridiculous dialogue when Alice says, "I say what I mean and I mean what I say," to which the Duchess replies, "Nonsense! That's like saying that I see what I eat is the same as I eat what I see"—and on and on wondered if Hetty had inadvertently mouthed the same words without realizing the source? Were there, after all, some happy memories of their shared childhood that Hetty couldn't suppress?

What was behind all that fury? What did Hetty *really* mean by saying she didn't want Aurelia to be "different"? Would reading, enjoying good books, make Aurelia grow up dissatisfied, discontent, unhappy in this environment? What was Hetty really saying? Was she talking about Aurelia or herself? It seemed that everything she tried to do, every time she turned around, she met Hetty's opposition. How could she possibly go on here with Hetty?

Frustrated, she shoved the box of books under the bed, took off her bonnet, and pondered the bleak prospect of the year ahead. If there were any place she could go, Holly would have packed up and left on the spot. There seemed no way to get along with Hetty. But with no viable alternative until she could figure out what to do next she would just have to accept it. Only a miracle could change the situation. And were miracles a common commodity in 1882?

Out of the blue, or so it seemed, help came from an unexpected source. One evening a few days later, when Ned came home from the store, he handed Holly a note. "Mrs. Dodd left this for you."

Surprised, Holly opened it and read it eagerly. True to her promise, Mrs. Dodd had written,

My dear Miss Lambeth, I cannot tell you what pleasure reading *Silas Marner* afforded me. I am indebted to you for the enjoyable hours I spent with the book you so graciously lent me. I would like to return my thanks by having you to tea, Wednesday next at three o'clock if you are free to come? I always take Wednesday afternoon off, and so look forward to entertaining you. You may send word by Mr. Thornton, as I plan to be in the store on Tuesday to pick up some material he ordered for me due to arrive that day.

With kind regards,
Viola Dodd.

On Wednesday afternoon Holly dressed with special care, aware that she would be viewed by a professional who would notice every detail. She chose a simple but stylish ensemble, a jade-green velvet hat trimmed with a cluster of feathers. When she emerged from the bedroom and came into the kitchen, ready to leave for Mrs. Dodd's, Aurelia looked up from the floor where she and Teddy were building with blocks and asked, "Oh, Holly, are you going to a party?"

Hetty was at the ironing board, but at that she looked up. Her narrowed glance at Holly revealed her curiosity, but her tightly pursed lips said she would rather be tortured than ask Holly where she was going.

Determined not to let Hetty's manner bother her, Holly spoke pleasantly, "I'm going over to Mrs. Dodd's; she's invited me to tea."

"Viola Dodd may put on fine manners, but after all, all she does is sew for other people!"

Although usually Holly made a point of not getting into arguments with her cousin in front of the children, this, however, was too much. This mean-spirited remark shocked Holly into responding, "What an unkind thing to say, Hetty!"

Hetty turned crimson.

Afraid that this could escalate into a full-blown argument or worse, deliberately, Holly controlled herself. Smiling at the children, she went to the door. "Good-bye, then, I'll see you later." Aurelia's sweet little voice followed her—"Have a nice time, Holly!"

In Viola Dodd's parlor there was none of the clutter of the popular decorating style, influenced by the English Queen Victoria, found in most houses of the time. It was not overloaded with the prevalent trend for crocheted antimacassars, China dogs, painted seashells, artificial flowers under glass domes. Instead it had the quiet taste of its owner.

When Holly remarked on a silver-framed photograph on top of the piano, showing a lovely young girl, Mrs. Dodd said simply, without further explanation, "My daughter, Avesta; she's away at boarding school."

Mrs. Dodd—"Please call me Vi,"—served a delightful tea consisting of egg salad sandwiches cut in triangles and a moist lemon sponge cake. Holly relaxed at once in her hostess's warmth. Soon they were chatting as if they had known each other a long time. Holly had spent many hours in her bedroom reading to avoid Hetty during the day without Ned's presence as a buffer. So, books were a natural topic of their conversation. Holly discovered Vi loved the novels of Sir Walter Scott and that they shared a very favorite author in Charlotte Brontë.

All too soon the melodious chiming of Vi's mantel clock reminded Holly that she had stayed past the acceptable time for a first-time call. However, it had been such a pleasant respite from her tension-filled existence at Hetty's that she hated to leave.

"Oh, do you have to go?" her hostess said, seeming almost as reluctant to have her leave. "There are so few ladies here in Riverbend I find I have enough in common with, although I'm sure there must be others who enjoy books and reading as much as we two, but most are married with small children which puts me—*and* you—out of their circumstances, doesn't it?"

"But does it have to?" Holly demanded. "At home, back in Willow Springs, I know my mother and aunts have friends in their Garden Club, for instance, who are all ages and in different walks of life—some of them are spinsters like me and—" She halted suddenly saying, "Oh, I'm sorry. Of course, *you're* not a spinster, I forgot you have a daughter."

Vi only smiled and went on to say, "You're quite right. I'm sure that's the best way to look for friendships. Not age nor situation but common interests." She paused as though thinking for a minute. They were now standing in the little hallway. Then Vi said slowly, "I don't know whether you'd be interested or not but just suppose—"

"Suppose what?"

"Suppose—we had some sort of book club. Invite some ladies to get together maybe once a month to discuss books, exchange them, and so on?" Vi suggested.

"Why, yes! But whom would we ask to join?"

"We'd first have to find out who in Riverbend likes to read. Sadly enough, there is no library. . . ."

Just then Holly thought of the box brimming with books under her bed. Hetty's disdain of having them around, the letter from Mama saying she was sending *more*—

"I'm getting an idea!" she exclaimed. "But I guess I better think it through a little bit."

"If it's on the line of a book club, I'm all for it." Vi smiled as she opened the front door for her, "I'm so happy you could come today, Holly. I haven't enjoyed an afternoon so much in—I couldn't tell you how long. Please come again soon."

"As soon as I get my idea figured out better, I'll talk it over with you," Holly promised as they walked out onto the porch.

"Pray about it!" was Vi's surprising suggestion.

"You sound just like my Great-Aunt Ancilla!" Holly laughed as she went down the steps.

"I hope that's a compliment?"

"It *is!*" Holly assured her.

The afternoon was well along, and Holly hurried through the gathering autumn dusk, filled with enthusiasm about her new friendship and excited about the plan stirring in her mind. But when she stepped inside Hetty's house, she was greeted by a smoldering look from Hetty and her announcement, "You're late. I'm serving supper now. Ned's been home a half-hour."

Holly started to apologize but Hetty's next words chilled. "Ned brought *another* box from your mother. If it's books . . ." the implied threat was in Hetty's voice, but Holly did not wait to hear it. She went back to the bedroom to take off her hat and jacket and saw the large carton at the door. *Oh, dear Lord, what now?* Holly murmured to herself, not knowing it was a prayer.

Later that evening, upon opening the box, she found a note from her mother inside: "Dear Holly, I trust by this time you are settled in at Hetty's and things are going smoothly." *Oh, Mama, if you only knew,* Holly sighed, then read on: "I hope it won't upset you to know that Jim Mercer and his bride are here visiting his parents. . . ." Reading this, Holly felt a dart of pain. Surprised by it she wondered if it was wounded pride she felt or regret? Would any mention of Jim always hurt her in some way? She read on: "—and I heard she was going to remain here since his next post is in some unsuitable place for wives."

Her mother had written something more, then scratched it out heavily. Curious, Holly held it up to the light so she could read through it. "Jim's mother introduced me to her after church on Sunday, and she is quite pretty."

She would be! Holly thought miserably, then continued with the letter: "Well, your father wants to take this box to the post office, so I shall close now. Hoping you are in fine spirit and good health, everyone sends love."

Squeezed at the bottom of the closely written page was a post-script: "Great-Aunt Ancilla just came by and wanted me to enclose these for you." Several small tracts fell out of the envelope. Holly fanned them out in her hand seeing a picture of the dear little old lady in her mind. Across the top of the first one in bold black type was the Biblical instruction: "Whatever your hand finds to do, do it with all your might." Slowly she reread it; wasn't this the same tract she had found in her hanky that day in the woods?

Her one hand was resting on the top of the new box of books, and she repeated the quotation to herself: "Whatever your hand finds to do, do it with all your might. . . ."

The half-formed idea that had come to her as she left Viola Dodd's burst into full possibility. Vi had said, "Pray about it." Great-Aunt Ancilla had sent the tracts! Maybe this was the answer to her unspoken prayer? Why not? This might well be the guidance she had been seeking, the direction she was looking for. *Could* it *actually* be? It *did* seem more than coincidental that this tract with the same message had come to her *twice*.

Feeling that Ned would know how such a project would be received, a few evenings later Holly decided to tell her idea at supper and find out his reaction. She had hardly finished speaking when Hetty let out a sound suspiciously like a snort. "A lending library!" her tone was derisive. "Who in Riverbend has time to read silly novels?"

Holly held on to her temper. "They wouldn't be *all* novels, Hetty. Mama sent a variety of books—and she's sending more—"

"My land! Where does she think you're going to put them, for pity's sake?" Hetty demanded. "Does she think we have a house as big as the Lambeths'?"

"That's just it, Hetty. I *know* you don't have room here. That's why I thought, perhaps . . . ," and Holly glanced hopefully at Ned who was listening intently, ". . . that Ned might have a small corner at the store where we could keep the books and I could be there certain hours to take care of lending out books. I would think some of the mothers would particularly like the nice selection of children's books Mama sent—"

Before Hetty could interrupt again, Ned spoke up, "I think that's a really good idea, Holly. I could put up a few shelves for you. I think people might be very interested. As long as they're in the store anyway. I know the copies I get of the *Farmers' Almanac* go almost as soon as I put them out. With no town library here, I think we'd be providing a great service for people."

Hetty's mouth pressed into a straight line. If Ned was for the idea, she wasn't about to contradict him no matter how much she opposed it.

Chapter 8

*A*lmost from the first week after Holly put up her carefully lettered sign, LENDING LIBRARY, the venture was a success. Contrary to Hetty's dire predictions and confirming Holly's hope, the women in Riverbend were starved for books and welcomed the project.

The first day the women who had come into the store to purchase flour, sugar, and salt, and other staples, to finger the bolts of bright cloth or leaf through one of the mail order catalogs Ned kept on hand, only eyed Holly's corner curiously. Initially, most seemed too shy to investigate.

As the hours passed with no customers, Holly tried to act busy, dusting the shelves, rearranging the books. Then she got the idea to make an attractive display of some of the books with illustrated covers and print out brief plot summaries to place beside them. The next day one or two women wandered over, and Holly immediately engaged them in conversation, telling about the lending plan and encouraging them to browse and select a book if they liked.

From then on, probably by word of mouth, awareness of the library spread and grew rapidly. In two weeks' time, Holly was doing a thriving business and meeting quite a few Riverbend women.

One of the early and most enthusiastic borrowers was Geneva Healy, a plump, rosy-cheeked woman with a snub nose, bright blue eyes, and an endearing smile, who came into the store about once a week. She was the wife of a prosperous dairy farmer, Holly learned from Ned. She was usually accompanied by two small curly-headed little boys, ages eight and nine, and one about three at her heels.

The first morning she spied Holly arranging books behind the low counter Ned had built for the library, she came right over. After they had exchanged "Good mornings," she hoisted the smiling cherub onto her hip and declared, "Oh, I love to read! I've read the few books I have over and over, and here you are with a good dozen or more I've never even heard of!"

"You're welcome to take one if you like. Just pick out what you want, then sign this little card, and I'll mark the date and give you three weeks to return it. If you haven't finished it then, you can take it out for another two weeks. Does that sound fair?" Holly asked. She was rather unsure if she should bend the rules of the three-week "borrowing time" for a woman with small children and a household to keep. Hetty just *might* be right, Holly worried, maybe none of the Riverbend women *did* have the time or inclination to read.

But Geneva seemed delighted. She introduced herself, and when Holly did the same, Geneva looked astounded. "You're Hetty's cousin? I'd never have guessed. There's no family resemblance, not a bit! Not that I know her well. Not well at all, as a matter of fact. I've just seen her at church, and before she had her little boy she used to help out here in the store once in awhile." Geneva put her head to one side, regarding Holly again. "Well, well—"

Geneva must have told her friends because within the next few days Holly did, according to Ned, "a land-office business" in books. She always greeted the tentative customers pleasantly and asked them what type of story they liked, then suggested titles they might want to borrow, explaining they were allowed to keep them three weeks before returning them.

The response to the library was gratifying. Hetty had implied that many of the women, isolated on remote farms, burdened with endless chores, felt they didn't have time to indulge in reading. Holly found that most of the women had come to

71

Oregon, leaving family and friends in the east and midwest, and experienced real loneliness. But with Holly's encouragement they now discovered that reading gave them a welcome outlet and provided an interesting break in their otherwise lonely routines.

It was Geneva Healy who actually organized the Riverbend Literary Society, confirming Vi's original idea. "We can have the first meeting at my house," Geneva offered. "We'll keep it simple, just cake and tea so the hostess won't have to fuss; we can just have a good time talking books! What do you think?"

"I think it's a wonderful idea!" Holly agreed enthusiastically, and so the Riverbend Literary Society was formed. That day Holly came home excited about the idea and in her elation shared Geneva's suggestion with Hetty. "Won't that be lovely? A real chance to get together and talk about something other than recipes and babies!"

Hetty's response was caustic. "*Most* women think *those* are the most important things, *more* important than *books,* and *enjoy* talking about their children and exchanging recipes! But, *of course,* someone like *you* couldn't possibly understand that."

Whoops! thought Holly, *that was a mistake.* Another black mark against her in Hetty's book inadvertently made. Trying to make amends, Holly tried again, "I didn't mean that the way it sounded, Hetty; I meant it would give women something *different* not *better.* Remember how your mother and mine used to enjoy the Garden Club, which wasn't about gardening much at all, but gave them a chance to gossip and giggle and be girls again . . ." Seeing Hetty's frown she added lamely, ". . . at least that's what Papa used to say."

Hetty sniffed and went on folding laundry.

"Wouldn't you like to join, Hetty? The first meeting will be at Geneva Healy's on Monday afternoon."

"No thank you," Hetty said emphatically, and that ended the matter. Holly knew there was no use trying to persuade her. Hetty was not going to enter into any project or idea that Holly came up with, so she might as well accept that.

Ned had allowed Holly to put up a small poster with an invitation about the time and place of the first meeting. To everyone's surprise not only ladies showed up. Besides the Bodine sisters, who ran Riverbend's bakery, Mr. Clegg, the church organist, came, as did Mr. and Mrs. Phillips, the town watchmaker and his wife. Mrs. Phillips explained that she read to him while he worked; they both loved good books. It was a lively meeting with much discussion, and they all decided that at each meeting someone would give a book report to the group of the book they had just read.

The biggest surprise of all was that both Ad and Blaine showed up. Adam declared that he wanted to write an article about it for the *Monitor,* and Blaine came during the last half-hour when refreshments were being served, then offered to take Holly home.

So in spite of Hetty's reaction to the idea, the Riverbend Literary Society flourished. Viola Dodd was one of its most supportive members. She closed shop on the meeting days and was particularly insightful when critiquing the books under discussion. Through the Literary Society, she and Holly became real friends.

One meeting day, after the other ladies had left, Holly stayed behind and offered to help Vi clear away the tea things. What she really wanted to do was talk to her, ask the older woman's advice about the situation with Hetty, which seemed to get more intolerable with each passing day. Vi's warmth made it easy for Holly to confide. "I don't think she wanted me to come out here in the first place. She just did it to please her mother, my Aunt Dolly. I think she's always resented me for some reason. I'm not sure why," sighed Holly.

Vi regarded her over the rim of her teacup but didn't say anything.

Holly went on, "What could I have done to make her so—so unfriendly?"

"You really don't know, do you?" Vi asked, then set her cup down carefully, wiped her mouth daintily on the small white embroidered napkin. "It's nothing you've done, Holly. Don't you understand that?"

"Then why?"

"Jealousy."

73

"Jealousy? Why should Hetty be jealous of *me*? *She* has everything I don't: a husband, a home, children." Holly was genuinely astonished at such a suggestion.

A silence fell, and Vi calmly poured them each more tea, then asked, "Have you prayed about this, Holly?"

"Yes, of course I have. Well, a little, I guess. I've worried about it more than I've prayed, to be truthful. And especially because I love the children so much and I'd love to spend more time with them, but . . . I just don't know how to deal with Hetty."

On the way home from Vi's that afternoon Holly thought hard about what Vi had said. Was it really possible that Hetty was jealous? Back in Willow Springs when Hetty sat at home while Holly went out dancing, it might have been true. But here in Riverbend, where Hetty was the wife of a respected, prominent citizen, and she, Holly, was a stranger, an outsider? But Vi was the most sincere, truthful person Holly had ever met and had wisdom as well. If *she* believed that was the reason for Hetty's coldness, Holly should at least consider it a possibility.

She felt somewhat ashamed when Vi had asked her if she'd prayed about her relationship with her cousin. To be honest, she had mostly resented it, thought it unfair, and felt herself to be the injured party.

Slowing her step, Holly probed the situation more deeply. If Hetty had always been jealous of her and had finally made a new life for herself in Oregon and had thereby escaped the family's constant comparisons of the two cousins—and then that same cousin suddenly appeared on the scene—wouldn't *you* feel upset? Holly's conscience demanded. If all this was true, what could she do about it? Unless she packed up and went back home, Holly had to stay in Riverbend and make the best of it, and Hetty had to put up with her.

Chapter 9

To Holly's amusement Adam Corcoran became one of the lending library borrowers.

"I thought those bundles of San Francisco newspapers you pick up at the post office every week kept you supplied with enough reading material," she teased him one day as he looked over her titles.

"Well, you can get an overdose of murders, mayhem, and political skullduggery, which is what seems to be the content of most of the city rags these days."

She pretended to be shocked. "I thought you missed the big city."

"I do. Maybe I'm getting soft in the head. Maybe the bucolic life is getting to me. Or maybe, it's just possible, that Riverbend has grown more interesting since some *new* people arrived in town."

She was checking out Dickens' *A Tale of Two Cities* to Adam just as Blaine Stevens came into the store and started over to the library. At his approach, Ad placed his hand on his chest as if suffering a heart attack and gasped, "Don't tell me our dedicated physician has time to read books!"

"It's good medicine; I recommend it to all my patients. A good book occasionally takes them out of their pain and away from their worry for a few hours." His grin included Holly. "I write dozens of prescriptions for a good book to be taken regularly."

"I can understand your giving that advice to sick people or someone who's laid up with a broken limb and worrying about who's going to do his plowing, but what are *you* doing here?" Adam kept up the ragging.

"Haven't you ever heard the saying, 'Physician, heal thyself'?" asked Blaine. Holly was observing the two men, apparently good friends ribbing each other.

At length, Adam said, "Well, check this out for me, if you will, Miss Lambeth, and I'll be on my way. I've got a paper to put to bed."

When he had sauntered off, Holly, assuming her role of librarian, asked Blaine, "So, what kind of leisure reading do you enjoy, doctor?"

"Believe it or not, I enjoy poetry," Blaine told her, leaning his folded arms on the counter and surveying her pleasantly.

"Poetry?" She *was* surprised. Science and poetry seemed a strange combination. "What kind of poetry?"

"Narrative, heroic. Byron, Browning," he replied.

Holly frowned. "I'm sorry, I don't believe we have either of those. Mama doesn't approve of Byron and well—we *do* have the collected sonnets of Elizabeth Barrett Browning—but they're mostly love poems and . . ." For some reason Holly felt her face flush under Blaine's interested gaze. Trying to reshelve the book, she dropped it and thought crossly, *What is the matter with me to be so clumsy?*

Blaine did not seem to notice her fumbling and went on talking. "Actually, I own several volumes of both Byron and Browning—and to be truthful, I came here under false pretenses. I wanted to ask you to go for a drive with me this Sunday after church—if the weather's still fine, and I thought maybe I could show you some more of the countryside."

Holly's head, which was bent to retrieve a dropped book, popped up in surprise. "Why, thank you, Dr. Stevens, I would enjoy that very much."

"Fine." Blaine's smile broadened. "Unless there's an emergency, and I can never be sure of that, and there are no sick calls, I'll attend service and meet you afterward."

Holly reshelved the book, smiling. "See you on Sunday then, Dr. Stevens."

Watching as Blaine departed whistling, Holly was amazed at herself for being so pleased at such an ordinary event as being invited for a drive. But at least it offered an escape from a long, stifling day, trapped at Hetty's. To be honest, Holly had to admit she had missed the company of young men, which she had always enjoyed. Of course, Adam Corcoran had shown some interest in her. But he tended to be sarcastic, which sometimes wore a little thin. So what harm could spending an afternoon with Dr. Stevens do? He was interesting and amusing. She most certainly had no intentions of becoming involved in any romantic way with anyone in Riverbend, whatever Hetty might think!

The rest of the afternoon passed quickly. Holly's spirits had lifted immeasurably at the prospect of an outing with Blaine. The Bodine sisters, Miss Eva and Miss Emmeline, who ran the local bakery and who had become regular lending library devotees, came in to chat and brought a little basket of cupcakes for her. Mr. Clegg, the church organist, also came by to return his book and take out another. Holly helped two new ladies who were interested in selecting books, and by the time Ned was ready to close the store, Holly realized that the day had flown by and had been especially pleasant.

Sunday morning, Holly was standing in front of her mirror, critically checking her appearance. She was wearing an outfit that she had not worn before in Riverbend. Now she wondered if it mighty be too dressy for a country drive. While she wavered about changing into something simpler, an impatient knock came at the bedroom door, followed by Hetty's querulous voice, "What's keeping you, Holly? Are you coming with us to church or not?"

Opening the door, Hetty peered around it. Her gaze swept over Holly from the bonnet trimmed with tiny blueberries down the scalloped bodice and flounced skirt of her blue faille walking suit. "My, my!" was all she said, but acid dripped from

77

her voice. Then she quickly withdrew, saying, "We're in the wagon, waiting. Hurry up if you're coming."

Holly gathered up her gloves and handbag and hurried out, wondering why Hetty always somehow managed to make her feel guilty. When she got into the wagon beside the children, Aurelia gave her an awed compliment. She squeezed the little girl's hand appreciatively and smiled, but it only made Holly feel worse. Hettty's unspoken but obvious criticism had done its damage. At least she'd be gone for the day and out from under it for a few hours, she thought gratefully.

It wasn't until they were going up the steps of the church that Holly informed Hetty in a whisper about her invitation from Blaine. Hetty's startled look was her only reply. Holly had not wanted to make too much of it by telling her beforehand, because Hetty always managed to spoil things by her sarcasm. Holly did not want this day to be ruined by one of Hetty's disparaging remarks.

After the service, Blaine was waiting for her at the bottom of the church steps when they came outside. "Sorry, I couldn't make the service," her told her as he took her arm and led her over to his small buggy. "Just as I was leaving, I got a message that one of the Findley children was running a high fever, so I had to make a sick call there. Did I miss a good sermon?"

Truthfully, sitting next to Hetty, Holly was too distracted by her cold disapproval to have paid much attention. So she fibbed guiltily.

"Oh, yes, it was very good."

Blaine glanced at her with mischievous eyes. "Care to give me a summary? What was the Scripture the text was taken from?"

Caught unawares by his question, Holly's eyes widened, then seeing that he was teasing her, she attempted to sound contrite, "I'm afraid I don't remember enough of it to tell you."

"Maybe it was something like 'This is the day the Lord hath made, let us rejoice and be glad'?" prompted Blaine.

"That sounds just right," Holly laughed.

Soon they were out from town, riding through some of the loveliest country Holly had ever seen. The woodland on either side of the winding road was glorious with autumn color, lush and green, and the river that ran parallel sparkled like silver in the sunlight.

Holly found Blaine thoroughly enjoyable. He was totally natural as he spoke of growing up back in Connecticut, of his family consisting of a mother, a stepfather whom he admired, and two married sisters. His own father had been killed in the Civil War, he told her, when Blaine was only nine years old.

"Regrettably, as so many of the War casualties, his was unnecessary. He bled to death on the battlefield because they didn't get him to a field hospital in time. My uncle was an Army doctor, and he told me that. Maybe it was the thing that motivated me to become a doctor myself. I wanted to know how to keep things like that from happening to people. My uncle said he saw so many soldiers die for lack of knowledge and the right treatment during the war." Blaine stopped. "Pardon me, Holly, I didn't mean to get on to an unpleasant subject like that on such a beautiful day. So, tell me, how do you like Oregon by this time?"

Holly wondered how she could possibly tell him. On this lovely fall day she almost thought that she could learn to love living out here, but then there was Hetty. How could she explain *that* situation?

Lately Holly had been debating whether it might not be better to leave Riverbend and go back to Willow Springs, even if Jim's bride was now there, to face whatever she had to face in the way of snide gossip. Would that be any worse than to go on living in that strained atmosphere at Hetty's? Since Holly had started the lending library and made some friends of her own, Hetty seemed to resent her even more. Was it worth it to remain under these circumstances?

Before Holly could tactfully answer Blaine's question, he suddenly jerked the reins and pulled the small vehicle to an abrupt stop.

"What's the matter? What is it?" Holly exclaimed in alarm, grabbing the seat handles.

"I don't know, I'm not sure, but look over there!" Blaine pointed to a figure slumped against a tree at the side of the road.

"Who is it?"

"It's Larkin!" Blaine said grimly. At that name Holly recalled the scene on the street when she was with Adam Corcoran and they had seen him reeling drunk.

"You mean the schoolteacher?"

"Yes. Poor devil."

"Is he—?"

"Dead? No, but dead drunk." Blaine threw the reins about the brake handle, sat for a moment as if trying to make a decision. Then he turned to Holly saying, "We can't leave him here like that. At least *I* can't," his mouth tightened. He gave Holly a long, evaluating look. "If someone else finds him, it will mean his job for sure. I've got to get him back to his place where he can sleep it off."

Holly felt an inner trembling. She had rarely seen anyone intoxicated. A few times at some public event or at an occasion like Fourth of July celebration she had seen someone slightly tipsy. Then, somebody always escorted the inebriated person off the premises with a minimum of fuss. But Larkin was something very different indeed. However, her reservation was fleeting. Hesitating only a second, she asked, "How can I help?"

"Good girl," he commented briefly. "I'll see if I can convince him that he needs to go home. Maybe he can make it on his own. Unless he's too far gone. Then I may need you to help prop him up."

Blaine got out of the buggy, and Holly followed him. Larkin was sitting on the ground, leaning against the tree trunk, his disheveled head sunk onto his chest. His horse had wandered a few yards and was grazing on the meadow grass. Probably this was not the first time he had been left to his own devices.

Blaine crouched down beside the man. Speaking in a low voice, he gently shook his shoulder. "Larkin, it's Doc. Come on, fella, wake up. Time to go . . ."

The man groaned, raised his hand, and moved it limply as if brushing away an annoying fly. "Lemme alone—go 'way," he mumbled.

Blaine looked up at Holly. "Looks like it's going to take more than persuasion." He stood up, plunged his hands into his pockets, tilted his head back and skyward as if for inspiration.

Then, sighing, said, "I guess the only thing to do is try to get him into the buggy. I think, between us, we can manage. He doesn't weigh much." He looked at Holly questioningly. "I know it's a lot to ask—a lady." She shook her head vigorously.

"Of course not. What about his horse?"

Blaine glanced at the placidly grazing animal. "We'll tie his reins to the back of the buggy," Blaine said and went over to the horse. Rubbing his nose and speaking to him softly, Blaine led him back and secured him. He then brought his own horse and buggy around closer to the tree where Larkin was slouched.

"Now, if you can get his arm over your shoulder, Holly, we'll get him on his feet, I think we can drag him over and into the buggy."

Drawing up her skirt with one hand, Holly leaned down and with some effort pulled Larkin's arm across her back and over her shoulder, grasping his wrist with her hand. On the other side Blaine was doing the same thing.

"All right now, slowly straighten up," Blaine directed. I'll take most of the weight; now grab him around the waist; let him fall toward me—I don't want you hurting yourself, Holly."

Larkin was a small man, almost skin and bones. Even so, Holly was breathing hard by the time she and Blaine half-dragged, half-carried him over to the buggy. He was mumbling and protesting by then. Finally, with Blaine pulling and Holly pushing, they got him into the buggy seat.

"Hurry and get on the other side, Holly," ordered Blaine. Holly obeyed, running around to catch Larkin before he slipped down. By the time Blaine got in and picked up the reins, Larkin was coming to, slightly. Gradually he seemed to become aware of his situation but just barely.

"It's not far to the schoolhouse," Blaine told Holly as he skillfully got the buggy turned with the added encumbrance of Larkin's horse behind and moved back onto the road. "I just hope we don't meet anyone on the way—especially a member of the Town Council or School Board."

They rode the short distance in tense silence, with Larkin mumbling and eventually snoring, lurching heavily from one

81

to the other. The smell of liquor was so strong that Holly wrinkled her nostrils distastefully and felt almost nauseous.

As they pulled into the schoolyard Blaine said, "I'll go around to the back where his living quarters are in case anyone riding by should see us."

When at last they halted, Blaine had to rouse Larkin again. When that proved impossible Blaine rummaged in Larkin's pocket, located his keys and tossed them over to Holly. "Would you please go unlock the door? I guess there's only one way to settle him safely." With that Blaine simply slung the man over his shoulder in the famous "fireman's carry."

Holly hopped down from the buggy and ran ahead to the back of the building. Fitting a key into the lock, she opened the door, holding it for Blaine to walk through with his inert burden. She stood there on the threshold, then heard the creak of mattress springs as Blaine must have dumped Larkin onto his bed, the clump of boots being dropped. A few minutes later Blaine reappeared.

"This binge must have started here, possibly as early as Friday afternoon after school." He pushed back his hat, rubbed his brow with one hand, frowning. "Couple of empty bottles around. When he ran out of booze he must have decided to go into town. . . ." He paused, pressing his lips together. Then he said thoughtfully, "I think I should try to straighten up some of this mess before leaving. Be sure to get rid of any unopened bottles there may still be around before he wakes up enough to start drinking again. On the other hand—" Blaine halted mid-sentence. "I probably should take you home, Holly. This has all been a pretty sordid spectacle for you to see. I know that poor Larkin would be humiliated if he thought that you—or anyone, for that matter—but particularly a *lady* like yourself had not only seen him like this but—"

"Oh, Blaine, don't! I understand. I *do*, really," Holly assured him, recalling the times she had seen Mr. Larkin in town perfectly sober, always neatly dressed. If he had come into Ned's store whenever she was working at the lending library, he always tipped his hat politely and addressed her with the greatest courtesy. Now she said, "Please, let me help. Tell me what to do."

The expression in Blaine's eyes changed from uncertainty to frank approval. "All right. Come in and together we'll make quick work of it."

While Blaine collected a number of bottles and disposed of them, Holly tidied the general disorder of the schoolmaster's small apartment. From the adjoining bedroom she heard the loud rhythmic sound of snoring as Larkin slept, oblivious of his rescuers.

As she picked up garments, carried used tumblers and half-filled mugs of old coffee into the kitchen, wiped table tops, and folded rumpled newspapers dropped on the floor, Holly also noticed the book-filled shelves in the tiny parlor. Pausing to read the titles, Holly realized Mr. Larkin was unlike her preconception of a drink-sodden derelict, a well-read man whose reading choice tended to the classics. There were books in Latin, philosophy and essays, Shakespeare plays. How had such a man of intelligence and taste ended up here teaching grammar school in a remote Oregon town?

On the table beside a well-worn leather reading chair was the scrolled silver-framed photograph of a pretty, stylishly dressed woman holding a beautiful baby. Holly had never even thought that Larkin might be married. That photograph seemed the most poignant evidence of all to Holly how much he must have lost through his addiction to drink.

Blaine's voice brought her back from her pitying thoughts. "Well, I think that's it. He'll sleep for hours and when he wakes up, he'll find nothing to drink to get him started again. He'll feel miserable. But he'll have time to get himself together by tomorrow morning. At least, I *hope* so. I'll ride out here early and check on him to be sure." Blaine's tawny hair had fallen forward onto his broad forehead from his exertion and he brushed it back with an impatient gesture. "You all set? Ready to go?"

"Yes," she replied, looking at him with new eyes. What compassion he had. His clear blue eyes were clouded now with concern; what strength of character in his face. How lucky Larkin was to have the doctor as a friend.

83

On the way back into town, Blaine said quietly, "I'm sorry our day together had to have this kind of ending."

"Please, don't apologize, Blaine. It wasn't your fault, and besides, I'm glad it was *us* who found him."

"I am, too. Only how long I can keep protecting him, I don't know. More for his own sake than for any other reason. It's a sickness, you know, contrary to what some self-righteous people would have you believe. It's not a moral weakness or a sin. One drink, and Larkin, for all the promises he makes to me and to himself, is off."

"I guess he could just not take that first drink?" murmured Holly.

"Of course, that sounds sensible to people to whom it isn't a problem. But so far, no one has come up with a way to really help someone like Larkin. At least not yet. There doesn't seem to be any cure or any medicine to take that will do the deed."

They went on a little farther, then Blaine turned to Holly and said softly, "You were a brick, Holly. Not many ladies would have handled the situation as well as you did. Thank you."

Holly felt a pleasurable warmth spread all through her; she could feel her face glow. Why, for heaven's sake? Hadn't she received dozens of compliments from gentlemen before? Flattering words about her dancing, her dimples, her hair, eyes, and complexion? Why did this unflowery comment from this practical doctor mean more to her than anything anyone had ever said to her?

Well, for one thing, she was rather gratified at how ably she had conducted herself in this really bizarre set of circumstances today. She had even surprised herself. And for another, she'd never been called "a brick" before! At this Holly almost burst out laughing.

Chapter 10

*H*olly had never known anyone to hold a grudge as long as Hetty! On Wednesday morning Hetty was still angry because Holly had returned late from her drive with Blaine and missed Sunday night supper. Bound by Blaine's request to keep the incident with Larkin secret, Holly could not explain. She knew that Hetty probably thought she was out "sparking" with the doctor instead of assisting him on his "errand of mercy." So, after her offer of household help was curtly turned down, to avoid another scene with Hetty, Holly left for the store earlier than usual to open the lending library.

A heated discussion was taking place around the potbellied stove where a group of "regulars" were gathered. Holly hung up her shawl and bonnet and slipped behind the counter of the Lending Library. She had discovered that Ned's store was the hub of the town. Here rumors, facts, whispers of scandal, tidbits, and tittle-tattle, along with reports of real events, were argued about, examined, and retold. Not a thing happened in Riverbend that did not eventually get thoroughly chewed over there long before it became a news item in the *Monitor*. Ned, as usual, remained a silent bystander, listening, but rarely offering an opinion or comment.

Today the voices were raised loudly and Holly could not help hearing every word. When she heard the name "Larkin" over and over, her ears pricked up.

"Well, it's the last straw, I guess," declared one of the men.

"We can't let it go on, that's for sure. Bad example for the young people." This next voice was indignant. "We've overlooked it long enough. But it's gone too far this time."

"Too many people know—"

"Too many people have *seen* him—"

"My Lorena said he fell asleep in class on Friday. Put his head right down on the desk and slept! Well, when her ma heard *that*—well, you know *my* wife, Tilly, is a 'Temperance'!"

Holly drew in her breath. Larkin! It was Larkin they were talking about. How had they heard about his latest binge? Her second thought sent a chill down her spine. Had someone seen him? Had someone, maybe, seen *her* and Doc with Larkin? *If so*, her next thought was, *Oh dear! Wait until Hetty hears about it.*

Another voice said emphatically, "You're right, we've got to do something about it."

"But school's just got started a few weeks. At this point in the school year, where're you going to find a teacher who hasn't already got a position?" This mild query came from Ned.

Concealed by the counter, Holly peered cautiously over the edge and saw that two of the men were Owen Roberts and Ed Morrison, two members of Riverbend Town Council. This elected body also served as the school board who did the hiring and firing of the Riverbend grammar school teacher.

Poor Blaine! He had tried so hard to protect Larkin. But the children had to be protected, too, didn't they? You couldn't blame the parents for being upset.

She had better go see Blaine, Holly thought, talk to him about how the word got out. Holly reached for her bonnet, tied it under her chin. The men around the stove were too involved in their conversation to notice her as she slipped by them, went out the door, and crossed the street to Blaine's office.

At her knock, he called, "Come in," and she entered his small waiting room. Through the open door to his inner office she could see him standing at his desk and packing his medicine bag. When he looked up and saw her, his face lit up.

"Why, Holly, good morning! How nice to see you. I hope this isn't a professional call?"

86

She shook her head, then looking left and right to be sure that they were alone, moved over to the door, and lowering her voice, said, "Blaine, have you heard about Mr. Larkin?"

The smile on his face faded, replaced by a worried frown. "Yes, he came by here last night. It seems that on Monday he was still pretty hungover and that evening came into town to the Nugget—as he explained it, 'to get a hair of the dog that bit him'—in other words, to get over the shakes." Blaine paused, his mouth grim, "Well, as luck would have it, the Town Council meeting was just breaking up as he came out of the saloon— he'd had more than one hair, it seems, and he ran right into them. He was nervous as well as a little gone in drink, and the encounter was not a mutually happy one, to say the least." Blaine shrugged. "Yesterday, he was notified they were demanding his resignation as schoolteacher, effective immediately."

"Then it's true," Holly said. "I heard them talking over at Ned's store."

"Yes. Poor fellow, he came by here, all remorseful, repentant, swearing off, and asked me if I'd speak for him to the council. But I had to tell him it was no good. They've given him his last chance, and he's out."

"Then, what will he do? And what about the school?"

Blaine shook his head again. "I put him on the morning stage. He was too ashamed to show his face in town, particularly to face the children. I sent him to a doctor friend of mine in California who may be able to help him get over his addiction. He's had some success with chronic alcoholics. I pray to God he'll get the help he needs."

Poor Larkin, Holly thought, remembering the books and the picture of the woman and child in his cluttered little living quarters in the schoolhouse. Her pity and concern must have shown in her face because Blaine stopped putting some small vials and bottles into his medical bag and gave her a long look. "Don't look so troubled, Holly," he said gently. I know this comes as a shock. But life is full of these kinds of tragedies. I'm sorry you had to—"

"Oh, no, Blaine, it's not that—it's just all so sad. . . ."

After a moment, Blaine said, "You look like you could use a

little diversion. Larkin asked me if I'd go out to his place, pack up his belongings, and send them to him in care of Dr. Logan. As a matter of fact, I'm riding out there right now before I make my other rounds. Would you like to ride with me?"

She nodded. It was true, the whole experience had affected her deeply. She looked up into Blaine's concerned eyes. "Yes, I think I would like to come with you, Blaine."

She was quiet as they rode out in the brilliant sunshine of the fall morning. The air was so clear, the sky so blue, the changing colors of the trees so beautiful, Holly felt that it was too bad for anyone, like Larkin, to be unhappy on a day like this.

The schoolyard was empty. In the absence of a teacher, school had been suspended temporarily. Maybe indefinitely, unless Riverbend could find a new one. Blaine unlocked the door and they stepped into the one large classroom. It smelled of chalk dust, charred wood from a stove that had been left to burn out, the mustiness of old books, unswept floors. The whole place had an air of neglect and indifferent care. *What a shame!* was Holly's first reaction. How hard it would be for children to try to learn in this kind of atmosphere. A schoolroom should be neat, clean, colorful.

"We can go through here," Blaine said, turning a key in the door behind the teacher's desk.

Holly followed him into Larkin's living quarters. The smells from the classroom were intensified by the sour odor of whiskey, unwashed clothes, and accumulated dirt. Holly looked around in dismay, unconsciously picking up her skirt. How could Larkin have made everything worse just since Sunday?

Blaine went ahead of her and opened the door into Larkin's bedroom. He was gone so long that Holly went to the door to see what he was doing. Blaine stood in the center of the room as if undecided where to begin. He held up his hand to halt her. "Don't come in here, Holly. I shouldn't've brought you into this! I'd forgotten how it can be when Larkin's been drinking steadily. Now, I don't want you to do anything—I'll see to it." He dragged out an old trunk from under the sagging mattress of the iron bed and told her, "Just wait there for me in the other room or go outside into the fresh air," he said as he began to toss things into the trunk.

Holly went back into the front room. When she had been here on Sunday she had been too nervous to notice much beyond the awful mess. This second time she took a closer look. This room was the same size as the schoolroom. There was an alcove with a table and chairs and, beyond that, a tiny kitchen area with a stove, a hutch, and a window. Larkin had as much space here at the back of the schoolroom as one would find in a cottage. Of course, it was in shambles now, but with a good cleaning, some paint and polish, it could be quite—cozy and charming. An idea began to stir in Holly's mind.

The more she thought about it, the more sense it made. Why not? Her heart began to race. *She* had as good an education as most women—perhaps better than some. She had finished the twelfth grade and then had two years at Blue Ridge Female Academy. Of course, to be truthful, Holly had not applied herself diligently or very seriously there. For one thing, the Academy had been too close to Penrose College for Young Men, and invitations to the parties, the fall and spring "Germans," and the social activities had occupied a great deal of her time.

Still, she *did* have a smattering of botany, geography, history and, certainly, as fond as she was of reading, she could teach spelling and reading! Arithmetic was another matter, however. But she was sure that if she brushed up on her multiplication tables she could manage reasonably well.

Of course, the main incentive for the idea growing in Holly's imagination was that with the job of teacher came living quarters. At such a possibility Holly's excitement soared. If she applied for the job of Riverbend grammar school teacher she could move out from under Hetty's inhospitable roof and be independent! Within those few minutes Holly decided that's just what she was going to do. Apply for the position of teacher at Riverbend grammar school!

Right then Blaine reappeared carrying out two boxes belonging to Larkin, then came back for the trunk, and took it out and lashed it to the back of his buggy.

"I wish we could take advantage of this lovely day and go on

89

a drive," he smiled regretfully as he helped Holly back into the buggy and picked up the reins. "But I've got to get this into town so it can be placed on the next stage, and I've patients to see."

Holly did not reply, only smiled vaguely. She had only half-heard the remark. Her mind was too busy plotting how she could go about the plan of acquiring the job of teacher and thus her freedom.

When Blaine let her out again at Ned's store, instead of returning to her task at the lending library, she crossed the street and hurried over to Vi's house. By the time Vi answered the doorbell, Holly was trembling with excitement. Vi had a customer being fitted in her sewing room, and suggested that Holly go into the kitchen and "make herself at home" until she could join her.

Vi's kitchen was like the rest of her little home, sparkling, spotless, serene, painted a sunny yellow and smelling slightly of herbs and spices. But Holly was too restless today to sit down on one of the pressback chairs and calmly await her hostess.

Of course, Holly had never thought of being a teacher before. Guiltily she recalled that she had always equated women teachers with plain, prim, proper spinsters who had no other choice but to teach! But as she'd often heard, "desperate times demand desperate choices," and Holly had become desperate enough living with Hetty to take any chance.

She knew that her educational qualifications lacked certification. But then her qualities compared to the failings of poor Larkin would be taken into consideration. What she did have she would use. Her ability to get along with children, her imagination, and storytelling talent could be put to good advantage. Surely there were textbooks she could read to help prepare lessons. The most important thing was to convince the Town Council that she was capable of doing the job. When she got it, then she could figure out how to go about teaching. -

Vi's clear voice floated from the hall out to the kitchen. "Yes, Mrs. Abbott, your dress will be ready next week."

Abbott? thought Holly. *Wasn't her husband, Miles Abbott, on the Town Council?*

She heard the murmur of more conversation then the front

door clicked shut, and Vi came into the kitchen, her tape measure still hanging around her neck. "What a nice surprise, Holly. What brings you here today for a visit?"

"Oh, Vi, I know I shouldn't have just popped in like this during the week when you have ladies coming for fittings, but I just had to talk to you. Actually to ask your advice!"

"Well, if I am to be your oracle today, I believe we better have some tea, don't you?" Vi went to fill the kettle with water from the hand pump on the counter and placed it on the stove to boil.

"Oh, Vi, the most wonderful opportunity has come up. Well, I mean, due to certain sad circumstances, there may be a chance for me to move out of Hetty's, be on my own. I'm so thrilled at the possibility, but I'm also scared and—"

Vi held up her hand. "Slow down, Holly, I haven't the slightest idea what you're talking about."

Holly took a long breath then very deliberately told Vi about Larkin's leaving and the post of teacher being left vacant as well as the little apartment behind the schoolroom.

While listening attentively, Vi got down two china cups, arranged some thin wafer cookies on a plate, and set them on the table.

"So, what do you think?" Holly asked breathlessly.

"Have you ever taught before?"

"Well, no, but I'm sure I could. After all it's only grammar school. Certainly I could teach six-and seven-year-olds!"

"You'll have *all* ages, Holly. Or at least for part of the year. The older children attend during the winter. But in the spring the big boys are usually needed to help out on their families' farms, plowing and planting and so on. Strapping farm boys of twelve and fourteen can be a handful—"

"Oh, I've got dozens of young cousins that age, Vi. I don't think that would bother me," Holly said confidently. "My real worry is getting the job! I suppose I'll have to apply and go for an interview before the Town Council."

Vi didn't say anything right away. She poured their tea and offered Holly the plate of cookies, then she looked over at her friend seriously. "Have you prayed about this, Holly?"

91

Taken aback by Vi's question, Holly replied, "Well, no, not really. I haven't had time. I just got the idea."

"It's a pretty important step for you to take. Don't you think you should have God's guidance?"

"Yes, I suppose so. I just thought *you* could help me decide what to do," Holly said. Then she asked shyly, "Is that what *you* do, Vi? I mean, pray about it before anything else?"

"When it's something that's going to change my life as much as this would change yours, Holly, I think it's the wisest thing to do."

"But if I pray and do seem to get a 'go ahead'—will you help me, Vi? I mean, you do think it's a good idea, don't you?"

"Of course, I'll help you every way I can, Holly," Vi promised.

Holly breathed a sigh of relief. "Thank you." She stood up. "And I will do as you say, Vi."

As they walked to the door, Vi put her arm around Holly's shoulder. "I'm sure the children would love having you for a teacher—that is, if you decide to do it."

"After I *pray* about it, you mean?" Holly smiled.

"Of course, *after* you pray." Vi gave her a mock reproachful look.

At the front door, Holly asked, "Seriously, Vi, how should I pray about it to expect an answer?"

Vi hesitated a moment before replying. "Well, I don't recommend this practice as a general rule, but I must admit that when I've been under pressure to make a decision and have been at a loss for direction, I *have* done it. First, pray earnestly for guidance, then open the Bible at random and read the pages where it falls open. Search there for what God may be showing you in His Word. That's all I can tell you, Holly. I feel that somewhere in those two pages you're going to find your answer."

Something stubborn in Holly resisted this idea. It seemed too chancy. With all her heart she wanted this job. Mainly, of course, because it provided an avenue of escape from Hetty. Actually, when she thought about it, didn't it seem almost Providential? Great-Aunt Ancilla always said that it is sometimes in *circumstances* that God makes His will plain. Wasn't *this* just that sort of *circumstance*?

Back in the cramped bedroom at Hetty's house, Holly decided she might as well follow Vi's advice. After all, if Vi relied on this method of discovering God's guidance when unsure of what direction to take, why shouldn't she try it?

Holly got out the little Bible that Great-Aunt Ancilla had tucked into her trunk that day when she was packing to leave for the West. Holding it in both hands, she squeezed her eyes tight shut and prayed, "Dear Lord, show me what to do, and *please* make it plain!" then flipped open the Bible. When she opened her eyes again and looked down at the pages, she was surprised to see she had turned to the Book of Isaiah.

If Holly was familiar with any Scripture, it was mostly the New Testament, and this seemed very strange to her. But remembering Vi's instruction, she began reading from the top of the left-hand page, relying on the possibility that at some point a verse would "quicken" to her, as Great-Aunt Ancilla used to say.

The pages that lay open before her contained Chapters 49 and 50. Running her index finger down line by line, she came to this one: "This place is too small for me; give me a place where I may dwell," and almost laughed.

If that wasn't to the point, she didn't know what was! Did God have a sense of humor? Quickly hoping that He wouldn't think her irreverent, Holly read on. A kind of quiet settled over her as she did, and she realized that the Scriptures had effects other than just giving answers. Then her finger stopped on a verse, and as she read it over two or three times, she began to feel it *was* her direction to pursue the position of schoolteacher. Chapter 50, verses 7–8: "For the Lord will help me, Therefore I will not be disgraced—Therefore I have set my face like flint and I know I will not be ashamed. He is near who justifies me, who will contend with me?" If she was interpreting this as an answer to her own question, it seemed to Holly that she was to step boldly forward, with a "face set like flint," and God would help her.

She closed the Bible thoughtfully. This was all new to her. She had never before exercised faith in such a manner. But she admired Vi Dodd, and if Vi thought this was how to go about it, who was she to argue?

That evening at the supper table Holly took a deep breath and announced her intention. "Well, that's splendid, Holly," was Ned's immediate response. "I think that's a great idea, you'd make a fine teacher."

"Oh, Holly, will you teach me when I go to school?" Aurelia almost bounced off her chair in her excitement.

"I haven't got the job yet, honey. I'm just going to apply for it." Holly smiled across the table at her, then glanced at Hetty, whose fork had stopped halfway to her mouth; she had paled, her expression blank. For politeness' sake Holly asked, "What do you think, Hetty?"

Hetty put down her fork, got to her feet, and picked up her unfinished plate, took it over to the drainboard and said over her shoulder, "I never thought you were much for school when you were a pupil, so how come you think you can teach?"

Holly felt her face burn at this barbed comment. She knew that she had not been a prize student as Hetty had been. Still her marks were reasonably good, and she certainly was no dunce!

Suppressing her indignation at Hetty's attempt to embarrass her, Holly replied gaily, "Well, isn't there an old saying, that 'if you become a teacher, by your students you'll be taught'? I'm open to learning all I can even this late in my life."

"I think you'll do just fine, Holly," Ned said heartily, which was a brave thing to do in the wake of his wife's blatant disapproval.

Hetty said nothing more, but her opinion was obvious in the way she brought the dessert dish of blackberry cobbler and slammed it down on the table.

PART 2

I a small house and large garden have,
And a few friends, and many books, both true,
both wise and both delightful, too!

Abraham Cowley

Chapter 11

*T*aking some liberty with the Scripture, Holly "set her face like flint" toward the coming meeting of the Town Council. Making many false starts and revisions of the text, Holly labored over her letter of application for the position of grammar school teacher until she was satisfied. Writing in her very best penmanship, she stated her qualifications and addressed it to the membership of the Riverbend Town Council acting in its capacity as school board. Within a few days Holly received a letter from Mayor Ed Morrison that her application was being studied and considered by each member. A decision would be announced at the next town meeting.

It was the longest week of her life. Finally on the morning before the meeting, Holly hurried along Main Street on her way over to consult with Vi on an appropriate outfit to wear. Preoccupied, she nearly collided with Adam Corcoran as she rounded the corner.

He took off his hat, made her an exaggerated bow, and greeted her, "Good day, Miss Lambeth. Rumor has it that you will be Riverbend's new schoolmarm in place of the lately departed but not lamented Larkin."

"Well, it certainly has not been decided, Mr. Corcoran, but I have applied for the position."

Regarding her with a skeptical smile, he said, "Perhaps I'm wrong, I often am, but my first impression of you was not of a schoolmarm. Probably that might be colored by the fact that I don't remember my own schooldays with much pleasure, due in large part, I'm sure, to a series of teachers who were neither pleasant nor charming nor even, I might add, erudite."

Although Holly knew he was teasing her, she was aware of a sense of irony in the situation herself but affected an air of indignant dignity and replied, "I find that very unfortunate, indeed, Mr. Corcoran. I myself have most happy memories of *my* school days *and* my teachers. And if I am awarded this important position, I certainly hope to emulate those paragons of wisdom and kindness." With satisfaction at matching Adam at his own game, Holly bestowed one of her most winsome smiles on him and moved past. "Now if you will excuse me, Mr. Corcoran, I have an errand to complete."

Holly might have been both flattered and disturbed had she seen the mixture of admiration and challenge in Adam Corcoran's glance following her.

At Vi's the two women put their heads together to decide just what Holly should wear the night she appeared before the Council. "You want to look well but not too fashionable," Vi told her. "That might put them off since most of them have wives who are busy, hard-working mothers with very few opportunities to dress up."

"Should I look drab, dowdy?" asked Holly worriedly, already thinking of the wardrobe of bright-colored stylish clothes she had brought with her.

"No, not that, but . . ." Vi hesitated. Looking at Holly, she could not help wondering how in the world this pretty, vivacious young woman could convince five middle-aged men she was capable of overseeing thirty or more children—no matter what she wore!

"Maybe, I can remodel something. I mean, take off the trimmings or flounces," Holly suggested, mentally reviewing her possibilities. Perhaps the blue traveling suit or her gray walking dress or even the cinnamon brown wool—she wrinkled her brow and asked Vi, "You think I should look more reliable and serious, don't you? Not flighty or—more Quakerish, right?"

"Well, not exactly, Holly," Vi laughed. "But I think you get the idea. You've got good taste and judgment. Just don't show up with too many feathers or flowers on your hat!"

Monday was the regular meeting night of Riverbend's Town Council. As usual the time and agenda was published in the *Monitor* with the added notice that the subject of hiring a new schoolteacher would be discussed after the previously announced items on the agenda.

Riverbend, so newly evolved from its raw mining camp beginnings, now had a citizenry eager to exhibit responsible civic interest and pride in its development. Therefore the Town Council meetings were usually well-attended. *This* Monday every seat was filled a half hour before the meeting would be called to order, extra chairs were even brought into place on the side aisles. It seemed that everyone in Riverbend had a personal reason to be present for this particular meeting.

It had already circulated around town that Ned Thornton's wife's cousin was applying for the teacher's job. Those who had met Holly through the lending library were pleased at the idea, confident that anyone who knew so much about books had to be a good teacher as well. Others who only knew her by sight had their own unexplored opinion that she was "too citified" and probably "stuck up." If she wasn't, why was it she never came along with her cousin Hetty to their Sewing Circle or Missionary Society? It didn't occur to those who held this attitude that Holly had never been invited. Others, mainly those with children in need of a teacher, were anxious to have the vacancy filled as soon as possible and had come to hear and see for themselves what the young lady from "back east" had to say for herself. Certainly no one who came to the meeting was disinterested in the outcome.

Holly herself had been in a frenzy of nerves all afternoon and at five went over to see Vi, who was going to accompany her to Town Hall, to get her final approval on her appearance. As she left for Vi's house, Holly paused in the kitchen and trying to keep her tone light, said, "Well, Hetty, I'm off to the lion's den, wish me luck!"

Hetty looked up from the bread she was kneading for the

99

next day's baking. Surveying every inch of her cousin, she replied coldly, "Hmmph, you'll need more than good luck."

Holly pretended to adjust the scalloped cuffs of her coffee-colored boucle-wool jacket and ignored Hetty's mean-spirited remark. What else could she expect from her cousin? Hetty had made no secret of how she felt about Holly's ability to get the job.

Keeping her voice even, she said good-bye and went out the door. As she walked briskly toward Vi's house, Holly thought she would never understand Hetty, not if she lived to be a hundred. *You'd think Hetty would hope I'd get the job and get out of her hair!*

But she had more important things now to be concerned about than Hetty's predictable attitude. She had to concentrate on making a good impression on the members of the Town Council, convince them that she was their best possible choice for teacher.

Holly knew that even if she embellished her educational qualifications it would not be enough. Her lack of references and experience were the first obstacles she had to hurdle. But then after the Larkin debacle, plus the fact that the school year session was already three weeks behind, put great pressure on the council to appoint someone soon. The time needed to advertise the position, receive and check applications, vote on the one to be selected, plus the expense of sending for someone were factors to be considered. Paying train or stagecoach fare for the person to get to Riverbend would seem prohibitive to the frugal council members and would strain the town coffers. All this might stand Holly in good stead, she told herself as she went up the porch steps of Vi's house.

Vi was dressed and ready to go when she let Holly inside.

"So, how do I look?" Holly asked her, spinning around slowly. "Like a potential, proper schoolmarm, I hope?"

Vi's critical eye reviewed Holly's outfit. The suit with its high collar over which a narrow rim of silk ruching peeked was subdued enough. Since Holly had taken Vi's suggestion to remove the small blue-feathered bird nested in green velvet leaves, leaving only the dark brown grosgrain ribbons, her bonnet was now acceptable. Vi nodded.

"Very nice indeed."

"Good! If you approve of my appearance, the Town Council will surely agree." Holly's eyes sparkled. "Come on, let's go."

On their way to the Town Hall, Vi tried not to let her own anxiety about the outcome of the meeting dim Holly's enthusiasm. "What a night!" Holly exclaimed. "Look!" she said pointing up to the stars glittering in the sky. "This is the kind of night that good things happen," she declared squeezing Vi's arm.

Inwardly Vi's heart sank. She was afraid that Holly's attractiveness might be the very thing that would do her the most damage. Even with her outfit carefully chosen for its conservative effect, Holly Lambeth was hardly anyone's idea of a schoolteacher.

There was a definite autumn crispness in the air and as they hurried up the steps leading into the brick building, Vi shivered. But it was more from nerves than cold.

Standing just outside the entrance was Adam Corcoran. "Why, Mr. Corcoran," Holly exclaimed, "What are you doing here? I shouldn't think you'd care who was hired for schoolteacher."

"Good evening, Miss Lambeth, Mrs. Dodd," he tipped his hat to both women. Then smiling at Holly said, "Of course, I'm interested in everything that happens in Riverbend. Especially who is appointed to the important position of teaching our young people. As I'm sure *you're* aware, a schoolteacher has great influence in a community. I wish you the best, even though I'm not quite sure why you are doing it."

He regarded her in that half-amused, half-skeptical way she had come to expect whenever they met. She felt sure that he knew about Larkin, probably knew about her helping Blaine the day they found Larkin inebriated along the side of the road. He may even have put two and two together and figured out why she was applying for the job. He had seen firsthand Hetty's ill-humor, perhaps even read between the lines of her cautious answers to his often pointed questions about her situation at the Thorntons'.

Adam had not come to call on her as he had first asked permission to do. Holly was certain this was because of his wish to

101

avoid Hetty. But on the days she worked at the lending library he visited her frequently there. Of course, he made all sorts of excuses for doing so: returning books, looking for recent arrivals, then lingering to chat. In spite of his cynicism and sometimes barbed comments, Holly had come to know and like Adam. She even thought she could see through that veneer of superiority he affected. So now she replied in the same vein, "It is very encouraging to realize that the editor of the town paper is so interested." Then she added candidly, "I'm glad you're here. I need all the support I can get."

"Rest assured you *do* have my support, Miss Lambeth. Only I'm afraid I don't have the power to sway any votes on the Council. I'm here in the capacity of editor of the *Monitor*. I always cover the Town Council meetings."

"Nevertheless, it's nice to feel I have some friends in the audience."

"I'm sure you do, Miss Lambeth," he said and opened the door for them to enter the building.

Watching Holly as she walked inside, Adam thought, *What a plucky little creature she is!* He hadn't imagined that she had it in her to face a five-man board and a room full of strangers, some of them probably hostile, ready to criticize or condemn her for her Eastern looks and manners.

Adam sauntered to a place on the left-hand side in the front row where he could get a good look at the members, try to judge their reactions, see and hear everything he could. He was betting on Holly to win, but he was also hedging his bet. The men of the Town Council took their roles very seriously. No doubt they'd been coached, argued with, and given opinions about the last item on tonight's agenda from everyone and anyone who had cornered them, bent their ear, or buttonholed them in the general store.

The thought of the country store naturally brought Ned Thornton to Adam's mind, and he twisted around to look at the people still filing into the meeting room. He spotted Ned's rangy figure in the doorway, talking to someone, then making his way forward to find a seat. Well, at least Ned had come to lend familial support to Holly's application. Adam wondered

102

where Ned's "gracious, honey-tongued" wife was? Not even for appearance's sake would she come to wish her cousin well? The harridan!

Fiercely Adam hoped the vote would go Holly's way. She deserved better than putting up with Hetty's petty cruelties, her spiteful nonsense, just because Holly was personable and charming. Women, the gentler sex? Adam gave a scornful grunt and the man sitting beside him looked alarmed. Adam immediately pretended to stifle a cough just as Mayor Morrison pounded the gavel, bringing the town meeting to order.

When Holly entered the hall, two dozen or more heads turned in her direction. But to her, all the faces were so blurred that she did not recognize any of them. Fully aware that she was the focus of all eyes, she moved up the aisle. Vi pointed out two seats in the front row on the right, and Holly quickly sat down. She tried to control her breathing, which was rapid and shallow, and to look composed.

Behind her she could hear the buzz of voices. Without doubt she was the subject of much of the conversation and comments. Knowing that she was being discussed was torture. Closing her eyes briefly, she thought miserably, *What am I doing here? How in the world did I ever get into such a situation?* Tonight seemed far removed from any other experience in her entire life.

Glancing over at Vi, she wished fervently that she had her serenity and inner strength. Vi was the only really serene person she had ever met. Vi always seemed poised, collected. She always spoke quietly, purposefully, never said an idle word nor made an irrelevant remark nor made a useless gesture, which gave force to everything she said or did.

Holly's stomach knotted. Desperately she tried to pray and could think of nothing but "Help!" To calm herself, she applied the comforting thought that she used when she had to go to the dentist: *In an hour or so this will all be over!* As the five members took their places on the platform, she folded her hands in her lap and tried to look both intelligent and attentive.

When Mayor Morrison picked up the gavel and brought it down with a loud bang and the meeting began, some of the apprehension, the timidity that Holly had experienced earlier,

103

began to vanish. A surge of determination replaced it. This was something she wanted, something she *needed,* something she intended to get. Unless she did—Holly firmly stopped that train of thought. She *had* to be appointed schoolteacher; for her to go on at Hetty's was out of the question.

Conscious that the hall was more crowded than usual because of the interest in the decision they were being called on to make about a new schoolteacher, Mayor Ed Morrison began going through the order of business more quickly than usual, initiating a quick consensus on several of the items and allowing for a limited amount of discussion on each. He was able to get a unanimous decision on most. All the members of the Council were acutely aware of the one subject everyone was waiting for, and each of them was conscious of the young woman seated in the front row, who was the most anxious of all.

Owen Roberts, a rough-hewn rancher in his fifties, had grown children and grandchildren. He'd seen plenty of schoolteachers come and go, some good, some bad, most pretty indifferent as far as that went. As a man who raised cattle, loved horses, he had taken the position on the Council reluctantly, and rarely came into town. Owen needed to have Holly pointed out to him one day when he was in the store where she was working at her lending library. Now as he squinted down at her he wondered—was she too pretty? Too young?

Miles Abbott, a surveyor, practical and close-fisted, figured the lady must have plenty of spunk to want to take on the mixed group of youngsters who would troop into her classroom at least six months of the year. Why not let her try if she wanted to? It would save money and time. It would cost the town both if they tried to fill the position otherwise.

Theodore Winsbrook had been trained as a lawyer back East but came to the West for his health in his youth, stayed to become a farmer, had observed Holly in the lending library, had privately looked over her selection of books, and had come to the conclusion she was "smart as a whip." He was willing to give her a chance. His own children, a boy and a girl, needed to have their minds stretched. And Larkin had been a disaster.

Matthew Healy, a short, rotund, ruddy-cheeked man, settled

104

back in his chair complacently. He already knew how he was going to vote. Before he left for the meeting tonight, he had been given orders by his wife, Geneva (who belonged to the Riverbend Literary Society and, of course, knew and liked Holly), to hire her.

Ed Morrison, the mayor, who would cast the deciding vote in case of a tie, had his doubts that anyone as dainty as Miss Lambeth looked could handle the big boys. He recalled enough of his own rambunctious boyhood, when school days were colored by plenty of sessions with the hickory stick, to feel uncertain about hiring a woman teacher. Those big fellows needed discipline, most often wielded by a strong man. Of course hiring a man, in Larkin's case, hadn't worked. She could probably do as well as Larkin had, dazed as he was with drink half the time.

"We will now consider the application of Miss Hollis Lambeth for the position of schoolteacher of Riverbend Grammar," Ed announced. "Will Miss Lambeth please take her place at the podium and present her credentials for this job."

Afterward, Holly could not remember a word she had said. She had rehearsed dozens of times in front of the mirror and also for Vi. She had planned to give a brief background of her school attendance history, enumerate the subjects she had studied, and finish with a little speech about the value of education and her love of children. When her mind went blank, she decided she must be finished, and she resumed her seat amid a nice spatter of applause. She hoped she had covered everything she wanted to say, but she wasn't sure. Vi reached over and squeezed her hand.

"How did I do?" Holly whispered anxiously.

"Fine, just fine," Vi reassured her. The waiting had been agony.

Mayor Morrison stood up and told the assembly that the council would retire to a private session to discuss their decision, and the five men filed out. There was an immediate breaking-forth of voices that was almost deafening.

Rigid with tension, Holly watched the five men come back onto the platform. Mayor Morrison moved to the edge of the

105

stage and held up both hands for quiet and the hum of noise ceased.

"The Town Council of Riverbend has voted to award the position of grammar school teacher to Miss Hollis Lambeth." He turned to the other members, and asked "So say we all?"

Five resounding "ayes" were raised, and an enthusiastic clapping of hands followed. Vi hugged Holly, and afterward Holly went up to the council members and shook each hand and thanked them individually.

Her sense of relief was almost greater than her elation. It was only later that she realized that this was the first time in her life she had ever gained something important—not because she was pretty, pleasant, popular, or because she was a Lambeth! This time she had got it on her own—and maybe even in spite of those very things.

Chapter 12

*M*oving day for Holly came on the loveliest autumn day she had yet seen in Oregon. The morning was bright as a new gold piece, the sky a cloudless blue, a brisk breeze rustled leaves of trees along the road out to the schoolhouse. The minute Holly awoke that morning, a feeling of joy soared through her. Today she would actually be leaving Hetty's house and going to her own place. This definitive step of independence gave her intense satisfaction. Surely this *was* "the day the Lord hath made," and she fully intended to "be glad and rejoice in it."

Ned had offered to take her with her belongings over to the schoolhouse, and Vi, along with Geneva and Matt Healy, had promised to meet her there to help her. Even Blaine told her that he would try to come by if no patient needed him.

In spite of her own good spirits, Holly dreaded the actual time of departure when she would have to say good-bye to Aurelia and Teddy. She had come to dearly love her little cousins in spite of the tension with Hetty. And what was she to say to Hetty before she left?

The night before, after the children were sound asleep, Holly had quietly packed all her things and had Ned place them in the wagon. Pretending to be still asleep, she waited until the children woke up and went out for their breakfast before getting up and dressing. She then delayed going out to the kitchen until she heard Ned go out to hitch up the wagon. One look at her woebegone face, however, and Holly knew that Aurelia realized this was the day she was leaving.

"Do you *really* and *truly* have to go, Holly?" the little girl asked plaintively.

Teddy's spoon of oatmeal stopped halfway to his mouth, and his large blue eyes widened.

"Go? Go where?"

"Today Holly's moving to the schoolhouse," Aurelia informed him.

Teddy's lower lip began to tremble, his eyes grew bright with tears. He dropped his spoon, spattering his porridge. "No!" he said, thumping his little fist on the table. "No! I don't want her to go."

Quickly Holly tried to avert a scene or, worse still, a Teddy-tantrum.

"But, Teddy, you can come visit me, you and Aurelia; we'll have a tea party and . . ."

Aurelia, always sensitive to a possible storm, added, "And next year I'll be a pupil, and Teddy can come some days with me to school, right, Holly?"

Knowing that next year was problematic, to say the least, that *she* might be a long way off by next fall when Aurelia would be six and ready for first grade, Holly attempted to divert an onset of tears. "Teddy, you can come anytime and visit the school, look at picture books, and play with the children," she said appeasingly. Then glancing at Hetty, she added tactfully, "that is, anytime your mama says you may."

Hetty maintained a stoic silence.

"Can I, Mama?" asked Teddy. "I want to go. Now."

"You can't go now," Hetty said sharply. "Sit up there and finish your porridge." Teddy opened his oatmeal-rimmed mouth and a wail began to emerge.

Hetty turned a furious face to Holly. "Now, see what you've done?"

Holly knew there was no use arguing or trying to explain. She hurried over to Teddy, kissed his round little face contorted with unhappiness, and said over the howls, "Teddy, please don't cry! Do what your mama says, and I promise you a 'nice surprise! I'll send it back with your papa," With that, after giving Aurelia a quick hug, Holly made her exit.

From the kitchen window Hetty watched them, the anger still like a hard fist in her chest. She saw Ned put his hand under Holly's elbow and assist her into the wagon. Hetty's lip curled scornfully even as her heart wrenched. Ned probably admired Holly, and that admiration would make him offer comfort and support to her. Men had always admired and helped Holly even when she didn't deserve it. *Especially* when she didn't deserve it, Hetty thought resentfully.

Things usually happened just the way Holly wanted them to; she always had the last word. Men had always flocked around her, wanting to do her bidding, *asking* to do whatever she pleased. Why? What made Holly so—so attractive to men? Even in Willow Springs, there had been far prettier girls, yet Holly had been the most popular. She did not even flirt—well, at least, not as blatantly as some of the other girls did, Hetty had to admit. Still, Hetty could never figure out just what it was that Holly did that men so liked, to make them circle her like moths around a flame. She did not even seem to have to lift a finger—

But she'd lost Jim Mercer, hadn't she? *That had brought her crashing down all right*, Hetty thought with some satisfaction. She remembered how she used to envy Holly when Jim came home from West Point in his dashing cadet uniform, with the red-lined gray cape and the jaunty cap. She recalled how indifferent Holly had seemed to his adoration, how casually she had accepted his worshipful eyes, his eagerness to do her bidding.

Well, Ned was twice the man Jim Mercer had been. And *she* was the one who had caught *him!* Suddenly Hetty was convinced, recalling Ned's remonstrative look when Holly announced so hopefully that she was going to try for the schoolteacher's job. All that week, in spite of his gentle prodding, *she* had remained aloof, unhelpful. Even last night he had gently asked if she wasn't even going to wish Holly well as she started her new endeavor. But why should she? Stubbornly Hetty justified her actions. It was all right for Ned to say. But what did *he* know? Ned couldn't possibly know what Holly was really like or what it was like for Hetty, all the years of being in Holly's shadow, being compared to her, and envying her while watching everyone else—even family—under her spell.

Hetty's hand shook slightly as she drew the curtain back just enough so she could peer around it. Ned and Holly were both seated in the wagon now. Ned was bending solicitously toward Holly. Listening? Or was he sympathizing? Hetty saw Holly's pert profile turned to him, her hair, upswept from the slender neck, gleamed like rich mahogany in the autumn sunlight, the blue bonnet tipped coquettishly forward, the small plum-colored plume fluttering in the brisk wind. Hetty felt the sour taste of jealousy rise up within her.

The wagon started out, and at the same time Hetty became aware of the scorching smell of something burning. Her biscuits! She whirled around, snatched up a pot holder, grabbed the oven door open, and pulled out the blackened baking sheet. She ran with it to the back door where she banged it down on the porch railing. Somehow she had also burned her fingers, and as she dropped the pan and shook her hand, scalding tears sprang into her eyes and coursed down her cheeks. It seemed the last straw.

Hetty leaned her head against the porch post and sobbed.

Outside, Holly climbed into the wagon where Ned waited patiently. She felt bad that there had been no mutually pleasant last words with Hetty. But there certainly had been no opening there. Unconsciously, Holly sighed. Ned raised his eyebrows. "Storm brewing in there?" he inquired, jerking his head toward the house.

"'Fraid so," Holly sighed.

"The kids adore you, Holly," he said as he lifted the reins, clicked his tongue for the horse to start forward. They rode a little way before Ned said sadly, "I'm sure sorry about Hetty—" He halted as though not sure that whatever he said might not seem disloyal to his wife. But then he went on, "You know Hetty hated Willow Springs, and I guess, in a way, you're being here reminded her of all the things she hated most about it."

"It's all right, Ned, I understand. I'm just sorry she can't let bygones be bygones. I realize now that back home I was pretty thoughtless sometimes."

Ned didn't offer any more, and they went the rest of the distance with only a few words exchanged. When they got to the schoolhouse, Ned unloaded Holly's trunk and boxes and carried them into the little apartment behind the classroom. "I wish I could stay and help, Holly, but I've got to go open the store. Saturday's one of my busiest days," Ned said as he stood awkwardly in the doorway.

"Oh, of course, Ned. I understand. And thank you for all this." Holly gestured to her assorted boxes and bags and her trunk. "You've done so much for me already. You go ahead. There are others coming to help."

"I wish you all the luck in the world, Holly, and if things don't work out—you can always come—" he broke off, turning beet red. Holly knew that what he had been about to say was something he really couldn't offer with any assurance.

"Thanks, Ned, I appreciate that. But it's going to work out, don't worry." She smiled confidently, adding mentally, *It's got to work out!*

Holly was only alone a short time when the Healys arrived.

"We're here to get you settled right," Geneva declared as, armed with scrub buckets, brushes, brooms and big cakes of yellow soap, she mounted the steps and set to work. "You, Matt, start on the windows outside," she ordered her hefty, muscular husband who winked at Holly as he saluted his wife and went to comply with her instructions.

Annie Olsen and Elly Rogers, both members of the Literary Society, came soon after, and then Vi. Holly was so grateful. All these women knew exactly what to do to turn the dusty, dirty place into clean, sanitary, and shining living quarters. Less experienced in housework skills, she was glad to follow their expert directions.

At noon they stopped for a hearty lunch. Besides cleaning equipment, Geneva had brought a hamper of delicious food: ham, deviled eggs, potato salad. Annie had brought a jug of sweet apple cider freshly pressed from their orchard's fruit, and

Elly provided home-baked bread and a custard pie. Vi's contribution was one of her delicate lemon sponge cakes.

"What a feast!" exclaimed Holly. "You're all so wonderful! How can I ever thank you."

"You're thanking us aplenty by teaching our children," Geneva said.

"Maybe you won't be so grateful after a couple of days with our two rascals!" laughed Matt.

"Matt's right, Holly, that's the truth. And I know *my* Billy and Tom can be as mischievous as a barrel of monkeys, I can tell you," Annie shook her head.

"Don't be afraid to use the proverbial hickory stick, Holly," counseled Elly who had five children, all under the age of twelve.

"I just hope I can do the job!" declared Holly.

"You'll do just fine," Vi told her, and they exchanged a look.

Holly was reminded of Vi's advice, "Pray hard and let God do the rest." She meant to take it.

After they ate, they all went back to work. Early in the afternoon, to Holly's astonishment Adam Corcoran appeared.

"What in the world!" she gasped as she saw him dismount and approach the schoolhouse, holding a bouquet of autumn flowers. She met him at the door and surveyed him with mock severity. He was immaculately groomed as always.

"Oh, no, Adam!" she shook her head, "you'll never do! This is hard, dusty work, and you're not dressed for it."

He looked momentarily abashed; then, pointing to Vi, with her head tied up in a scarf and wearing a coverall apron, he asked, "Why can't I have one of those?"

Holly giggled, "I guess we can find an extra one for you if you really want to help."

"Why else would I have come?" he demanded. With that he handed her the flowers, took off his gray broadcloth jacket, and rolled up the sleeves of his white shirt.

At four o'clock Geneva said that she and Matt would have to leave. She had left her brood with a neighbor, and, this being Saturday night, there were baths to be given in preparation for the Sabbath and church the next day. Holly thanked them pro-

112

fusely, and they departed. Elly and Annie, who had come together, gave their particular job a final "lick and promise"; then they left, too. Vi was next to leave. Promising to come to visit soon, she got into her small buggy and rode off.

Adam was the last to leave and seemed almost reluctant to go. He pulled an immaculate linen handkerchief out of his pocket and wiped his forehead. "Whew, you were right. I never saw so many cobwebs, so many spiders. What did old Larkin do with them, I wonder, raise them for scientific experiments?"

"You're not quitting?" Holly, hands on her hips, demanded as if shocked.

"Isn't everything done? The place looks like it underwent a complete transformation. But if there's anything else, it'll have to wait until I just have a little rest before tackling it," he told her, adding, "The spirit indeed is willing, but the flesh is weak."

Holly blinked her eyes, "Why, Adam Corcoran, quoting Scripture?"

"Every educated man knows plenty of appropriate quotations, as many from the Bible as Shakespeare."

"But you know who quotes Scripture for his own purposes, don't you?" she teased.

"I am also aware of that," he answered, nodding his head sagely. "And I only quote it rarely when the occasion calls for it."

Holly found his coat for him and gave it to him.

"I was joking. Everything is done. I can't thank you enough for lending a hand. I didn't expect it."

"Life is full of surprises, isn't it?"

"And thank you, too, for the flowers," she said as they walked out onto the schoolhouse porch.

"You're more than welcome. And I really *do* wish you . . . well, everything you need to succeed . . ." here his voice changed into his supercilious tone, ". . . at this enterprise you've so rashly undertaken."

He went down the steps and untethered his horse from the hitching post. For a moment he stood by his horse's head, adjusting the bridle then tightening the stirrup buckle. Then he turned and looked up at Holly standing on the porch steps above him and asked doubtfully, "Sure you won't be lonely here?"

"Lonely?" she repeated his question, and paused before answering slowly. "I'm really not sure. I've never lived completely alone before. But to be quite honest, I hadn't given a thought to being lonely. I just wanted to be free."

His smile was slightly sardonic, but his eyes were understanding, and he did not comment.

After Ad had ridden off, Holly went back inside her new domain. Smiling, she looked around. She had never worked so hard physically in her life before; she had never felt so tired, but she knew she had never felt so happy.

The entire place smelled of scouring powder, ammonia, and vinegar, and of furniture polish and wax. Holly drew a long breath. The clean astringent odor seemed as sweet as any perfume. She circled the room, trailing her fingers along the tops of the polished double-desks, stopping to straighten a picture, then she paused to gaze out the clear windows onto the schoolyard and the surrounding hills.

She'd read somewhere that it takes a person at least three weeks or twenty-one days to get accustomed to a new place, a new set of circumstances. In time, she knew, all this would become as familiar to her as her room at home in Willow Springs.

She had come to Oregon with no other purpose than to escape the swirl of gossip around her, of "hiding out" comfortably until she felt she could slip quietly back into town, no longer the target of wagging tongues. She remembered her feeling of dismay when she arrived—"end of the line"—how bitterly she had regretted coming. Now, instead of regret, she was filled with hope. It wasn't just by chance she was here. She was more and more convinced there was a plan, some kind of Divine plan to all this.

Holly smiled. She seemed to be thinking in clichés: end of the line, closing one door, opening another, turning over a new leaf, or starting a new chapter. This experience would be a blank page. Nothing had been written on it yet. Its contents would be up to her. Until now, Holly had spent a lot of time looking back.

But, no more. Now was a new beginning—Holly felt a tingle of real excitement—she spun around, pirouetting several times— and she was going to enjoy it, make the most of it.

Several loud knocks on the schoolhouse door jolted her out of her unaccustomed reverie, and Holly heard a man's voice shouting, "Anybody here? Where's the new schoolmarm?"

Holly stood still, startled, listening.

"Miss Lambeth! Hello, are you here?"

It was a voice she recognized, vibrant, pleasantly pitched. For some reason Holly's heart skittered!

The voice came again, "It's me, Blaine Stevens!"

Blaine Stevens! That's what had been missing today, she thought. Blaine! She ran through the hallway joining the small apartment in back to the schoolroom, feeling unreasonably happy to see his tall figure standing in the doorway. He was holding a huge orange pumpkin.

"I guess I missed the housewarming party?" he asked abjectly.

Holly tried to look severe. "You missed the *work* party."

Blaine looked sheepish. "Sorry."

Holly laughed and put her hands on her hips and eyed the pumpkin, saying, "So! You think bringing *that's* going to make up for it?"

"I guess you could put it like that," he drawled.

"You know what they say about Greeks bearing gifts, don't you?" she demanded.

"Well, not being a Greek—I'm not sure—but it doesn't sound good."

"If I were a Trojan, maybe not—," she dimpled, "but under the circumstances . . ."

Blaine shook his head. "What those poor, unsuspecting children are in for! A teacher who knows the classics."

"Only by hearsay!" Holly smiled, then with her head on one side, she examined the size of the pumpkin and asked warily, "I hope you're not expecting me to bake a couple of pies with this?"

"Not at all. I thought I'd show off my surgical skill and carve you a jack o'lantern—thought it would be a nice touch for your first day of school."

115

"Why, Blaine. what a delightful idea. Shall we go into the kitchen?"

"No, let's sit outside on the porch and I'll do it there. It's such a nice afternoon, and from the looks of this place you've spent enough time inside today. It'll do you good to get some fresh air and sunshine!"

Holly put a finger under her chin as if in obedience. "Yes, Doctor. Thinking of my health, I see. So, what do you need?"

"Just some old *Monitors*, if you've got them. I come equipped with scalpel," he joked and walked out onto the front porch while she hurried into the kitchen and gathered up a stack of newspapers in a box by the stove.

Watching Blaine's hands as he first outlined triangular eyes, nose, and a wide, grinning mouth with the point of his knife, Holly thought how strong and capable they were, blunt-tipped, flexible. She was fascinated by how quickly and smoothly he cut into the flesh of the pumpkin, neatly scooped out the meat and seeds, then finished off tne comical face, leaving two jagged teeth on the top and bottom of the smile.

"There! How's that?" he asked leaning back and surveying his handiwork.

"A work of art!" declared Holly. "You're a genius!"

"Ah, madam, you exaggerate!" he murmured with mock humility.

"Only slightly. It is certainly one of the handsomest jack o'lanterns it has been my privilege to meet—the children will love it!" she assured him. "Now, I'll just gather up this mess and reward you with a piece of lemon sponge cake."

"That sounds great—if it's no trouble."

"None," said Holly starting to fold up the remains of the pumpkin.

"Wait! Don't throw away the seeds," cautioned Blaine. "Rinse them thoroughly, put them on a baking sheet with a little butter and into the oven for about fifteen minutes and—"

"Then what?"

"Eat them! They're delicious and *very* good for you besides. Very healthy!"

Holly teased, "Always the doctor!"

"'Fraid so." Blaine looked abashed. "I guess it goes with the territory—, as they say."

"Never mind. I should be glad you're concerned about my health! All this good medical advice for free," she said laughingly over her shoulder as she started inside.

"Don't be so sure of that," Blaine retorted.

"Sure of what?"

"That it's free. I may present you with a bill."

"Oh, so what is your usual fee?"

"Well, it's not *usual,* not what I *usually* charge my patients," Blaine said as he followed her into the kitchen.

"So? What is it?"

"Would you like to go on a picnic with me next Sunday afternoon?"

Holly was glad that her back was turned to him so that he couldn't see how his question had brought the warmth rushing into her cheeks, starting her heart thumping.

She tried to keep her voice steady as she replied casually. "Why, yes, that sounds like fun—that is, if this good weather lasts."

After Blaine had gone, Holly lighted a candle and placed it inside the grinning jack o'lantern and stood looking at it for a long time. Was she becoming too interested in Blaine? Everything about him appealed to her. his strength, his confidence, his manner, and underneath all that, his quiet sense of humor. She realized that when she was with him, things seemed to fall into place as if it were all as it should be. Strange?

For awhile that evening she puttered around, setting out her personal things to make the little parlor more hers. She set out the double-framed pictures of her parents, the watercolor of their home that her Aunt Sylvie, the "artistic" sister in her mother's family, had painted, and then she placed her photo album containing all the special pictures on the small chest of drawers.

The flowers Ad brought, the white and gold chrysanthemums, were already filling the room with their spicy scent, and the pillow that Vi had needlepointed for her went on the rock-

117

er. Holly looked around with infinite satisfaction and drew a long breath of contentment. She couldn't remember feeling so happy for a long time.

That night before getting into bed, Holly stood at the window, watching a harvest moon move slowly across the sky. After she blew out the lamp, the moon shining in the window made square patches on her bedspread.

After this eventful day, sleep didn't come easily. She missed the feel of Aurelia's warm little body curled beside her and realized the one thing she would miss from moving out of Hetty's house were the children. Finally she closed her eyes and whispered the childhood prayer that Great-Aunt Ancilla had taught her, "I will lay me down in peace and sleep, for Thou, Lord, only, makest me dwell in safety."

PART 3

If ever I am a teacher,
it will be to learn more than to teach.

Madame Deluzy

Chapter 13

The first morning that Holly was to take charge of the Riverbend grammar school so many butterflies were fluttering in her stomach that she could hardly manage to swallow a half cup of coffee. And not very good coffee at that. She had been so distracted making it that it tasted more like bitter hot sand than anything else.

Dressed in what she hoped was a "schoolmarm" outfit, over her plainest blue merino dress with a simple white collar, she put on the patterned calico pinafore Vi had made her to protect her dress from chalk dust and ink and "whatever the children may have on their hands when they tug at you." She swept her hair up and back into a prim knot and looked in the mirror to assure herself that at least she looked the part, then Holly went out into the schoolroom for a final check before school started.

Everything in the schoolroom looked perfect. The worn, scratched pupils' desks had been cleaned and varnished, the scarred floor was waxed, blackboards washed. The teacher's pointer hung neatly by the wall map of the world, chalk was in the boxes, the slates were on each desk, pencils and erasers on top of the polished teacher's desk at the front of the room. The finished result was all due to the help so generously given her, Holly recalled with gratitude. For the short time she had been in Riverbend she had made some really good friends.

In spite of Hetty. That last awful scene with her cousin flashed into her mind and Holly gave a little shiver. She quickly banished the memory. She refused to think about it now. Or to think about it any more, for that matter. She wanted to forget it. She had enough on her mind without thinking about Hetty.

Morning sunshine poured through the sparkling windows and, peeking out, Holly saw a few of her students were coming into the schoolyard. She consulted her fob watch pinned to her apron bib for at least the dozenth time. It wasn't yet eight o'clock, the time she was supposed to go out on the porch and ring the bell announcing the opening of school.

Suddenly Holly felt the grip of doubt. Perhaps she had underestimated the pitfalls of what she had undertaken. In less than an hour twenty-five children would be thronging through that door. And *she* was expected to teach them! In the euphoria of privacy and freedom she had experienced over the weekend, obtained with the schoolteacher's position, the responsibilities of it, only dimly perceived, had floated somewhere on the periphery of her mind as "next week." Now *next week* was *now!* The first day of school was *here!* Her first day of teaching was about to begin.

All at once came a terrifying vision of this room filled with children of varying ages, noisy, squirming, staring at her curiously while she was supposed to not only keep everything in order but teach them something as well. Oh, why had she ever thought she could do this? What on earth was she doing here?

Then suddenly, out of Holly's past came a memory of something her father had told her when she was a little girl and refused to go by a neighbor's house because they had a big black barking dog, "Holly, a dog senses when someone is afraid of it, and that's when a dog will bite!"

Why that came back to her now, Holly couldn't imagine. However, it did the trick of steadying her. "If I look as scared as I feel, the children will see it, and it will all be over for me," she told herself, the ridiculous image of the children pushing through the doorway jumping on her with bared teeth almost made her laugh out loud.

Her feeling of panic subsided. Holly walked over to the teacher's desk and picked up the handle of the heavy teacher's bell, walked out onto the schoolhouse porch, and, pumping back her arm, began to swing it. The loud clanging ring reverberated into the clear morning air. Riverbend Grammar School was now back in session.

At the end of the day Holly's head was throbbing. As the last little "scholar" trailed out of the classroom, she sank into the teacher's chair with a sense of infinite relief and total exhaustion. *How did people manage to teach year after year?* she wondered wearily, thinking of the grammar school teachers she knew in Willow Springs who after forty years were still teaching—like old Miss Wilkins who had taught Holly's own mother!

She had moved through the day in a whirl. The projects she had planned for the children to do that she thought would take twenty minutes were either completed or ruined in five! The variety of ages and diversity in ability of her pupils was confusing. The tasks that she thought would be simple proved difficult. The ones she thought would occupy them long enough to give her a breather were completed in record time. She would go to help one group with something, repeat instructions, and get them started, when another group would need help.

And always at the back of the room were the big boys! She had been warned about them. It seems once a boy got to the age and strength he was of real use on the farm, he only attended school haphazardly and regularly failed to appear during spring planting and fall harvesting. These fellows, ranging in age from twelve to fourteen, were a continual source of interruption. They carried on a constant conversation between themselves, talked through her directions, and asked for repetitions just, Holly suspected, to divert her from her explanations and irritate her. She would have to find some system to get them under control. But right now she was too worn out to think how.

She was so tired that she went to bed early that night, then overslept the next morning. She had to rush, with only time to grab a quick mug of coffee and a few bites of bread and jam, to be ready when the first little pupils arrived. They were the Healy twins, scrubbed and shiny-faced, eager to begin their day of learning.

At the end of her second day of teaching, Holly concluded it was far worse than the first had been. *Why did I ever think I could do this job? Was having the little apartment in back really worth all this?* she demanded of herself as she sat slumped at her table sipping tea that afternoon.

If it hadn't been for Vi's unexpected arrival with a meat pie and a pan of cornbread wrapped in a padded cloth to keep warm, she might have been tempted to write a letter of resignation to the Council right then.

"Oh, Vi, why did I ever take this on! I'm not up to it! I don't think I can ever get the hang of it. A teacher I'm not!" she moaned as they sat at the kitchen table together.

"Nonsense, you're going to do fine. It's always hard starting any new venture," Vi assured her.

"I don't know," Holly said, gloomily shaking her head.

But the next day things went a little better. Some of the children were really eager to learn, quick to follow directions, and touchingly sweet. Holly decided to separate the big boys, give them physical tasks to do, like bringing in water from the well and filling the drinking bucket in the classroom each morning, splitting kindling, and chopping wood to keep the woodbox for the stove filled even though the days weren't cold enough yet to have a fire going.

She found a box of *McGuffey Readers* that Larkin had evidently ordered and never unpacked, and these were a great help. For the children who knew how to read, she could assign them a lesson while she taught the younger ones their ABCs. By Friday, although her nerves were frazzled and she was physically spent, Holly felt she had gained a little more confidence that she would survive the year ahead.

It would only be until spring, she encouraged herself. The school year in Riverbend only went until the first of May; then Holly would make plans to go home to Willow Springs.

Chapter 14

$\mathcal{T}$he second week of school had gone incredibly well, Holly thought, as she stood at the schoolhouse door on Friday afternoon, watching the last group of children leave the play yard and start their meandering way home. None were in any hurry, probably because they knew the chores that awaited them there.

Little Joel McKay and his sister, Cissy, were the last to leave. Cissy turned at the gate to wave one more time to Holly before hurrying to catch up with her brother. These two had already made inroads into Holly's affection. Skinny and under-sized for their ages, with threadbare clothes and bare feet. She worried about them now especially when early fall frost covered the grass.

Holly was just about to close the door when she saw a familiar small buggy and horse coming down the road toward the schoolhouse. Her heart gave an unexpected little leap as the buggy turned into the schoolyard. *Blaine!* she thought happily.

He reined up in front of the porch, leaned out, and greeted her. "Well, Miss Schoolmarm, how's it going?"

She placed a hand on her breast and heaved a dramatic sigh. "Better than I had any right to expect!" she admitted with a laugh.

He reached into a basket beside him on the floor of the buggy then held out his hand, "An apple for the teacher?" he grinned, opening his palm revealing a round bright red apple.

"Why, thank you, Blaine!" Holly took it and dropped a curtsy.

"Thank the Fosters; they gave me a whole bushel in payment for taking care of their last baby," Blaine laughed.

"Ummm, delicious!" Holly said as her white teeth bit into the rosy skin and took a bite of the sweet, tart fruit.

"Know someone who can bake a superior pie? I can't possibly eat all of these myself."

Holly thought a moment, then warned laughingly, "Well, don't look at *me*, Blaine, I never was able to get the crust right. But I was thinking you could leave some of the apples here to share with the children. Some of them seem to forget to bring lunch sometimes or else come without it, and it would be nice to have something on hand for them to eat."

"Good idea!" agreed Blaine. "I'll bring the basket inside for you." He got out of the buggy and led his horse over to the edge of the yard where there was some scraggly long grass for him to nibble on; then he lifted out the split-oak basket of apples and carried them into the schoolroom.

Holly held the door open for him and he set them down behind the teacher's desk.

"I'd say it's more likely some of them come without lunch because there isn't enough in the larder at home to spare," Blaine told her frowning. "A few of the families around here have quite a struggle to make a go of it. A lot of folks came out here from the East without much farming experience, just wanted to get a new start, maybe; when offered land to homestead they grabbed on to it. Turned out to be a lot harder than they had any idea it would be—"

"The proverbial Promised Land?" Holly commented.

"Something like that." Blaine shook his head. "Only for some of them it hasn't worked out all that well."

Then turning to Holly, his serious expression was replaced by an engaging smile. "Since this is Friday and the youngsters get a holiday from school on weekends, so how about the teacher? What would you say to going on that picnic we talked about, tomorrow?"

"Oh, yes, I'd love that."

"While this weather holds—it might be really nice farther up

126

on the river—I might even do a little fishing. That is if you wouldn't object?"

"Object? I like to fish myself; my Grandfather used to take me fishing with him. And I've caught a few nice trout myself a time or two!" Holly gave her head a little toss.

"Were you a tomboy, Miss Lambeth?"

"You *might* say that, Doctor." She lowered her voice conspiratorially. "Would you believe that my mother quite gave up on me several times! She would say to my grandfather, 'Papa, how do you expect me to bring Hollis up a lady if you keep encouraging her this way?'"

"Well, I'd say she managed to do that just fine," Blaine commented as he gazed at Holly appreciatively, adding with a mischievous grin, "But then I've never seen you with a fishing pole, have I?"

"You'll have your chance tomorrow."

As they walked back to the door she asked, "What about the picnic food? What shall I bring?"

"Yourself. I'll provide most of it." He held up his hand when she started to protest. "Really, most of my patients pay me in wonderful ways—you'll see." He went down the steps. At the bottom he turned and looked up at her. "So, then, I'll come by—say ten o'clock tomorrow morning?"

"Yes, fine."

Blaine started walking to where he had left the buggy, and Holly's eyes followed him. *If* she planned to stay in Riverbend, Holly could not think of a nicer "beau" than Blaine—good-looking if not handsome, intelligent, gentle, and with a fine sense of humor—but then, she amended quickly, she wasn't planning to stay. There was certainly no point getting any ideas about the doctor.

True to his word, Blaine arrived promptly at ten next morning, and Holly was ready and waiting in a blue calico dress with a pattern of tiny flowers, her hair out of its coil and gathered with a blue ribbon at the nape of her neck.

"I feel like a kid playing hooky from school!" he told her as he helped her into his small gig, picked up the reins and they started off.

"But that's impossible! You're *with* the 'schoolmarm'!" Holly laughed gaily.

"That's right! I almost forgot or else you don't *seem* like a schoolteacher to me!" he looked at Holly, thinking how lovely she looked with the sun's sending dancing gold lights through her hair, the rose color of her softly curved cheeks. "You see, Miss Lambeth, I never had such a pretty teacher as *you* when I went to school."

"Why, thank you for the compliment, sir," Holly replied. "It's hard for me to believe, too. I never thought I'd end up a schoolteacher."

"What do you mean 'end up'?"

Holly hesitated. Surely she didn't know Blaine well enough to reveal her sorry story, to tell him that by this time she had expected to be an Army officer's bride, not teaching school in a frontier town. No, she couldn't confess her humiliating experience of being jilted. Instead, she answered, "I just never *planned* to teach school. It just never occurred to me that I would. But I'm discovering as they say that 'life is full of surprises,' right?"

Blaine gave her a searching glance as if he knew she was holding something back, but he didn't ask anything more. Instead, he spoke of himself. "I always wanted to be a doctor. My uncle was a doctor and as a little boy I used to go with him in his buggy when he made his calls. The whole idea of being skilled enough to help people when they were hurt or ill seemed a great way to spend my life."

"From what I hear, Riverbend is very lucky to have you."

Blaine shrugged, "I'm just glad I can be of use." Then he changed the subject. "I'm going to pull off the road here, we'll have to leave the buggy and walk down to the river bank. I started to get another horse from the livery stable and a sidesaddle for you to bring out, but I didn't know whether or not you rode. Do you?"

"Yes."

"Next time, we'll do that. Then we can ride right to our picnic spot."

Holly felt a little spurt of pleasure that Blaine had said "next time."

Blaine unhitched the horse and led him over to a shady spot to graze, tying him loosely to a small aspen. Then he got the wicker hamper and his fishing gear from the back of the buggy and said, "Come on, it's not far."

It could not have been a more beautiful day for a picnic. Holly had never seen deep forests like these in Oregon. She loved the feel of the pine needles under her feet like a soft brown carpet on the path through the woods to the river. The sun was warm on their backs as they came to a clearing over-looking the clear, rock-rimmed river. They both stood for a moment, savoring the quiet, the only sound being the rush of the water below, the gentle swish of wind high above in the trees.

Blaine set down the picnic basket, and Holly spread out the blanket for them to sit on. It was so lovely and peaceful that nei-ther of them spoke for a few minutes.

"Are you hungry? Or do you want to try your luck at fishing first?" Blaine asked after awhile.

She considered her choices, then said, "Eat? I am rather hungry."

"Good! So am I." Blaine opened the hamper and began putting out the food.

"My goodness, such a lot!" Holly exclaimed.

"I have a lot of grateful patients!" he laughed as he continued bringing out a loaf of home-baked bread, sliced ham, a choco-late cake, and peach pie.

Holly opened her own much smaller basket and brought out her contribution. "And *I* have a lot of *grateful students!* Or at least their mothers are!" she announced putting down a dainti-ly arranged plate of deviled eggs and a square of gingerbread. Blaine looked surprised, and Holly explained, "Danny Glenn's mother sends me a dozen eggs every week, and Geneva Healy always bakes something extra for me on her baking day."

"If I were the suspicious type I'd say some of your pupils are angling for good grades," he commented as he sampled one of the eggs.

"And it pays, doesn't it?"

"Hmmm." Blaine rolled his eyes as he popped the rest of the

129

egg into his mouth, then licked his fingers. "I'd give them all A's for sure."

They made sandwiches of the ham and thickly buttered bread, drank the lemonade, and finished with cake.

"What a feast!" declared Blaine, leaning back against a large rock, his arms folded beneath his head. "It's a real treat for me, I can tell you. I usually get my meals at the Hometown Cafe, and believe me, I don't know *whose* hometown they're advertising with that name, because the food leaves a great deal to be desired."

"Well, maybe we should go on picnics more often!" Holly quipped then blushed. Immediately she wished she hadn't said that. It was the sort of thing the "old Holly" would say, coy and flirtatious. Wasn't she done with that sort of foolishness? She hoped Blaine wouldn't take it wrong. She looked over at him. His eyes were closed. He seemed to be entirely relaxed, maybe even dozing.

Holly got up and walked over to the edge of the river and looked down at the clear, sun-dappled water. How peaceful, how beautiful it was. She felt a kind of awe at the splendor of this country. The surprising thought came to her of how lucky she was to be here. She couldn't remember ever having been so touched by the majesty of natural beauty before. Maybe she really was changing, becoming a different kind of person. Someone who was aware of beauty, able to appreciate nature, capable of reflection.

"Ready to try your luck fishing?" Blaine's voice behind her made Holly turn. He was on his feet, roused from his short nap and getting out his fishing rod.

"I think I'll just tag along down the stream with you," she said.

She followed Blaine as he moved from one rock to the other, casting and spinning. She saw the flashes of gold and brown of the plentiful trout in the crystal water. Blaine landed several but released them, explaining offhandedly that he didn't cook enough to take them home, and besides it was just the fun of testing his skill that he enjoyed most.

All too soon, the shadows began to lengthen, the towering trees soon hid the lowering sun and the wind off the river turned chilly. "Guess we better get started back," Blaine said reluctantly.

They repacked the hamper, folded the blanket and walked slowly to where they had left horse and buggy earlier. Holly debated whether or not to invite Blaine back to the schoolhouse for a pick-up supper from the remains of the picnic, make a pot of hot tea. Would it be proper for a spinster schoolmarm to entertain the town's bachelor doctor alone?

Vi had warned Holly that a small-town schoolteacher had to be careful about her reputation, so, regretfully, she decided against such an invitation. But with someone like Blaine it seemed such a silly rule to be kept.

In the buggy on the way toward town, Blaine said, "I hated to leave. I haven't enjoyed a day so much in . . . well, I don't know how long."

"It was lovely, Blaine; I'm glad you suggested it." Holly smiled at him.

As they jogged along, they carried on a bantering conversation, while Holly enjoyed the scenery of meadows fenced with rails where placid cattle grazed and where orchards were now heavy with autumn fruit: golden pears and russet apples. Suddenly the peaceful scene was shattered. Coming down the road toward them was a horse in a frenzied gallop with its rider waving one arm frantically and shouting. Blaine pulled on his reins. "Whoa!" He leaned forward as the breathless rider slid his mount to a stop alongside.

"Thank God, Doc! I found you! You gotta come quick! It's my boy Chad! Fell off the hayrack, split his head near clear open—he's bleedin' somethin' awful—please, come, right away!"

"Sure thing, Jesse," Blaine clicked his reins, and as the man whirled his horse around and started galloping ahead, Blaine urged his jogging horse forward. "Come on, fella, let's get going!" They started off at a fast clip.

"That was Jesse Renner. His farm is not far from here. A widower with three boys all under twelve who do a man's work along with their father."

"Oh, you mean Ev and Henry? They come to school. But I don't think I know Chad," Holly replied.

131

"He's probably been helping his father by not attending school since their mother died last spring."

"Ev and Henry don't come regularly either. But I didn't know why."

"A motherless home has a lot of problems," Blaine said grimly. "I'm sorry, Holly, you'll have to come along. There's no time to take you back into town."

"Of course not, Blaine. I understand."

They were going so fast that the fragile little buggy swayed perilously from side to side as they bumped down the rutted country road. Holly had to grip the side handles of the seat to avoid being tossed from the jolting vehicle. Swerving, almost on one wheel, Blaine turned into the gates of the Renner farm. Near the barn, lying on the ground, she saw the prone figure of a boy; two other boys, looking pale and frightened, stood over him. The father, who had made it back only a few minutes before, handed the reins of his horse to one of his sons, with a terse order, "Take him in and rub him down," then knelt beside the inert body of the boy.

"He's still a-breathin' Doc, but I dunno." The man's voice broke as Blaine jumped out of his buggy and ran to where the man was kneeling beside his son.

Over his shoulder, he called back to Holly, "Get my medicine bag, it's under the seat."

Mechanically, Holly ducked her head and saw the black medicine bag, dragged it forward, grabbed it. Gathering up her skirt, she got out of the buggy and hurried over to Blaine. Looking down at the child, she saw blood all over his face, matted into a shock of sandy hair. Instinctively she shrank back, fighting down the instant nausea at the sight, the scared pounding of her heart, and the flinching of every nerve. She set down the medicine bag beside Blaine and stepped back, quelling the urge to run away.

Blaine made a quick examination of the boy, running his hands over his limbs, arms, taking his pulse; then, placing practiced fingers on the base of the boy's throat, he bent his head close to scrutinize the still bleeding gash on the boy's forehead. "He'll be all right, Jesse, but we've got to close up that wound.

He's lost a lot of blood and will go into shock if we don't act fast." He turned aside and snapped open his bag, brought out a square of cotton gauze, and applied it. It immediately turned crimson and Holly felt herself gag.

Blaine spoke again. "We'll take him into the house. Jesse, get on the other side and easy now, gently. Careful—," he instructed the father. To Holly he said, "Bring my bag, please."

Like an automaton Holly followed them. They entered the house into the kitchen. It was dim, dingy, smelled of old grease, dirt, and the odor of cabbage and fried meat hung in the air. A widower, Blaine had said. Certainly no woman lived in this fetid atmosphere.

Blaine issued orders like an army drillmaster, and Holly scurried to obey. "Clear that table. Scour the top, see if you can find a clean towel—"

She found a large cake of lye soap in a cracked dish on the counter, and there was some water in the kettle on the stove. It was almost impossible to get a lather up, but she did her best; then, as rapidly as she could, she washed off the surface with a wadded dishrag.

There wasn't a tablecloth in sight. Blaine and Jesse were still holding the boy, waiting. Realizing that every minute counted, Holly made an impulsive, instantaneous decision. Blaine and Jesse both had their backs to her, still holding Chad. Quickly Holly moved into the corner and lifted her skirt to one side and unbuttoned the waistband of one of her petticoats. Holding it so it wouldn't drop on the floor, she stepped out of it carefully, then whipped it over onto the kitchen table. Then the two men eased the boy on the top.

Outside, the autumn evening was rapidly darkening. The kitchen was full of shadows.

"Light a lamp," Blaine said to Jesse. "I need to see what I'm doing. I'll have to suture that cut; it will take stitches—" Blaine was almost talking to himself.

The boy began to moan. Blaine put his hands on the boy's shoulders soothingly. Holly could hear Jesse fumbling as he lighted an oil lamp with shaky hands.

"Jesse, hold the lamp right here so I can see," Blaine said calmly.

The father stepped up to the table. Then Blaine spoke directly to Holly. "Chad will have to be held absolutely still so that we don't start the bleeding all over while I sew up his head. Think you can hold his head for me?"

Holly's face whitened and her eyes darkened with fear. She knew she had no time to hesitate. She was needed in a way she had never been before in her entire life. The only thing that deeply troubled her was whether she was up to this task that had been thrust upon her. She swallowed over a throat dry with fear and nodded.

"All right, just step here and put your hands on either side of his head, hold it steady," Blaine ordered. He gave her one long look, then he seemed to forget her and concentrate totally on his patient.

Holly clamped her teeth together, so they wouldn't chatter and she wouldn't scream. Eyes riveted, she watched as Blaine removed the blood-soaked cloth, wiped the child's forehead gently, then began his skillful surgery. His hand never shook as he expertly, quickly moved the needle back and forth closing the gaping gash.

It wasn't until she heard Blaine speaking to Jesse that Holly snapped back to consciousness and knew the ordeal was over. She heard Blaine say, "Let's wrap him in a blanket, get him into bed, heat some bricks, and place them at his feet; see that he doesn't get a chill. He'll be fine. I'll look in on him in the morning, but I don't think you have to worry, Jesse. He may have a mild concussion from the fall, but the wound on his forehead will heal, and he'll just have a slight scar, that's all."

Left alone in the dark kitchen, Holly stripped off the blood-spattered petticoat from the table, rolled it into a tight ball, and stuck it under her arm. Shuddering, she walked over to the door, opened it, and stepped out onto the porch and took a long, shaky breath.

Every muscle in her body ached with released tension. She began to tremble and felt suddenly cold. How had she ever been able to do what she had just done? The Holly *she* knew was one

134

who grew faint at the merest drop of blood on a pricked finger and turned away from a plucked chicken or a dead mouse!

Within a few minutes, she felt a firm hand on her arm and Blaine's voice saying solicitously, "You all right?"

She nodded.

"Come on, then, I'll take you home."

They drove back to the schoolhouse in silence. When Blaine took her up to the door, he asked softly, "Will you ever go on another picnic with *me?*"

Her laugh sounded slightly hysterical. "Of course."

"You were splendid, Holly. Thank you."

"You're welcome," she said faintly.

There was much left unspoken, but there seemed no adequate words to be said. This was the second time they had shared something for which there seemed no words.

"Good night, Holly. Bless you."

"Good night, Blaine."

One morning about two weeks later Holly was awakened out of a sound sleep by an unusual sound outside. Reaching for her wrapper, she got out of bed and padded barefoot to the window and looked out. To her surprise she saw Jesse Renner and Chad unloading a cart of firewood and stacking it beside the schoolhouse.

She realized it was their way of saying thanks for her part in helping Blaine when Chad was injured. She rapped on the window, and they both looked up; and she smiled and waved her appreciation. Jesse shook his head as if to say "No need!" and went on working.

Somehow the incident made her feel a special bond with Blaine. This was the kind of payment for "services rendered" he usually received. They had shared something important, and now she understood something else about him: the warmth of people's gratitude. It made her feel a new closeness to Riverbend's doctor.

Chapter 15

*R*iverbend, Oregon, October 1882

"Dearest Mama," Holly wrote,

I have now been a full-fledged teacher for over a month! From your letter, which I received today, I am aware of the full extent of your and Papa's surprise at the news. It is so like Papa to say, as you quote him: "Well, well, maybe all the hefty fees I paid out to Blue Ridge Female Academy are being put to some practical use after all." I can just see his eyes twinkle while he says that. But in all seriousness I seem to have taken to teaching like the proverbial duck to water.

Of course, I would not be entirely truthful if I didn't relate some of the mishaps that have occurred, although in retrospect some of them have been quite comical. For example, I have certainly been put to the test as people tell me all new teachers are. Particularly by some of the older boys. Because they only attend school sporadically, when they are not needed on the farms, they do not have the desire to learn as do most of the other children. The three who are most troublesome have played some tricks. I will not go into full detail but just mention a few—such as putting old rags in the classroom stove so that one chilly morning when I decided to light a cozy fire, it smoked terribly creating such a cloud of fumes that I had to evacuate the building and conduct the rest of the school day outdoors. Thankfully, the weather here is still warm in the middle of the day so we all rather enjoyed the change of location! Another time a small garter snake was found in the bottom of the drinking water bucket, much to the horror of two screaming little girls.

But I think my stern reprimand and threat of worse has straightened these youngsters out sufficiently—at least temporarily. Nothing untoward has happened recently. They are woefully behind in their studies, so I have separated them from their usual places in the back of the classroom and set them to practicing their letters and doing sums.

The children who come to school are all ages, so I have to be quite versatile in planning each day's schedule. On the whole, I find them all anxious to learn and attentive. I try not to have favorites, but two of the children are especially appealing—a little boy named Joel and his younger sister, whom he calls Cissy. He is about eight, I think; she about six. Both have angelic expressions on not-always-too-clean faces, curly golden hair, large brown eyes. Sadly enough, they are the poorest-dressed children at school. There is an air of neglect about them, although it is touching to see how Joel, such a manly little fellow, is so protective of his sister.

Holly stopped writing for a minute as she thought about Joel and Cissy. How to explain children like these to her comfortable, well fed family? How could they possibly understand? Try as she might, Holly could not remember having seen any *really* poor people in Willow Springs. Had she actually been *that* sheltered or too-self-centered to notice if there were?

These two children had become a matter of concern to Holly. Both came to school barefooted even now when the weather was getting cooler. Holly had worried what they would do when winter really set in. She soon found out. One particularly chilly, damp morning Cissy was wearing shoes, much too big for her little feet, but no stockings.

They both looked small and underweight for their ages, and Holly wondered if they got enough to eat. Most of the other children came with full lunch buckets, but one day Holly had seen Joel sitting with Cissy at recess, sharing what appeared to

137

be a meager one. It looked as though it might only be a piece of crumbly cornbread. Another time she had seen Joel picking up one of the Healy boys' discarded thick ham sandwich and giving it to Cissy, who devoured it hungrily. After that, Holly felt she must do something.

She remembered one of her favorite folk tales from her childhood: "Stone Soup"—the story of a beggar who came into a poor village and cleverly got everyone to contribute something to what was only a stone in a pot of boiling water until a rich concoction of meat, potatoes, carrots, lentils, and beans was soon bubbling over the fire with enough to feed everyone. So Holly told it to the children one afternoon and suggested that the next day they make some stone soup and each child could bring something to put in it. The idea delighted them, and the following morning Holly, who had purchased a nice soup bone with plenty of meat on it at the butcher shop, placed it in a pot on the schoolroom stove. It was sending up a delicious smell as the children filed into the class. Each child had brought something to add; Joel and Cissy had brought wild onions. By lunchtime, Holly ladled out a delicious bowl of soup for everyone, and she felt *this* day Joel and his little sister had gone home with full stomachs. The children were so enthusiastic about stone soup that it became a weekly treat.

When Holly confided in Geneva that she felt some of the children did not have adequate lunches, Geneva suggested putting potatoes in the warm ashes of the stove at the end of each day and letting them roast overnight. That way any of the children who wanted one could have one the next day with no one being pointed out as not having enough to eat.

Holly realized she was learning something every day: how to deal with problems, meet challenges, use good judgment in ways she had never before been called upon to do. She had been used to living in a world where all her wants had been met, where there was always someone to take care of things, see that food was provided, that her clothes were not only warm and comfortable but fashionable as well. All that was changing for her; she was seeing things with new eyes; a different kind of world was coming into focus for her. This new awareness in her feelings seemed to be centered on Joel and Cissy, not only because of their physical needs but they also seemed hungry for care and affection. What was their home life like? Holly wondered.

One rainy morning she found them both wet and shivering on the schoolhouse porch long before time for school. Holly brought them inside, back to her own warm little kitchen, dished them each a bowl of oatmeal and hot tea with plenty of sugar. While she dried Cissy's hair and rubbed her cold little feet in her own hands, she noticed the bruise on Joel's forehead and his swollen eyes. What kind of parents did these children have?

When she asked Geneva what she knew about the family, Geneva just shook her head. "Not much. No one does. The McKays always keep to themselves. They don't attend church. I do know he came out here originally to mine, and when that didn't work out he tried farming. But I don't think he was ever much of a farmer; he's sold off his land piece by piece, cut most of the timber too. The few times I saw her, she looked a poor, beaten thing. When I tried to be friendly and talk to her, she just scurried away. Not much I can tell you, Holly."

For not being able to tell her much Geneva had given Holly a lot of information about the McKays. However, it was nothing that made her feel very good about the children. Holly frowned and said, "Joel is so bright. He's one of the smartest children in school. Eager to learn, wants to recite—," she halted midsentence as Geneva regarded her curiously. Holly could guess what her friend was thinking—what her own good sense told her, that it was unwise getting emotionally involved with her students. Especially since she'd be leaving in the spring. Holly knew she was already growing almost too attached to the little boy and his sister.

But it was true. Joel was always the first to raise his hand, first to volunteer for any little job she wanted done around the schoolroom. They were always the first children to arrive at school and the last ones to leave in the afternoon. It was as though *this* was a place where they felt warm, happy, and safe. Safe? *That* thought that came unbidden into her mind troubled Holly most.

Holly decided not to write any more about Joel and Cissy in her letter home. It would only distress her soft-hearted mother to hear the things that bothered *her* so much. Dipping her pen in the inkwell, Holly went back to writing an "edited" version of her life in Riverbend.

As to my "social life," Mama, about which you inquired, I cannot say my calendar is crowded! I find I need much time to prepare my daily lessons and have only the weekends for "fun and frivolity," of which there is not a great deal in Riverbend! I keep the lending library going one Saturday a month so I get to see some of my acquaintances, and the Literary Society meets once a month. I've told you about Viola Dodd and Geneva Healy, both have become dear friends.

Her pen halted a second, then she wrote, "I don't see as much of Hetty or the children as I would like, but she has a busy life and, as you can see, my own is quite full." Here Holly's pen stopped moving across the page. She had never been able to tell her mother about the situation between her and Hetty or that it had been the spur that moved her to apply for the teacher's job. It would grieve both her own mother and Aunt Dolly to know that their daughters did not get along, that, in fact, there had been a clear break in their relationship.

Holly tapped her teeth with the end of her pen thoughtfully for a moment. "Well, it isn't *my* fault!" she said to herself before starting to write again.

I have also attended performances of two plays put on by a traveling acting group who were in Riverbend for two nights. Both were well-attended and received enthusiastic applause from the audiences. One presentation was of Shakespeare's *As You Like It.* So you see we are not completely without cultural amenities here. I was escorted to this performance by Adam Corcoran, the editor of the town newspaper, a gentleman of refined taste and intellectual background.

Holly halted the flow of her pen; *that* description did not *exactly* describe Ad. Actually, she knew that his sophistication and his satirical bent in conversation would make her mother uncomfortable, and she might not consider him a suitable escort for her daughter. However, Holly found Adam intensely attractive and interesting and enjoyed hearing his comments, listening to his views, and sometimes arguing with him. He took delight in prodding her to defend her opinions and that was stimulating to Holly, who spent most of her time with minds under the age of twelve.

The other, a modern melodrama, was *The Fate of Jenny Osborne,* and to this one I went with Dr. Stevens, our town physician. He was, however, called out in the middle of the performance by a seriously ill patient and had to leave. He made arrangements for me to be escorted safely home by our mutual friend Mr. Corcoran.

In her letter Holly did not mention the other times she had spent with Blaine. Her mother would have been shocked to know about her helping Larkin and that she had assisted him in an emergency surgery! How could she put into words her relationship with Blaine? She and Blaine had established a special bond that was more than friendship but a little less than love. At least there was nothing the least bit romantic between them—

Quickly Holly dipped her pen into the inkwell, unable and unwilling to explore her own feelings about Blaine. She went on to finish the letter, saying,

I will take this into town to the post office now so that it will go out with the mail on the morning stage. I don't want you to worry about me if it is a long time between my letters. From what I have described of my life now you will understand. Do not imagine for one minute that you are not all often in my thoughts and always in my love. Your affectionate daughter.

Just before Holly sighed it with a flourish, she scribbled a postscript along the margin.

Afterward, when Holly thought about it, she told herself that perhaps she should have been more alert to the restless atmosphere in the classroom that afternoon. But when the children had filed back in from lunch hour, she was preoccupied with finding written work for the fourth- and fifth-graders to do while she drilled the third-graders on their times tables. She had received a letter of intent from the District that the County School Supervisor was making his annual rounds of the grammar schools of the area and would be in Riverbend within the next few weeks. Holly was anxious that her students would make a good showing.

Still, if she had been a more experienced teacher, she might have sensed an unusual undercurrent in the classroom. It wasn't until she had to interrupt her drills three times to quiet the other children and settle a squabble between the Healy twins, that she had noticed that the three older boys, Sam Durkin and Ben Hostler and Wes Spurgeon, were missing.

She stood up and looked around. She hoped that all three of them hadn't gone to the "necessary" behind the schoolhouse at the same time. If they had, that meant they were probably jostling and roughhousing outside instead of coming straight back into the classroom. She frowned; now that she came to think about it, she didn't remember having seen them since before lunch. She usually put them to doing more sums than she knew they could finish before the day's end when they got back from recess. This usually settled them down quickly after their vigorous outdoor playtime.

But no, they weren't in the classroom. Walking to the back of the room, she looked at their desks and saw no open workbooks. Where had those rascals got to? Holly heard snickering behind her, and she turned around to see all heads swiveled in her direction, all eyes upon her. Aha! Everyone knew something that *she* didn't. She marched to the front of the class and, folding her arms, glanced around. Sly glances were exchanged one to another, a few hands were suddenly clapped to mouth, cov-

142

ering guilty smiles, and a few suppressed giggles could be heard. Something was definitely afoot.

Holly employed her sternest schoolmarm voice. "If anyone is keeping the whereabouts of Sam and Ben and Wes a secret from me, he or she will be punished as severely as they will be when I find out."

Dead silence. Holly scanned the room, searching out her most vulnerable prey. Who would break first? She maintained her severest expression and began to pace up and down, then walk slowly along the aisles between the desks. The silence grew heavier. Finally reaching the front of the classroom again, Holly casually took down her pointer and tapped it on the teacher's desk. At this, one or two tentative hands were raised. She spotted Suzanne Rogers.

"Well, I see that one of my pupils is honorable enough to speak up." She gave the rest of the class a scathing look, then said, "Suzanne, do you know where the big boys went after lunch?"

"Yes, ma'm, I-uh, I *think* so," the little girl stammered.

"I do! I do!" Tommy Mason waved his hand wildly.

"So do *I!*" shouted Fred Kohl, not to be outdone, and jumped up. "I heard them talking at lunch."

"Well, then?" Holly waited.

Full of himself, Fred squared his fat little shoulders and announced, "They said they wuz goin' to a saloon and get them a beer!"

A shock wave of gasps and titters echoed throughout the room. Holly blinked and tried to maintain a straight face. "You're sure, Fred, that they really said that's where they were going? They weren't just showing off? Teasing you younger boys?"

Fred shook his head from side to side vigorously. "No ma'am, I sure as anything heard them say that. And so did Billy, didn't you, Billy." Shy Bill Sanders nodded solemnly.

"So did I hear 'em, Miss Lambeth," piped up Bucky Jensen.

Holly took a deep breath, trying not to lose her composure. This was a serious matter. This was insurrection at its worst. If the Town Council learned that three of her students had taken

143

off, heading for one of the town's drinking and gambling establishments during the school day, they would be convinced that she had lost control. They would dismiss her without a doubt. Holly knew a couple of them had had grave reservations that a young female teacher could not handle the big boys who worked on farms alongside the men who didn't think much of "school larnin" anyhow.

Holly knew this was a crisis. She had to take action. But what? She was fully aware that she was the focal point of every child in the class room. They were all watching her to see what she would do.

"All right, children. Settle down," she said automatically although nobody was making any noise. It just gave her something to say while she tried to put her thoughts in order. "Back to your lessons."

She must do something right away. Bring back those truants, make them an example. Inwardly, she quailed. Ben was big, brawny, and although Wes was thin he was wiry and strong, and Sam towered over her. How in the world could she order those huge farm boys back to school, make them come?

Well, she had to try. A half-hour before the regular time for school to close, Holly rapped for attention and said, "Children, we are going to dismiss early today. Tell your mothers there was an emergency that teacher had to attend to. That will be all then; bring your readers up to the front and clean your slates," she told them in a voice that she tried to keep from sounding wavering.

As usual, some of the children dawdled. She noticed Joel eyeing her curiously, taking time helping his sister on with her jacket and edging slowly to the classroom door. She knew they were trying to figure out what she was going to do. Very deliberately she put on her bonnet and took her shawl down from the hook beside the door. "Hurry up, Joel. Time to go. I have to leave, lock up. I have an errand to do downtown."

Reluctantly he took his sister's hand and went out the door. Holly quickly closed the schoolhouse and shooed the children lingering in the play yard out, urging them homeward; then she set out for town. She knew that some of the children who lived

144

in town quickened their lagging steps to follow her. She almost had to laugh, thinking she probably looked like the Pied Piper of Hamlin with a line of children behind her.

A saloon, eh? If that was true, which saloon? When Holly reached Main Street, it had its usual middle-of-the-day deserted appearance. She halted for a minute, squinting at the signs proclaiming the business that had enticed the boys to try out the wares inside. The Nugget, Last Chance, the Doggone Best.

Her heart bounced like a sledgehammer gone wild as she started down the street. She would just have to check each one, she guessed, and pray that the Lord was with her. She was about do something that she never in her imagination had dreamed she would do! But gritting her teeth and with only one last-minute panicked hesitation, Holly pushed through the slatted, swinging doors of the Doggone Best and took a few steps inside.

The first thing that hit her was the stale air. The combined strong odor of cigar, sour whiskey, sweat, and sawdust wrinkled her nose in distaste. The interior was so dense with smoke, so murky and dim that it took Holly a full minute to adjust her eyes enough so that she could see. As soon as she could, what she saw was a blur of startled faces—the weathered faces of old miners standing at the long bar, the open mouths and widened eyes of the cardplayers huddled at the tables, the dropped jaws of the cowboys holding brimming beer mugs half-raised, and the painted masks of the "girls" hanging around at the pool table.

The stunned, bald bartender, in a striped shirt was the first one to find his voice. He leaned forward, his elbow on the bar top. "Can I do something for you, lady?"

Holly's gaze was still circling the room, searching for the boys as he spoke. A second later she spotted three pairs of scared-looking eyes gazing back at her. They stumbled up from the table where they were sitting with some rough-looking characters and started backing up against the wall.

In a clear, strong voice Holly spoke. "Sam Durkin, Ben Hostler, Wes Spurgeon, get over here at once. Get yourself out of this place and home. Tell your folks I'll be there to talk to them later."

145

She had managed to put more authority and command in her tone than she would ever have thought possible. Her words snapped in the air like firecrackers going off on the Fourth of July. To her own amazement she saw the three shame-faced truants, shoulders hunched, slouch forward and slink past her and through the doors.

Then Holly, hands on her hips, swirled around and swept the room with a long, slow, disgusted look. Turning back to the bartender, she riveted on his now-reddening face. She tried to make eye contact, but he averted his head. Still, Holly had her moment.

"All you men should be ashamed of yourselves. You had to *know* those boys were underage. They should have been ushered out the minute they came through those doors, not encouraged and plied with drink." Her tone was scorching. "I don't know how many of you have children, but if you do, how would you feel if someone served them an alcoholic drink that could start them on the road to ruin." She took another long breath and, pointing her finger at the bartender, said, "There's a law in this country about selling strong drink to minors. If I report this to the sheriff, this place could be closed."

Holly wasn't at all sure that this was the case, but it sounded threatening and rang true enough.

By now she was trembling. Doing this had taken all her energy. Her knees felt so weak that she wasn't sure she could manage to walk out the door. Somehow she did, and once she stepped outside and was able to draw her breath again, the three culprits were nowhere in sight. There were, however, a few of her students gathered at a little distance from the entrance of the saloon as well as a few interested adults who evidently had been told what was going on. As Holly started down the steps and back toward the schoolhouse, there was a light smattering of hands clapping. She didn't look back but walked on.

146

Chapter 16

$\mathcal{T}$he next Sunday morning at the door of the church, Owen Roberts, the head usher, greeted Holly and, handing her a bulletin, whispered, "That was a splendid thing you did, Miss Lambeth. Everyone is mighty impressed." Remembering that Mr. Roberts had been one of the members of the Town Council who had been most reluctant to appoint her to the position of schoolteacher, she appreciated his comment all the more.

Holly found a seat at the end of one of the rear pews. The Macready family, already seated in it, moved over with nods and smiles to make room for her. The Willis family in the pew in front of her all turned and smiled.

Holly recalled with what trepidation she had attended church the first Sunday after she had assumed the job of schoolteacher and moved to the school house. She knew that the town's schoolmarm was expected to attend church. When she had first arrived in Riverbend, she was forced to accompany Hetty and Ned and sit with them. Already aware of Hetty's feelings about her, Holly had felt very uncomfortable. Locked in her own misery, surrounded by strangers, filled with resentment and a critical attitude toward her cousin, Holly knew that her heart had not been right for worship.

She had spent the entire hour feeling sorry for herself and thinking of the neat white clapboard-and-stone steepled church at home. By contrast, in Willow Springs, church had been a pleasant weekly event with the enjoyable hymn-singing and an inspirational sermon followed by fellowship after the service that was almost a social occasion. That month of miserable Sundays was now past, Holly realized with a sense of relief and gratitude.

Of course, the story of the incident at the Doggone Best had made its rounds, probably embellished each time it was retold. Its effect had been apparent almost immediately as the very next day children had brought presents from grateful parents to a teacher who knew how to take charge. Gifts of home-baked bread, canned peaches, sweet potatoes, and plantings had all been shyly offered by her students. Why, her cache was beginning to rival Blaine's, she thought with some amusement. Well, it was nice to be appreciated and complimented and feel accepted. Now when she came to church, she was greeted with shy smiles from students, approving nods from their parents. She felt welcomed and enveloped by their friendship.

But just as she was basking in this new security, she saw Hetty and Ned enter. Hetty marched first down the aisle, looking neither to the right nor left; Ned was behind, holding Aurelia and Teddy by the hands. As Aurelia passed her pew, she twisted her head around and smilingly waved with a wiggling of all five fingers. Holly smiled and raised her hand in a demure wave back. How she loved those children. And how sad it was that she and Hetty had so much animosity between them.

The congregation rose for the opening hymn. As she stood, Holly noticed that some of the elders were preparing a table for the Lord's Supper and realized that it was Communion Sunday. The Reverend Mobley took his place in the pulpit and announced, "We will now take up the tithes and offerings. Before we do, let me remind you of the biblical admonition in Matthew 5:23 to meditate on: 'Therefore when you bring your gift to the altar and there remember that your brother has something against you, leave your gift there before the altar and go your way. First be reconciled to your brother, then come and offer your gift.'"

Conviction tingled through Holly at these words. She

glanced over at the back of Hetty's head, but the stiff black bonnet never quivered. Hetty remained staring straight ahead. What *did* Hetty have against her? Holly wondered. What had she ever done to her to make Hetty so resentful? Oh dear, sighed Holly, what was there to do about it? What *could* she do about it?

The day's sermon didn't help. Reverend Mobley took his text from Mark 11:25 and read, "And whenever you stand praying, if you have anything against anyone, forgive him, that your Father in heaven may also forgive you." Convicted, Holly listened carefully to what the minister said. As he ended with— "Forgiveness is the key to the Christian life, let us always be aware of all that the Lord has forgiven us and not be in judgment of anyone else," Holly bowed her head and, with as much sincerity as she could muster, forgave Hetty.

When the Communion tray was passed and she partook of the elements, she promised that she would make an attempt to speak and be as pleasant as possible to Hetty after the service.

It became a promise impossible to keep. Before she could leave, one of her pupils' mothers tapped her on the shoulder and engaged her in a long conversation about her Billy's progress. By the time Holly was able to get away and hurry out to the church steps, she saw Ned's wagon pull out of the churchyard. So Holly missed the hoped-for opportunity.

For the rest of the afternoon Holly was very thoughtful. In Willow Springs she had never seemed to need time alone to think, reflect, and pray. But today she felt newly troubled about the rift between herself and her cousin. She knew that both their mothers would be grieved if they knew how deep and wide was the chasm separating their two daughters. Should she go to Hetty? Try to somehow bridge the gap? What could she say that would help?

She needed someone to talk to about it, someone whose advice she could ask, someone she could trust. Naturally, Vi came to mind. Holly bundled up again, for the day had clouded over, and walked to her friend's house. Vi was always comforting to confide in, sensible yet sensitive, practical yet inspiring.

"Come in, come in!" Vi welcomed her. "What a pleasant surprise!"

"I'm not sure you'll think it's so pleasant when you hear what I've come to complain about."

"Well, what are friends for anyway but to lend a listening ear or a shoulder to weep on, if that's called for?" Vi took Holly's coat and waited while Holly unpinned her hat and veil. "You'll have some tea, won't you?"

"That sounds lovely. It's getting colder outside." Holly rubbed her hands as she followed Vi out to her neat little kitchen.

After the tea brewed, Vi put her pink and white pot, two cups, and a plate of caramel cookies on a tray and carried it into the parlor. Vi's parlor, with its starched lace curtains, dark- blue velvet love seat and curved "lady" chairs, was as feminine and fashionable as she was.

"Now, what's the trouble?" she asked as she handed a cup of the fragrant steaming tea to Holly.

Trying to divide the fault as equally as she could, Holly poured out the still unresolved situation between herself and Hetty, confiding the conviction that she now felt she had to do something about it.

"She won't even let Aurelia and Teddy come to see me. I do miss them and . . ." Holly lifted her chin defensively, "I think they miss me, too. Ned says they do."

Vi's eyes were sympathetic. "I understand. So what do you plan to do to heal things between you?"

"Well, today at church what the minister said really hit home. Do you remember the Scripture passage he used?"

"About forgiveness?"

"I intended to make a point of going up to Hetty after the service and as the quotation says 'be reconciled,' but I didn't have a chance."

"Maybe you're going to have to make the opportunity yourself," Vi gently suggested.

Holly made a face. "Oh, I really dread doing that, Vi. You don't know how Hetty can be—"

"No, but I know everyone can be difficult at times. Some of the ladies I sew for can be *very* difficult, *indeed.*"

Holly was thoughtful for a moment then finally said, "Other

than going to see Hetty, is there something else you think I should do?"

"Praying is the most important thing, Holly. Since you don't feel ready yet, ask the Lord to prepare your heart to go to see Hetty."

"I *have* prayed, Vi, but so far it hasn't done any good. Maybe I'm praying the wrong way."

"I'm not sure there *is* a really wrong way to pray, Holly. I do think when there is something between us and someone else, we need to ask God to do the necessary healing. He knows both hearts. If you're sincere in your desire to make things right between you and your cousin, ask him to prepare *her* heart to receive whatever you say to her. Your part is praying; God will do His."

"Oh, Vi, how did you get so much wisdom?"

Vi laughed. "Through lots of trials and tribulations, Holly, and *lots* of praying!"

As the afternoon was getting late, Holly said she must be going. She gave Vi an impulsive hug before she left and thanked her for her tea and her advice.

That evening Holly got out her Bible and decided to try Vi's method, the same one she had successfully followed when she started the lending library. It wasn't foolproof, as Vi had warned her, but Holly didn't really know what else to do about herself and Hetty. This time the Bible fell open at Proverbs, Chapter 27. Holly squeezed her eyes tight shut and ran her finger down the page, then stopped. Opening her eyes, she glanced at the verse on which her finger had landed, verse 19: "As in water face reveals face, so a man's heart reveals the man." That didn't seem to make much sense or at least didn't satisfy her with the direction she was searching for. Disappointed, Holly closed the book and blew out her lamp and got into bed.

Lying there in the dark, it came into her mind that Hetty had been in church that morning just as she had! Had the minister's words touched *her* heart? It seemed to her that there was fault on both sides, but Holly didn't know how to end the impasse. She sighed, turned her pillow over, and bunched it under her head.

151

But she couldn't sleep. Although her experiment to get guidance had not seemed to work, the words "be reconciled with your brother" kept repeating themselves in her head. In biblical times a cousin was considered a "brother." Hetty was, after all, her "brother," and she should try to make peace with her.

That was her last thought before going to sleep. In the morning the verse still remained foremost in her mind. By the end of the week Holly knew she must take the first step toward reconciliation, as hard as that was going to be for her to do.

So, on Saturday morning she resolutely walked over to Hetty's house. She took with her a new picture book, from the latest box sent by her mother, for Aurelia and Teddy. The children's presence would break the ice if her cousin met her with the same degree of chill she usually did. Whatever her reception, Holly was determined to get to the bottom of the problem and achieve some kind of truce with Hetty.

To her dismay, Ned had taken the children to the store with him, and Hetty was in the midst of a vigorous end-of-week housecleaning. She met Holly at the door, enveloped in a "coverall" apron, a dust scarf tied around her head, and a stormy expression on her face.

At first Holly did not think Hetty would even ask her in, for she stood there arms crossed, glaring for a full minute before grudgingly opening the door for her. Finally, Hetty stepped back, and Holly walked inside.

Already intimidated by the hostility in Hetty's eyes, Holly realized she was trembling. Holly prayed for courage.

"I brought a lovely new book I'm sure Aurelia and Teddy will enjoy," she began. "Mama sent it, and she sends her love, too, Hetty."

Hetty did not respond immediately, then reluctantly offered, "Would you like some coffee; there's some left from breakfast."

Hardly a gracious gesture, Holly thought, feeling her temper rise. Forcing a tight smile, she said, "Yes, that would be nice." She was determined not to leave before she had a chance to straighten out whatever grudge Hetty was holding against her.

She took a seat at the kitchen table and groped desperately for something noncontroversial to start the conversation.

152

Nothing came. She began to feel tense as Hetty silently got out two cups and then shook the blue-enameled coffeepot before filling them.

Holly saw that Hetty was going to do nothing to make this easy, so in total frustration she just blurted out, "Hetty, why do you dislike me?"

Hetty put the coffeepot back on the stove with a bang. She stood with her back toward Holly for what seemed a long time. When she whirled around, her eyes were flashing. "Dislike you? I don't *dislike* you. Sometimes I even feel sorry for you," she sneered. "You're so pitiful! For the first time in your life you found out that you couldn't have everything you want, so you run away, come out here and then try to take over here just like you did back home. You think you can sweet-talk your way just like you did in Willow Springs, have everyone eating out of your hand. I don't blame Jim Mercer one little bit. In fact, I applaud him. You treated him like dirt, like you did any fellow that was fool enough to show he was interested." She gave a harsh little laugh. "Oh, I've seen you plying your little tricks, using people—my husband included—just like always. Maybe you think you're foolin' folks here, but they'll catch on pretty quick. They'll see through you. Just the way I do."

Shocked, Holly stared at her cousin. "I don't know what you mean, Hetty. When did I ever hurt you?"

Red blotches were coming out on Hetty's face now, her hands were clenched into fists at her side, her lip curled as she continued, "You hurt me plenty. Lots of times. Dozens of times. You ignored me, treated me like I didn't matter—"

"If I did—and I don't remember doing it, I never guessed—"

"How could you?" Hetty demanded furiously. "You were always too busy playing the belle of the ball to notice anyone else!"

"If I did, I'm truly sorry," Holly said contritely.

"Sorry? What good does it do to be sorry *now?*"

"Well, that was *then*, Hetty, this is *now*. If I was a thoughtless, self-centered girl who didn't know she was doing it—we're both women now, can't we possibly put all that aside, be friends?"

Hetty shook her head. "It's too late, Holly. I don't need your

153

friendship. I don't need *you*. I've made a place for myself here. I've got a husband and children, my own friends, and I don't need you anymore."

Holly felt sick and shaken by the bitterness in Hetty. Gone was any pretense of relationship, cousinliness, now even the possibility of friendship. Holly got to her feet, not knowing what more she could say. Then before her horrified gaze, Hetty's features began to break up; she turned away and put her face in her hands and began to sob, the harsh, painful sound of someone who had not cried since childhood.

Helplessly, Holly stood there, knowing if she reached out in comfort she would be rejected. Then Hetty's muffled voice said, "Please go—"

"Hetty, I—"

"I said *go!*"

Unsteadily, Holly made her way to the door, then she turned and looked once more, struggling for something to say. All that came was a broken, "Believe me, I *am* sorry."

But Hetty did not move, turn, nor reply, and Holly left.

Once outside she realized she had been so upset that she had forgotten to leave the book for the children.

She walked through town in a daze, the things Hetty had said ringing in her ears. Had she really been that indifferent, that selfish, that unsympathetic? Vaguely she remembered Mama's urging her to see that Hetty had a good time at one of the impromptu gatherings of young people that seemed to happen so often at their house. She couldn't honestly remember making any concerted effort on Hetty's behalf. With belated realization, Holly knew she had found it flattering and enormous fun to be the center of attention herself and gave little thought to any of the other girls who might be longing for some of the spotlight she had always taken for granted.

How hard that must have been for someone like Hetty, painfully shy, awkward, tall and skinny, and insecure. Holly was genuinely sorry that she had been the cause of some of Hetty's unhappiness, but she couldn't take the blame for all of it. Holly recalled how she had once overheard Aunt Dolly, Hetty's mother, complaining to Holly's mother that Hetty was "impossible, glum, moody, uncooperative—"

Mounting the schoolhouse steps and letting herself into her own apartment, Holly said aloud, "Well, at least I *tried*, didn't I!" She made herself some tea and feeling rather sorry that her sincere efforts for reconciliation had been so rebuffed, she went over some of Hetty's accusations, trying to justify herself.

Unkind? Indifferent? Unfeeling? Maybe she *had* been. She thought of the Scripture she had found at random: "As in water face reveals face, so a man's heart reveals the man."

She had gone to see Hetty to try to make right the difficulty between them. In her heart Holly had believed it was all Hetty's fault. But instead of getting the expected apology from Hetty, she had heard a lot of unpleasant things about herself.

Maybe *her* heart wasn't right. Maybe *she* needed to think about all the things Hetty had said. Whatever Hetty had perceived her to be she *was* different now. She remembered her feelings upon her arrival in Riverbend when the stagecoach driver had shouted—"End of the line!"

In a way, it had been the "end of the line"—at least of one part of her life. That frivolous life she had led with all the careless abandon of a butterfly, the life that had ignored people like Hetty. Things had happened to change her. She had closed that chapter of her life, and she had opened a new one. New things were being written in it. Why couldn't Hetty see that?

Maybe, in time, she would, Holly sighed but with little hope. Hetty had told her to leave. Would she ever feel comfortable returning to Hetty's house after today? When would she get to see Aurelia and Teddy? Sadly, Holly drew the beautiful new edition of *Alice in Wonderland* out of her basket. Idly she turned the pages, looking at its colorful illustrations, pausing to read some of its amusing verses. She had loved *Alice* when she was a child and had wanted so much to share it with Aurelia and Teddy. She stopped at one of Alice's encounters with the White Queen and read, "Consider what a great girl you are. Consider what a long way you've come today. Consider what o'clock it is. Consider anything, only don't cry!"

She too had come a long way from Willow Springs. She had

managed and coped, accomplished and overcome a great many things she would never have thought she could before. She had even often "imagined six impossible things before breakfast!"

God bless Lewis Carroll, Holly thought, closing the book and feeling much better.

If, in spite of all her attempts, Hetty refused to be friends, hadn't she gone the extra mile? Holly shrugged, What else could she do?

Just then she heard the sound of horses hooves, buggy wheels outside. Blaine! Holly felt her heart lift immediately. She jumped up, took a quick glance in her mirror, patted her hair, straightened the brooch on her collar, and hurried to open the schoolhouse door.

Her eager smile faded when she saw that it was *Ad!* He had just thrown the reins over the hitching post and was putting the block on the ground when he looked up and saw her standing at the door.

"Good afternoon, Miss Lambeth," he greeted her making a sweeping bow. "It was such a pleasant day, I rented this and took the liberty of coming out to see if you were free and to suggest we take a nice ride through the countryside? You look like you could use a little outing—or did I mistake the expression on your face for something else? Disappointment?" his smile was slightly sardonic. "Were you expecting someone else?"

Quickly Holly assured him. "No, of course not! And I'd enjoy some fresh air and sunshine! Wait until I get my bonnet and shawl," she told him and ran back inside.

So what did it matter if she had hoped it was Blaine? Holly scolded herself. Ad was always amusing and took her mind off her troubles. And she was foolish to spend time thinking about Blaine Stevens who was a man totally dedicated to his career and far too busy to spend a Saturday afternoon frivolously.

PART 4

Heap on the wood! The wind is chill!
But let it whistle as it will,
We'll keep our Christmas merry still.

Sir Walter Scott

Chapter 17

*O*ne Friday early in December as school was dismissed, there was a little more than the usual scramble for the door. As was her practice, Holly followed her students out onto the porch to see them off, to make sure that the older boys didn't start a scuffle or fight. But the excitement that erupted as the children poured through the door, down the steps, and out to the play yard were for a different reason. "It's snowing!" came glad shouts. Holly looked up into the pewter-colored sky. When she saw large snowflakes drifting lazily down, she, too, experienced the same childlike thrill at the sight of the first snow of winter.

Holly had always loved snow, perhaps because her birthday was in December, and at home it had always been celebrated festively. In her happiest memories of childhood, it always seemed to be snowing. Maybe because her parents always gave her a wonderful party. There had been one birthday she remembered with particular joy. She must have been about eleven, and her father had rented a sleigh and all her friends had been invited for a sleigh ride. She could still feel the cold air that made it almost hurt to breathe, the bite of the wind in her face that made her eyes sting, and the merry sound of the sleigh bells ringing as the sleigh skimmed over the icy roads and fields. . . .

Holly wondered if anyone in Riverbend owned a sleigh or if there ever were sleighing parties or carol sings? She put some wood into the stove and got the fire going again, glad she had the whole weekend to herself with no lessons to prepare for the next day.

The following morning when she woke up, the room held a peculiar brightness. Had she overslept? Then she realized that it was Saturday, and there was no school today. She could look forward to a day all her own, a welcome break in the routine of the week. When she finally got up, she saw to her delighted surprise that the ground was covered with a light powdering of snow, and it was still snowing.

It was still snowing when, after her leisurely breakfast, she decided to indulge herself and spend the day reading. It was a perfect day to reread one of her favorites, Charles Dickens' *A Christmas Carol*. Before settling down with it, she looked out the window again. The snow was coming down thicker and faster now. Maybe she'd even get snowed in! She had plenty of wood and food and lots of reading material, so she smiled to herself as she pulled her rocker close to the stove and opened to page one. "Marley was dead, dead as a doornail. . . ."

The next thing she knew, the room was gray, and it was getting hard for her to see. She got up to light her lamp and, at the window, saw that it was still snowing, and in the quickly falling darkness the pine trees at the edge of the road were new shapes of white pyramids. It looked like a Christmas scene, Holly thought. Christmas! An unexpected wave of homesickness surged through her. She'd be spending this Christmas thousands of miles from home. . . .

At Christmas the Lambeth home was very Dickensian. As they had said of Scrooge at the end of the book, her family "really knew how to keep Christmas!" There was a gaily trimmed six-foot cedar in the front hallway by the staircase, its banister and post entwined with evergreen boughs and red ribbons, the mantelpiece in the parlor decorated with red candles and poinsettias, and in the dining room, on the sideboard, was a big cut-glass bowl of eggnog to be offered to the many guests who came calling during the holidays, to be served along with slices of Mama's heritage fruitcake.

There had been parties every night of the week between

160

Christmas and New Year's and the annual Christmas pageant and program at the church—

A Christmas program! That's what this school needed—a project in which everyone could have a part! One that they could put on for the parents to come and see the children perform. Why, they could have carol singing, and after the Nativity play she could have a party right here in the schoolhouse—

What an inspiration, just the thing to bring parents and children together. Of course, it would mean a lot of work, but it would have such rewards that it would be worth it.

In the weeks that followed, Holly would have to remind herself often of her first enthusiasm. There were days when nothing went right and everything went wrong. The children were inattentive, couldn't remember their lines or the lyrics of the simplest, oldest carols, some of which, to Holly's astonishment, they had never heard before. The old piano badly needed tuning, but she struggled along with it to keep the various-ranged voices on key or at least partially so.

She divided the Christmas story into what she judged were basic scenes with minimal lines for each of the speaking parts to memorize. Even so, such phrases as "Lo, I see yonder Star" and "Be not afraid" proved almost impossible for some to learn or remember. There were moments when Holly was close to desperation that it would not all come together, and many times when she was ready to give the whole thing up.

But the excitement of the children, their eagerness to participate, their anticipation of wearing costumes, and the idea of performing before an audience was contagious. And when Holly was at the point of losing heart, something or somebody rescued her from the brink of despair.

Holly sent notes home with the children, announcing that there would be a Christmas program and a party afterward on the evening of the last school day before the ten-day holiday period.

After that, the days seemed to fly by. Every day Holly used the incentive of play practice and carol singing to get through the regular lessons with dispatch and inspire more effort on the part of the children. She was encouraged by the willingness of most of them to cooperate. Although there was much discussion about the role each one was to play, there seemed to be less squabbling, shoving, pushing, and general naughtiness with the prospect of the Christmas program always ahead.

"I'd like to think it's the Christmas story itself having an effect," Holly sighed half-humorously to Vi one afternoon when she went over to consult with her about costume descriptions to send home to the children's parents.

"Don't underestimate the power of the Word," Vi replied as she went through her scrap bag, getting out materials Holly could use to put together shepherd's robes and strips of sizing to stiffen angel wings.

"While you're here, come see what I've done," Vi suggested, her eyes shining, and she beckoned Holly down the hall and opened a door at the end. "I've redone Avesta's room for a surprise when she comes home for the holidays!" Vi said excitedly watching for Holly's reaction.

"Oh, Vi, it's any girl's dream!" declared Holly stepping into the room and gazing around. There was a white iron bedstead with gracefully scrolled enameled loops and gilded curls covered by a white matelasse woven spread, and a white painted bureau and washstand on which stood a china pitcher and bowl covered with painted pansies. The windows were curtained in gauzy white organdy tied with lavender ribbons. "Oh, she'll love it, Vi," Holly exclaimed.

"I hope so," Vi beamed. "Avesta likes things pretty, feminine, and she loves this color." Vi touched the lace pillows threaded with lavender satin ribbon.

Holly hoped Avesta appreciated her mother and knew she was the center of Vi's life. Now that she was so far away and on her own, Holly had begun to realize how much her own mother had done for her when she lived at home, all the little things that went unnoticed and unacknowledged. Holly left Vi's and headed for Ned's store.

She was anxious to find out if the small Christmas gifts for the children had arrived yet. She had ordered them from one of Ned's catalogues: spinning tops in all colors for the boys, hair slides and ribbons for the girls. She was going to wrap them with each child's name and then tie them to the branches of the Christmas tree in the classroom.

One new experience that Holly was particularly enjoying was managing her own money. At home she had gone to her father whenever she wanted money. Although the Riverbend teacher's salary was small, it gave Holly a feeling of independence to know she had earned it and could spend it any way she liked. She loved using a small part of it to plan the Christmas party.

Before, when Holly ran the lending library, she had discovered that the little world of Riverbend revolved around the General Store. There was always a group of men discussing the weather, the crops, the current topics. Even the women shopping for groceries or dry goods often gave their opinion, made a comment, or expressed their views.

This Saturday when Holly entered there seemed more hubbub than usual in the voices of those gathered around the pot-bellied stove in the center. The jangle of the bell over the door seemed to go unheard, and she moved immediately over to the counter where Ned was ringing up a purchase. As she waited for Ned to finish with his customer, she overheard the men, inasmuch as none of them were making any attempt to lower their voices. In fact, it seemed they were raised, indignant, and argumentative.

When Ned was free, he smiled and greeted her. "Good morning, Holly, what can I do for you?"

He came over to where she stood, and she leaned toward him, nodding her head to the group at the stove and asking in a low tone, "What's all that about?"

Ned lifted an eyebrow, slipped a folded copy of the *Riverbend Monitor* in front of her, tapped his forefinger to the bold-faced column headed "Editorial."

"Oh, dear, what's Ad been up to now?" she sighed, her eyes racing down the rows of print.

WHO STILL BELIEVES THE RAILROAD IS COMING THROUGH RIVERBEND?

Only the people who will benefit continue to perpetuate this

163

myth; namely Miller's Brickyard, Tidwell's Lumber Mill, Bankers, Realtors, possibly the politicians if they can convince their constituents that their clout will make the planners and the Eastern owners of the railroad companies change their minds—which of course won't happen! These decisions are usually made in Washington, D.C., and that's where the "Big Boys" play.

All the usually "reliable sources" we've checked have told me the railroad is NOT coming to Riverbend; the town of Medford will get the proposed branch line from San Francisco to Portland, NOT Riverbend.

"Uh-oh!" Holly said softly as she raised her head and met Ned's eyes. "Ad's in big trouble now." Ned nodded solemnly and gave a shake of his head.

The store was filling up with people getting their weekend supplies so Ned and Holly had no more time to discuss their friend's latest published opinion. Ned checked the shelves of the post office, found Holly's package, and she left.

The day was windy and overcast, and Holly's thoughts were as storm-tossed as the clouds overhead as she walked home. Why did Ad always stir up something, "trouble the waters"? Maybe it was his "exile mentality," the thing that he claimed was *their* bond, that neither one of them really belonged in Riverbend, that their stay was temporary and they had no stake in what happened, that they were both "birds of passage."

But Ad was wrong about her, Holly thought, as she turned into the school yard. Something definitely had happened to her. She wasn't sure just what. She could feel it. Everything was drawing her in, deeper, closer—almost as if she was becoming part of everything—the hills, the river, the town, the people— like the Healys, the members of the Literary Society, the friends she had made, Vi, the Bodine sisters, Mr. Clegg, and Rupert Benson—and the children, especially the children—Aurelia and Teddy, of course, and Joel and Cissy, *and—Blaine Stevens*.

Holly let herself into the schoolhouse door. No matter if she left in June, she *did* care about this community, about the people.

Since Vi had volunteered to make the more elaborate costumes

164

needed for the Three Kings, having, as she did, a great many odds and ends of trimmings for the robes of these potentates from the Far East, Holly was left with the more mundane task of fashioning costumes for the lowly shepherds. She was busily sorting among piles of flour sacks that had been washed then dyed, mounds of old curtains, and pieces of quilting on the Saturday before the program was scheduled when Ad dropped by the schoolhouse.

"Oh, it's you," she said offhandedly when she opened the door.

"Well, that's not much of a welcome," he pretended offense.

"I'm sorry. I'm just feeling rather cross. I'm not a great hand at sewing, and I have a half-dozen shepherds to garb properly for the Christmas play," she explained, settling down again.

Ad sauntered around the kitchen, stopping at the table where some of the material and balls of varicolored yarn were stacked. He picked up a piece of material at random. "What are these for?" he asked curiously.

Holly looked up briefly, then back at the stiff cloth through which she was trying to push her needle. With one finger free, she made a circle around her head. "It's for one of those towel kind of things they wore on their heads, and we'll braid the yarn for what goes around it to hold it in place."

"Oh, you mean a 'kufiyya' and an 'iqal,'" nodded Ad.

Holly blinked a couple of times, demanding in astonishment. "How do you know that sort of thing?"

"Oh, editors have all sorts of sources of information," Ad shrugged. "Or bored bachelors do crossword puzzles to wile away lonely evenings, read dictionaries, peruse encyclopedias."

Holly threw him a quizzical look. "Maybe that's time better spent than writing inflammatory editorials."

"So, you heard about that, huh?"

"Who in Riverbend hasn't?"

Ad scowled. "People don't like to hear the truth."

"Well, you sure started a firestorm with this one. You should hear what they're saying at Ned's store."

Ad did not reply. He walked idly around the room, then stopped at the chest where Holly's photo album was placed.

165

Busy with her work, Holly did not notice at once that he was looking through it. After a few minutes she realized he had stopped turning the pages and was studying one in particular. She glanced over, and he turned his head to meet her gaze. His tone was indifferent, but his eyes held hers intently as he asked, "Who's the dashing soldier boy?"

For a second, Holly was tempted to retort, "None of your business." But then she thought, *Why not?* and with a slight shrug replied, "Lieutenant Jim Mercer. We were engaged."

"To be married?"

"No! For the next dance!" she said flippantly, then, "*Of course,* to be married."

"What happened? Did you change your mind?"

Holly hesitated then blurted out, "No. He did."

"When was this?"

"About two months before I came to Riverbend."

Ad closed the album abruptly. "Then why do you still keep his pictures?"

Again Holly shrugged, "I'm really not sure."

"He must be some kind of fool," Ad said quietly.

"Oh, no, he's very bright, very smart. He graduated way at the top of his class from West Point," she said continuing to take stitches.

"Then why—?"

Holly put down her sewing with an exasperated sigh and said, "Adam Corcoran, did anyone ever tell you that you ask too many questions?"

"It's the reporter in me; it's in the blood."

"Well, if you want to know the truth, he married someone else."

As soon as the words were out of her mouth, Holly was surprised that it didn't hurt. The old feelings of humiliation and shame seemed somehow to have disappeared. In fact, she felt an unexpected sensation of freedom as if she had shaken off an old burden.

"I'd get rid of the pictures if I were you," Ad said casually. He sauntered over to the door. There he turned back and looked at Holly for a long minute. "You're a very special lady, Miss Holly

166

Lambeth." At that he made an obeisance, said, "Shalom," turned on his heel, and walked out of the room, then she heard the schoolhouse door shut.

The last day before the holidays was the date of the Christmas program. That week was fraught with mishaps and anxiety. Holly had always heard dress rehearsals were usually disasters, and that a bad one guaranteed a wonderful opening performance. Considering how terrible theirs was, she fervently prayed that the old adage was true. The children stumbled over lines that had been word-perfect in practice; some tripped over the unaccustomed shepherd's robes; angel wings fell off; the Kings' crowns toppled; and the beard refused to stay glued to the Innkeeper's chin.

When Adam had come by to get the details of the program so he could do a preview article and announcement for the paper, Holly told him about the party she was having after the performance. "I want to have a tree and all the trimmings. I'm sure some of the children have never had a *real* Christmas," she confided. "I've sent away through one of Ned's catalogs for paper cornucopias, colored crepe paper. I'm going to have the children make their own decorations, cut and paste rings to drape on the boughs, and we'll pop corn and string cranberries too."

"You really love doing all this, don't you?" Ad asked her with an appraising look.

"Yes, I do," Holly replied almost defensively. "I always assumed that everyone had the same kind of childhood I had, but I'm finding out that people coming to settle out here had so many other things—*survival* things—to do, that some of the fun things, the things that give flavor and lightness to life—got lost." She paused for a minute, then said, "I guess they were considered less important, and maybe they are—but, no, not really. I *do* think they're important. And it's so much fun for me to see how happy these things make the children."

At last the night of the program arrived. The schoolroom had been turned into a theater. Matt Healy had donated chairs from the Town Hall and brought them over in his wagon the afternoon of the performance. As he helped Holly set them in rows, he said, "Riverbend children have never had something like this, Miss Lambeth. Everybody's mighty excited about it. I think the parents don't know what to expect, but they're proud that their kids are being treated special."

"I'm glad. I hope everything goes well!" Holly said. She couldn't remember ever feeling more nervous.

Geneva had offered to help backstage, where a flimsy curtain had been strung across one end of the schoolroom. As the parents began to assemble, Holly greeted them at the door, trying not to let the sounds of loud whispers and shuffling behind the stage distract her too much.

Holly was even pleased to see people who didn't have children in school arrive to support this first dramatic effort on the part of the school. When she saw Ned come with Aurelia and Teddy, Holly thought that perhaps in the spirit of the season, her cousin had put aside her animosity and come. But Ned mumbled that Hetty had a sick headache and wasn't up to coming. Holly sympathized even though she knew it was only an excuse.

Her rueful feelings were fleeting, however, because her attention was needed elsewhere. With everything in readiness, she had to begin the program. As she stepped forward to make her opening announcement, she saw, with happy surprise, Blaine step into the back of the room. She was glad she had chosen a very becoming red taffeta dress frilled with Irish lace to wear for the occasion.

To her amazement and everyone else's delight, the production came off without any hitches—at least none that were visible to the audience. Of course, there were actors whose minds went blank at the novelty of wearing a toga or the sight of his or her parents' faces in the crowd; loud promptings from Holly were seemingly unheard by the rapt viewers. The audience, at Holly's invitation, joined in the final singing of "Hark, the Herald Angels Sing" with reverent gusto, and then rose to give the players a standing ovation.

When the grinning cast had taken three curtain calls, Holly held up her hand to quiet the applause and spoke, "I want

168

everyone to please stay for refreshments and for each child to take a gift off the tree."

The party started in full force and the little schoolhouse rang with voices, laughter, and merriment as people mingled, greeted one another, helped themselves to the variety of food provided by the parents; and the actors and actresses, still resplendent in their makeshift costumes, enjoyed being the center of attention. There were cries of excitement as the children found their presents from Holly tied to the tree; the boys began top-spinning contests immediately, while the girls helped each other with the hair slides and ribbons.

Ad complimented Holly and remarked dramatically, "I shall give this a four-star review in my newspaper. Theatrical agents and managers from all over will be beating a path to the door, wanting to sign up all these youthful thespians."

"Oh, Ad!" Holly dismissed his teasing. "But do be sure you check with me so that you get all the children's names and spell them right before you print it in the paper. I know every parent will want to save the clipping when they see it."

Just then Blaine came up and joined them. "Great show, Holly. Everyone did splendidly. You have a real gift for working with children."

"Why thank you, Blaine." Pleased and flattered by his comment, Holly was annoyed to feel herself blushing and even more annoyed to see that Ad noticed it.

After the evening was over one particular incident stood out in Holly's mind. During the party she had felt a tug on her sleeve and turned to see Joel standing beside her holding the hand of a pale, hollow-faced woman. Cissy, looking anxious, stood beside her. "Miss Lambeth, this is our Ma," Joel said.

"Oh, I'm so pleased to meet you, Mrs. McKay," Holly exclaimed. She extended her hand to the shabbily dressed woman and felt a thin, work-roughened hand in her grasp. "Your children are so bright, a real pleasure to teach."

The woman seemed ill-at-ease and hardly looked up as she stammered something in reply.

Holly wanted to talk to her more, try to draw her out, see what she could find out from the mother, but one of the other parents, who was leaving, tapped her on the arm, and Holly had to give them her attention. By the time they had left, so had the McKay's.

Later, as she tidied up the remnants of the party, Holly found among the presents that some of the children had given her, a booklet Joel had made for her of carefully pressed leaves. With it was a small card, soiled by much redoing, laboriously printed lopsided letters, "Luv from Cissy." Both gifts brought tears to Holly's eyes. Most of the presents from the other children were the handiwork of their mothers—crocheted pot holders, jars of candied peaches, boxes of homemade fudge—Holly knew *these* were the ones that she would cherish most.

With school closed for two weeks for the holidays, Holly enjoyed the first free time she had had for months. Knowing the slowness of the mails, Holly had sent her Christmas gifts to her friends and family in Willow Springs right after Thanksgiving. But some things she had ordered by catalog had only just arrived. Even though she knew they would get there late, she wrapped them and planned to mail them anyway. She was on her way into the post office, located at Ned's store when she met Vi coming down the steps.

One look at her friend's face and Holly knew immediately that something was wrong. Usually so poised, Vi seemed distracted and distressed. Holly had to catch her arm and speak to her or else Vi might have gone right past her. "Oh, sorry, Holly, I didn't see you—"

"What's the matter, Vi? Has something happened?"

Vi's eyes brightened with unshed tears. She quickly tried to blink them away.

"Oh, it's nothing really! I just got a letter from Avesta, and she's not coming—"

"Not coming?" gasped Holly, knowing what a keen disappointment this must be to Vi. "After all you've done to get ready for her? Why not?"

Vi whisked out a handkerchief and dabbed her eyes before the traitorous tears could overflow. She tried to smile, but her lips quivered at the attempt. "She's had a lovely invitation to spend the holidays with one of her classmates. The girl's family lives in California, and they've asked Avesta to come with them to San Diego to stay at the Del Coronado. It's a beautiful place, a luxurious resort. They have all sorts of things planned for the girls—it's a wonderful opportunity for Avesta to meet the right people." Vi's voice cracked a little, and Holly pressed her friend's hand.

"I'm sorry, Vi, I know how much you were looking forward to Avesta's coming," was all she could think to say to comfort her.

"But, I'm really happy for her, Holly. Really! I mean that's why I sent her away to boarding school. I wanted her to have nice friends, girls from good families who would open doors for her—" She smiled bravely. "There wouldn't be much for her to do here during the holidays, anyway. What girl of sixteen wants to sit home with her mother and sew, for goodness' sake, when she could be horseback riding and dancing and going to parties and balls?"

Holly nodded sympathetically. She felt a sharp twinge, remembering her own former life of parties and festivities—she, too, would probably have chosen the same option as Avesta had at that age.

"It's all right, Holly. I'll be fine. I think I'll have a party on Christmas anyway. You'll come, of course, won't you? Unless you have other plans."

"Yes, of course. I mean, no, I have no plans," Holly agreed, sure that no invitation from Hetty was forthcoming. "I'd love to come, Vi."

Chapter 18

*W*hen she first heard about the town's annual Christmas Dance, Holly wasn't sure she wanted to go. But she discovered there was no way of getting out of going. The town schoolteacher was expected to be there along with everyone else in Riverbend. Once she had resigned herself that her attendance was, in fact, a "command performance" due to her position, she found she was looking forward to it. She began to think that it might be fun. It had been such a long time since she had had a chance to get dressed up and step out.

As she thought about what to wear, she remembered with some chagrin that it was only at her mother's insistence that she had brought a suitable party dress with her. Now, as she got it out from her trunk, Holly recalled the day she had watched indifferently as her mother carefully packed it in layers of tissue paper. Then, feeling utterly rejected by Jim, she had felt she would never want to go to another party or dance as long as she lived. She was going to Oregon to "lick her wounds," not to dress up or go to parties! How long ago that seemed. Her life had changed so much since she had left Willow Springs, brokenhearted. Strangely enough, days went by when she hadn't even thought of Jim.

Holly shook out the dress, spreading the skirt across her bed and trying to see it through the eyes of the other ladies who would be in attendance. She knew that as the schoolmarm she would have to pass a gauntlet of criticism as to the appropriateness of what she wore. Examining it critically, she decided that it was much too frothy, too ruffled, too much décolletage for Riverbend. She would have to do something about the neckline for sure—

Maybe she should consult Vi, ask her expert opinion, Holly decided and bundling the dress up in a box, she walked over to Vi's.

Vi ushered her into her fitting room and had Holly put on the dress.

"It's such beautiful material, I'd hate to do anything drastic to change it," she murmured. "But, truthfully, it is a little dressier than most of the Riverbend ladies would wear to the Christmas party—"

"Well, I certainly don't want to wear anything inappropriate."

"No, of course not. Let me think what we can do," Vi circled Holly, "Uh-huh. Well, now, just let's see." Narrowing her eyes Vi surveyed the dress critically. With another "Uh-huh," she held out the material and, nodding, began snipping here and there, making a few tucks with pins taken from the red tomato pincushion strapped on her wrist. Her "magic" needle did the rest.

"How's that?" she asked Holly turning her toward the full-length mirror. Holly saw that Vi had filled in the scoop neckline with some judiciously placed netting, removed some of the roses and rearranged them, and taken off two rows of ruffles. "There now, you'll look pretty as a picture, but you won't cause any 'green-eyed' remarks about looking too citified. A schoolmarm has to be as 'without reproach' as Caesar's wife—or in *Riverbend*," she added dryly, "—as the minister's wife."

"Thanks, Vi!" Holly gathered up her things and started to leave, then asked, "You're coming, too, aren't you?"

"Oh, yes, I will for awhile. The Bodine sisters asked me to go with them, so we'll be there."

"Good! Then, you'll see me in all my finery. Thank you so much, Vi." Impulsively Holly gave her a hug. "You're a wonderful friend. I don't know what I'd do without you."

"Good-bye, Calpurnia," Vi laughed, and Holly went out the door.

As she walked down the street toward the schoolhouse, the

173

door of the *Monitor* opened and Ad stuck his head out and greeted her. "Afternoon, Holly. Just wanted to make sure you were going to the dance tomorrow night?"

"Yes, I am, are you?"

"Wouldn't miss it," he grinned. "Polishing up my dancin' shoes."

She regarded him skeptically. "I thought you didn't mix socially."

"Well, I've got to cover it for the paper since I don't have a society editor," he said straightfaced but with twinkling eyes.

Holly shook her head, smiling.

"Be sure and save me a dance," Ad called, as with a wave of her hand she walked on.

The morning of the dance, Holly washed her hair in the newly collected rain water, then sat in front of the stove, drying and brushing it until it crackled and shone with russet lights. Early in the evening she bathed, lavished herself with her rose cologne, put on two petticoats, one cotton and one taffeta that rustled and swished with each movement; then she slipped into the remodeled gown.

Holly did not realize how her new life had enhanced her looks. The rigorous routine of keeping up the little apartment and schoolhouse, chopping wood, carrying pails of water from the well, the exercise of playing games like "Run, Sheep, Run" and "Drop the Handkerchief" with the children outside in the schoolyard, her long walks in the woods and back and forth to town, all had contributed to not only a feeling of well-being, but a radiantly glowing complexion and a slenderly rounded figure.

Even with its altering, the dress was very becoming. For an added effect, Holly tucked some of the silk roses removed from the skirt into her hair.

The dance was not scheduled to start until nine o'clock. Party or no party, farm chores had to be done, cows milked, livestock brought in and fed. Town folks had to close their stores and places of business. Men working in the woods, the local "lumberjacks," had to get into town, pick up their paychecks, patronize the barber shop and hotel baths before going over to the

174

Town Hall. People living in outlying areas or coming from other districts had to drive their wagons long distances. But no one would miss this annual event, the high spot of the year for most people, a chance to get together for some fellowship and fun no matter how far they had to come or what the weather was like.

The weather was clear but with a definite bite in the air, Holly discovered after sticking her head out the door, trying to decide whether to wear her fur tippet and carry her muff or just her hooded cape. She decided on the cape. The fur ensemble might appear too fancy, as if she were showing off. Her acceptance in Riverbend had been too hard-won to gamble on losing the ladies' goodwill.

It was after eight-thirty when the pounding on the door announced the arrival of Matt and Geneva Healy, who were to take her to the Town Hall.

"Well, if you don't look like a picture, all duded up," was Matt's hearty comment when she opened the door.

"Thanks, Matt—I *think!*" Holly laughed. "I'll be with you in a minute."

"I'll wait for you in the wagon."

Holly flung her cape around her shoulders, wound the delicate knitted "fascinator" over her hair, gathered up her gloves and small velvet evening bag, and hurried outside. The sky was a satiny dark, pin pointed with a few brilliant stars. Matt assisted her into the wagon alongside Geneva who exclaimed, "My, oh, my, Holly, you smell good enough to sprinkle on my best linens!"

"Oh, Geneva, I love the way you put things! I hope it's not too much!"

"Not a bit, darlin', just lovely like a spring garden." Geneva reassured her. "And like Matt said, you look so sweet; you're not going to have a chance to set down all night, you'll have so many dance partners."

A chorus of greetings came from the back of the wagon where all the little Healys were bundled down, scarfed and mittened. In Riverbend children were welcome at every event; besides, there was usually no one to leave them with at home.

175

After returning their greetings, Holly turned to Geneva and asked, "Tell me what to expect at this party."

"Well, first we just sorta socialize, you know, just mix and mingle with folks, some of the ones that come from Mills Flat we don't see but once or twice a year; then the music kind of gets agoin', and the dancing begins—"

"And then we eat, and that's the best part!" Matt chuckled.

"Now, Matthew, you know you like to square dance as much or more'n anybody," Geneva chided. "Well, around eleven or so, when folks are gettin' a little hot and tired, we set out the food—I brought my fried chicken and my marble cake—all the ladies try to bring their very finest recipe—"

"Oh, dear, should I have brought something?" Holly worried.

"Oh, no, honey, nobody'll expect *you* to bring anything!" exclaimed Geneva.

"Single gals are there to set their caps for the bachelors in the bunch!" Matt put in.

"Now, you hush, Matt, you're goin' to have Holly all nerves 'fore we get there. Listen here, Holly, there's going to be so much those tables are going to be groanin'. Not only desserts but hot dishes and pies, and I don't know what all."

"I'm sure countin' on Annie Olsen's bringing her stack cake and Hazel Burrows her 'Impossible' pie—" Matt smacked his lips in anticipation.

Ignoring him, Geneva patted Holly's hand again. "Believe me, Holly, you're going to be a special guest at this party. You're just there to enjoy yourself. You've worked hard all this time with all our young'ns, and everybody's so grateful you took over and done so well. Why, everyone's still talking about the Christmas program. We never had one like it before. All the parents are so pleased that their youngsters had a part and did them proud."

As Matt pulled the wagon up into the row of buggies and wagons lined up at the fence in front of Town Hall, lights were shining out of the oblong windows. They could hear the sound of voices, laughter, and the squeak of band instruments being tuned. Holly felt her spirits lift happily.

"Give me a hand with this basket, Matt," Geneva directed,

176

and Matt helped her down, then offered an arm apiece to both and escorted them toward the hall, with the Healy youngsters trailing along behind.

Outside, ranged along the steps, were a number of young men. All heads turned in their direction as they approached. A wave of sound, muted whistling, and mumbled comments reached Holly's burning ears as she felt at least a dozen pairs of eyes upon her. Geneva squeezed her arm and whispered, "Don't pay them no mind, Holly; they don't have polished manners, but they're all nice fellows. That's just their way of admiring a lady."

Inside it was bright, noisy, and warm. All along the sides of the big room were plank tables resting on sawhorses covered with white paper and festooned with crinkly yards of twisted red and white paper ribbon. Women were busily scurrying about putting all sorts of platters, bowls, and covered dishes out on each one.

"I'll just take my things over there and see if I can help out," Geneva said and went bustling off, the youngest Healy child holding onto her skirt while the others ran to be with friends they had spotted. Matt had stopped at the door to talk to some men, and Holly found herself left standing alone.

Then, directly across the room she saw Hetty in conversation with another woman. Hetty must have seen her come in with the Healys, but when Holly tried to catch her eye, her hand raised in a little wave of greeting, Hetty turned her head. Deliberately! Holly was sure.

Holly felt the old rage rise up in her. Where was her cousin's holiday spirit? Couldn't she at least make an effort at Christmas? Holly knew that her mother and Aunt Dolly would be sick at heart if they knew the situation between their daughters. Well, she certainly wasn't going to walk over and barge in where she obviously was being ignored.

Embarrassed to be snubbed so blatantly, Holly pretended to admire the festive appearance of the room. The decorating committee had done a fine job. Boughs of cedar tied with shiny red ribbons were draped all around, wreaths bright with holly, and glistening gilt bows hung over the doorways and in the

177

windows. The little band on the raised platform at one end of the room was tuning up, sawing at their fiddles, plucking the strings, and twisting the tuning pegs, as the piano player tried to help them by striking one key.

Still smarting from Hetty's snub, Holly looked around for a friendly face and saw the mother of one of her pupils nearby. After exchanging greetings, she asked where she should put her wrap and was directed to an annex that had been utilized as a cloakroom for the ladies. Besides a coat rack, makeshift cots lined the walls so that sleeping babies and worn-out tots could be put to sleep if the hour got late and the party was still in full swing. In one corner were piled quilts, blankets, and pillows belonging to those who had come from so far away that they would stay overnight rather than face a cold ride home in the chilly dawn.

On the far side of the room a mirror hung over a long shelf. Loath to return immediately to the main room and perhaps experience again the humiliation of having her cousin ignore her publicly, Holly spent longer than necessary fussing with her hair and checking the tiny buttons on her gloves. For the first time in her life Holly understood what used to puzzle her back in Willow Springs—why some of the less popular girls had virtually hid out in dressing rooms at dances and parties, afraid to venture back to the ballroom where their dance cards might be left blank and they would be relegated to being "wallflowers."

When she could delay no longer without being conspicuous, Holly swallowed her pride and reentered the main room now filled with people. To her relief just then, she saw Adam walk in the door. Dressed in a fine dark suit, a frilled white shirt, and a flowing black tie, he could have been on his way to some fancy San Francisco social event. She was grateful when she saw him heading toward her.

He greeted her with a lavish compliment. "Good evening, Miss Lambeth, if you aren't looking as dazzling as a star on top of the Christmas tree! And may I have the first dance and sign your card for a few other dances before those rascals lining up over there fill it all up?"

178

"Of course, you may, but I don't think this will be a card dance."

"No, I don't suppose so. It's just first come, first served, I understand. I just wanted to make you feel at home where, I imagine, you barely get inside the door of any ballroom before your dance card is filled."

"Oh, Ad, don't tease!"

"Homesick?"

"Not exactly. But Christmas is a kind of sentimental time, don't you think? Thoughts of home and family and that sort of thing."

"But you have family right here. Aren't you spending the holidays with your cousin?"

Holly lowered her eyes, biting her lip, wondering how to tell the truth without making Hetty a pariah for not inviting her. "Oh, the music seems to be starting!" she exclaimed, skillfully diverting the conversation and the necessity of answering Ad's question.

There was immediate comprehension in his eyes. Ad held out his hand to her and as he spun her out onto the dance floor, he said, "Well, don't fret about it. I believe Vi is having a party for all of us who are a long way from home, and I'm *sure* you're invited there."

"Aren't you going, too? I know Vi mentioned that she was inviting you."

"Yes, she was gracious enough to do so; however, I don't plan to be here over the holidays. I'm going out of town."

"On a rail? After that editorial I wouldn't be surprised!" Holly teased, her eyes sparkled wickedly.

"No, folks have been surprisingly tolerant—or maybe it's just the Christmas spirit. So far no one has volunteered to provide tar and feathers. But just between me and thee, I may look around, test the waters, so to speak, for another position while I'm gone."

"In case the town fathers are secretly searching for a new editor?"

"Not that either. I think I may just be ready to end my exile."

"We'll miss you," Holly said, realizing that it was the truth.

179

"Perhaps absence will make the heart grow fonder."

"On the other hand: Out of sight, out of mind!" she laughed.

Ad pretended a scowl. "There's no verbal sparring with a schoolmarm."

Although they had some trouble measuring their steps to the band's first halting attempts at a waltz, Adam was a superb dancer with a strong-lead and was able to make the set enjoyable in spite of the struggling band. Gradually the musicians seemed to get their instruments into harmony, and the next set, consisting of a lively polka then a popular schottische, was better. That was the last of the round dances because after that, Bill Hanum got on stage and began calling, "Gentlemen, choose your partners; we're going to do some high-steppin' square dancing."

At this there was applause, and before Adam could offer his arm to Holly, Matt Healy had come up and claimed her for his partner.

People lined up, men on one side, women on the other; then the command "Circle round" was shouted, and everyone joined hands and started moving. It was great fun, exhilarating and energetic. "Do-si-do, round you go, find yourself a pretty gal and swing her to the right." Sounds of clapping hands and shuffling feet were mingled with shouts and much laughter. Holly had to listen to get things straight because there were some new calls here in Riverbend she had never heard before. She found herself being swung right off her feet by some hearty man at times and giggling as she made mistakes and was pulled into line by others as she tried to keep up with the dance.

Finally the music reached a high crescendo and, with a loud twang of a fiddle, stopped at last; everyone was flushed, breathless and nearly exhausted.

"Just so you *old folks* can take it easy for awhile 'fore the next Virginia reel, we're goin' to have a Paul Jones," Bill Hanum announced, and the band began playing a soft, gentle melody. The idea of this dance was that when the caller blew his whistle and the band stopped playing, whoever you were facing became your partner. Whether by accident or design, Holly was never sure, but she found herself in front of Blaine.

Surprised, she said, "Why, Blaine, I didn't know you were coming!"

"I wasn't sure myself. I just got here, as a matter of fact. I had to make a call out on the old Mine Road. But now I hope everyone in Riverbend is alive and well, and from the looks of things, they are all right here!" he laughed.

There wasn't time for any more talk then because the circle began to move again, the music flowed and then stopped again. Holly had a succession of partners until the end of the piece. When intermission was called, Blaine magically appeared at her side again. People were thronging toward the tables, where cups of refreshment were being ladled out of huge punch bowls.

"May I see you home, Holly?" Blaine asked as they left the circle.

Pleased that he had asked, Holly wasn't sure if it would be considered proper since she had come with the Healys. As she hesitated, a look of disappointment crossed Blaine's readable face. "You've promised someone else?"

"Oh, no, it's not that; it's just that I came with Geneva and Matt and—well, actually, it's really out of their way to go around by the schoolhouse since their farm is out in the other direction—"

"You don't need an excuse to say yes, Holly," he teased. "I'm sure that Geneva and Matt won't mind; in fact, they'd probably approve."

A little embarrassed that it was so transparent she *had* been doing exactly that, Holly unfurled her little fan and fluttered it, murmuring, "My, it is very warm in here, isn't it?"

Still looking amused, Blaine said, "I'll go get us some punch; you wait here." With his hand under her arm, he guided her to one of the chairs along the wall and headed toward the punch bowl.

With the press of people and all the exertion of the lively dancing, the room did seem very hot. Holly fanned briskly to cool off while she looked around. As she did, she saw Ad's towering figure pushing through the crowd, carrying two cups of punch.

"Here you are!" he said triumphantly as he handed one to

181

her. "I wasn't sure I was going to make it through that mob," he sighed as he sat down in the empty chair beside her.

"Thank you, Ad, that was very kind of you, but Blaine just went to get me some," Holly said, a little apologetically.

Ad frowned. "Well, you can drink two cups, can't you? It's hot enough in here."

Holly took a sip, knowing that Adam was miffed.

"Well, I better ask you for the next dance *now*, I guess," he grumbled.

"I *think* I heard somebody say it's going to be a Paul Jones."

Ad made a sound of disgust. "I'm not sure I approve of this kind of dance rather than card dances," he growled. "Well, the first one after the Paul Jones then?"

Before she could reply, they saw Blaine approaching. Ad stood up, leaving the chair next to hers empty for him. While the two men exchanged greetings, Holly gulped down the rest of the cranberry punch, then she quickly slid her first empty cup out of sight under her chair and accepted the one that Blaine handed her. Ad left them, and a few minutes later the Paul Jones was announced.

During the dance Holly had several partners because every time the music stopped she was standing in front of a different man. This way Holly had a chance to chat with some of the fathers of her students, and she enjoyed hearing them say that their children were enjoying school.

When the Paul Jones ended, the band played a fanfare and the caller shouted, "Gentlemen, claim your ladies for the last dance."

Ad was at her side instantly and, making a great show of checking a nonexistent dance card and giving an elaborate bow, said, "I believe this one is mine."

"Well, I . . ." began Holly, looking uncertainly at Blaine who had also come up.

Blaine motioned toward the Healys and said, "I'll give you the pleasure, Ad, since I'm taking Holly home. I'll just go tell Matt and Geneva. I'll meet you at the door, Holly."

Ad said nothing, just bowed and held out his hand to lead Holly onto the dance floor, but his expression was ironic as he remarked, "I thought the proper etiquette was for your partner for the last dance of the evening to escort you home. Evidently I was wrong."

Holly tried to soothe his evident irritation. "Weren't you the one who informed me that Riverbend affairs followed no prescribed pattern?"

He made a grimace. "Hoisted on my own petard."

"Or 'snared by the words of your own mouth'," she retorted, reminding him of his contention that he knew Scripture.

"I'm just a little surprised that our serious, dedicated young doctor has time to attend dances and see young ladies home!" He glanced over her head around the room, asking in an aggrieved tone, "Why couldn't one of those overfed men or chubby children suddenly get an attack of food poisoning? Or one of the ladies faint and need the ministrations of our town physician? I'd counted on seeing you to your doorstep myself."

"I'm sorry, Adam. Thank you, anyway," Holly said, feeling a little rush of satisfaction. *How* flattering having two such attractive men vying for her favors. It was like old times in Willow Springs!

Almost at once she felt the prick of conscience. Wasn't she over all that sort of foolishness? Had she only thought she was? *What a silly shallow person I am after all!* Yet she still couldn't help the little bubble of excitement inside as the music ended and Ad reluctantly released her to Blaine.

"Ready?" Blaine asked.

"I'll just get my wrap," she told him.

"I'll wait for you at the door."

Holly hurried to get her cape, but when she came out, Blaine had disappeared. In another minute or so he reappeared and apologized, saying that one of the women had asked him to take a look at her child who seemed feverish. As Blaine took Holly's arm to assist her down the steps now coated with an icy glaze, he said, "Sorry about that."

"I hope it wasn't anything serious."

"No, probably too much cake, pie, and punch. He'll be fine in the morning. A doctor's never 'off duty' even at a party."

"It's all right. I understand," Holly said.

183

"Do you? Most women—I mean, most people don't." He helped her into his buggy then went around and took the blanket off his horse. He folded it over his arm and, as he patted the horse's neck, Holly heard Blaine speak to him. "What a good old fella. Long time out here in the cold. Well, we'll be getting warmed up, trotting out Lincoln Road to take the schoolmarm home." Holly smiled in the darkness, touched by Blaine's unselfconscious concern for his horse, his gentleness.

He got back into the buggy, picked up the reins, flicked them a couple of times, and they started off through the night. At least a hundred thousand more stars seemed to stud the sky since earlier, and the horse's hooves on the frost-skimmed road made a crunch sound in the stillness.

"Nice party. At least the end of it," Blaine remarked. "I hadn't planned to get there so late, but just as I was leaving my rooms Seth Hilliard rode in to say all three of the children had real bad coughs and the baby was having trouble breathing, so I went out there to take a look at them." Blaine shook his head. "Never can understand why folks wait so long to call a doctor. I could have given them something days ago and none of them would be this bad—" He broke off. "Sorry, shouldn't bore you with shop talk."

"You're not, and Denny Hilliard is in school. How is he— and the others? Are they going to be all right?"

"Yes, the older ones, certainly. I'm a little worried about the baby. I'll take another ride out there tomorrow and see," Blaine said, then changed the subject abruptly. "—You warm enough?"

"Yes, it is very cold, though. Think it will snow again?"

"Possibly." Blaine turned to glance over at her. "That's right—this will be your first Oregon winter, won't it? I almost forgot. You seem to have become a part of the community, fit in so easily, like you'd always been here."

"Why, thank you, Blaine. That's nice of you to say so."

"Well, of course, your coming has made a difference."

"*Really?*"

"Sure you have. The parents really liked the Christmas program; I've heard nothing but good about it."

"That's nice to know. I hoped they would. It means a great deal to have the parents think I'm doing a good job with the children and all."

"And of course, you've also brightened up the place, prettied the scenery too, as they say around here," he laughed.

Pleased, Holly smiled in the darkness. Blaine didn't toss compliments around lightly. Not like Ad, whose charm was second nature; flowery phrases came easily to him.

Even though her toes were freezing in her thin dancing slippers, the ride to the schoolhouse seemed to Holly to come to an end too soon.

"Whoa!" Blaine reined to a stop at the side of the school building, then jumped out of the buggy, came around, and held out both hands to help Holly down. He accompanied her up the steps and unlocked the door for her.

As he handed her back her key, their fingers touched. For a minute, Holly could not breathe. All at once everything became dazzlingly focused: the snow-scented wind, the brilliance of the stars overhead.

Both of them stood very still, their frosted breath mingling in the darkness. Holly swayed slightly toward Blaine, felt his hands tighten on her elbows as he steadied her. Holly felt that Blaine was about to kiss her, and instinctively she started to close her eyes—

Then, suddenly, through the clear night air came the sound of horses, the jangle of harness bells, voices ringing out Christmas songs, and around the bend of the road came a wagon load of merry-makers from the Town Hall, the swinging lanterns sending arcs of light onto the snow and throwing the two figures on the schoolhouse porch into full view.

"Howdy, folks!" the voices called heartily as the wagon lumbered by. "Merry Christmas, Miss Lambeth, Merry Christmas, Doc!" The laughing faces were illuminated, and Holly recognized most of them— all people she knew, parents and pupils alike, folks she had met through the lending library.

After the merry group had passed by, their songs still echoing, an awkwardness descended on them for a full minute. Then Blaine said with a chuckle, "Small towns! God bless 'em." He

185

started down the steps, saying, "Well, Holly, I guess I better say good night."

Conscious of keen disappointment, Holly managed to keep her voice light, "Good night, Blaine; thanks for seeing me home."

Once inside, Holly watched as Blaine got into the buggy and turned it around. After awhile, with a last look out, she sighed and walked back into her bedroom. Slowly, one by one, she began discarding gloves, slippers, cloak, and fan. The Christmas dance was over, the sound of the toe-tapping music faded away. Suddenly she was left with an awful sense of emptiness.

Tonight she had felt so happy being with Blaine as if they were on the brink of something—falling in love? What? Was she beginning to think of Blaine romantically?

Oh, what a perfect fool you are, Hollis Lambeth! What did it matter whether Blaine kissed you or not? Blaine was undoubtedly handsome, warm, sincere, understanding, but—after all, in the spring, when school was over, she was going home—home to Willow Springs. Wasn't she?

Chapter 19

A few days before Christmas, when Holly was in the store, Ned had issued an embarrassed invitation for her to come to Christmas dinner at their house. Aware of the probable discussion with Hetty that must have preceded it, Holly tried to make her refusal as easy as possible for him. "Oh, Ned, thank you, but I've accepted an invitation to Vi Dodd's. It turns out that he's going to be alone for Christmas after all, and so she's having a few friends to share the holiday with her. I do have some gifts for the children and for you and Hetty, too. So I'll stop by on Christmas Eve before the service at church if that will be all right?"

Ned's face flushed as he shifted the glass candy jars on the countertop nervously and said, "That's mighty nice of you, Holly; I'll tell Hetty, and the children will be so happy to see you."

Holly could see that he wanted to say more, obviously struggling with his own need to be honest with her and his loyalty to his stubborn wife. Holly felt sorry for him, but she felt sorrier for her cousin. Why was Hetty making life so difficult for everyone? Her husband and children especially? What possible pleasure could she be getting out of this feud?

Holly dreaded the prospect of the encounter with Hetty. It was enough to spoil Christmas Eve for her. But since she had promised Ned and did not want to disappoint the children, there was nothing to do but go. It had been fun, picking out their presents, poring over one of Ned's catalogs, selecting just the right gift, anticipating their happiness at what she had chosen. Afraid that anything of a personal nature she might give Hetty would not be acceptable just because it had come from her, Holly decided to give Ned and Hetty a joint present, something for the house. She hated thinking that way about her cousin, but in her heart she knew it was probably true. After much deliberation, she had chosen a cranberry glass bowl suitable for flowers or fruit or to be used as a decorative centerpiece. She wrapped all the presents in paper she decorated with holly leaves and berries and tied with scarlet ribbon.

She delayed going until late afternoon when, she knew, the children would be up from their naps. She did not want to be alone with Hetty. On the walk over, Holly kept thinking, *What a shame it is that things aren't normal between us.* It would have been so much fun to be included in all the traditional Christmas plans, trimming the tree, the holiday baking, filling the children's stockings. That's certainly the way things *should* have been for two cousins, both so far away from home.

Hetty's greeting was about as frozen as the ground over which Holly had trudged to get there. But the affectionate welcome Holly received from Aurelia and Teddy, who flung himself into her arms, made up for the iciness of their mother. "Will you have some tea or coffee?" Hetty asked stiffly after a few minutes. Holly would have loved to stay longer, talk and play with her small cousins, but the atmosphere was too stifling. Hetty's attitude made relaxing and enjoying impossible. Making the excuse that she had other stops to make and some last-minute shopping to complete, Holly moved to the door. Before she reached it, Hetty thrust a small, wrapped package toward her. "Here," she said shortly. "Fruitcake, made from Grandma Granville's recipe."

Holly managed a "thank you" even as she thought, *What an impersonal gift from one cousin to the other* and, at the same time, of the half-dozen same such fruitcakes sent by some of her pupils' mothers, lined up on her own kitchen table!

Back outside in the crisp December air, Holly felt incredibly let down. As she had known it would, her visit to her cousin had depressed her. A sudden wave of homesickness and nostalgia for other Christmases struck her, and she fought an overwhelming urge to cry. Holly hurried along toward town, her head bent against the wind.

"Whoa there!" a familiar voice rang out, and Holly came to an abrupt halt. She had almost collided with Blaine coming from the other direction. "And where are you off to in such a hurry?" he asked, grinning. His face was ruddy, and his blue eyes merry as he held out both hands to steady her from her sudden stop.

"Well—eventually to the Christmas service, but it's a little early yet."

"Believe it or not, I had the same thing in mind. Would it fit your plans if I offered you a little holiday hospitality before attending church? One thing I'm good at is making coffee, and you should see my waiting room. It's absolutely filled. Not with patients but *payments*. Most of which look and smell suspiciously like fruitcake."

"Sounds like *my* kitchen!" Holly laughed, feeling her heart already lifting. "And Hetty just gave me another one!"

"Well, come along," Blaine said heartily, offering his arm. Linking arms, they walked the short distance to the doctor's office. While Blaine moved briskly about stirring up the fire in the stove and brewing coffee, Holly examined the framed certificates on the wall. Ad was right. Blaine's qualifications were impressive.

"I'm surprised you're not spending Christmas with the Thorntons," Blaine remarked casually as he handed her a mug of steaming coffee. "It seems such a family time."

Holly accepted the coffee and took a sip before answering. Why not be honest? Surely Blaine would understand.

"The truth is, Blaine—, Hetty and I are not on the best terms. Please don't ask why. I really don't know, myself. I've tried to figure it out, but—" She shrugged.

"Hetty doesn't seem to be a very happy person," was his only comment. Then he deftly changed the subject, for which Holly was grateful.

"You will be at Vi's tomorrow, then?"

"Yes, it was lovely of her to invite me."

"And other homeless folks as well," Blaine smiled. "Vi always takes pity on us."

"A very fitting way to celebrate Christmas, don't you think?"

They chatted easily together for a half hour or so then left to walk down the street to the church to the simple but meaningful Christmas Eve service. Afterward, Blaine took Holly back to the schoolhouse in his buggy and escorted her to the door. "I'll see you tomorrow at Vi's? I have to make a few house calls first, but I'll be there." He started down the steps then turned back, grinning. "You know something? It's been years since I've looked forward to Christmas the way I'm looking forward to tomorrow." With that, he ran the rest of the way down the porch steps, whistling "Jingle Bells."

And so am I, thought Holly, smiling to herself.

Christmas Day at Vi's was lovely. As Holly had expected, Vi served a meal that was both a pleasure to the palate and to the eye. The table was spread with an embroidered cutwork linen cloth, silver candlesticks, and ivory china. She had fashioned a centerpiece of red-berried pyracantha and white geraniums in a milk-glass bowl. Turkey roasted to perfection, mounds of snowy potatoes, glazed carrots, pearl onions in cream sauce, and fresh cranberry relish was followed by a frothy lemon sorbet, and later by mince pie and coffee.

Holly, whose own culinary skills had not evolved much further than necessity required, thoroughly enjoyed being in a real home, eating delicious food, and being with pleasant adult company for a change. After dinner they had all had a fine time playing "Quotations" and "Charades." Although Holly knew Vi had been sadly disappointed about Avesta's not coming, she covered it well and could not have been a more gracious hostess.

Blaine helped Holly on with her cape and handed her her muff as they both thanked Vi and said good night. "It was a lovely party, wasn't it?" Holly commented as they walked along the darkened, quiet streets of town. "It reminded me a little of Christmases at home. Our family always held open house on Christmas Day with friends and relatives flowing in and out, my father presiding proudly over the eggnog punchbowl—" She

190

broke off, hoping she didn't sound homesick. "Do you have Christmas memories, Blaine?"

"Yes, of course, I suppose everyone does. The lucky ones do, anyway, those of us who had good parents, happy homes."

"Yes. I'm surprised I haven't missed things as much as I thought I might," she said thoughtfully. "Do you miss yours?"

"Not so much anymore. Of course, I've been away from my childhood home for a good many years. First, away at college, then in Scotland and Germany for two years for further study— then I came out West," he replied, then looked at her. He smiled and said, "And I must say that Riverbend has its compensations—especially recently."

When they reached the schoolhouse, it was only early evening. Holly hated to see the lovely day end. She especially wanted this time with Blaine to last a little longer. Remembering Vi's caution about how careful the schoolteacher must be about her reputation, Holly hesitated to invite Blaine into her little parlor. As she debated about its propriety, Blaine made the decision for her. "Would it be improper for me to suggest that you might offer me something warm before I brave the chill again on my walk back to town?"

She knew —, he must have been reading her mind.

"Not improper at all but very probably inhospitable!" she declared with a toss of her head. "I might even offer you a slice of fruitcake!" she teased.

She took off her bonnet, hung it up, and Blaine assisted her with her cape. They walked into the parlor.

"Certainly *I've* found things I used to think were so very important don't really matter a fig to me now," she said. "Why don't you sit down here, and I'll bring us some tea?"

In the few minutes it took Holly to heat the water in the kettle, arrange a tray with teacups, and pour the water into the teapot, Blaine had picked up her photo album and was turning its pages. He looked up as she entered with the tray and said, "Hope you don't mind? It was lying here open, so I thought it was all right to look."

"Oh, sure. A little bit of Willow Springs I brought with me.

Have you ever seen so many aunts, uncles, and cousins?" she asked gaily as she proceeded to pour out the fragrant jasmine tea.

"I'm curious about all the empty spaces. Have you banished or disowned some of your relatives. Don't tell me *your* family has black sheep?"

"Doesn't everyone's?" She dimpled, eyes mischievous. "Or are all the Stevens clan impeccable pillars of society?"

"I don't know about that; never have been one to go into genealogy." He paused for a minute as he accepted the cup she handed him; then he regarded her thoughtfully and said, "You haven't answered my question."

Holly recalled Ad's same inquiry, and also that afterward, acting on his advice, she had removed all Jim's pictures from the album. How freeing it had been! She had taken them all out the very same evening Ad had been here, and since then she had rarely given Jim a thought.

Now, looking into Blaine's frankly interested eyes, she found it almost easy to say, "They were pictures of someone who's no longer in my life. It seemed a good idea to take them out. You see, we were engaged, and he broke the engagement. It pains me to confess that I have only myself to blame. For quite a while I spent time in futile regrets. It's over now, and it seems a long time ago and actually sort of unreal to me now."

"Did you love him very much?"

Holly thought a minute before answering. "I'm not sure I even knew what love is. As painful as it is, I must confess that I was to blame for what happened to us. I hurt him deeply—but it's all in the past now. Taking the pictures out was just a step in realizing that and going on with my life."

Telling Blaine was much easier than it had been telling Ad— Ad performed the surgery, the sharp cutting advice; Blaine's sympathy, understanding, brought healing. Then Holly said, "I was very young, and it seems a long time ago. So much has happened; I've changed so much." She took a sip of tea then quoted softly, "'When I was a child I thought as a child, I spoke as a child—now, I've put away childish things.'"

"Good for you. Out here you grow up fast, or you don't survive," he said quietly.

As Holly met his eyes, she felt disconcerted for a moment. She saw something in Blaine's eyes that she had seen in them earlier in the evening at Vi's. She had been asked to play the piano, and Blaine had come over and leaned on it while she played. He was looking at her now as he had then. His eyes regarding her with a mixture of admiration and incredible tenderness. Or was it something more? Before she could answer her own question, he went on, "It would do for all of us to put the past behind us—painful or otherwise. As a doctor, I've learned that life is precious—too precious for wasteful lingering over mistakes we've made or having vain regrets." He smiled, then drained his cup, set it upon its saucer, replaced it on the tray, and said, "And that's enough unsolicited philosophy from a country doctor. Now, I must be off." He stood up and started toward the door. "Thank you for a most delightful ending to a particularly happy Christmas Day."

Holly rose and went with him into the hallway and handed him his coat. Around his neck he wrapped the red-and-purple striped muffler the Misses Bodine had given him for a Christmas gift, and he plunged his hands into his pockets for his gloves. Then a slow grin broke across his face as he said, "Well, well, what do you know? I wonder how this got in here?" and instead of his gloves, he brought out a small sprig of mistletoe.

Still smiling, Blaine dangled it above her head.

Tilting her chin up and leaning down, he kissed her. Her response was instantaneous. Slipping her arms around his neck, she returned his kiss. She felt his arms tighten, and he kissed her again. She closed her eyes, savoring its sweetness. This was the kiss she had hoped for after the holiday dance, but it was much more tender, more intense than she could have imagined. With a little sigh, she looked at him. When she saw Blaine's expression, a tingle of alarm went through her. She recognized something in his eyes that frightened her a little. They were searching for some—what? Encouragement? Confirmation? Commitment?

She recognized something familiar in the way her heart was beating, too! Was she—*could* it be?—she was falling in love? Or was this the old Holly's response to the thrill of being the object

193

of a man's admiration? Especially a man like Blaine Stevens? She stepped back out of his arms, feeling confused. Before she could say anything, Blaine said, "Merry Christmas, Holly, and good night." Then he was gone into the dark, chilly night. She remained standing in the doorway, still feeling the warmth of his lips on hers.

The week between Christmas and New Year's flew by. There was fresh snow, and Holly was invited out to the Healys' farm to go sledding on the hill behind the house; then she stayed for one of Geneva's bounteous suppers.

One day Ned brought Aurelia and Teddy to the store, where Holly came to meet them and take them out to her little school-house home to spend the day. Aurelia wanted to play school in the classroom, and Holly let her draw on the blackboard to her heart's content while Teddy sat on the floor, looking at picture books and playing with the bean bags the school children used at recess.

Holly served them a "pick and choose" lunch made up of all the gifts of cakes, pies, fruit jams and preserves, nut loaves, and candy she had been given by her pupils. The children had a glorious time and didn't want to leave when Ned came for them after he closed the store.

"Why don't you live with us anymore, Holly?" Teddy asked plaintively as she helped him into his warm jacket.

"It's not fun any more at home without *you*, Holly," Aurelia added wistfully.

Holly's eyes met Ned's over the children's heads and then looked away quickly. She said, "But, I have to live at the school because I'm the teacher, Teddy. And, Aurelia, you and Teddy can come and visit during a real school day sometime if your mama says you may."

That seemed to cheer them up a little. But as Ned led them down the steps and out to the wagon, they kept turning back and waving to Holly, who stood at the door.

Returning to her apartment, it suddenly felt empty. She had loved having the children here. Why was Hetty so stubborn? Why couldn't they all be pleasant and happy and *family*, for goodness' sake! Holly sighed with frustration. It ought not to be like this. She thought of the fabricated letters she wrote to her mother to pass on to Aunt Dolly. Did anyone read between the lines? Probably, if anyone did, it was Great-Aunt Ancilla. If not, why then in the latest batch of tracts from her were ones with such Scriptural admonitions as: "Ephesians 4:31: Let all bitterness and wrath and anger and clamor and evil speaking be put away from you with all malice," and "Proverbs 15:1: A soft answer turneth away wrath, but grievous words stir up anger"?

New Year's Day dawned crisp and clear and blue. There were still patches of snow on the ground, but the sun was shining brilliantly. To Holly's surprise, she received an unexpected New Year's caller: Adam Corcoran, looking dapper, as usual, in ruffled white shirt, string bow tie, dark blue coat, and a biscuit-beige waistcoat.

"Why, good morning and Happy New Year, Adam!" Holly greeted him at the door.

He leaned against the door frame, looking at her; then from behind his back he brought a package tied in bright paper and ribbon and handed it to her. "Happy Birthday."

"What on earth makes you think it's my birthday?"

"Everyone has a birthday every year, right? Since I don't know the exact date of yours, New Year's Day is as good a day to start a new year as any, don't you agree? So let's just say, it's a little gift to give you a good start on your year." He held it out to her.

"Why, Ad, that was very sweet of you—"

"Not sweet at all. I enjoyed doing it very much. I never do anything I don't enjoy," he said. "Well, hardly ever—as I recall one moving day doing a lot of things I didn't particularly enjoy."

"Yes, I know, and you were quite marvelous, and I appreciated every grubby unpleasant chore you did. Come on in, sit down, and I'll make us some tea." Holly carried the gift box over to the table and set it down. She placed the kettle on the stove.

"Aren't you going to open it?" he asked.

"Of course. Just delaying my pleasure."

195

"What a martyr you are," he remarked, seating himself on one of the straight chairs and stretching out his long legs with his shiny boots out in front of him.

Holly poured the boiling water into the teapot. While it steeped, she put the honey jar in the center of the table and cut two slices of the stack cake Rebecca Clay had brought her the day before on a plate.

"What do you suppose the year 1883 will bring us?" Ad mused.

"Is that a rhetorical question, or do you expect an answer?"

"I hope it means the end of my exile," Ad said, stirring honey thoughtfully into his cup.

"Has it really been that bad for you here?"

He lifted an eyebrow and gazed at Holly across the table for a second, then said slowly, "I'd say it's been better since sometime—about the end of August. . . ."

Ignoring his implication, Holly said seriously, "You've done a great deal with the paper. Everybody reads it; there's always lots of talk about your editorials!"

Ad shrugged. "Maybe start a little brush fire now and then. But that soon dies down. Besides, there's not much the locals can get too excited about. This Town Council's made up of the proverbial 'salt of the earth,' all upstanding, honest types. My meat is usually corrupt politicians. Not that *that* did me much good!" he remarked ironically. "Going after one particularly bad one landed me here! That should have taught me something, right? What do they say, teacher, if you don't learn by your mistakes, you're doomed to repeat 'em? Maybe I'm a slow learner." Ad made a dismissing gesture. "But that's enough about me. Open your present."

Affecting a simpering smile Holly pretended coyness. "Oh, Mr. Corcoran, you *shouldn't* have!"

"I know I shouldn't have but open it anyway!" ordered Ad.

Laughing, Holly untied the ribbons, pushed away the paper revealing a small, square box. Lifting the lid, she brought out a tiny rosewood clock. "Oh, Ad, thank you."

"It not only tells the time, it shows the date," he pointed out the small dial on the face.

196

"How clever! I never saw one like this or one so pretty. Thank you very much."

"Well at least now you can keep track of your prison sentence," he said gesturing to the schoolroom.

"I don't think of it *exactly* like that," she protested.

"Maybe not, but it takes one to know one, as they say, and I believe you're counting your time in Riverbend as much as I am."

"No, Ad, I'm not. You're wrong."

"If I am, I stand corrected. Has something happened to change your attitude about this town?"

Holly hesitated. Would Ad understand if she tried to tell him? Truthfully, she knew *much* had happened. It wasn't just one thing; there were many turns of events that had changed her thinking about Riverbend. Some she knew, some she only guessed, some she didn't want to admit. At least not to Ad.

But he was looking at her so curiously, she had to say something. "Well, for one thing I found I love teaching! That's a big surprise and probably accounts more than anything else for my change of attitude. And the children. They're wonderful."

Ad yawned elaborately, tapping his hand over his mouth, "Ho-hum, now I have heard everything!"

Holly pretended indignation. "But it's true!"

He frowned and gave her a long, scrutinizing look, then said, "Yes, I believe it really is. Who would have thought it?"

He finished his tea, put his cup down, and got up to leave. "Well, I guess I better be on my way; I have an important editorial to write—predictions for the New Year I think will be my subject."

"Do try to be optimistic, Ad," Holly begged as she walked with him to the door.

With his hand on the doorknob, he lingered as if he were about to say something else. Instinctively Holly braced herself for what might be some last cynical comment on Riverbend, its banality, its provincialism, its lack of excitement. She had no idea his mind was on something else altogether. She was unaware that the pale afternoon sun streaming in through the narrow windows created a golden aura behind her head.

Unexpectedly, Ad reached out and softly touched her hair;

his finger trailed down her cheek. Holly sensed that perhaps she should step back, but she didn't.

"You know, your eyes are extraordinary," he murmured. "I thought at first they were hazel, then I thought they were blue, but in this light—they're almost green, like Chinese jade—"

Then he leaned down and kissed her on the lips, with a gentle sweetness.

Automatically Holly had closed her eyes and when she opened them, Ad was smiling at her.

"Just a birthday kiss, Miss Lambeth. You know, everyone gets kissed on their birthday, don't you?" he asked in a low teasing voice. "Happy Birthday, Holly," he said, going out the door, "Happy New Year," he called over his shoulder as he went down the schoolhouse steps.

Holly stood there looking after him, not sure how she felt about the kiss or about the man who had kissed her.

PART 5

If suffering is life's teacher,
then let us learn courage, patience,
tenderness, pity, love and faith.

—Anonymous

Chapter 20

*A*fter New Year's, the weather turned bitterly cold. In the morning Holly had to crack a crust of ice off the top of the water in the rain barrel to get enough to bring inside to wash with and to boil for her coffee.

At night the wind whistled around the schoolhouse like a wild thing, crept in through the cracks and around the window frames. It was hard for her to keep the woodbox filled and to have a fire going to heat the classroom in daytime and her own rooms in the evening. Mostly she huddled, wrapped in a quilt, reading or writing her lesson plans; and then got into bed early to stay reasonably warm.

In the morning she would wake, trying to bolster enough grit to get up, teeth chattering and shivering, to start the fires in both stoves. Wearing a shawl, muffler, and gloves, she kept moving until her blood was circulating and it was time for the children to start arriving for school.

To add to Holly's general feeling of let-down during the second week of the New Year, when she went to the post office to pick up her mail, there was an official-looking envelope. Upon opening it she found it was from the District Superintendent of Schools informing her of the date of his visit to Riverbend to evaluate the progress of its pupils in comparison to the rest of the elementary schools of his district.

At first, this threw Holly into a complete panic. Although she had been pleased at the steady, if slow, progress of most of the children, she had suspected they might fall far below some of the other schools in the district. After all, the school had undergone the disruption of changing teachers. How long had they been exposed to the erratic tutelage of Larkin with his frequent absences? Even if he was present physically, due to his hidden drinking he had certainly not been in condition to control and teach.

Holly was well aware of her own inadequacy as a teacher. Even though she was making every effort to increase her own knowledge and skills she feared she would fall far short in the estimation of the District Superintendent. Therefore she began an intense campaign of readying her pupils for the scrutiny of Mr. Lanier and the examination in reading, spelling, and arithmetic he was sure to give them.

Teaching was hard-going after the excitement of the preparation and performance of the Christmas program followed by the ten-day holiday. The children seemed lethargic and uninterested in their lessons. To Holly's bewildered frustration, they seemed to have forgotten everything she had so laboriously taught them before the vacation. School days were narrowed to endless arithmetic drills and tedious spelling tests. At the end of each trying day, Holly felt exhausted.

The closer the date of his coming, the more nervous Holly became. Her prayers became desperate as her temper grew short. Her students paused, stumbled over the simplest words, and even the brightest among them seemed stumped at recitation of times tables they had rattled off with ease before. Daily spelling drills became routine and were greeted with moans each day.

It occurred to Holly that her reputation as a teacher might be at stake. But that was the least consideration. After all this was only a "way station" along her own path of life. Being Riverbend's teacher was not a career goal. It had simply been a means of escape from an unbearable situation. A straw she had grasped at for self-preservation.

Consideration of her own reputation paled beside the benefit and encouragement the children would receive by doing well in the District rolls. As one of the smallest and newest schools, Riverbend's status was in question.

Nerves frayed, Holly woke up on Monday the week of the superintendent's expected visit with a feeling of dread. She dragged herself out to the kitchen. While the water in the kettle boiled, she stared gloomily out the window. The scene did nothing to lift her spirits.

The sky was heavy, gray with clouds, the wind gusty. As she dressed, she heard the patter of rain and knew a rainy day meant the children would be inattentive, restive, and distracted.

As one by one they straggled in, Holly tried to be especially cheerful, promising that if everyone knew their times-tables and spelling words, she would read them another chapter of *Robin Hood*, a story they all particularly enjoyed, both the boys and the girls.

Outside, the wind was rising, hurtling rain in increasing violence against the schoolroom windows. The storm mounted during the early afternoon and, since some of the children had to walk long distances home, Holly decided to dismiss them early.

If Holly had known the storm would work to her advantage, she might have spent a more peaceful night. But she slept fitfully, awakened often by the wind shrieking around the edges of the schoolhouse and rattling the windowpanes. It was still raining hard when she awoke the next morning.

Only a few students showed up for school. These were mostly children who lived in town. The Brysons were the only ones from the outlying farms who came, and that was because their father delivered milk to customers in Riverbend. They told of ankle-deep mud on the roads that had become quagmires and were flooded in some places.

It rained steadily all through the day and throughout the week. On Thursday she received a letter from the District Superintendent stating that due to the weather and the impassable condition of the roads he would be unable to make his annual visit and would have to postpone it until spring. If she hadn't been so relieved Holly might have been angry. All that preparation, all the anguish, all the punishing, grinding repetition she had put the children through for nothing!

As it turned out, it hadn't been useless. Within a week Holly realized that every one of the children had benefited in some way from her insistence on their learning their lessons. Happily she sent away her order for the second volume of the *McGuffy Reader* to replace the ones they had all passed successfully.

Later, when discussing the entire matter with Vi, Holly complained, "And to think of all my prayers about the superintendent's visit going perfectly, and then it never even happened!"

Vi smiled. "Remember, Holly, God *always* answers prayers even if not the way *we* think He will." She paused significantly. "Who do you think is in control of the weather?"

One day, three weeks into the new school term, Holly sensed there was something indisputably wrong. She felt it almost from the moment she opened the school door and rang the bell. The children came in sluggishly, in a disorderly line, shoving and pushing. There seemed to be more confusion and quarreling than usual as they put down lunch buckets and slung their outer garments on the hooks at the back of the room. There was more than the usual amount of noise as they shuffled to their places, banged slates on desk tops, and dropped books.

Holly had difficulty getting the children's attention. The big boys were unusually disruptive during the geography lesson. Every time she turned her back to the classroom to point out something on the map, she would hear scuffling and whispering.

Beside herself as to what to do to get control of her pupils, Holly called an early lunch period. Since it was too cold for them to play outside, she read them aloud a chapter from *Robin Hood*. This time, however, it seemed to have lost its flavor. Even Molly Spencer, one of her best and brightest students, put her head down on her crossed arms on the desk during the reading.

Holly was really concerned as the wall clock inched to dismissal hour. When asked to erase the blackboard, Luke Healy moved without his typical energy, and Holly noticed he was flushed. Little Cissy McKay's eyes were glazed, and when Holly touched her cheek with her hand it felt like fire.

As Holly watched them straggle out the door and walk out of

the schoolyard, she was worried. Were these children all coming down with something?

Within forty-eight hours Holly's premonition came true. Only a handful of children showed up for school the next week. They each told of a brother or sister who was sick. Each day it seemed one or two other children failed to appear. By the end of the week it was known that the cause of these absences was the dread disease—smallpox.

Holly had been vaccinated as a child and so was in no danger of contagion from exposure to her pupils. Since vaccination had been prevalent in America for at least 150 years, Holly wondered why some of the Riverbend people had not been vaccinated. At first no one seemed unduly concerned. The parents Holly spoke to about it seemed more worried about the possibility of diphtheria which had taken its toll of Riverbend children in past years.

But the relative calm with which most people were taking the epidemic was soon altered when the number of deaths became known. First there had been two, then five, suddenly thirteen deaths were reported from the disease. Word spread quickly, rumors of rampant infection followed, and panic came in its wake. Riverbend was swept with a full-scale epidemic.

This change of attitude was further brought to the public concern when Ad printed a letter to the editor from Blaine in boldface type, outlined in black on the front page of the *Monitor* with an editorial admonition to the Town Council to take appropriate action for the protection of the community's health.

Holly read what Blaine had written, with growing alarm,

The present eruptive disease in the patients I am treating now is a far different type of smallpox than any I have seen before. There is no reason to panic if certain preventive, hygienic measures are taken. Homes of people already infected should keep a quarantine, and those not infected should avoid them. I have vaccination serum for those who have not been vaccinated and want to be vaccinated. In the houses where sickness is present, a dish or plate containing chloride of lime or other disinfectant should be placed.

205

The infected person should be kept quiet in bed, cooling drinks offered for fever, mild laxative given if required, liquids should be administered to patient as he can tolerate.
Meticulous cleanliness in the sickroom and in the care of the infected person keeps the disease from worsening. Linens, clothing, bedding, etc., should be washed and changed frequently. To prevent pitting of skin, the most effective remedy is to paint the face with collodion.

Under Mayor Morrison's leadership the council reacted promptly. They established a Board of Health to enforce precautions to contain the spread of the disease. School was suspended, all meetings were banned, yellow flags were placed on the gateposts or porches of all houses where there was infection. Someone suggested the idea of burning pitch pine in the streets to purify the air. Carbolic acid was recommended to disinfect buildings.

When it was realized that whole families were coming down with it and there was no one to care for the sick if the mother of the home was ill, an emergency "pest house" had to be found. The town itself was quarantined with citizens of Riverbend prohibited from traveling into other nearby counties.

The day the mayor's proclamation to close all public gathering places was posted, only five children had showed up for school. As Holly told the subdued little band there would be no school the next day, Suzie Briggs put her head in her hands and began to sob heartbrokenly. Holly was at her side in a minute. Kneeling down next to the child's crouched figure, she put her arms around the little girl's shaking shoulders and tried to soothe her, "As soon as everyone is well again, Suzie, we'll have school again."

Suzie kept on sobbing. Her older sister, May, fighting tears herself, told Holly, "Pa told us to come here, Teacher; said you'd take care of us. He's bad sick, and Ma hasn't moved from her bed all day yesterday."

A chilling realization clutched Holly. These children's parents were desperately sick, perhaps dying, or maybe even dead! They had nowhere to go, no one to take care of them. She would have to check it out but in the meantime—Holly got to her feet and saw the other children all standing staring at her with wide, frightened eyes. She looked from Joel to Cissy, who was clinging to him, to gangly Sam Durkin, looking as lost and scared as the younger ones. With cold certainty Holly knew what she had to do.

Thus, the schoolhouse was turned into a haven for the suddenly homeless as well as an infirmary as one after the other of the children, except Sam, came down with the smallpox. Fortunately, all but Cissy had light cases. The little girl, already weakened by malnutrition and neglect, suffered severely. Holly sent Sam for Blaine while, with the delirious Cissy in her arms, she paced agitatedly and prayed frantically.

At last, Blaine arrived, his coat stained with rain. "Thank God, you've come, Blaine; I think she's very ill." He looked as if he had not eaten nor slept in days. She was weak with relief that he was here and would know what to do.

He took the child out of Holly's arms and laid her gently down on the pallet of quilts Holly had made for her in her own bedroom. Holly hovered anxiously as he examined the little girl. Afterward he turned to Holly and said quietly, "All you can do is keep her as comfortable as possible, I'm afraid."

"What do you mean 'you're afraid'?" Holly whispered, feeling a rush of fear, the beginning of panic.

Blaine looked at Holly with sudden sympathy. Her wide eyes were shadowed with dark circles; she was pale and looked thinner. This woman, hardly more than a girl, had without warning been thrust into a crisis that demanded maturity, judgment, and emotional strength, as well as physical strength. "I mean that Cissy is very weak, Holly; I don't think she has enough strength to fight the infection—"

"Oh, no, Blaine!" Holly put her hand to her mouth.

"You've got to stay calm, Holly, be strong," he told her. "Those children in there are depending on you. I know you'll do fine. I've seen you in emergencies before. And I *know* you *are* strong, competent, brave—"

Holly shook her head, "No," she said. "You're wrong, Blaine. I'm not brave at all. I'm sickeningly frightened."

"That's what real bravery is," Blaine replied quietly. "To be afraid and to go on doing what has to be done, when there is nobody else but you to do it—in spite of how you feel. In wartime, men get medals for that kind of fear."

"Can't you stay longer, Blaine? Can't you do something for Cissy?" Holly pleaded.

"I'm sorry, Holly. Cissy is beyond help now. I can't stay, but I have other sick people I may be able to save."

She was torn between being selfless and selfish. What she really wanted was for Blaine to stay with her, give her the support she needed so badly, but she understood others needed him more. She also realized he was the only doctor in Riverbend and was taxed to the last ebb of his strength. He looked so weary and drawn, so sorrowful, that Holly longed to reach out, comfort him.

After Blaine drove away, Holly went back inside. Sam was standing at the door leading into the classroom, now an improvised dormitory of sick children. Sam, who had been one of the ringleaders of the trip to the saloon the day she had had to march in after them. What a miracle turn-around. He had been a staunch help during these troubled days.

Holly had to remind herself that Ad, too, had been an unexpected source of help. Vaccinated himself, he had no fear of infection and almost daily brought her boxes of needed groceries, medication, and extras.

"Take care of yourself, Holly," he'd told her sternly. "Don't play Florence Nightingale until you drop from exhaustion yourself. That won't do anyone any good." His eyes were concerned. "We don't want to lose you."

"What can I do to help, Miss Lambeth?" Sam asked in his gravely adolescent voice. Distractedly, Holly glanced at him and saw an unexpected understanding in the boy's eyes.

The Briggs girls were recovering and restless, Holly had noticed. They were finding it hard to lie quietly, which was imperative for them to do until all the eruptions had disappeared.

"Thank you, Sam. Maybe you could read to Suzie and May? That would help keep them still," she suggested.

"Yes'm." Sam grinned and started toward the bookshelves.

Holly went back into the bedroom, lifted Cissy, and wrapped her in a blanket; then holding her on her lap, she sat in the rocking chair and gently rocked her. From the other room she could hear Sam haltingly struggle to read *The Adventures in Sherwood Forest*. The child in her arms moaned faintly, and looking down at the once angelic, now blackened face of the little girl, Holly felt stinging tears cloud her eyes and run unchecked down her cheeks. For some reason the words "Suffer the little children . . ." came into Holly's mind. "Oh, dear God, why must these little ones suffer so?" She felt her heart was breaking.

She knew the little girl in her arms had in some way filled the place left lonely when Hetty had deprived her of being with Aurelia. But then Cissy had created her own special niche. After Holly's first week as her teacher, Cissy had never come empty-handed to school. It was only something she found along the way, a bunch of wild flowers clutched in her tiny, birdlike hand, or a pretty rock, or a handful of acorns. It didn't matter what it was, Holly thought, choked with grief—it was a gift of love. A gift that was given completely without any thought other than to be just that—an expression of love. "Unless you become as a little child . . ."—Cissy had taught her so much about love, real love, unconditional love, the only kind of love that really mattered.

Holly never knew how long she sat there rocking Cissy, humming the old familiar hymns of her childhood. Outside, the daylight faded, and the room slowly filled with shadows. She could hear the murmur of children's voices in the next room, and she thought she should really put Cissy down and go see about getting some kind of light supper for the recuperating patients. Cissy was very still, and Holly's arm had grown numb holding her head. Instinctively, Holly held her breath and, in a minute, realized that the little sufferer was no longer breathing.

Sometime later, Blaine returned. When she heard his buggy wheels, Holly threw a shawl around her shoulders and stepped out onto the porch. When he reached the top step, she told him, "Cissy's gone, Blaine; she died this afternoon."

Without a word, Blaine took Holly gently into his arms. She leaned against his shoulder, felt his hand stroke her hair, heard him murmuring her name. Holly let the tears come at last, and Blaine's embrace tightened. She felt the blessed comfort of his arms holding her, and from deep within her came an aching to stay within his embrace, draw from his strength—always. Words rushed up inside her, begging to be said. Words of love and need and longing. Holly had to bite her lip to keep from saying them. Finally, she gave a long shaky sigh and lifted her head.

"I haven't told Joel yet," she said. "I don't know how."

Blaine wiped her cheeks with his thumbs and said softly, "You'll find the right way. I trust you." Then Blaine took her arm, saying, "Come outside with me, Holly, there's something else you have to know." Blaine's voice sounded infinitely weary. Holly followed him to the porch, wondering what new tragedy he was about to tell her.

Blaine's voice was heavy. "I've just come from the McKay's cabin—Joel and Cissy's parents are dead, Holly."

"Oh, no, Blaine!"

"Maybe Cissy's better off. . . ." Blaine shook his head sadly.

Holly was too stunned to speak at first, then she whispered, "What will become of Joel?"

"I don't know."

"Why is life so hard?" she asked brokenly.

"I don't know that, either, Holly."

She searched his face for another answer but saw only the sorrow and shock in his eyes. With sudden insight Holly realized that Blaine was vulnerable to pain and unanswerable questions, too. Finally he said, "I have to go, Holly."

"Yes, I know," she said with difficulty.

"Try to get some rest. It won't do if *you* get sick," he said as he turned up his coat collar and went out into the rainy night.

Holly felt a tremendous ache to see him go. The truth she had denied so long to herself clearly surfaced as she watched him wearily mount into his buggy. She knew she loved Blaine whether or not her love would ever be returned.

The *Monitor* posted the number of cases and also repeated the information Blaine had given to the paper so people would be aware of the symptoms and know what to do if they or members of their families fell ill.

When it became necessary to clear out one of the older buildings in town as a place where victims with no one to care for them could be placed, this was also reported along with the news that some nurses had come from Portland to help in the emergency.

A dark pall seemed to settle over the town, streets were empty, business in the downtown stores of all kinds was practically nil, people only ventured out for the most basic supplies, afraid of contamination or infection from others about to succumb. Social life of every kind had totally ceased, there were no gatherings of any kind—not the sewing circle, quilting bees, or church meetings of the Missionary Society or Bible studies. Fear ran amok, no class of society was protected from this dread scourge. It struck rich and poor alike, and although it might be possible for the more affluent to nurse their sick at home, provide a few more comforts, the dreadful ravages of the disease itself knew no social barriers.

The stagecoach now only brought mail, and no longer did drivers linger at the Doggone Best or the Nugget to revive themselves. Instead, they made their stop as brief as possible in the place now known throughout the state as "plague town." Once the ban was posted on people from Riverbend leaving because of the fear of other counties in the area that they might spread the disease, there were few passengers on the stage.

The "pest houses" were crowded. Mops and pails smelling of chloride and alcohol could hardly contend with the peculiar smell of the illness itself. Makeshift beds of straw pallets were laid end on end beside cots; as the dead were lifted off and out, new cases were placed upon hastily cleaned ones.

The hillside cemetery was the only place in all Riverbend that saw daily activity. With gravediggers working round-the-clock, the Town Council allotted two new parcels of land for cemetery space, which had been previously earmarked for the expansion of business in town when the railroad came.

All day long on Main Street the steady sound of the hammering of nails on wood could be heard as Joe and Bill Slyder

211

made coffins, stacking them and then unloading them onto carts almost as soon as they were finished.

There were now more obituary notices in the *Monitor* but fewer flowery eulogies written by relatives of their deceased, and funerals were quick and without many mourners outside the immediate families; sadly enough, fewer and fewer people showed up as whole families were stricken and perished.

The only light in the darkened *Monitor* office wavered as the solitary oil lamp on the editor's desk sputtered. Ad looked up, threw down his pen, and rubbed his eyes wearily. Then he reread what he had just written: "This is a town under siege. The smell of burning pitch through the night is a macabre reminder that people—children—are dying—"

He planned to dispatch this article in the morning to his former editor at the San Francisco newspaper where he used to be a reporter. How could he make anyone understand what it was like to live in a "plague town," to stir their compassion, their goodwill, to compel them to dig into their pockets and to send much needed medicine and supplies to this beleaguered community?

He ran his hand through his thick dark hair. His neck and shoulders ached; he straightened and stretched. Just then he heard a plaintive *meow*, and Chester leaped onto the pile of papers in front of him, his paws skidding a little, then made a dainty leap into Ad's lap. Absently, Ad's long fingers kneaded the soft fur of the tabby, who settled down with a contented purr.

A sizzling sound alerted Ad that the coffee pot he had set on top of the potbelly stove had boiled over, and he got to his feet, unceremoniously dumping Chester. The cat voiced an indignant yowl and marched off, tail switching, to find a more accommodating place to snooze.

Ad lifted the blue-speckled pot, stained by a dozen or more similar accidents of forgetfulness, but as he did, he burned his fingers and swore. He grabbed a greasy cloth hanging near the handpress mainly used to wipe the printer's devil's inky fingers, wrapped it around the pot handle, and poured himself a cup of the foaming brew. While waiting for it to cool so as not to scald

212

his tongue as badly as he had his fingers, Ad stood morosely staring out into the darkened street. Ironically, on this Saturday night, when the saloons would usually have done a "land office" business, Main Street was deserted. The lights from the pitch fires mounted on hastily erected posts, cast an eerie illumination on the street where no one walked.

He hoped he had made the situation, the circumstances he had written about, real to the people who would read them. But how could he adequately convey the courage and selflessness of some, the humanness of the citizens of Riverbend during this crisis?

Ad's thoughts turned to his friend Blaine, who had worked tirelessly and without thought of his own health among the stricken people of this deadly plague. And Holly Lambeth—something uncharacteristically soft and tender touched Ad's heart thinking of how Holly had reacted during this time. Who would ever have dreamed she had the strength, stamina, and fortitude needed to care for those children? He had been wrong about Hollis Lambeth, and Ad wasn't usually quick to admit mistakes. In fact, he had always rather prided himself on having correct first impressions. But Holly had turned out to be no pampered Southern belle. She was—in Ad's opinion—the genuine article, a real heroine.

Holly woke in the gray, chilly dawn. She hadn't slept much. Not that she wasn't tired these nights; she just wasn't sleepy. It was more than physical. It was a feeling of exhausted weariness that came from some deep inner core of hopelessness and sadness. Cissy's death and Joel's heartbrokenness had made her aware of the uncertainty and fragility of life.

She lay in bed listening to the rain, knowing that it fell, too, on the new little grave on the hillside. She closed her eyes again, lying inert for a few minutes, unwilling to get up and face yet another terrible day, one more in an endless line of unendurable days. And yet, she had endured, she *had* survived. Was it that Blaine had expressed his faith in her that had kept her going more than her own determination? Why was his opinion of her so important?

At last, reluctantly, she pulled herself up, went over to the

213

window, pushed back the curtain and saw that the day looked as gray and cheerless as she felt. Then all at once she saw someone swathed in a long cloak turning into the schoolyard, carrying two large baskets. There was something very familiar about that walk—the figure coming toward the schoolhouse.

Grabbing her shawl and wrapping it about her, Holly rushed to the door and stood barefoot and shivering in her nightgown as Vi mounted the steps. She looked up and smiled, "Thought you could use some help," she said.

"Oh, Vi, you better not come in here, we're *quarantined!*" Holly protested.

"That's all right. I've been vaccinated! My father was a pharmacist, you know, and he insisted on it. I've also had some experience nursing children."

"Oh, Vi, thank you!" cried Holly giving her friend a welcoming hug. "You're an answer to prayer. And I thought God wasn't listening!"

One night not long after Cissy's death, Holly was roused from an exhausted sleep by an insistent pounding on her door. She threw back the covers, struggled out of bed, flung her wrapper around her, and hurried to answer. An ashen-faced Ned, carrying Teddy and holding Aurelia by the hand, stood in the eerie light of a cold moon.

"Holly, I hate to bother you like this, but Hetty's real sick. I'm afraid it's the smallpox or maybe something worse. She's out of her head with fever, and I thought I better get the kids out of the house. I didn't know what else to do but bring them here. Then I've got to go for Doc."

"Of course, Ned," Holly said. "Here let me take Teddy. And Aurelia, honey, you come inside with me. They can stay here as long as they need to, Ned," she assured him.

"Thank you, Holly, I can't tell you—"

"Don't try, Ned. You just go on, find Blaine, and I hope—I pray Hetty's all right."

Looking at the calendar, a dazed and worn-out Holly suddenly realized that six weeks had passed. It was as though she had been living in a long, dark tunnel. Most of the children were now in various stages of recovery. But this was almost harder than when they were feeling really sick. They were cranky, listless, homesick, as well as easily bored, easily upset. It was hard just keeping them amused and quiet until they were completely well or their families were recovered sufficiently to come to get them.

Vi went home, and one by one the other children were fetched home by grateful parents until there was no one left but—Joel.

As the last wagon with the last happily reunited child and parent drove out of the schoolyard, Holly saw Joel's small forlorn figure standing at the schoolroom window watching it leave.

The harsh reality of the little boy's fate gripped Holly. With a wrenching sensation she asked herself, *What was to become of Joel?*

Chapter 21

*B*y the end of February the epidemic had subsided sufficiently for the town to resume its normal activity. The
temporary infirmary, where the worst cases had been put and
for those who had no one at home to care for them, was closed.
Within another few weeks the Health Board, after enforcing all
the emergency mandates to prevent the further spread of smallpox, was dissolved.

Relatives had come to settle affairs, sell the property and
belongings of their family's victims of the deadly smallpox
scourge, and to take orphaned children with them when they
left. However, there were some who had no relatives; no one to
provide them with care or give them a home.

Joel McKay was one of those. He had remained at the schoolhouse with Holly, and no immediate action had been suggested
for his future. Through Geneva Healy, Holly found out that the
Town Council had already sent some of the children orphaned
early at the height of the epidemic to the orphanage at the
county seat. The word "orphanage" sent a cold shiver of alarm
through Holly's heart.

Joel in an *orphanage!* She could not imagine that lively,
inquisitive, precocious child institutionalized, regimented, and
made to conform to the necessary rules of a place already
crowded with too many children— no individualized attention,

no affectionate care. The thought of this little boy who had grown so dear to her in such a situation was too much for Holly.

School was not yet back in session on the March day when Ned had come to get Aurelia and Teddy. Joel was at the Healys', playing with their children, and Holly was alone. Although Hetty was still weak, she had recovered enough to want the children home. "I don't know how I can ever thank you, Holly," Ned said. "We are both very grateful. As soon as Hetty is able, I know she wants to thank you in person."

"Oh, Ned, I was just happy I could help," Holly reassured him as she hugged both the children good-bye.

In spite of Ned's assurances, she didn't count too much on hearing from Hetty, but it didn't bother her. Her mind was too preoccupied with another problem at the moment. What to do about Joel? She decided to go and talk to Vi about it. Vi would give her good advice.

Seated in Vi's sewing room, while Vi sat and continued to work at her treadle machine, Holly voiced all her jumbled thoughts. Finally, she sighed and said, "I can't just let him go to an orphanage, Vi. He's too special. He'd be lost there, I don't know what would happen to him."

"Lots of children grow up in an orphanage, Holly. They seem to survive. They're not starved or beaten, they're taught a trade. It might be the best thing for Joel. Anyway, what can you do about it? Ad had a piece in the paper yesterday about the children who had lost parents in the epidemic. They're now wards of the county, didn't you know? The Town Council decides what to do, where they go."

"No!" Holly exclaimed emphatically. "I can't possibly allow them to send Joel away! He's lived all his life here in Riverbend, all his friends are here—*I'm* here!"

Vi stopped pushing the treadle and held the wheel. "*You're* here? What do you mean, Holly?"

Holly stood up and started pacing back and forth, then looked out the window. It had begun to rain. She watched the rain pelting the old leaves on the oak tree in Vi's yard, and as they hit the window they ran down the glass pane in tiny rivulets. "I guess I mean I'm here for Joel," she said slowly, then turned around and faced Vi. "I could adopt Joel."

Vi's mouth parted in surprise. "You can't do that. You're not married; the Town Council would never place a child, especially a little boy, with a single woman."

"Why not, I'd like to know?" demanded Holly. "What about all the widows in the world who raise their children alone?"

"That's different."

"Why is it different? Most of the time they have to work to support their fatherless families. I work, I teach, and Joel would be right there with me all day."

Vi stared at her. "But I thought you were leaving in June to go back to Willow Springs. Do you mean if you got Joel, you'd stay here?"

Holly started pacing again. "I don't know. I mean, I hadn't thought that far ahead. But, I do know I'm going to try to adopt Joel." She halted, whirled around, and said, "Why aren't you supporting me, Vi? *You* brought up your daughter by yourself, didn't you?"

"It wasn't easy, Holly," Vi said quietly. "It was, in fact, very hard."

The two women stared at each other for a full minute without saying anything more. Then Vi said gently, "Let's go have a cup of tea, and I'll tell you how it was with me."

An hour later Holly walked back to the schoolhouse in the pouring rain under the umbrella Vi had lent her. The story that Vi had told her weighed heavily on her heart. It had made her admire her friend even more. It seems Vi had been the late child of middle-aged parents, was the proverbial "apple of their eye." They lived comfortably in a small town where her father, a pharmacist, was a well-respected pillar of the community and her mother a prominent church leader. Vi was given everything. When at a young age she had shown musical talent, she was given piano lessons; later she played the organ in church. Under all this loving care she had grown up in every way a model daughter.

Then the summer she was nineteen, Vi's whole life changed. A handsome pharmaceutical salesman with smooth manners, irresistible charm, came to town. Vi fell head over heels in love. Her parents were terrified of losing her and discouraged the romance. But dazzled and headstrong, Vi agreed to elope with the man. Only weeks later she found herself deserted in a San Francisco hotel with just a note of explanation that the man at least had the decency to leave for her. It revealed the sad truth that he was already married.

Vi was devastated, especially when soon she discovered she was pregnant. She could not return home because she knew it would break her parents' hearts, disgrace them. For days she walked the city streets dazed, depressed, desperate. Finally, she apprenticed herself to a dressmaker, who took a liking to her and when her pregnancy became advanced, offered to help Vi. This kind woman allowed Vi to continue working out of her home after the baby was born. Nearly a year later, she secretly contacted a friend in her hometown to get an idea of what the situation with her parents might be. To her sorrow she found out that her father had had a stroke and died and her mother was in fragile health and doctors felt she had not long to live. Vi knew if she made the decision to go home with her baby, that would be the last straw for her aging mother. It would be far better to let her die in some peace without ever knowing. So she wrote, saying that she was well and happy and would be home when she could. Her mother died without ever knowing the truth.

"I hated living in the city, and I didn't think it was a good place to raise a child," Vi told Holly. "By this time I had become an expert seamstress, so I knew I could make a living for us. So I packed Avesta and myself up and bought a stagecoach ticket to—"

"Riverbend—'the end of the line'!" Holly finished for her.

"Well, yes, that was almost the way I decided to come," Vi agreed. "I wanted to go somewhere where no one knew me, no one knew my story, where I could create a whole new life for myself and my daughter."

"And you did," Holly said. "So, why can't I?"

"Holly, I've just told you the bare facts of my story. I haven't told you what it's like to live with no family, no background, to have to be careful what you say, what you mention, or that you might slip and name a town or a place that someone can connect with your past—I have made up a life for my daughter, too. I don't want *my* mistakes to ruin her life."

"How did you manage, Vi? I mean, the lonely nights, the times when you needed someone to turn to?"

"I had to build on a faith that I'd almost lost," Vi sighed. "I literally spent nights reading the Bible almost blindly, crying out for help." She paused. "Remember, when I told you to read until some verse or even just a line of Scripture quickens to you? As if it was meant for you? Well, finally it was one from Isaiah that spoke to my heart and that I came to lean on—Isaiah 54:4: 'Fear not, you will not be put to shame, for you will forget the shame of your youth and you shall not remember the reproach of your widowhood. For your Maker is your husband, the Lord of hosts is His name. . . .' I just kept repeating those verses over and over."

Holly reached the schoolhouse and hurried up the porch steps, closed the umbrella, left it on the porch, and went inside. She was conscious of a new hope, a new determination. There must be a way to keep Joel, and she was going to find it. Almost from the first day of school she had felt a special bond between herself and the little boy. It had grown even stronger through the last few weeks, after the epidemic, certainly after Cissy's death and the death of his parents. Whatever she had to do to convince people that she was capable of bringing up a child, Holly was determined to do.

And if she couldn't—well, then she would take Joel home to Willow Springs. She felt certain that her mother and father would make him welcome as part of the family. Holly tried to imagine how a homecoming like that would be. Would there be as much gossip about her return as there had been before her leaving?

Holly's imagination took her no further. There was no use imagining circumstances that might never happen. She should concentrate on the positive. Take the first step, whatever that was, to adopt Joel, then worry about what to do next.

The first thing she had to do to reinforce her qualifications with the Council was to prove that she could offer Joel a stable home. For that she would have to apply to have her teaching contract renewed for another year. That would establish the fact that she would have a regular income and a permanent place to live.

It surprised Holly to discover that she had no qualms whatsoever about writing a letter of intent to teach at Riverbend for the coming year. She had no misgivings, no lingering regret that she wouldn't be returning to Willow Springs in June. It was the right thing to do. If there was a reason other than to ensure the granting of her petition to adopt Joel, she was not yet ready to admit it. It was her only purpose for wanting to remain in Riverbend, she told herself as she filled out the application to the School Board.

When Holly told the Healys what she intended to do, she asked Matt how she should go about petitioning the Town Council to grant the adoption and name her Joel's legal guardian.

Matt shook his head, warning her warily that nothing like that had ever come before the Council before. That did not deter Holly's resolve. She immediately followed his instructions as to how to place an item on the Council's agenda for decision at the weekly Town Council meeting. This was duly printed in the *Monitor* in the regular column as "News of Public Interest"—the usual procedure of publishing the business before the Council—in case anyone wanted to speak for or against the item.

On his way out to the schoolhouse, Ad felt strangely disoriented. He was still ambivalent about the decision he'd come to after a great deal of uncharacteristic self-debate. He left Main Street and turned onto the road leading out of the center of town, gave the horse its head, sat back in his saddle, and let his mind wander back to almost a year ago—to the first time he had set eyes on Holly Lambeth, just off the stagecoach, the evening she arrived in Riverbend.

He had known at first glance, *here* was a real lady. There had been an unmistakable aura of class about her from her quality clothes to the look of breeding and background about her, an air of independence and spirit that Ad particularly admired in a woman.

But for all her independent spirit and determination, Ad knew the odds could be stacked against her. No matter that it was now 1883, people in Riverbend had not all moved ahead with the times. In some places, the cities, for example, women were allowed all sorts of privileges once limited to men. Why there was even a woman reporter in the city room at the San Francisco newspaper where Ad had worked before coming here. Women owned their own businesses, negotiated their own contracts, managed their own property, bought and sold real estate. But here—Ad knew firsthand, some of the attitudes about a woman's "proper place" were still archaic. Unless there was a man—a husband—in the picture, Ad doubted that Holly's chance to adopt the little boy was very good.

He had come to admire Holly, her intelligence, the strength that she had shown during the epidemic, as much as he enjoyed her wit and her clever conversations. More than that, Ad knew he had come to care deeply for Holly. It was more than friendship if he allowed himself the truth. Maybe it wasn't love, but it was a deep affection that maybe eventually—who knows? Much as it went against Ad's long-held freedom, the kind of future he had always taken for granted, he could not let Holly face the possibility of losing Joel. If this step could help—even if it changed his life forever, which it certainly would, it would be worth it.

Ad turned his horse into the schoolyard, dismounted, and slung the reins over the hitching post. He brushed dust from his knees with his wide-brimmed hat, straightened his string tie, and checked his vest buttons, then marched toward the porch, took the steps two at a time, and knocked at the door.

When Holly came to the door, Ad was newly conscious of how attractive she was. Even with her rich brown hair slightly disheveled and a smudge of chalk on her cheek, she looked utterly charming.

Feeling suddenly awkward under her curiously direct gaze, he said, "Hello, Holly, I'd like to talk to you about something. But if you're busy, I could come back another time?"

"Do come in, Ad. I'm not really busy. Just the usual after-school cleanup, wiping blackboards, filling inkwells, and—what I have to do can wait. Come on in. What do you want to talk to me about?"

Ad twirled his hat absent-mindedly as he glanced around the schoolroom. He hadn't been in it since New Year's Day. He remembered how they had discussed what the coming year might hold for both of them. That seemed a long time ago, now. *A lot has happened since*, he thought, his eyes coming to rest again on Holly. He took a few steps around looking at everything: the children's pictures, the bunches of flowers in glass jars on the windowsills, a low tier of shelves filled with books behind the teacher's polished desk.

"Looks nice, Holly. You've sure done a lot, made some real changes," he commented, continuing to slowly circle the room.

"Thanks, Ad. The children help. It's fun," she said, giving a final swipe to the blackboard before wiping her hands on a cloth and folding it. "Why don't we go into my parlor, and I'll make us some tea? We can talk in there," she suggested, leading the way through the door into her own part of the building.

Here, too, Ad saw things he had never noticed before. Crisp curtains hung at the windows, some plants and flowers in a pretty bowl on the round table covered with a bright cloth. All the touches Holly had made to make it, well— cozy, homelike. An alarm sounded in his brain, and he shut it off quickly. Isn't that what women do? The "nesting instinct"?

Leaning against the doorframe, he watched Holly go about setting the kettle on the stove, getting down the tin canister of tea, and spooning out tea in careful measures into the teapot, enjoying the sheer gracefulness of her movements, Ad thought Holly looked especially pretty today.

She wore a simply styled dress the color of a robin's egg, its fitted bodice showing off a waist that Ad could surely span with both hands. Her hair was swept back and up from her neck, and here, too, the curls had escaped, making it hard to resist the temptation to run his finger the length of its slender column. Ironically, he wondered if perhaps Fate had ordained it that way to stiffen his resolve, the purpose of this visit?

223

"Cream and sugar?" Holly's question caught Ad off-guard, and he was brought abruptly back from the contemplation of her pretty neck to stammer, "Sugar, no cream."

"Tea's brewed," she announced and turned from the stove, her face flushed from the heat. Placing the teapot on the table, Holly motioned Ad to draw up a chair. "Now, what did you want to talk about?" Holly asked stirring her tea and fixing him with an interested look.

So, here it was, the moment that he had debated over and finally had come to the conclusion to act upon. But, not quite yet—

"I got an interesting letter the other day," he began, picking up his cup and studying the amber contents. "It seems I've won some kind of award."

"An award? How wonderful, Ad. What kind of award?"

"A rather nice one, and it has a bonus attached." Ad's voice betrayed a little of his own pride and excitement. "The series of articles I wrote about Riverbend during the smallpox epidemic and about how we survived it, about the extraordinary heroism of some of the people—" He let this sink in for a moment, gazing at Holly. "At any rate, it did have the effect of touching people and resulted in much of the help the community got—as you know, medical supplies came from the city, along with nurses and nuns to help with the sick." He shrugged. "Well, you know all this, but the main thing is that I've been offered a job. Not my old one but a better one, as a feature writer; they've even suggested a regular column, at a lot more money."

"Well, that's grand, Ad, I'm so happy for you."

"At least it means my exile is over."

"You mean you'll be leaving?"

"Yes. Of course, the job is in Monterey, down the peninsula from San Francisco. A smaller newspaper than the one where I worked before as a reporter in the city—but I'll have more clout and—" He halted. "But that's not really what I came to talk about, although I wanted to tell you that I would be going at the end of the month."

Holly leaned forward, her expression interested, slightly

regretful. "People here will miss you, Ad. Certainly at the paper—we *all* will."

"But you're leaving, too, aren't you, Holly? You only meant to stay until the end of the school year, right? Surely *you* never intended to stay in this backwater town."

"Well . . ." Her voice faded uncertainly.

"That's what I wanted to talk to you about—actually. Why don't we both leave—together?"

"*We?* Together?" It was a puzzled echo.

"Yes, you and I—and Joel," he finished slapping his hand on the table.

"Joel?"

"Look, Holly, I'm asking you to marry me. That way there'll be no problem about your keeping Joel. I mean, how can the Town Council refuse to let a married couple adopt a little boy?"

Holly's eyes opened wide, startled, then softened and warmed. For a moment Ad saw sudden hope leap into them.

"Ad, what a generous offer," she stammered. "I'm touched—flattered, actually." Ad shook his head as if to deny that, but she went on. "I realize what prompted you to make it and I cannot tell you how much it means to me that you—well, that you cared enough to do so. . . ."

Holly pushed back her chair, stood up, walked over to the window, and looked out. The last of the snow had melted; here and there tufts of new grass could be seen thrusting through the patches of brown earth, and the faintest hint of green buds were appearing on the trees. Both Vi and Blaine had told her that spring in Oregon was glorious.

If only Blaine had come to her with this proposal—*that* would have been easy. She had at last stopped denying her feelings for him. With Blaine, everything would be assured. She could happily stay in Riverbend, continue teaching, and together they could make an ideal home for Joel. *They* shared the same values, faith, the desire to make their lives meaningful, to count for something. Instead, it was Ad. Dear Ad. Her heart was deeply touched by his offer. It wasn't that she did not appreciate his motives. She did. But if she accepted it—on any basis—it would mean moving with him to California, starting all over in a new place, in a new role, and with a man she couldn't give her wholehearted love to—couldn't, because that love belonged to someone else.

What Ad was offering was tempting. She knew what he said was true. If she were married, there would be no question of the Town Council's letting her adopt Joel. Alone—there was the risk of losing him.

After talking with Vi, Holly had felt strong and brave and sure, but now the doubts and uncertainty returned full force, disquieting that hard-earned confidence. Ad, who certainly had his "finger on the pulse" of things in this town, knew how things worked, understood the probable masculine viewpoint held by the members of the Town Council, knew what her chances were. Was it *because* he had weighed them and found them wanting in this that he had gallantly proposed marriage?

On the other hand, was Ad's proposal the answer she had been praying for? "God Will Provide." That reassurance of Scripture for every need came into her mind. Was a *husband* what God was providing?

"You don't have to give me your answer right away, you know, Holly," Ad said and his voice sounded both hesitant and a little offended. "Take your time and think about it. . . ." He paused, then said, "Holly, how often have you told me that you've worried about going back to Willow Springs? That you thought you might have changed too much to fit back into that pattern?" He let this sink in for a moment, then he demanded: "You want Joel, don't you? And you're not sure the Town Council will permit an unmarried woman to adopt a child, are you? What I'm offering you is the best possible answer, isn't it?"

"If that were all there were to it," Holly said slowly, then she turned from the window to face him again saying, "But, Ad, that *isn't* all—"

A glint of humor showed in his gray eyes as he said, "I felt there was a 'but' coming."

Holly smiled. "Yes, an important 'but'—"

Ad's expression was a mixture of chagrin and reproach as he answered for her, "You don't love me."

Holly hesitated. Her feelings for Ad were almost love. She

226

understood and appreciated what the offer he was making her cost a man like him, to whom marriage meant giving up his cherished freedom. Also, Adam was offering to take her away from a town that she had never wanted to come to in the first place, from people who held her destiny in their hands, people she was afraid had too narrow a vision so that they would rather see a little boy placed in an orphanage than with an unmarried woman he loved and trusted. Accepting Adam's offer would give her that chance.

But did Adam really love her? Her woman's instinct told her Adam found her attractive, intelligent, enjoyable to be with, amusing. . . . But more important, even than that, did *she* love him? Enough for marriage? No matter what the reason?

As she hesitated Adam told her, "You know a lot of marriages are based on a lot less than we have, Holly. We're good friends, aren't we?" Ad asked, then got to his feet. "There's no hurry. Think about it—"

"Vi would say—*pray* about it," Holly said softly.

At these words Holly saw that veil drop over Ad's eyes. It was the same silent closure she sensed in him whenever she brought up anything about God or prayer or faith. In that moment, Holly realized she did not really know how Ad felt about the important things of life—at least the things that were becoming more and more important to her.

A smile touched Ad's mouth. "Whatever—think, *pray,* make a list of the pros and cons of my—proposal."

Had he almost said *"proposition"?* Like a business contract? Holly wondered. Was this *that* kind of an arrangement to Ad? How did he *really* feel about her?

He picked up his hat and moved toward the door, saying, "Well, I better be heading back to town. I have a letter to write—replying to the editor at the Monterey paper, accepting the position they've offered me. They want me by the end of the month. When I go, I'd like you to go with me, Holly—and Joel, too, of course."

After Ad left, Holly had the urge to rush over to Vi's, tell her of Ad's proposal, and beg her advice. But something checked her.

No one could make this decision but she—with God's help. The rest of her life—and Joel's—depended on her choice. If she accepted Ad, Joel's adoption would be guaranteed. If not, his future would hang in the balance. It would be up to her to convince the Town Council that she, a single woman, was capable of raising a child—a male child—by herself.

Involuntarily, a deep shudder shook her. Her thoughts went back. He had said, "We're good friends, aren't we?" But what was that friendship based upon? She and Ad had been first drawn together by a mutual feeling—the bond of "exile mentality." In a way, Ad had always mentally had "his hand on the doorknob," he was always on his way out, he had never allowed himself to put down roots in Riverbend—or anywhere else, for that matter. He didn't want permanence or commitment. And Holly realized this was exactly what she *did* want.

Although Ad might provide for her earthly needs, a home, protection, allow her to have Joel—and they could go away together, to a new place, start a new life—was that all that was necessary? And even if Ad thought he wanted that now—was that only temporary? Would that last? Could Ad, in all sincerity, all honesty, promise lifelong fidelity? Was he willing to stand before God and make the vows for an enduring relationship: "for better or for worse, for richer or for poorer, in sickness and in health"? Was what he felt for her—affection, respect, *friendship*—enough? For both of them? For *her?*

Holly knew it was not. In her heart of hearts she knew what she really wanted in a marriage, in a husband. And she knew Adam was not the one who could fulfill that meeting of mind, soul, and spirit that she knew now was what she really yearned for in a relationship. And she knew that without it, she would never be satisfied. She and Adam would always be "unequally yoked." How could she commit her life to someone who tolerated but did not share her deepest beliefs?

The following week she sent Ad a note at the *Monitor* asking him to come out on Saturday.

She met him at the door. "Hello, Ad, let's go into the kitchen," she suggested, leading the way.

Ad looked wary as he came into the room. He dragged one of

the chairs out from the table, straddled it, leaned his arms on the back, and looked at Holly.

"I have a feeling the other boot's going to drop," he said with an attempt at humor. "As I remember, our last conversation ended with the word 'but.' I suppose I'm now going to hear the rest of the sentence. I believe I'd just suggested that you don't love me. Am I right?"

Holly said gently, "Ad, I *do* love you—*but*—," here she smiled a little, "it's not the kind of love I believe it takes to marry someone. It's different from that but just as real."

Ad scowled. "Are we talking about the same thing?"

"Maybe not, but I think so," Holly paused, then continued, "I know and *you* know, too, a marriage has to be built on strongly held mutual beliefs. On faith. Some common center." She chose her words delicately, before going on. "I realize you don't share some of the things that are basic to my life, things I didn't even realize meant so much to me as they do. The epidemic was a kind of turning point for me. This whole year has changed me—deeply. You were right when you reminded me that I might not be able to go back to Willow Springs. Maybe I've changed too much—but I can't marry you, either."

A silence fell between them. Holly's eyes blurred as she looked at Ad across the table where they had sat so often talking, discussing, arguing. Even as her tears distorted his physical image, Holly saw him more clearly than she had ever done before. They had both walked together through a time of testing, and both had seen the realities of life and death, and both of them had been changed by it. Holly saw in Adam the sterling qualities that his old aloof cynicism had hidden before. She knew him now for his true self— strong, caring, fearless in the face of the most terrible possibilities.

Ad stared at a point over Holly's head as if he could not look at her directly while he absorbed everything she had said. Then after a minute or so, he leveled his glance and really looked across the table at her. The woman he saw was a different person from the person he had seen when he first met Hollis Lambeth, newly arrived in Riverbend. He saw a face, more interesting than beautiful; those eyes he had always found so extraordinary—greenish, golden brown—now blazed with honesty. There was no flirtatiousness in them now, no awareness of her own charm, nor artifice in her manner. Here was a true lady, tested in the fire of trials she had never expected to encounter, a woman of gallantry and character.

With a sudden unforeseen wrenching of his heart, Ad found himself wishing that she *did* love him. After another minute he spoke, "I got a letter from the editor of the paper in Monterey. They want me sooner than I thought at first. In fact, they want me as soon as I can come. So . . . ," he said slowly, "since there's really nothing to keep me here now, I guess I'll write them back and then . . . go."

Ad got up and Holly walked with him to the door. He put out his hand, clasped her small one in both his, and looked long and deeply into that face he had come to admire—yes, love. Something good had come out of their meeting, knowing each other, for both of them. He would not have gone through life without having known her, unaware of what she stood for, heedless of what was meaningful to Hollis Lambeth.

"Sure you won't change your mind?" he asked, half-teasingly, half-seriously.

"No, I'm sure," she smiled back at him.

They stood there for a full moment looking at each other, then Ad said almost sadly, "I'll never forget you, Holly. That's a promise."

"Nor I you," she said softly, meaning it.

"Good-bye then. I hope things work out for you—about Joel, I mean," he said. He made a slight movement toward her, and for a minute she thought he would kiss her, but he just smoothed back his hair with one hand, put on his hat, and went down the steps and across the schoolyard, where he had left his horse.

As he mounted his horse, turned, and headed back to town, Ad felt a mixture of disappointment and relief. He understood Holly's reasoning. They *did* hold different values. Her life pattern was different from the one he had always followed, one of self-sufficiency, independence, uncommitted; he could never follow hers unquestioningly. And yet, he believed with a convinced certainty that hers was the better way. But to his regret it was not his, nor ever would be.

Seeing him ride away, Holly realized she *would* always remember Adam Corcoran—debonair, skeptical, soft-hearted, reckless, courageous, all the things that made him who he was— and made him unacceptable as a husband.

PART 6

End of the line!

Chapter 22

*J*ust as school was closing one afternoon, Matt Healy showed up. "Official business, Miss Lambeth," he said, handing her an envelope.

Upon opening it, Holly learned that the hearing on her petition to adopt Joel was scheduled for the next Town Council meeting, at which time they would consider and make a decision.

"What do you think, Matt, will they grant it?" she asked as she replaced the letter into its envelope.

"I couldn't say," Matt said, but his expression was doubtful. "There's never been such a thing come up since I've been on the Council. There's many would say it ain't fittin' for a—if you'll excuse the term—a spinster lady to raise a child. But then, on the other hand, seeing you're a teacher, used to children—well, I jest dunno."

Matt's ambiguous opinion did not do much to bolster Holly's optimism. However, she tried to distract herself by finishing up the year's work and issuing "promotion" certificates for the children to take home when school closed for the summer. As she filled in the names of Eliza and Annie Bates, Tom and Michael Healy onto the cards in her best swirly writing one afternoon, she could not help wonder who would be checking them over, planning lessons next fall when school reopened.

Holly put down her pen stared pensively out the window. Her own plans were uncertain. It all depended on the decision rendered on Joel by the Town Council. If they didn't allow her to adopt Joel—she thrust the thought away. They *had* to. But if they *wouldn't*—the possibility persisted—what would she do?

Her mind suddenly in turmoil, Holly took up her pen again, determined to concentrate on the promotion cards, when she saw Ned's wagon coming into the schoolyard. But it wasn't Ned driving, it was Hetty! Holly dropped her pen with a sputter of ink and almost overturned the inkwell. She hadn't seen Hetty since before the epidemic. When Ned came to take Aurelia and Teddy home again, he said that Hetty was still very weak but recovering. Of course, that had been weeks ago. Now it was April. Why had Hetty come now?

Holly watched as Hetty got slowly down from the wagon seat. Holly hurried to open the schoolhouse door just as Hetty was coming up the steps. Under her arm Hetty was carrying something wrapped in brown paper. When she saw Holly, she halted; her hand went out to hold onto the railing as if for support. Hetty was pale but evidently unscarred by her attack of smallpox.

"Why, Hetty, hello. How are you feeling?" Holly greeted her, the surprise at seeing her cousin showing in her voice.

Hetty seemed to take a deep breath before she replied. "I wanted to come sooner but I wasn't up to it."

"Well, do come in." Holly realized Hetty had never seen her little apartment behind the classroom, had never come out to see her before. In fact, since the day of that awful confrontation she and Hetty had never been alone. She started to offer to make tea but then hesitated. Perhaps first, she had better wait to see what was the purpose of Hetty's visit.

Hetty entered the classroom and looked around. She saw the colorful posters, the pictures the children had drawn pinned on the walls, the old glass bottles they had made into vases to hold the wildflowers, the purple lupines, yellow daisies, and Queen Anne's lace they picked and brought in to Holly.

"It's very nice." Hetty nodded, then added a little awkwardly, "Some of the mothers I know have told me what a good job you've done here."

"Why, thank you, Hetty," Holly said genuinely pleased at the compliment. "Of course, I love the children, and I've found—of all things—that I love teaching!" she laughed.

"I thought you'd be good at it," was Hetty's unexpected comment.

It surprised Holly, remembering Hetty's negative response when she had announced her intention to apply for the schoolteacher's job. Suppressing the impulse to remind her, instead she asked, "Could I offer you a cup of tea, Hetty?"

Hetty's mouth worked nervously. "I really can't stay, Holly. I left the children at the store and Ned's pretty busy, so I said I wouldn't be long—"

"You should have brought them. I would love to see them."

"Yes, I know. They begged to come with me when they knew where I was going, but I needed to talk to you—alone," Hetty said stiffly.

"Well, then, won't you sit down?" Holly suggested, thinking how odd it was to feel so ill at ease with your own cousin.

"Here, this is for you," Hetty said, thrusting the package toward Holly. "It's . . . actually, it's a 'thank you' for taking care of Aurelia and Teddy while I was sick." She was struggling to get the words out. "I don't know what I can say to tell you how much—I mean, after all I said and did—well, it was more than I should have expected for you to do for me—"

"Oh, Hetty, please!" Holly protested. "After all, we're *family*, aren't we?"

At this the tears rolled down Hetty's cheeks. "Well, I sure haven't acted like it," she burst out. "I just don't know how to say how sorry . . ."

"You don't have to, Hetty."

"Yes, I do, Holly. I was mean and acted so ugly to you. I guess I had a grudge or, oh, I don't know." She broke off abruptly and fumbled in her jacket pocket for a handkerchief and impatiently wiped her eyes. Then she pushed the paper-wrapped bundle again at Holly. "Here, take it. Open it."

Holly took it and fumbled a little as she untied the string and pushed aside the brown paper. Folded inside was a beautiful red-and-white quilt. Holly remembered seeing the bright-

237

patterned calico pieces that made up the dozens of cartwheels on the diagonally stitched background months ago at Hetty's.

"Oh, Hetty, it's simply lovely!"

"It's the Star of Bethlehem design with twenty stars," Hetty explained. "Aurelia helped cut the diamond shapes to make into stars."

"Oh, it must have taken you hours to make it, Hetty! It's so beautifully done," Holly examined the tiny, exquisite stitches.

"It's the least I could do," Hetty said in her usual stiff way.

"Thank you, Hetty, it's something I'll always cherish."

"There's another thing I want to say, Holly. Ned and I have talked it over and agreed that if the Town Council doesn't approve your adopting the little McKay boy—we'll take him in. What I mean is, he can sleep at our house, and, of course, you can see him all you want and have him with you on the weekends or whenever—that is, if you think that would work out."

Holly was momentarily speechless then genuinely touched. "That's very generous of you and Ned, Hetty."

"Well, he's a nice little fellow, and it would be good for Teddy to have someone for a big brother," Hetty concluded, then started to the door. "I best be getting back."

"Next time bring Aurelia and Teddy, Hetty," Holly said as she followed her out to the door.

"Yes, I'll do that," Hetty promised and even managed a tight smile.

Then at the door, Hetty halted and turned back to face Holly. "There's something else, Holly . . ." she hesitated, ". . . I've had time to do a lot of thinking while I was sick. Time to go over things, things I didn't want to think about, look at—and what I saw—mostly in myself—well, it wasn't very nice." Hetty's inner struggle was apparent in her expression. "Jealousy is a very ugly thing. It's poison and if you let it, it goes all through you. I was deadly jealous of you, Holly. You were everything I wanted to be when we were girls. Then, by some miracle, Ned asked me to marry him and come out here with him. I jumped at the chance to escape from Willow Springs and all my unhappiness there."

Holly saw her swallow and she spontaneously put out her hand as if to stop the flow of words. But Hetty shook her head

238

vigorously, "No, Holly, I have to say it. Then when Mama wrote and told me what had happened to you—I mean, about you and Jim—I was glad! Yes, glad. I'm shamed to admit it, but it's the truth. I gloated about it. I thought, *So something bad can happen to someone like Holly!*" Hetty bit her lower lip and hung her head for a minute before continuing. "When Mama asked me to let you come out here to stay until the gossip died down, I didn't want to do it. And when you came—everything that I remembered I hated about growing up in Willow Springs in the shadow of my pretty cousin hit me! I hoped you'd be so bored and dissatisfied here that you'd leave soon!"

"Hetty, you don't need to tell me all this."

"Yes, I do, Holly, it needs to be said. I've got to let all this poison out," Hetty rushed on, "but that didn't happen. Instead, you charmed everyone, made friends, created a place for yourself in Riverbend, *in spite of me!* And I resented *that*, too!" Hetty sighed deeply. "Well, I've learned my lesson, Holly. Besides hurting you, I've not only hurt myself but Ned and the children, too. And I just have to ask you to forgive me."

"Of course, I forgive you, Hetty," was all Holly could say. She was too moved by Hetty's obvious grief and remorse. She started to give Hetty a hug but wasn't sure whether to or not. It might be too soon. After all, Hetty had taken the first step toward reconciliation. Maybe she should wait, let her cousin set the pattern of their future relationship.

Hetty opened the door and started down the steps, out to the wagon and climbed in. She raised her hand in a wave before she picked up the reins and turned the horse around.

Standing at the door, Holly watched the wagon as it went down the road. Many things were going through her mind. She realized she had written Hetty off as troublesome, abrasive, and tiresome, never taking time to weigh the reasons that her cousin so often manifested these traits.

She understood so much more now about her cousin. Hadn't she gone through feelings of isolation, of being judged, rejected, disliked, and without friends, since she came to Riverbend? She could understand how having enough of those kinds of experiences could embitter someone. *Maybe it has to be that way,*

239

thought Holly. *A heart that has never known pain can't empathize with someone else's.*

Back in the house, Holly took the quilt to her bedroom and spread it on the bed, but the sides trailed to the floor on either side of the narrow bedstead. It was a quilt made for a larger bed, a double bed. It was the kind of a quilt that a young woman usually made for her hope chest or the kind that one received as a wedding present. Holly felt a little twinge of wistfulness.

Almost at the same moment she thought of Blaine.

Holly had not seen much of Blaine. Was he avoiding her? She'd spent an inordinate amount of time worrying why.

When the date of her appeal for Joel's adoption was set, Holly was told that there were several documents she would have to present to the Town Council with her application to become Joel's legal guardian. Along with a verification of her contract for another year as Riverbend's schoolteacher and a recommendation from Reverend Mobley that she attended church regularly and was of good moral character, would be a health certificate. This presented Holly with the perfect opportunity to stop by Blaine's office.

The night before her appointment, Holly washed her hair in fresh rainwater and soaked for a long time in a tub lavishly scented with rose oil. Afterward she sat for a long time brushing her hair in front of the mirror, her thoughts as dark as the gathering evening outside. Why, suddenly, did the optimism she had been feeling seem wrapped in a pall of melancholy?

Things were actually working out very well, much better than she could have hoped. Systematically she counted her blessings: She had a contract for the following year, she had supportive friends, there was the reconciliation with Hetty, the very real hope that her adoption of Joel would be granted—why then this sadness creeping over her?

Was it because Ad was gone? Did she have any lingering regret that she had not accepted his proposal, ensuring Joel's future with her? No, Holly had never been more sure that turning down Ad's offer was the right thing to do.

Then what was it? It was Blaine. Holly put down her brush and looked deeply into the eyes of the young woman in the

240

mirror. Hadn't she matured, become self-reliant and responsible? Why, every time she saw or was near Blaine, did she become a fluttery schoolgirl?

Resolutely Holly reminded herself that Blaine had had a life before she had known him, before she ever came to Riverbend. A full, dedicated life. He was admired, trusted, respected; he did not seem to have a void in his life nor any need for someone to fill it. He was well-educated, widely traveled, had known personal loss, faced life-and-death challenges that she knew nothing of, had lived and known a whole existence of which she had no part, had a past that she had not shared.

Meeting such a man in this remote little town in Oregon had been such happenstance. Or—and here a little shiver trembled through Holly—was *anything* in life just happenstance or was there, as Vi believed, a plan, a Divine one, for everything—every meeting, every event, every person?

The next day as she got ready to go into town for her appointment with Blaine, Holly's hands shook as she pushed the pearl-headed hatpins firmly anchoring her bonnet on her head. Her hair was so shiny clean and silkily slippery that it defied her attempts to secure it neatly into a twisted coil. She wore a blue jacketed dress and a lighter blue blouse underneath with a ruffled jabot. It looked as though it might rain, so she carried her umbrella, recalling with a smile the first disastrous time she had set out for an appointment with Blaine.

Walking into his small waiting room, Holly was aware of its antiseptic smell, a clean, astringent odor that she always vaguely associated with him. On the desk to the right of the door was set a metal bell next to an open ledger, identified as "Patients Log," and a neatly printed sign that read, "Please sign your name and tap bell to let doctor know of your arrival."

After writing her name in the book, Holly gave the bell a tap then sat down, her hands clasped tightly over her small handbag in her lap. Almost immediately the door to the inner office opened, and Blaine looked out.

"Good morning, Holly!" he smiled. "I wish all my patients looked as much like they didn't need a doctor as *you* do!"

With a sudden little flash, Holly had a prescient vision of

241

what Blaine might look like in the years down the road. Traces of character were already forming around his eyes, the laughter lines would deepen, and there would be silver in the thick tawny hair. In that second a strange thought followed, *Will I know him then, will I share those years?*

Quickly Holly brought all her imaginings into subjection. In her most sedate manner she rose from the seat and said demurely, "Well, I certainly hope I'm well and healthy, Blaine. There's a great deal depending on it, you know."

"Well come into my examining room, and we'll soon find out. Although I've never been surer of my diagnosis," Blaine said heartily. He sensed her nervousness and was trying to reassure her. "Would you mind removing your jacket so I can listen to your heart and lungs?" he asked in a very professional manner.

Blaine took the jacket and hung it up on the coatrack; then indicated a small stool for her to sit down on, then put on his stethoscope. He listened to her heart and took her pulse. To her annoyance, both had accelerated the minute she had stepped into his office. Asking her to remove her bonnet, he poked some kind of instrument into her ears, checked her eyes, and had her open her mouth so he could look at her teeth and throat.

"My goodness, I feel like some kind of prize calf being readied for the county fair!" she exclaimed, flustered.

Blaine smiled as he folded up his stethoscope and returned it to his pocket. "Not at all. I give you a clean bill of health. You are as fine a specimen of healthy American womanhood as it has ever been my pleasure to see."

Blaine busied himself making notations on the certificate Holly had given him to fill out after the examination. Even as Blaine wrote the medical comments in professionally accurate terms in the appropriate spaces, he was keenly aware of Holly—the flawless skin of her softly curved cheek, the warm scent of her faintly reminiscent of summer roses . . .

Finally he handed her the certificate with a flourish. "There you go, Holly. With all the other good recommendations I'm sure you'll get, I feel very positive that the adoption will go through."

242

She drew on her gloves slowly, sighing and said, "I wish I felt that confident."

"Come on now, Holly, where's all that spunk? I don't think you've got anything to worry about. I *know* what my vote would be. Joel would be a very lucky little boy to get someone like you for a mother."

"Too bad *you're* not on the Town Council!" she declared.

"Everything's going to work out just fine. You'll see."

Holly got to her feet, and Blaine took her jacket down from the coatrack and helped her on with it. He followed her out to the reception room and opened the office door for her. At the door she held up the certificate. "Thanks, Blaine, for this. *And* your encouragement."

"Look, Holly . . . ," Blaine hesitated a second, then said, "May I take you to the meeting the day of the hearing?"

Holly was taken back by his offer. From the first, Blaine had not said very much about her plan. While everyone else had counseled, warned, advised, argued about it, Blaine had remained silent. Holly thought that perhaps he wasn't interested, or maybe he thought it a bad idea, or worse still, maybe he didn't really care about the outcome. She would have welcomed his opinion, wished he had come forward, made some suggestion. Of all the people in Riverbend, Blaine was the one with whom she most wanted to discuss it. Why not? She had been more hurt by this than she cared to admit.

But now she saw the genuine concern in his eyes, and it gave her a surge of strength and optimism. "Why, yes, Blaine, I'd like you to. Thank you very much."

Two weeks later, standing at the schoolhouse window, Holly waited anxiously for the sight of Blaine's shabby little buggy. Dressed in a simple olive green suit of light wool Vi had made for her, Holly checked her fob watch for the dozenth time, hoping nothing unexpected, some kind of emergency, would delay Blaine or, at the worst, prevent his coming to escort her to the meeting at Town Hall.

Joel was staying with the Healy family until the Council made its decision, and Holly missed him already. She had been

243

awake half the night, worrying and praying about the meeting today. At dawn she got up, wrapped herself in a shawl, sat in the rocker by the bedroom window with the Bible in her lap, turning its pages, seeking comfort and guidance. Over and over she had returned to the book of Joshua, relating very much to *his* apprehension of what lay ahead. It *had* to be God's will for her to have Joel, she told herself. There were too many "coincidences" about their relationship for it *not* to be so!

Her nervousness began to abate. She felt curiously calm. Once before she had had to go before the Town Council to plead her case. She had won then, against all odds, and now the stakes were even higher. *This* time more than her own self-interest depended on the outcome: Joel's life, his future, his bright little mind, his eagerness to learn, his outgoing personality, and his loving heart—all the things Holly saw in him that no one else had seen or cared about. Why wasn't it obvious to everyone that this homeless orphan would be better off with her than placed in an orphanage in another county? Why couldn't a single woman raise a child? Vi Dodd had.

Holly's hands twisted tensely. She wouldn't let Joel go to someone else, to a farm family who might use him as another field hand, consider him just an extra mouth to feed. She was determined to fight for Joel as she had never fought for anything in her life before. And if she lost, if the Council refused her request to adopt him—what then? She pressed her lips into a straight line. Holly dared not think of the alternative that had already presented itself to her rebellious spirit.

Just then she saw Blaine's gig pull into the yard. She hurried out ready to climb into it before he had a chance to get out and help her.

"Fortified to face the gladiators?" he greeted her, trying to lighten her mood.

"Yes," was all she could manage to say. She was too preoccupied, mentally rehearsing her speech, hoping it had the right mixture of conviction and appeal.

They were almost to the edge of town when Blaine looked over at her and remarked, "That's a mighty pretty hat."

Surprised, she touched the brim with one hand and said, "You noticed?"

"Of course, I noticed," Blaine said, then added quietly, "don't you know I notice *everything* about you, Holly?"

Suddenly, spending considerable time putting new ribbons on her bonnet seemed suddenly worth the effort. Breathlessly, Holly realized Blaine was looking at her the way she had always hoped he would. She started to reply, but they were too near town and there wasn't time. They turned into Main Street, and Blaine drew up in front of the Town Hall. He pulled on the brake, then got out and came around to the other side of the buggy to help her down.

"Good luck, Holly. I know you'll do a good job,"

"Aren't you coming in with me?" she asked.

"This is *your* moment, Holly. You're going in there as an independent, capable woman. You don't need me or anyone to make your case for you. Remember Larkin and the Renner boy and the day you walked boldly into the Doggone Best—you didn't need anyone then and you don't need anyone now. Nobody can forget what you did during the epidemic. Just stand up and be yourself, Holly. That's all you need to do." Blaine helped her down, held both her hands in a strong clasp for a single second.

Holly looked up into his face, a face she knew now that she loved. She longed to say, "You're wrong, Blaine, I need *you!*" But she couldn't. Not after what he'd said, not after what he believed about her. She swallowed her fear, straightened her shoulders, and started up the Town Hall steps, repeating under her breath the words she had read and memorized the night before from Joshua: "Be strong and of good courage, I will not leave you nor forsake you. Do not be afraid, nor be dismayed, for the Lord your God is with you wherever you go."

If Holly had been made to relate word by word what took place in the council meeting that day, she would have found it impossible to do. She recalled her name being called to address the members with her petition; she remembered Vi squeezing her hand for encouragement; then the next thing she knew, she was standing at the podium, clearing her voice to speak.

Others in that crowded meeting hall that day *did* remember the sight of the slender young woman, becomingly yet conservatively dressed, whose voice shook a little as she began but grew stronger as she went on, "Even though I do not have a husband, a protector, a provider, I feel that as Riverbend's schoolteacher, with the salary and living quarters allotted me, I will be able to give Joel McKay a stable home. More than that, I love him dearly. We have been through things together that many a mother has not experienced with a son born to her. I comforted him at the death of his own parents. I have nursed him through the sickness that took his younger sister, and I shared his grief. We have grown closer through these trials. If I am given the privilege of rearing him, I feel I can best help him learn and develop the abilities I see in him. Since he's been one of my pupils, I've become aware that he *is* extremely bright. Now, that I've had the opportunity of observing him more closely, I am convinced Joel McKay has the potential of becoming a fine man, a benefit to this community. With your help and the help of those other citizens of Riverbend who are sympathetic and supportive of my appeal to adopt Joel, I believe he will have a far better life with me than being made a ward of the county and sent to the orphanage. I have submitted the personal character references you required, and I earnestly ask you to grant my petition for legal adoption of the minor child, Joel McKay."

Mayor Morrison had to gavel down the spontaneous applause that erupted as Holly resumed her seat. When quiet was restored, the Mayor said gruffly, "The council will take a fifteen-minute recess to consider Miss Lambeth's petition. When we return, we will announce our decision."

Holly felt as though she were reliving the time she had applied to become schoolteacher, only this anxiety was more acute. It was hard to believe that had been nearly a year ago. She had arrived in Riverbend feeling as though she were about to serve a penal sentence. All she had hoped for then was to endure it long enough to let the gossip about her and Jim

Mercer's broken engagement die down. Now that seemed almost unimportant except as the reason she had come to Oregon in the first place.

Holly sat stiffly in her chair, hardly conscious of the people who came up to shake her hand or pat her shoulder and wish her well. Her mind was locked into that inner room where Joel's fate and hers was being decided. She couldn't even pray. No words came to her to plead except, "Help! Lord. Please, Lord."

Finally, a nudge from Vi alerted her that the members were taking their places on the platform. The mayor moved to center stage and, shuffling some papers, declared, "As you all know, the case brought before this membership was an unusual one, and under most circumstances such a petition would not even have been considered. However, since Miss Lambeth is known to us all, has established her name and reputation in Riverbend, and is held in high esteem by all who know her, we hereby grant an affirmative response to her appeal to adopt the minor child Joel McKay."

"You've won, Holly, you've won!" cried Vi, hugging her.

Relief made Holly weak, as the realization broke through her tension; joy filled her heart bringing both tears and laughter.

Caught up in the excitement, Holly felt dazed, astonished, still unable to believe that it had really happened. People she did not even recognize came up to congratulate her. Then, suddenly, Holly looked around—searching for the one face that was missing. Blaine! Where was Blaine?

The following week was the last week of school. After the rest of the children had left for the day, Joel helped Holly tidy up the classroom. Both he and Holly were finding it hard to believe that what they had hoped and prayed for had really come true.

"And will I be your little boy forever and ever after?" he asked her now as he had a dozen times since the hearing.

"Yes, Joel, and my *big* boy and my grown son and my great strong manly son when I am an old, old lady!" Holly told him, laughing and hugging him and tousling his hair.

"You'll never be old!" he declared, then added anxiously, "Will you?"

"Not for a long, long time," she laughed.

Holly had not told Joel that she had been offered a contract for another year to teach, because she was unsure of what she was going to do. Even that fact astonished her. Six months ago the thought that she would not be heading home in June never entered her mind. She had not yet written her family about the adoption. This presented another puzzling problem. Of course, she felt sure the Lambeth family would have welcomed Joel with the proverbial open arms. But Holly knew what her mother's and other female relatives' private reaction would be—a single woman with an adopted child would have a difficult time finding a husband!

"May I go now?" Joel's voice broke in on her thoughts. "Uncle Ned said I should come and work at the store after school today. He has lots of boxes to put away."

"Yes, go ahead, Joel. We're about finished here," Holly said. Good old Ned, he had been her staunch support right from the start and had taken Joel under his wing immediately. Holly was grateful, too, that the long breech with Hetty was finally healed. Although they were still careful with each other and would probably never be close—at least not like Holly and Vi were, there was now peace about their relationship, past and present.

After Joel left, Holly was so preoccupied she did not hear buggy wheels outside nor the sound of footsteps on the porch. The schoolroom door was open because the weather was mild, but it wasn't until he said her name that she looked up and saw Blaine in the doorway.

"Holly, may I come in?"

She was on her knees in the front of the low shelf, straightening books that the Primary pupils used.

"Of course, Blaine," she said and sat back on her heels, dust cloth in hand. "What brings you out here this time of day?"

He pulled up one of the wooden stools and sat down.

"Business."

"Business?"

"Yes, serious business."

"What kind of *serious* business?"

"The *most* serious business there is."

248

"And what is *that?*" Holly, smiled, knowing that Blaine enjoyed conundrums and word games.

"Love."

"Love?" Holly gasped.

Blaine chuckled, "You have a most annoying habit of repeating everything I say."

"Well, you say the most *amazing* things!"

"Yes, love is amazing, and it is also serious business," he paused. "I love you, Holly, and I'm not sure what to do about it."

Holly blinked, tried to absorb what Blaine had said.

"I guess I've known I was falling in love with you over the last year. I certainly respected you. Admired you. I respect you for your courage, your honesty, your independence," his smile broadened, "your sense of fun, your generosity, and your sweetness—"

Blushing, Holly got to her feet and Blaine stood, too. Twisting the dustcloth nervously, Holly moved to a safe distance, distractedly dusting the top of the teacher's desk. "You make me sound like a paragon of virtue!"

"Well, of course I do. Doesn't every man think the woman he loves is perfect?" He moved steadily toward her. She took a few steps backward, bumped into the blackboard and found herself trapped. "When I realized I really loved you—maybe it was the day of the picnic or the night out at the Renner's farm or maybe at the Christmas party or during the epidemic—who knows when it was? I just *knew.*"

"But you never said anything, you never spoke about—"

"What could I say? I thought that maybe Adam was in the picture. And then when he left town and you decided to petition for Joel's adoption as a single woman, I realized you weren't planning to marry Adam. I began to think there might be a chance for me. But I didn't want to say anything *before* the hearing for fear *you* might think I was just doing it to make the adoption possible."

Holly thought of Adam and his proposal. She glanced up at Blaine. She stared at him in disbelief. "But it *would* have—"

"Yes, but then *you* wouldn't have known you were able to do it on your own."

The meaning of what he was saying finally penetrated. Blaine cared, *really* cared, wanted her to have the confidence, the justifiable pride of accomplishing that alone, *wanted* her to have that victory for herself.

"But you could have said something—," she faltered.

Blaine plunged his hands into his pockets and stared over her head out the window. "I couldn't. I know the kind of background you come from. I recognized it the moment I met you. Maybe because I come from the same kind. I know what a family like yours expects of a husband, and it isn't the life of a country doctor in a frontier town." Blaine shook his head.

"I don't even know why I came out here today. I probably shouldn't have. I just kept thinking that school is ending and that you'd probably be leaving, and I might never see you again. I guess I thought I couldn't let you go without at least . . ."

"At least what?"

"Telling you how I feel. But what do I have to offer you? A doctor's life doesn't belong to him or his family, it belongs to his patients. Any time, any hour of night or day—it isn't much of a life to offer a woman. The truth is I didn't dare hope that you could love me. Didn't dare ask you—"

"Oh, *ask* me! *Please* ask me, Blaine!" the words were out of her mouth before she realized she had said them.

His expression showed the joyous shock. "Holly! You mean it?"

"I never meant anything more," she said softly.

He held out his arms and she went into them. Holly felt his strength enfold, envelop her. She felt infinitely safe, unconditionally loved. For a long time they stood, just holding each other, heartbeat against heartbeat. Then slowly Holly raised her face, looked into Blaine's eyes, and knew that at last she had found what she had been looking for all her life. Commitment, purpose, and a love that would last forever.

Westward Dreams Series

Promise of the Valley

WESTWARD DREAMS SERIES

Promise
of the Valley

JANE PEART

BOOK II

ZondervanPublishingHouse
Grand Rapids, Michigan

A Division of HarperCollinsPublishers

To Lloyd,
with gratitude
for his generous help and patience

Prologue

VIRGINIA

September 1870

Adelaide Pride looked up at the blackened structure—all that remained of her beloved grandparents' home, Oakleigh. Between two charred chimneys the roof lay open to the sky. Gutted. Torched by the Yankee invaders. All that was left of the once beautiful house were the burned, crumbling rafters, the sagging floors, and the scorched walls.

Her hands clenched in helpless fury. Why had it been necessary to destroy it? After the battle of Seven Pines, the Union Army had used it for temporary headquarters. Why had they felt it necessary to burn down the place when they left? Just another case of the wanton destruction that generated so much of the blind hatred throughout the South since the war's end.

From behind her came the soft voice of her aunt Susan waiting in the small one-horse buggy. "Addie, dear, better come along now. It'll be getting dark soon, and it's a long drive back to town."

"Yes, Auntie, I'm coming," Addie called. Still she could

not seem to move. Memories of the past held her prisoner. Oakleigh was her grandparents' home. There, as a child, she had in summer played on the velvety lawn under the sweeping boughs of the giant trees that surrounded it while the adults carried on leisurely conversations on the shady verandah. Images floated back to her hauntingly. Days of gracious hospitality, gaiety, laughter; lazy summer evenings of soft dusk and flitting fireflies.

Was it really possible that all that was gone? Was it all lost as surely as the cause for which so many of her cousins, her friends, her beaux, had fought?

"Adelaide, we must go," Aunt Susan's pleading reminder came again. "Honey, the livery stable closes at six, remember? We have to get the horse and rig back before then."

Addie sighed. She needed no reminder that they no longer could afford to keep horses themselves and had to rent them to drive out this afternoon. With sad reluctance she turned from the skeleton of the house and climbed into the buggy beside her aunt.

The older woman placed a sympathetic hand on Addie's arm. "I know, darlin', what you're feeling. There's no use standing around mournin'. It won't bring anything back— or anyone. The main thing is that *we* survived, and we have to go on."

"But it's all such a waste, Auntie! So much and so many lost. Like Ran." They were silent a minute, thinking of Randolph Payton, the man Addie had expected to marry, who was killed in the battle of Antietam. Addie also thought of her parents, both of whom had died by the end of the war.

Aunt Susan patted Addie's hand. "But *you're* young, Addie. You've still got your whole life ahead of you. Don't let what's happened embitter you. Too many have gone that route." Addie knew her aunt meant her own husband, Uncle Myles, whose unrelenting anger at the South's defeat

8

had transformed him into a twisted, emotionally crippled man—old before age sixty.

"I don't intend to, Aunt Susan. After today, I'm not going to look back." Addie drew on her driving gloves, picked up the reins, and clicked them. The horse moved forward. "That's why I've decided to take that position with Mrs. Amberly," she said resolutely, looking straight ahead.

Her aunt gave a little gasp. "Surely *not!* Not with that—that *Yankee* woman!"

"What choice do I really have, Auntie? Yankees are the only ones with any money these days. The salary she's offered is more than I could hope to make at any job here. And I need a way to support myself."

"But to go all the way out to California!"

Addie lifted her chin determinedly. "What else can I do?"

Her aunt shook her head silently, pressing her lips together. For the next few minutes, as they rode along, the only sound was the soft clop-clop of the horse's hooves on the dusty country road. She knew Addie was right. Her niece had been left without family, fiancé, or fortune. What else was there for an impoverished Southern gentlewoman to do? At twenty-five, in the South, Adelaide was considered hopelessly on the brink of spinsterhood. Particularly now that so few eligible men of her age and class had returned from the war. Marriage seemed a remote possibility. What alternative did she have but to take the offered position as companion to an elderly widow?

The job offer had come through a distant cousin of Susan's. One of his "new" Yankee friends had asked him if he knew of a refined young lady to be the paid companion of his great-aunt Sophia Amberly at a famous soda hot springs health resort in the Napa Valley of California.

Susan had refused to have anything to do with Cousin Matthew since he began doing business with their despised conquerors. Many affluent Northerners had swarmed into

9

Richmond since the surrender, buying homes and property the natives could no longer afford. Matthew, however, had assured the man he had the "perfect answer" to his elderly relative's search for a "young, healthy, intelligent, ladylike" employee. The salary offered was one Adelaide felt she could not turn down.

Susan glanced over at her niece's cameo-like profile. Before the war, everything would have been so different for a young lady of Adelaide's beauty and breeding. She had certainly inherited both parents' good looks, if nothing else. She had her Carrington mother's high-arched nose; winged eyebrows; dark, lustrous, and silky hair; marvelous eyes the color of cream sherry. Of course, her erect carriage and the elegant set of her head were all definitely Pride.

Pride! Her name could not have been more appropriate, thought Susan, although some called it stiff-necked stubbornness. But maybe that's what would carry Addie through whatever lay ahead of her now. Surely, she'd need all the strong will and strength of character she could muster as she set out on her new uncertain future.

The next few weeks were busy ones, full of preparations for Addie's long journey. Hours were spent stirring dye into pots of boiling water to renew or freshen faded dresses, turning hems, changing buttons, adding braid or bows, to get Addie's wardrobe ready to pack. She and Aunt Susan stayed so busy, in fact, that there was little time to dwell on the parting they both knew lay ahead.

A few days before she was to leave for California, Addie went out to the cemetery. The September day was warm Indian summer lingered. She opened the wrought-iron gate and entered the enclosure, then walked toward the Pride family plot.

At the foot of the two headstones engraved with the names Spencer and Lovinia Pride, she place the mixed bouquet of late-blooming fall flowers from Aunt Susan's garden: asters, cosmos, Queen Anne's lace. Standing there for a few moments, Addie was lost in affectionate remembrance of her parents: her tall, strong-featured father, with his kind eyes and humorous mouth; her gentle mother, known endearingly to all as "Lovey." They had given Addie a wonderful heritage, and she was only beginning to appreciate it. All the values they had lived, she silently promised to try to practice in whatever lay before her.

After a few moments of reflection, Addie moved on through the graveyard, pausing here and there to read inscriptions on the markers. Many names she recognized. Boys she had grown up with who had gone off as soldiers and never returned.

A cloud passed over the sun, suddenly darkening the afternoon as though mourning these who had died too soon, without living out their lives, finding love, having families.

Then she reached the grave she was looking for and placed her smaller bouquet on the granite stone marked "Randolph Curtis Payton, Lieutenant Confederate Army, 1840–1861." A smile touched her lips as she thought of Ran, his bravado, his laughter, his light-hearted optimism when he had told her good-bye on that long-ago day he had ridden off to join Lee's army. He had been twenty, she sixteen. A hundred years ago!

Her arms, now empty of flowers, fell to her sides. She had come to say her farewells, now it was time to go. In six weeks' time, she would be far away from all she had ever known. Slowly she turned and walked out of the cemetery, closing the scrolled gates behind her.

Her hardest good-byes were still to come. To leave her aging aunt and uncle, who had taken her in after her parents' deaths, would be the most difficult of all.

Mixed with her natural sadness at the parting, however,

11

Addie felt a faint stirring of excitement. After all, was this not going to be the great adventure of her life? Although Addie had always been considered imaginative, something blocked all but the faintest vision about California. The future seemed hidden by a dim curtain of uncertainty.

Oct. 10th, 1870

Well, here I am, off on my journey—"the greatest adventure of my life," as dear Emily described it. Emily Walker, who has been my best friend for as long as I can remember, gave me this leather-bound journal as a going-away present. She told me it was to be filled with all the wonderful and exciting things that are going to happen to me on this trip and in my new life in California. Emily has always been an incurable optimist. Even when Evan, her husband, a strapping six-footer, came home a helpless cripple after losing his leg at Gettysburg, Emily never gave way. Dear gallant Emily. We were to be bridesmaids at each other's weddings. I was hers, but she never got the chance to be mine. Ran died the first year of the war.

I do wonder with what I'll fill these blank pages.

Cousin Matthew, full of self-importance, came out to Avondale with his fine new carriage to drive me to Richmond and escort me to the train station. When he arrived, Aunt Susan treated him coolly. She has stated over and over that she cannot abide to be around him since he's "taken up with those carpetbaggers—even though he *is* kin." But I cannot afford that luxury. After all, he arranged for me to take this position with Mrs. Amberly, which will provide me with money enough to send back to Aunt Susan and Uncle Myles. It will be enormously helpful to them. It is more than I could earn any other way—especially here in the South, crushed and defeated and with a surplus supply of impoverished gentlewomen with few or no "marketable" skills. With the salary she is paying me, I can also accumulate a little nest egg for the future. A future as a spinster, in all probability!

Aunt Susan was teary but brave as we said good-bye.

When I gave her a last hug, I could feel her tiny birdlike bones under the thin shawl, and I almost said I wasn't going. But I knew I must. I climbed into Matthew's shiny buggy, with its new-smelling leather seat, and I nearly fell out waving to Aunt Susan as she stood at the gate.

When we got to Richmond, Cousin Matthew saw to my trunk and assorted baggage. As we waited on the train platform, he shifted from one foot to the other, hemming and hawing and trying to make conversation—feeling uncomfortable, but doing his "familial duty." Aunt Susan lamented that before the war, no lady would travel unless accompanied by a male relative or a maid. Since I have no maid, Cousin Matthew was my only option. Finally, when the whistle blew, he handed me a box of bonbons and pressed two twenty-dollar gold pieces into the hand I extended to bid him good-bye. Then he hurried off, obviously mighty relieved to have me safely on board and settled in my seat. Could he possibly feel guilty that he is sending his cousin off into the unknown?

Aunt Susan packed me a hamper, fearing I had to go three thousand miles without any food, and she also gave me plenty of instructions and advice. My very outfit is the result of her strongest admonition about journeying alone. She insisted that I wear black, declaring, "For a lady traveling alone, wearing mourning is the best protection to avoid unwelcome attention from undesirable fellow travelers." I agreed, not only to put the dear lady at ease, but also because it could not be more appropriate. I *am* in mourning. I have lost everything I once held dear in life: parents, home, inheritance, the man I was to marry.

But so has everyone else I know. Certainly Aunt Susan and Uncle Myles lost everything—property, servants, a splendid home where she entertained lavishly many notables, including President Jefferson Davis himself. Emily and Evan too are nearly destitute. Yet I look on these two couples with some envy. They may have lost everything material, but they still have each other. The love and devotion between them is so tender, so beautiful to behold, that

13

I find myself bereft. There's a longing within me for something to fill that void in my heart.

When I opened this book, I saw the inscription Emily had written: "Journeys end in lovers meeting." Didn't I say Emily was an optimist? She is also a romantic. But could she be a prophet as well? Only time will tell. On to California.

PART 1

CALISTOGA, CALIFORNIA

NOVEMBER 1870

Chapter 1

*C*alistoga! Next stop, Calistoga!" the conductor's voice rang out as he wove his way down the aisle of the passenger coach.

"Thank goodness, at last!" Addie murmured with heartfelt relief. Although the last few hours of winding through the beautiful Redwood-covered hillsides on either side of the railroad tracks had been lovely, she was glad to reach her final destination at last—after all these weeks of traveling.

Her cross-country trip had been an adventure to say the least. In 1870, westward-bound trains boasted none of the amenities of eastern trains, which now had dining and Pullman cars. The western railway companies made no effort to make travel easy or comfortable for passengers. Clean hotels were nonexistent. In their place were rustic buildings with cots, hardly a proper resting place for a genteel person. Meal stops were mostly at towns consisting of a shack, dignified as a "depot," a saloon, and a water tank. Food was beyond description. What meals were available were often inedible. They were usually served by a saloon keeper or bartender, for there never seemed to be a scarcity of "spirits" for those who would rather drink than eat the awful fare provided. The menu rarely varied: greasy meat fried to a crisp, canned beans, biscuits called "sinkers," rancid butter, bitter coffee. One either had to develop a sense of the ridiculous or a cast-iron stomach along the way. The last straw was that the "rest and refreshment" stops were limited to twenty minutes, just long enough for the train crew to take on water. This gave the harried passenger a choice of bolting what food he or she could eat or taking a few minutes of fresh air and exercise before reboarding and enduring another long, grueling ride in the cramped quarters of the coach.

Addie enjoyed the scenery, however, which was so different from anything she had ever seen. Still, after a while, the hundreds of miles of wild prairies and endless deserts became monotonous, and she longed for the sight of civilization.

When the train finally pulled into Sacramento, Addie, like most of the passengers, took the ferry to San Francisco. There, Addie decided to splurge. Using one of the gold pieces Cousin Matthew had pressed on her, she went to a fine hotel where she obtained a comfortable room, luxuriated in a warm bath, washed her hair, and had dinner sent to her on a tray. She didn't even feel guilty about it.

The next morning, after the first restful night's sleep she had had in weeks, she sought information about getting to Calistoga. She was told that the steamer left San Francisco twice a day. She had a choice of two departure times, morning or afternoon, to make the sixty-eight mile trip to the Napa Valley. Taking the 2:00 P.M. steamer would break up her trip so that she could spend the night in Vallejo; then, the next morning, she could board the train of the newly established California Pacific line, thus enjoying the scenic trip through the Redwood-covered expanse in daylight. Having read and heard so much about the giant trees, Addie decided that this is what she would do.

She spent the morning walking around the city, being

sure to keep within sight of the impressive hotel where she had stayed the night before. San Francisco amazed her with its many fine buildings. It was a city bustling with commerce. The streets were crowded with different kinds of vehicles, from large delivery wagons to polished coaches pulled by matched horses and driven by drivers in flashy livery. Elegant shops of every description lined the hilly streets, their display windows filled with all manner of expensive wares, millinery, fabrics of silks and satins, jewelry, fur-trimmed manteaus, beaded purses. Florist stalls stood on every corner and offered a profusion of flowers, some of which were long out of season back east: gladioli, phlox, chrysanthemums. The sidewalks were crowded with all sorts of people, from stylishly attired men in frock coats and top hats, and women in the very latest Paris creations, to roughly dressed workmen hurrying to their jobs. Construction seemed ongoing, buildings seemed to go up before your eyes, and the sound of hammers banging was constant in the misty, sea-scented air.

Addie window-shopped until it was time to take a hack to the dock to board the steamer. Living as she had for all these years in the small Virginia town, and deprived of seeing such luxurious abundance of merchandise, she felt quite dazzled by it all.

Therefore, she found the leisurely river trip relaxing by comparison. The steamer moved languidly over the placid sun-dappled water. Standing on deck, Addie was awed by the variety of fall colors in the trees that lined the bank. Now, in early November, they still retained abundant foliage in glorious array of polished cinnamon, old-gold, flashes of brilliant scarlet against the sage green of the pines. The river trip passed all too quickly for her, and the afternoon had grown chilly by the time they reached Vallejo.

Upon disembarking from the steamer, the passengers

19

were herded to the only hotel available and served dinner—if the food could be described as such. Later, Addie was shown to a small, dingy room with a narrow iron bed, covered with doubtfully clean blankets, into which she could not bring herself to crawl—even though she was bone tired. There was a little stove whose fire only smoldered instead of burning, and then she could not budge the window to clear the room of smoke.

If Addie had not been blessed by a sense of humor, she might have been totally undone by the situation. It seemed so ludicrous that she found herself having a fit of giggles as she tried a dozen different positions on top of the lumpy mattress. She awakened before dawn and went outside to walk to the train shed. There, alone in the misted morning, she breathed deeply the pine-scented air, as fresh and intoxicating as wine, and heard birdsong high in the majestic trees, and felt she had an idea of California at last.

The whole trip had been an education. She became accustomed to the casual camaraderie of travel, the heartwarming generosity of fellow passengers, and the willingness of strangers to share and help. Although the usual protocol required in polite society was often ignored or dismissed while traveling, there was an unexpected pleasure in mingling with others who were also enjoying the excitement and adventure of crossing the wide, varied country of America.

She felt the train begin to slow, and the chug and the grinding of metal wheels on steel rails began to lessen. They slowly passed orchards, vineyards, and farmhouses. People on the streets stopped to watch and sometimes waved as the train rolled down the tracks toward the yellow frame building with a sign that read "Calistoga."

As the train pulled to a stop, Addie adjusted her black-dotted face-veil on her black *faille* bonnet, securing it more firmly with a jet hat pin, then checked it critically in her small hand mirror before slipping the mirror back into her purse. She pulled on black kid gloves, picked up her valise, and started making her way down to the door of her coach.

A well-dressed man just ahead of her in the aisle looked over his shoulder and cast an admiring glance in her direction. Then breasting his hat, he stepped politely aside to let her go first, his eyes following her slim figure.

At the car's exit door, Addie halted for a moment and drew a long breath. Here she was, for better or worse. Then she took the conductor's hand, with which he helped her down the steps onto the wooden platform.

Calistoga, California—where she would spend the next year of her life.

Chapter 2

The town of Calistoga lay nestled in the Napa Valley, trimmed in rolling oak-studded hills, surrounded by acres of vineyards under the blue-purple shadow of Mount Helena.

As Addie stepped from the train onto the wooden platform, the first thing she was aware of was how warm it was. It had been cool in San Francisco yesterday, with wisps of swirling gray fog obscuring the tops of the buildings and with a chilly wind off the bay. Here it might as well be midsummer. She ran her forefinger under the edge of her high-necked basque and took a small hankie from the sleeve of her jacket and dabbed her damp upper lip.

The last communication she had received from the nephew of her employer-to-be was that someone from Silver Springs Resort would meet her train when she got to Calistoga. Addie looked around hopefully.

As she did, her gaze met that of a man standing a few feet away. For a moment, their eyes locked. Could he be the person sent from Silver Springs? Almost immediately, she decided no. He looked more like a cowboy from pictures she'd seen of the West. He was tall, over six feet, lean, broad shouldered, long limbed, wearing a faded blue cotton shirt, buff-colored breeches, and knee-high, worn leather boots. His brown felt hat had a dented crown, and its wide brim looked as if it had often been exposed to wind and rain. When he removed it, as if in greeting, it revealed a deeply tanned, strong-featured face, with deep-set light-gray eyes and a cautious expression. He took a tentative step toward her, as if he thought he knew her, yet wasn't sure.

Addie wondered if she should acknowledge him. Perhaps he *was* a hotel employee here to meet her. As their gaze held, Addie had an uncanny sense of recognition. But that was impossible. How could she possible know him? And yet . . .

As he continued to stare at her, suddenly she felt dizzy, almost faint. It must be the glare of sunlight, the unaccustomed heat, the long train ride over the winding hills, the sleepless night in the dreadful Vallejo hotel, the lack of food—all were combining to make her feel disoriented.

Just as he seemed about to approach and she started to speak, she heard her name spoken. "Miss Pride? Miss Adelaide Pride?"

Quickly she turned away from the man whose gaze had captured hers to see an elegantly dressed gentleman striding toward her, smiling broadly.

Reaching her, he swooped off his hat and announced, "Brook Stanton, your host at Silver Springs Resort, at your service. Mrs. Amberly told me she had received a message that you were expected today, but since she was scheduled for one of her health treatments, I volunteered to welcome you to Calistoga."

A little taken aback by this exuberance, Addie murmured an appropriate "thank you" while she took in his appearance. He was strikingly handsome with a smooth olive complexion, flashing smile, dark curly hair cut close to his head and slightly silvered at the temples, and he sported a flourishing mustache. In contrast, his eyes were a surprisingly vivid blue. He was dressed like a dandy, in a biscuit-colored broadcloth coat, brocaded vest, ruffled linen shirt, and highly polished black boots.

A sudden flash of memory reminded Addie of an incident out of her childhood. Her father had taken her on a trip to visit relatives in Mississippi on a paddle boat, the *Delta Queen*. On board, a darkly handsome man, wearing a white linen suit, with a sparkling diamond stud pin in his silk cravat, had been pointed out to her as a well-known "gambler." To her little-girl imagination, he had seemed a glamorous figure, but her father had told her sternly he was to be avoided as "not our kind." Mr. Stanton's appearance was remarkably like him.

"I'll see to your luggage, Miss Pride; then we'll be on our way to the resort," he told her, offering her his arm. Then they started toward the other end of the platform where the baggage compartment was being unloaded. Before they had taken more than a few steps, a voice behind them called, "Stanton!"

They both halted and watched as a man approached them.

"Mr. Montand!" Stanton greeted him cordially. "I didn't see you. Did you just get off the train from Vallejo?"

"Indeed, I did. I was visiting the Fleischers, looking over their winery and learning their process." The man's gaze moved over to Addie. "I believe this young lady and I were in the same coach." There was a questioning lift to his cultivated tone.

"Allow me," Stanton said. "May I present Mr. Louis Montand, Miss Pride, one of our guests at Silver Springs. Miss Adelaide Pride."

Addie looked into a face that might be considered handsome, but it struck her, despite its even features, as somewhat bland. Soft brown hair waved back from a high forehead, a well-trimmed beard outlined a narrow jaw. His brown eyes were alert and curious.

"I'm sure you'll enjoy your stay at Silver Springs. My sister and I have found it most comfortable, a pleasant place to wait out the completion of the home we're building in the valley." He looked at Stanton and shook his head. "These Californio carpenters and stone masons work at a snail's pace. It would be unheard of in Boston! I'm beginning to wonder if we shall become your *permanent guests*, Stanton."

"Oh, I'm sure not, although there could be worse fates!" he laughed jovially.

"Spoken like a true *hotelier!*" quipped Montand, including Addie in his smile. "Is this your first visit to the area, Miss Pride?"

"Actually, it is my first visit to *California!*"

"Ah, well, we must show you the beauties of the valley, then."

"Miss Pride has come to be Mrs. Amberly's companion, Montand," Stanton informed him.

Addie noticed a subtle change in Montand's expression as he darted a quick glance at Stanton. Something she could not discern seemed to pass between the two men at the mention of her employer's name. Or was it her imagination?

The awkward moment passed, and Montand directed himself again to Addie. "Well, I'm sure *you're* not here for your health, Miss Pride, and I hope you will have plenty of free time to enjoy the beautiful surroundings of the resort. I would like the pleasure of showing them to you." He smiled ingratiatingly. "Even my sister, Estelle, who is extremely particular, agrees that Silver Springs is one of the nicest places we've stayed on our travels—especially in the West."

"When will Miss Montand return from San Francisco?" Stanton asked.

Montand rolled his eyes dramatically. "When the stores there run out of merchandise or our bank funds are depleted, whichever comes first!" He threw up his hands in a hopeless gesture.

As both men laughed heartily, Addie felt sure, from the cut of Montand's splendidly tailored clothes, the gold cuff links, and the watch chain across his satin vest, that the latter was not about to happen soon.

"Can I give you a lift back to the resort, Montand?" Stanton asked.

"No thanks. My vineyard overseer is meeting me. I want to go out and see what progress has been made on the house while I've been gone." He turned to Addie, bowing again. "So, then, I'll bid you good-bye for now, Miss Pride, and look forward to seeing you again soon." He tipped his hat and spun on his heel to walk back down to the opposite end of the depot platform.

Stanton settled Addie in his shiny green two-seater buggy, then supervised a porter who was securing her small leather trunk to the back. She guessed he might find the meagerness of her luggage strange. Probably most of his wealthy, health-seeking San Franciscans arrived with handsome matched sets of luggage. However, she was coming as a "paid companion," not as one of the guests, she reminded herself. A fact that the gallant Brook Stanton seemed to overlook, for he treated her as if she were a member of Queen Victoria's court.

After tipping the porter, Stanton took his place beside her in the smart buggy, smiled at her, lifted the reins, then they started off at a quick trot down the street from the depot.

"I'm sure you are going to enjoy your stay in Calistoga, Miss Pride. Accommodations at Silver Springs Resort are of the very best. I pride myself on giving my guests luxurious rooms and amenities that compare favorably with any of the finest resorts in the east—some in your own state of . . . Virginia, isn't it, Miss Pride?"

"Yes," Addie answered. "How did you know?"

"I'm a connoisseur of accents." He smiled disarmingly, then added, "I'm a Southerner myself, although I've lived away from my native land for a good many years. I was born in Savannah, raised in Tennessee."

Addie glanced at her companion's aquiline profile, thinking how nice it was to find a fellow Southerner so far from home. It made her feel easier and warmer toward him. Up until now everything had seemed so strange, so new to her. Most of the people she had encountered on her trip almost seemed to have foreign accents—harsh, nasal, or twangy.

"You could not have come at a better time of year—Fall is one of the most pleasant seasons here, although our climate is extremely mild year-round and considered very healthful with just enough rainfall to keep our air fresh and clean and uncontaminated with some of the unfavorable elements in our cities."

Addie listened while she was busy looking from left to right as they turned onto the main street, which the sign indicated, she noted with some distaste, was named *Lincoln* Avenue.

Both sides of the road were lined with small stores of various types, interspersed with shade trees, some now beginning to show fall colors. It looked on the whole like a quiet but pleasant little town.

"And the resort itself is full of interesting, enjoyable things for our guests. Of course, most come for the wonderful treatments, which are even better than the great European spas, if I do say so myself. But besides that, we have a number and variety of social and cultural events, dances, musicales, lectures, poetry readings. Some of our

27

guests have been well-known authors themselves. . . . I would name them but most wish to remain anonymous while vacationing. And that is another thing about which I pride myself—honoring my guests' wishes, whatever they are. Our motto here at Silver Springs is that our guests are all treated like royalty."

They passed a building under construction. Stanton pointed with his buggy whip. "That is one of my newest projects. I'm building an opera house. Here I plan to invite some of the greatest internationally acclaimed artists of the opera and theater to perform. It is almost completed. I've ordered carpets from India, carvings from Italy, furniture from France. It will be a showplace. Opera buffs from San Francisco will buy season tickets and flock here. . . ."

Addie realized that Brook Stanton was a true entrepreneur, a man of ambition and vision. She had been in the company of so many defeated men in the last few years, men who had lost their zest, their hopes, and dreams. It was refreshing to meet someone so full of enthusiasm and ideas.

Addie was totally unprepared for Silver Springs Resort. She hadn't expected anything nearly so grand. As Stanton's high-stepping, gleaming black horse trotted through the gates, Addie saw a sweep of velvety green lawn. It was beautifully landscaped, dotted with sculptured flower beds, bright with a mixture yellow, bronze and russet chrysanthemums, marigolds, and deep purple stattice. A winding gravel drive serpented through the parklike grounds. It led to a white Colonial-style building with white pillars and green shutters. A balcony fronted the upper story, and a deep verandah circled the lower floor.

"This is the main building where many of our social events are held. There are some guest rooms upstairs, but you and Mrs. Amberly are lodged in one of the cottages," Stanton told Addie as the buggy came to a stop. "First, I'll

show you the lobby before I take you over to your cottage."
He pulled out a handsome gold watch and consulted it.
"Mrs. Amberly still has at least forty-five minutes before
she's finished with her treatment. One of the bathhouse
assistants will escort her back to the cottage, and she'll rest
for a half hour there, so there's plenty of time before you
have to begin your duties." His eyes twinkled as they
regarded hers.

He got out and came around to help her down from the
buggy. Then he offered his arm, and they walked into the
lobby together.

Addie looked around with surprised pleasure. She wasn't
sure what she had expected, but nothing like this. She had
never dreamed Silver Springs Resort would be this luxurious. Brook Stanton seemed to sense her reaction and stood
beside her for a few minutes, looking pleased.

The lobby was furnished tastefully: pale green painted
walls gave it a restful atmosphere, graceful furniture was
placed in small conversational groups around the large
room with many windows, curtained in sheer lace, draped
in cream taffeta swags, letting in the filtered afternoon sunlight.

"Now that you've admired my pride and joy sufficiently,
I'll escort you to your cottage," Stanton told Addie teasingly. Back in the buggy, with the horse slowed to a walk,
they proceeded around a flower-bordered circle over to a
group of white cottages, which all had peaked roofs and
small, elaborately fretted porches.

"Here we are then," announced Stanton, braking the
buggy. He sprang lightly out, then came around to hold
out his hand to assist Addie down. As if by some silent call,
a young man in a short green-jacketed uniform appeared to
unload and carry Addie's trunk inside.

Stanton took off his hat and bowed slightly, saying,
"When Mrs. Amberly has completed her treatment at the

bathhouse, one of the attendants will accompany her back here. In the meantime, may I suggest you make yourself comfortable? I'll have some refreshment sent over, and perhaps you can rest a bit before dinner. I trust you will find everything to your liking. If you have need of anything— anything at all—simply ring the bell, and one of our chambermaids will come at once."

"Thank you, Mr. Stanton, you have been most kind, most gracious."

"My pleasure, I assure you, Miss Pride." He bowed again and left.

His manners were so perfect. Why was it he reminded her so strongly of the "riverboat gambler" her father had strenuously told her to avoid? Even at age eleven, Addie had thought the man dashingly attractive—just like the illustrations of the swashbuckling pirate in her storybook. And without doubt, Brook Stanton resembled him. Was Stanton also a gambler? And would her father have warned her against him as well?

Chapter 3

The front door opened into a small parlor. Stepping inside, Addie looked around with immense pleasure. She had been on the road for so many weeks, dealing with all sorts of discomforts, inconveniences, and all manner of accommodations from wretched to passable, that this cottage was a welcome change. Lace-trimmed curtains hung at the shuttered windows. The furniture was not as elaborate as the furniture in the lobby, but it was in excellent taste. A love seat and two armchairs were placed in a conversational arrangement, and fresh flowers in cut-glass vases were set on the marble-topped table.

An archway led into a narrow center hall, with a door at its end and two doors on either side. The door at the end was a bathroom, equipped with modern conveniences and a white porcelain tub mounted on claw-footed legs. The other two must be the bedrooms.

She knocked lightly on the closed door but, receiving no answer, assumed this must be Mrs. Amberly's bedroom. The door opposite had been left open, and in that she saw her trunk had been placed.

In there everything was light and fresh. The sleigh bed of bird's-eye maple was banked with ruffled pillows, and covered by a white embroidered coverlet, which matched the curtains at the windows. Outside, the garden was bright with autumn flowers, and Addie could see the blue ridge of mountains beyond. An armoire, a bureau, and a washstand of the same golden wood, a small desk and chair, and a comfortable upholstered armchair completed the furnishings.

Addie circled the room. She looked at everything and stopped to touch the soft, clean towels on the rack beside the washstand. She picked up the lavender-scented cake of soap in the fluted dish and sniffed it appreciatively. What luxury! After last night, how glorious it would be to wash off all the gritty soot, grime, and dust of the train.

She was tempted to use the tub in the pristine bathroom, but she was not sure she had time to do so before Mrs. Amberly returned. Meeting her employer was a rather daunting thought. What if the woman hated her on sight! That was too foolish a thought to waste any time about. Whatever happened, she had signed a year's contract with Sophia Amberly, only to be broken if Addie proved dishonest, immoral, or committed anything deemed injurious to her employer's reputation or property—none of which was likely to occur. Still, Addie wanted to freshen up so that she could look her best.

Untying the veil, she took off her bonnet, then unbuttoned the tiny covered buttons of her basque, unfastened the hook and eye of her waistband, and stepped out of her skirt. She unlaced her corset and tossed it aside. It was a relief to be rid of the whalebone stays for a few minutes. What an instrument of torture! Stupid! How cruelly the current fashion dictated the ideal woman's waist to be twenty inches or less!

Pulling out her hairpins, she shook her hair down and dug into her valise for her brush. Bending over, she brushed her hair until it crackled. She fastened it back from her face with a ribbon, then poured water into the bowl and began

32

to scrub away the residue of her journey until her clean skin glowed and tingled. Quickly she rewound her hair, drawing it up into a figure-eight chignon at the nape of her neck.

The surprising warmth of the November weather prompted the decision to unpack something lighter weight to wear.

She unlocked her trunk and lifted the lid. On top of her neatly folded petticoats was a tissue-paper-covered square. She hesitated a few seconds, knowing what it was. Then she slowly unwrapped it and drew out a silver-framed photograph. For a long tender moment, she looked at the picture of the handsome young man, resplendent in his newly acquired Confederate uniform. Lt. Randolph Payton—how proud he had been the day he rode over to Oakleigh to show off the splendid spotless tunic, the yellow silk sash, the gilt epaulettes, his then-unused sword. And how tragically soon that uniform was battle soiled, blood-soaked when he fell, his horse shot from under him, himself mortally wounded, at Antietam. . . .

Gazing at the clear-eyed, untroubled face, Addie felt a hard lump rise into her throat. Feeling a deep sadness for all that he represented, all that was lost, a mist of tears blurred his confident smile. . . .

What had Aunt Susan said over and over? "We must put the past behind, forget, and go on—" Addie shook her head, saying to herself, "Auntie's wrong. If I did that, who else would remember him? If I did—it would be like Randy never existed. I don't want to forget him—or anything else. It would be like saying it had all been for nothing. I can't. I won't."

Holding it a minute longer, Addie studied his image, then put the picture on the top of the bureau beside her silver-backed dresser set. Determinedly, Addie continued unpacking, putting away her things in the bureau drawers, and hanging her dresses and jackets in the armoire. Then

33

she emptied her valise. In it were the three books she had traveled with: her small leather Bible, the George Eliot novel *The Mill on the Floss,* and her journal.

For some reason, Addie suddenly thought of the tall stranger at the train depot. Would she ever see him again or learn who he was? An involuntary shiver passed through Addie as she thought of that uncanny sense of recognition she had had when their eyes met—as though they had met and known each other somewhere before—almost as if he had been waiting for her to arrive!

What foolishness, like a schoolgirl's daydream. Sternly, Addie jerked herself back to reality, reminding herself that she was nearly twenty-six and long past such silliness. She put the three books on the bedside table and took out a cotton blouse with a tucked bodice and demure collar and cuffs, suitable for her new position as "paid companion."

She had just added her mother's cameo brooch for a finishing touch when she heard voices and footsteps outside her open window coming up on the cottage porch.

"I hope all this is doing me some good!" a high-pitched female voice complained. "What possible benefit is it to soak three times a day in that bubbly mineral water, I'd like to know—it's bad enough to have to drink that stuff without then being steamed in it like a lobster—"

"Well, ma'am, Dr. Willoughby is convinced that these treatments are *very* beneficial, and you will feel like a new person entirely when you leave here in the spring—," a quiet confident voice replied.

Addie stood quite still in the center of her bedroom. Should she go out and introduce herself right now? Or should she wait until Mrs. Amberly was back in her own bedroom? Possibly she was in some measure *dishabille* if she were returning from treatments at the bathhouse. Caught in anxious uncertainty, Addie asked herself if it would seem too forward if she did. Or if she hesitated and did not make her presence known to her employer, would Mrs. Amberly think she was sly or devious or worse still, awkward, without social graces?

As she hesitated, she heard huffing and puffing, the shuffling of slippered feet along the hallway; then a door was unlocked, opened, then closed again.

Addie let out her breath slowly. For the moment, the decision had been taken out of her hands. She felt, however, that she should speak to the attendant, let her know she had arrived, and perhaps ask her what she should do about meeting Mrs. Amberly.

Opening her door, she waited until a white-uniformed figure emerged from the other bedroom and came down the hall.

"Hello!" the rosy-cheeked, middle-aged woman greeted Addie. "I'm Letty, the maid assigned to this cottage, as well as one of the bathhouse attendants. You must be Miss Pride. Mrs. Amberly's expecting you. In fact, she's been fretting, wondering when you'd get here. I guess she was expecting you sooner?"

"Well, transcontinental travel does have its drawbacks!" Addie declared with a smile. "The trains don't always leave on time or get there when they're supposed to either. I've come from Virginia and there were quite a few unpredictable delays along the way."

"I suppose so. I came when I was little girl with my family in a wagon train, so I don't remember much about it. I was only three years old, but I know my poor mother said never again. And she never did."

"Should I go in to see Mrs. Amberly now?" Addie asked.

"I'd give her a few minutes, if I were you. I helped her get dressed, but I wouldn't disturb her right away." The woman lowered her voice. "She's probably having her little toddy." She gave Addie an elaborate wink. "Strictly against doctor's orders, of course. But *at the prices,* who's going to stop her?"

35

Addie did not know what to say to this unexpected piece of information.

"Well, I best be on my way. My day's done. And I suppose *yours* is just beginning. Good luck, dearie. I think you're going to need it."

With this, Letty went out of the cottage, leaving Addie wondering what awaited her beyond the closed door at the end of the hall.

Chapter 4

*A*ddie knocked tentatively on the door and heard a voice whose tone was to become familiar in the days ahead. "Yes, it's open. Come in."

Addie hesitated a second before turning the knob and entering the room. It seemed to be empty with curtains drawn. The room was shadowy. Addie took a few steps further, looking around for the person who had spoken. Then someone said sharply, almost accusingly, "Well, so you've come."

Addie whirled around to see a large, round figure seated in the corner in a chair, feet propped up on a hassock. A grossly fat woman, overdressed in a tasseled, bell-sleeved purple taffeta of enormous frills, pleats, and braided trim. Her small pig eyes were almost lost under the puffy lids. Her small flat nose and down-turned mouth were bracketed by ballooning cheeks. Addie's immediate first impression of her employer was the woman's resemblance to pictures she had seen of the aging English Queen Victoria.

"Mrs. Amberly?"

"The same," came the curt reply. "And *you*, miss, I presume are Adelaide Pride."

"Yes."

"Well, first things first, I suppose. I am here because of my health—very precarious—I have dropsy, a swelling of the tissue, as you can see, as well as rheumatism—all of which I have been told—practically promised by Mr. Stanton, these mineral water baths and so on—will cure!" She gave her head a little shake, setting the ruby and diamond pendant earrings swinging from her drooping earlobes. She waved one pudgy, heavily ringed hand impatiently. "But I've heard that kind of fairy tale before at other spas in Europe, as well as back east. I'm simply hoping the California climate will help."

"I'm sorry," murmured Addie, not knowing what else to say.

"You needn't be sorry. I don't like people who talk a lot of nonsense. Now, let's get your duties straight. I do need help walking to and from the main lobby—the attendants fetch me and bring me back from the bathhouse after my daily treatments. So, there really isn't that much for you to do, so I expect you to spend your time profitably. I like to be read to, so you will avail yourself of the local library, which Mr. Stanton assures me is well supplied, and get me my hometown newspaper, which comes by train from San Francisco. It's a week late, but I still like to keep up on things—stock market report and such.

"I want you available if I want something extra—morning and evening snacks, that sort of thing. I have a hard time hobbling around on these poor feet. That's the reason I don't like being waited on, but I do like to have what I want when I want it." She pursed her lips for a moment before continuing. "Do you play cards, whist? You may have to fill in if we cannot get a fourth, or if some of the guests I've been playing with should leave—that's always a possibility. If my health improves, I may want to take some short side trips—to the Lake Country or Saint Helena. You would see to those arrangements. I may think of some

38

other things, but for the present that is all, I suppose." Mrs. Amberly frowned. "I dislike change, and my cousin Ella was my companion for a number of years, but when I decided to come out West, she refused to accompany me. Afraid of Indian attack, she said! Ha! Can you imagine such stupidity in this day and age?" Mrs. Amberly looked disgusted. Then she jangled the jeweled necklace that hung around her neck and lifted the magnifying glass attached to it and checked a watch pinned to her shelf-like bosom with a diamond bow knot. "It's almost time for dinner and since I move slowly, we better get started."

It took Mrs. Amberly a number of attempts and several minutes to heave herself out of her chair. Addie had not known whether to move forward to assist her or wait until she was asked. Mrs. Amberly was an uncertain quantity just now. Addie realized she would have to bide her time, learn to know when to offer help or when to resist the urge to do so. Mrs. Amberly seemed easily offended, so that, at the moment, tact seemed the best thing.

Once on her feet, Mrs. Amberly leaned heavily on Addie's proffered arm, and they made their slow, ponderous way across the courtyard to the dining hall.

Mrs. Amberly made little attempt at conversation, even omitting the questions about Addie's trip that one might expect out of ordinary courtesy or even curiosity. Instead, she kept up a running commentary, mostly negative, on the other guests at Silver Springs as they entered the dining room.

All through the long dinner, Addie was more and more appalled by her new employer's comments on everything and everybody, from their waiter to the other guests dining in the large, windowed room. Everything she said was critical or sarcastic. She complained about the service, and declaring that her meat was too rare, sent it back; when it was brought back, she said it was "burned to a crisp." It didn't take Addie long to realize Mrs. Amberly was a selfish, self-centered person who cared little for anyone but herself.

Addie had noticed the curious looks in her direction from the other diners and knew she was under speculation. As they were finishing their dessert, two of the other guests, the Brunell sisters, Elouise and Harriet, stopped by the table. Mrs. Amberly was saccharinely sweet and amiable. Of course, since Addie's presence could not be ignored, an introduction was unavoidable and done with very poor grace. Addie stifled the rush of resentment, finding it galling to be introduced as "my hired companion." From the Brunells' rather startled reaction, Addie realized that designation put other guests at Silver Springs in an awkward position of not knowing exactly how to treat her. She felt humiliated and inwardly outraged by it.

Addie was relieved and grateful that almost immediately after the Misses Brunell had left, Brook Stanton came over to the table.

"Good evening, ladies." He included them both in his smile. "I hope you are finding everything satisfactory."

Mrs. Amberly immediately became a different person. Simpering coyly, she waggled a fat finger a him, saying, "So where have you been the last few days, Mr. Stanton? None of us have seen you."

"In the city on business."

"Visiting some lucky ladies there, I'll wager." Mrs. Amberly screwed up her small mouth into a smile she must have thought looked teasing but only looked malicious.

"Afraid not, Mrs. Amberly. You give me credit where none is due. Rather they were several portly gentlemen with whiskers and beady eyes, inclined to be more parsimonious than gracious." His eyes moved admiringly over to Addie. "It seems I must return to Calistoga to be in the presence of charm and beauty."

Mrs. Amberly darted a glance at Addie, and for a

moment, her mask slipped. As Brook turned toward her again, she quickly rearranged her expression. Only Addie had caught the look of open indignation. In the snap of a finger, she knew with alarm and surprise that her employer was capable of petty and unprovoked anger.

She had no time to dwell on the realization, however, because some of the other guests leaving the dining room passed by and nodded to Mrs. Amberly, saying, "Come along, we're ready to play."

Brook took that as a cue. "I'm sure you must be anxious to get to your regular game, Mrs. Amberly, and I'm also sure Miss Pride must be weary from her day's travel, so suppose I escort her to the cottage this evening for an early retirement. Later, when you are finished with your game, Mrs. Amberly, I'll see you safely there."

Mrs. Amberly seemed as if she were about to object, but Brook had already moved to her side and was assisting her from her chair. He continued a smooth line of pleasant conversation as the three of them strolled out of the dining hall and over to the main building.

They left Mrs. Amberly at the door of the game room where card tables were being set up, and Brook, with Addie on his arm, went out the front entrance. It was a beautiful evening, mild, with stars overhead sparkling.

"Calistoga welcomes you with one of its lovely evenings, Miss Pride. We sometimes get early fog this time of year in the valley, but not tonight."

They walked along in silence. Addie realized suddenly that she *was* very, very tired. But also that it was an emotional weariness rather than physical.

Her mind was numb, and she could think of nothing to say to the gallant Mr. Stanton and thought he must think her either rude or completely lacking in the minimal social graces. That, however, did not seem to be the case because before leaving her at the cottage porch, he said, "You are going to bring something to Silver Springs that I hadn't realized was missing before you arrived, Miss Pride. Youthful beauty, grace, and a certain instinctive charm that have been sadly lacking among my guests."

A little flustered by this unexpected compliment, Addie murmured, "How kind of you to say so. Thank you."

"Not at all, Miss Pride. I feel we will all be in your debt before this winter is over. Just don't let anything stifle your natural cheerfulness and good humor—" There was a hint of humor in this.

"I'll try not to," she replied, realizing Brook Stanton read Mrs. Amberly like the proverbial book.

"Good! Now, have a good night's sleep. This clear air is the best insurance one could possibly have for complete restoration of body and spirit, I guarantee it," he told her, then laughed. "Spoken like a true innkeeper, right? Good night to you, Miss Pride. Sweet dreams."

With that he gave her a little salute and went off into the night humming under his breath. Addie looked after him thinking Brook Stanton was far more than an innkeeper. He was a man of considerable talents, many of them probably hidden.

Chapter 5

*I*t was after midnight and at Addie's desk the wick of the oil lamp sputtered, the light flickered as her pen moved across the pages.

November 24th, 1870
Only two weeks have gone by and I still face months of putting up with this insufferable woman. And this evening was the worst yet. Usually I just manage to sit out the hours she spends at the card tables until she's ready to be helped back over to the cottage. Tonight, however, one of the "regulars" pleaded a headache and retired, and I was ordered to fill in for her. I find the game not only stupid—to say nothing of the shallow chit-chat carried on between plays—but discussion afterward of every play is so boring. By the end of the evening my head ached. I felt like screaming.

Addie was gripping her pen so hard that the point dug into the paper, causing the ink to splatter across the page. She flung down her pen in frustration, rubbing her aching forehead.

November 27th
Mrs. Amberly pretends she has forgotten her promise to reimburse me for travel expenses. The small fund of cash I brought with me from the sale of some of Mama's jewelry

has dwindled alarmingly. Finally I had to mention it, and a more humiliating scene has never been my experience to bear. Mrs. A. acted as though she could not recall such an offer. I was forced to produce her letter in which she *had* made such a statement. Confronted with the evidence she turned beet red, and with obvious reluctance wrote out a cheque, giving it to me like tossing a bone to a dog! I dread to think I may have to go through this sort of thing each month for my salary!

But being able to send Aunt Susan and Uncle Myles a nice sum every month will make up for any cross I must bear in this hideous situation. But very honestly, I feel— trapped! That's how I feel. Perhaps this is the way slaves in the old South felt.

Dec. 2nd

Today I went to the Post Office to mail the money order to Aunt Susan. As I was doing that, I saw the man I first noticed the day of my arrival at the depot. I was standing at the corner getting ready to cross the street when he came down the street mounted on a fine, gleaming chestnut horse. As he passed he lifted the brim of his hat and nodded—as if he knew me! The strangest part is that I felt the same extraordinary sensation I'd had before. That we had met somewhere before, been parted a long time, and were only just now seeing each other again.

It is so ridiculous, I do not know why I even record it.

Involuntarily, Addie shivered. She closed her journal. It had been a long, wearying day, and tomorrow there would be another one to face.

As she got undressed for bed her feeling of depression deepened. How could she endure this year of employment to a woman she had come to dislike heartily. Mrs. Amberly's abrasive personality was bad enough, but her arrogance was worse. Her treatment of the resort employees, the maid assigned to their cottage, the bathhouse attendants, the waiter in the dining room, the desk clerk in the lobby, made Addie wince inwardly. Addie felt embarrassed to be associated with Mrs. Amberly, as though she were, as they say, "tarred with the same stick!"

To counteract Mrs. Amberly's actions, Addie went out of her way to pleasantly address the various employees by name, though she had little opportunity away from the scrutiny of her employer.

Addie lay awake praying for patience. She knew she had to make the best of the bad bargain she had made. She had signed a contract. Her word must be her bond. After all, she was a Pride, wasn't she? The Pride name stood for something. It stood for integrity, truth, and above all honor. She must honor her word that she would stay out the year. Whatever it took—and Addie had the feeling she would be tested far beyond anything life had ever before demanded of her.

Addie determined to try harder to put up with the situation. It was a mere matter of will, she told herself. She would try to be cheerful. If she could not overlook the things that bothered her most about her employer, she would simply grit her teeth and bear it. What else could she do?

Dec. 8th

The weather is still mild with the exception of intermittent days of rain. But the sun seems to manage to come out for a portion of every day at least. My escape from the drudgery of my job and the stress of being around someone like Mrs. A. for hours at a time is to take long walks. While Mrs. A. is at the bathhouse taking her heated mineral water treatments, I leave the resort and walk to town. Calistoga is a small town, very new. The houses look freshly painted and the gardens are a wonder, full of all sorts of flowers, some blooming profusely, even this late. The trees are beautiful, all sorts of ones that I cannot name, but think I shall get a book and try to learn what they are, so many different kinds. It does refresh me to do this. Still I cannot help feeling lonely. As I walk along these pretty streets, I keep thinking, people live in these nice houses, people it would be nice to know, perhaps be friends with, but I know no one except the maids and no one knows me. It has been a long time since I've even heard anyone call me by my Christian name. It is certainly a change from Avondale where I knew everyone and everyone knew me and my family.

The guests at Silver Springs were mostly middle-aged, many of them in poor health, who had come there seeking some recourse in the beneficial mineral water, the heated pools, and the mild climate. There were no young people with whom Addie could make friends, even if her ambiguous position as a "paid companion" made that possible.

Oddly enough, it was Brook Stanton with whom Addie found rapport. Busy as he always was as manager of the resort and many other entrepreneurial projects that occupied him, Brook always seemed to have time to stop and chat with Addie whenever he saw her.

Brook was entirely different from the Southern men she had known all her life, who took affluence, position, and privilege for granted as their right. For all his casual affability, Addie suspected that underneath Brook's charming manners was a driving ambition, perhaps even a ruthlessness to succeed. This he skillfully kept hidden under an engaging personality.

He had great style in everything: his attire, his management of Silver Springs. His insistence on perfection was evident everywhere. The tasteful furnishings in the lobby and lounges, the exquisite table settings in the dining hall, the crisp white linens, the gleaming china, the sparkling glassware, the spotless cottages, and the excellent service all compared favorably with any prestigious eastern resort.

Addie enjoyed her contacts with Brook, who provided her with intelligent, witty conversation—a welcome relief from the usual shallow chatter of Mrs. Amberly and her cohorts. The problem was that she soon became aware that her employer resented Brook's attention to her and reacted to any special notice by him with increased orneriness and petulant demands. Addie soon discovered what a petty, childish woman Mrs. Amberly could be.

At least on Sundays Addie had some respite. The first time Addie suggested church attendance, Mrs. Amberly appeared flustered. It amused Addie to see the inner struggle taking place as her employer debated if she could get away with refusing Addie time off for worship service. Since even the hotel employees were allowed to attend church on Sunday mornings, there was really nothing Mrs. Amberly could say.

Addie wondered if it were not that Mrs. Amberly felt some guilt about not going to church herself. After grudgingly assenting to Addie's going, she rambled on at some length about the impossibility, in her rheumatic condition, of sitting in the hard pews during the long sermon. Addie listened, trying charitably to give the woman the benefit of the doubt, but it occurred to Addie that Mrs. Amberly seemed to have no trouble sitting for hours on end playing cards most evenings. Nevertheless, with the tug of wills finally over, Addie had won the freedom of a few free hours on Sunday mornings.

Sunday morning began like any other morning. Addie rose, dressed, knocked on Mrs. Amberly's bedroom door to see if she was ready to walk over to the dining hall for breakfast.

When her employer appeared, she was puffy-eyed, her cheeks creased from sleeping on massed pillows, her mouth in its perpetual downward pull. Addie greeted her. "Good morning, Mrs. Amberly."

"Humph," was all Mrs. Amberly could muster in response as she took hold of Addie's arm.

"I hope you slept well," Addie murmured the comment

47

she made every morning as if they were lines she'd learned in a play.

"Tossed and turned all night," complained Mrs. Amberly, as she always did not knowing that sometimes her loud snoring could even be heard through the walls and down the hallway to Addie's astonished ears. When they stepped out onto the little porch and saw the light mist rising from the ground, Mrs. Amberly exclaimed crossly, "I thought the sun was always supposed to be shining in California!"

"I'm sure it will burn off before noon," Addie replied, having noticed this seemed to be the weather pattern of valley days.

Ignoring that optimistic prediction, Mrs. Amberly droned on, "I should have gone to Florida or Italy. It wasn't *my* idea to come here. Now I suspect my nephew must have had some investment here and that's why he persuaded me that *this* would be a good place to spend the winter. It's just like him. He's a sly one, a great talker, he is. Money is what he's interested in most—*my* money most likely—and here I sit shivering in *sunny* California while he—I think he went to Bermuda—but how should I know? He never contacts me unless he's got some scheme for me to invest in—but he don't fool me. No, indeed. Somebody'd have to get up pretty early in the day to pull the wool over *my* eyes—my, but my neck's stiff, and my legs—I dunno whether this whole thing is doing me a bit of good—"

Addie groaned inwardly. Was there no end to this petty whining and complaining? This spoiling of every new day?

Settled at their table in the dining hall, Mrs. Amberly surveyed the breakfast menu with a jaundiced eye while the waiter greeted them and poured them coffee. Mrs. Amberly had been advised to eat lightly before her treatments which were scheduled for ten o'clock. But, regardless of that sage suggestion, after a great show of resignation she would go ahead and order sausage and eggs or griddle cakes.

48

"Stanton should get a new chef. This food is getting monotonous," Mrs. Amberly said as she shoved the menu back at the patient waiter. "His cook is one of them Chinese, you know. What on earth could a China man know about what *Americans* like to eat, I'd like to know!" She sniffed disdainfully.

To avoid commenting, Addie took a long sip of the steaming coffee. She was often at a loss for how to reply to her employer's innumerable complaints. If she said nothing, Mrs. Amberly stared at her belligerently until she said something.

Luckily, this morning Addie was saved by Brook. He was just entering the dining hall and saw them. As he approached their table, Mrs. Amberly immediately stirred in her chair like a pigeon fluffing her feathers and put a smile on her face.

"Good morning, ladies," he said cheerfully. "You two will be the first to hear my news! I've got a surprise that is going to set this town on its ear and give you a chance to enjoy a performance that brought the crowned heads of Europe to their feet in wild applause!"

"What on earth is it, Mr. Stanton?" Mrs. Amberly asked.

"It's a secret. And until I have all the details I will just have to leave you ladies guessing—but I promise you you're going to be thrilled."

With that he went on his way. Mrs. Amberly's false smile faded and her face slumped into its usual petulance.

"Humph, that man's all bluff!" she said grumpily. "I don't believe a word he said."

To save herself from commenting, Addie took a bite of scrambled eggs. *She* had no doubt that Brook would carry out his promise to set this town on its ear. Whatever his surprise, Addie was anticipating it.

After breakfast Addie left Mrs. Amberly in the lounge to

chat with one of her bridge partners and went to get ready for church.

Addie decided there was no longer any reason to wear the "protective" mourning attire she had worn so effectively on the long journey west, and instead put on a walking suit Aunt Susan had made for her from a lovely length of soft wool, purchased in England before the war. It had been put away during the war years when any kind of extravagant show was considered unsuitable or unpatriotic. A skillful seamstress, her aunt had fashioned a stylish outfit for her. The Prussian blue color was vastly becoming, the fitted jacket trimmed with soutache, her bonnet refurbished with new ribbons and a bunch of wax cherries. As a last touch she buttoned up her best pair of gray kid boots with French heels that she had bought on impulse in San Francisco the day before boarding the steamer.

Leaving the cottage, she went down the path around the arboretum, aware of several admiring glances from gentlemen guests out strolling, even though they had their wives on their arm. Flattered, Addie lowered her eyes as was proper, smiling demurely, as she passed them. She had almost reached the gates when she heard footsteps hurrying along the gravel path behind her and a voice calling her name.

"Miss Pride, good morning!"

Surprised, she turned to see it was Mr. Louis Montand, the guest Brook Stanton had introduced her to on the day of her arrival. She had not seen him except from a distance since then.

He caught up with her and asked, "Where, may I ask, are you off to on this bright morning?"

"To church," she replied.

"Isn't it rather a warm day to walk? You look so utterly charming I would hate to see you get overheated."

"Thank you, it's lovely and cool, besides I have this—" She unfurled her silk parasol and prepared to move on.

"Would you mind if I walked along with you? It is a lovely day at that."

Addie hesitated only a second. After all they had been properly introduced, and he was a guest at the hotel.

"If you like," she murmured.

"I've just returned from San Francisco," he told her. "I must say it's nice to be back in this bucolic setting. How are you enjoying being in Calistoga by now?"

Truth or a polite lie? What if she told Mr. Montand how really miserable she had been? But of course that was impossible. Instead, she said, "There is much to enjoy here, the mild weather is delightful, unusual, at least to me, for this time of year, and the scenery is awe-inspiring."

"I believe you are a diplomatic person, Miss Pride," Montand replied, amusement in his voice. "You are not bored, then? Not with the provincialism, the stultifying lack of stimulation at the hotel, the vacuity of most of our fellow guests?"

Addie looked at him surprised by the underlying sarcasm in his comment. "Well, Mr. Stanton has promised us some special sort of entertainment soon," she began, then stopped, remembering Brook had said it was a secret.

"Ah, yes, well, we shall see. Ever since my sister and I came here, he has been saying there would be more social life at the hotel, assured me he is making all sorts of arrangements so his guests will not get bored. I trust you are not bored, Miss Pride?"

Addie was saved from answering as the white-steepled church came into sight. "I must cross the street here, Mr. Montand," she said, gesturing to it with her gloved hand.

"Ah, that's where you attend? I am not a regular churchgoer, Miss Pride, or I might be tempted to accompany you," he chuckled softly. "But I hope you will not hold that

51

against me. I would like very much to become better acquainted. Perhaps you could have luncheon with me after church services? I would be happy to meet you in an hour or so? I would be waiting right here when you came out."

"Thank you very much for the invitation, Mr. Montand, but I am really not free to make social engagements. Perhaps, you did not understand that I am employed by Mrs. Amberly as her companion, and as such I must be available to her except for when she has her treatments and Thursdays and now—on Sunday mornings to attend services."

"Ah, I see," Montand looked thoughtful as he regarded Addie. "That must become a rather tedious occupation—dancing attendance on a woman so—" he hesitated as if searching for the right word, "—crippled with arthritis, is it? She did tell me one time just what her ailment was and why she was here—but I'm afraid it slipped my mind." His mouth twisted in a mocking smile.

Addie pretended not to notice. She would not for one unguarded moment reveal her own feelings about Mrs. Amberly or risk having Montand realize she agreed with his accurate if uncharitable assessment of her employer.

His sarcastic remarks struck Addie as ironic because she knew, even though Mrs. Amberly had met them only briefly, she admired the Montands inordinately. She had often mentioned both Louis and his sister, Estelle, telling Addie several times that they were the only people at Silver Springs worth cultivation—"They're *real* class!" Addie had soon learned that Mrs. Amberly had a rating system to designate who at the hotel was worth her time or effort. At Montand's obvious disdain for her employer, Addie felt almost pity. From his words it was clear that neither brother nor sister had any desire to socialize with *her*.

"Well, perhaps another time," Louis said. "I'm so happy I saw you and we had this chance for a little chat. I do hope you will consider dining with me some evening when my sister returns from the city? I would like you two to meet."

The church bell began to clang and Addie said, "I must go or I'll be late for the service."

"Yes, of course, but before you go, I must say your ensemble is stunning; you look absolutely charming, and your bonnet is one of the prettiest I've seen in quite awhile."

"Coming from a gentleman who has just been to San Francisco that's quite a compliment. Thank you," Addie smiled. "I really must go now." She closed her parasol.

Intuitively, Addie knew Louis Montand found her attractive, and her old self-confidence, dampened daily by her ignominious position, re-emerged. She crossed the street aware that Louis Montand's eyes were following her.

Holding her skirt gracefully with one hand, she went up the church steps, knowing he was still watching her. For the first time since her arrival she felt like herself, Adelaide Pride of Oakleigh. As she reached the church door, she lifted her head.

Just as she entered the vestibule, one dainty heel of her new boots caught on the doorstep. She tripped and would have lost her balance, maybe fallen, had not a solicitous usher at the entrance caught her elbow and steadied her.

Blushing, she whispered a thank you. Hot with embarrassment, she was shown to a pew and seated. Trying to cover her confusion she opened the church bulletin she had been handed. When she saw the announcement of the text for today's sermon, Proverbs 16:18, "Pride goeth before destruction, and a haughty spirit before a fall." Addie had to suppress a giggle. How humorously the Lord sometimes admonishes.

Across the street Louis Montand stood watching as Addie mounted the church steps then disappeared through the church door. There was no question about it, Adelaide Pride

53

had an air of quality about her. Something that, in his experience, was rare even in the well-bred young women to whom he had been exposed at the rounds of debutante parties when he was an undergraduate at Harvard. She possessed a natural refinement and understated elegance that he certainly had not met since coming to California. Friends had introduced him to any number of daughters of gold- and land-rich families, hopeful mamas hovering, aware of his enormous wealth and his background. However, none had appealed to him. And Louis was determined he would only marry on his own terms. He must feel something. If not passion, at least there must be real attraction. Anything less would only bore him. If he were going to fulfill his own vision of life here in this valley, he wanted to share it with a woman of whom he could feel proud and who would make other men envious of him, someone who could grace the kind of home that would establish him in this tight-knit community. A woman of beauty, breeding, some intelligence, and ability to understand and appreciate his plans.

Possibly Adelaide Pride could be the one. But what on earth was she doing here with that vulgar social climber? Louis's lip curled in contempt.

Well, he would wait until Estelle had a chance to meet Miss Pride. He valued his sister's opinions and advice although he did not always take them.

A few nights later, Addie wrote in her journal:

I have now been here and in the position of "paid companion" (as Mrs. A. never lets me forget!) a full month. I feel like a prisoner marking off the days of his sentence on the wall of his cell! Never have I met anyone who is so universally unpleasant and rude to anyone she considers inferior, which includes me, along with the hotel employees, the waiters in the dining room, the desk clerk, and maids. I wince inwardly whenever Mrs. A. addresses anyone. Only

54

Brook Stanton and Louis Montand escape her razor-sharp tongue.

Mrs. A. is, in my opinion, interested only in people she thinks are superior in some way. Almost upon my arrival here, she pointed out Mr. Montand saying he and his sister, whom I have not met as yet, were the only guests worth "cultivating." "They're *real* bluebloods," she confided. "From Boston." As if I cared.

Besides, I have discovered that in California what is important is to claim you are descended from "pioneers," the earliest settlers. Just as in Virginia a family who could trace their ancestry to Jamestown was considered among the most prestigious F.F.V. In that case, Letty's, our cottage maid and bathhouse attendant poor mother who came out in 1849 by covered wagon, should be on top of Mrs. A.'s list to cultivate!

To my embarrassment, Mrs. A. pursues Montand and keeps asking him when his sister will be returning to the Springs. Mr. Montand is certainly polite and pleasant enough. I had a chance encounter with him Sunday morning on my way to church.

Dec. 27th

Christmas has come and gone, a more dreary one I have never spent. Well, maybe the ones during the war were worse—in some ways. But at least I was surrounded by family and friends and we all tried to make things as merry as possible under the circumstances.

Many people left to spend Christmas with relatives for a week. The Montands left to spend Christmas in southern California with friends at the famous Del Monte Hotel in San Diego and will not return until after the New Year.

So there were only a few of us left, the Misses Brunell, and several older people, invalids in wheelchairs or walking with canes.

I must give credit to Brook who made things as festive as possible for those guests who remained during the holidays. Brook had a seven-foot cedar tree put up in the lobby, decorated lavishly with glass balls, flittering tinsel, and gold garlands, and each evening tiny lighted candles made the gilt baubles and cornucopias filled with hard candies sparkle. He said it was a custom first started in Germany and brought to England by Queen Victoria's Prince Consort, Albert, and now was becoming a tradition in America. At each table in the dining hall he had placed red candles and a wreath of greens and holly. One evening a choir from one of the local churches came to sing carols, another evening a quartet gave a concert in the lounge. He told me he had planned to give a Christmas ball but with so many guests leaving, it had not worked out.

January 1, 1871

New Year's Day. I cannot believe it is six years since the war ended and my strange new life began. It has all passed so quickly and I don't remember as much about it as I remember about the five long years of the war.

Now I am in a whole new phase of my life and the future is a kind of blur. I cannot imagine what awaits me in this New Year.

I don't know why I even mention this, but a few days before Christmas I saw the man I now call my "mysterious stranger"—again. I was doing a little shopping and saw him coming directly toward me along the sidewalk. For some reason, I became so flustered, I simply ducked into the nearest store. My heart was like a wild bird beating its wings. So rattled, I bought a silk scarf and a pair of gloves I didn't need and couldn't afford.

January 23

My Christmas box arrived from Aunt Susan along with a letter from Emily filled with news of friends and events in Avondale—which now seems to me like another world. Sometimes I ask myself what I am doing here, so far from everything I knew in my life. Just this morning when I was reading my Bible I turned to Jeremiah 29:11 and read, "For I know the plans I have for you, says the Lord, of peace and not of evil, to give you a future and a hope."

How comforting that is; how I wish I could believe it.

One thing of which I'm sure is that what I'm earning is helping provide Aunt Susan and Uncle Myles with a few extra comforts. That thought is worth all I have to put up with in this ignominious position.

PART 2

SILVER SPRINGS RESORT

Chapter 6

*U*pon her arrival Mrs. Amberly had outlined Addie' duties to her. Among them was to read aloud to her. Because of her own love of books Addie assumed this would be one of her easiest tasks. But although Mrs. Amberly sent her on weekly trips to the library to select books, it turned out that newspapers were what her employer most liked having read to her. She loved nothing more than hearing accounts of deaths and disasters; murder and mayhem were her special enjoyment. She eagerly relished the details of survivors' firsthand stories of excursion boat sinkings and train wrecks. Floods, fires, and tornadoes she savored vicariously.

Although her employer's tastes continued to dismay Addie, she constantly reminded herself of her purpose in taking this job, of how important it was that Mrs. Amberly be satisfied with her. Addie determined to give Mrs. Amberly nothing to complain about—not her attitude, nor unwillingness, nor any failure to accommodate.

Addie even conquered her distaste for reminding Mrs. Amberly when her salary was due. This demeaning scene was repeated on the first and fifteenth of every month. It was an ordeal each time, but Addie faced it without flinching. She learned to stand impassively while Mrs. Amberly emitted a small grunt or two, frowned as she wrote out her check. It was for Aunt Susan and Uncle Myles' sake, and for them Addie would have gone through much worse.

Twice monthly Addie walked to the post office and sent off the money order. Knowing how gratefully it would be received made up for all the humiliation in earning it. Afterward she would walk to the library and check out several titles of her own choosing.

One such afternoon, as she arrived back on the resort grounds from town, Addie met Brook. He was smiling broadly and seemed in especially high spirits.

"Well, Addie, I've brought it off!" he greeted her. "Come sit down on one of the benches, and I'll tell you all about it."

Curious, Addie followed him over to one of the white iron-lace benches circling the arboretum and sat down, eager to hear at last what Brook's secret was.

"It's confirmed. *She's* coming. *Della DeSecia!*" he announced triumphantly. "She's just finished a concert engagement in San Francisco, and I've persuaded her to come here for a rest *and*—" he paused significantly, "—*and* to give an informal concert for our guests."

"That's wonderful, Brook. I know how pleased you must be."

"I'm planning to send out invitations to people in town, as well—engraved ones. Make them feel they're singled out to attend." He smiled mischievously. "There's nothing people like more than feeling they're getting into something exclusive. And Madame DeSecia will get what she enjoys most—all the attention, not having to share curtain calls with a tenor she dislikes or a contralto who's jealous of her!" Brook rubbed his hands together gleefully. "Ah, it will be quite an occasion. I shall put on a reception like this town has never seen before—champagne, caviar . . ."

His eyes shone with excitement, his voice buoyant. He

was obviously elated by his accomplishment. It confirmed what Addie had intuitively felt about Brook: when he wanted something he went after it. He let no obstacle stand in his way. She couldn't help wondering what he had offered, what he had promised to get the famous opera star to come.

Brook's eyes took on a kind of glaze as he continued. "You know, Addie, this means the beginning of a dream I've had for a long time for this town. To bring well-known theatrical figures, actors as well as opera stars and concert artists here to perform. It's the perfect place, and if we treat them like royalty—this will become as fashionable as any resort in the east!" He sighed. "I've always loved the theater even though I was brought up in a home that considered it a sin and I was forbidden to go." Brook gave a little laugh, shook his head as if at the futility of such a prohibition. "Of course, I used to sneak out and spend whatever change I could scrounge up—selling newspapers, shining shoes, running messages—yes, my dear, since you might never guess it to look at me now, but I was a little street urchin. And then I'd go to the Saturday matinees. Sit in the balcony; I bought the cheapest tickets, but I loved it all—sitting in that darkened cavern on uncomfortable, moth-eaten seats, with smells all around me—the smell of over-ripe fruit most of the audience brought with them to eat—or throw—along with the smell of the oil lamps along the side of the aisles dimly illuminating them. All that is mixed in with the thrill of theater—yes, I was conscious of all that and yet, the minute the curtains parted and the flickering stage lights came up, I was in another world.

"The stories and songs unfolded before me, even as I began to see the shoddy costumes, be aware of the bad acting, realize that the comedy and comics were second-rate—still—" Abruptly Brook broke off as if suddenly conscious of how much he had revealed about himself. Suddenly the shining little-boy look on his face vanished and his eyes hardened. He gave a short, harsh laugh.

"I assure you my taste has risen from that of a little lad. One of the joys I find in going to the city is seeing great performances—drama, opera. And that is what I hope to bring here to Calistoga. I want to make it so attractive to the leading stars of the stage, concert halls, and, yes, opera—that they will all be willing to come—even consider it an honor to perform here."

As if he realized she was looking at him sympathetically, Brook smiled, stood up, and said less intently, "That's my dream. And I'll do whatever it takes to make it happen."

There was a flurry of excitement the day Della DeSecia was to arrive at Silver Springs. The rumor spread among the guests that she would come before lunch. An unusual number of bathhouse appointments were changed, and plans for drives and other activities were canceled so guests could be in the main lounge to catch a glimpse of the opera star. Although everyone tried to maintain an air of casual indifference, as though she were just any other guest arriving at the hotel, the electricity of anticipation was contagious. Mrs. Amberly was as bad if not worse than the rest, though still expressing negative opinions about the famous diva.

"She's past her prime, you know. Why else would she accept an invitation to come here, this out-of-the-way place, if she could go to some big city and have a huge audience?"

Addie said nothing. Besides, the question was rhetorical. Even so, Mrs. Amberly had no intention of missing Madame DeSecia's arrival. She positioned herself in a chair facing the entrance to be sure to have a good view. When Brook's carriage came up the driveway all conversation in the lounge stopped. All eyes turned toward the front door as Brook escorted Madame DeSecia inside. Her white-gloved hand rested on Brook's arm, and she talked animatedly to him as they walked into the lobby.

Addie thought her the most beautiful woman she had ever seen in spite of Mrs. Amberly's stage-whispered comment, "That color *can't* be *real!*"

Under question was the mass of lustrous red-gold hair visible beneath a hat with a sweeping brim trimmed with lilac blossoms. A lavender suit, with wide satin reveres showed off her figure, voluptuously curved, as befitted an opera singer.

Behind them, scurrying with mincing steps, came a small, thin woman, drably dressed in gray, carrying two hat boxes and a velvet case—containing, one assumed, Madame's jewels. This must be her maid, speculated the whispers behind Addie.

After her was one of the hotel porters laden with tapestried luggage. It was, Addie thought, quite a parade. Impressed, Addie watched as Madame DeSecia, apparently unaware of her audience, swept up the stairway to the suite Addie knew Brook had prepared especially for the use of such celebrated guests.

During her sojourn at the Springs Hotel no one saw much of Madame DeSecia. She had her meals in her suite, and if she had any of the treatments they must have been taken at night or at dawn for no one encountered her coming or going to the bathhouse. However, they did hear her. Sometimes the sound of her vocalizing penetrated the lower floor of the hotel, and everyone stopped whatever they were doing to listen. Even when it was only scales, it seemed remarkable that such a talent was actually on the premises.

At last the date of her concert came. Early in the evening the hotel started filling up. Local people who had received Brook's fancy invitations came dressed in their finest. In the lounge, chairs had been set in two semi-circular rows.

65

A grand piano brought from San Francisco was placed in shiny, black magnificence at one end of the room. Madame DeSecia's accompanist had arrived two days before, and the room was closed for hours at a time so he could practice.

Since Brook had made such a point that the evening would be the most elegant affair ever held at Silver Springs, Addie decided to wear a dress she had been saving—for what she wasn't sure. But now it seemed appropriate. Excitement flushed Addie's cheeks and brightened her eyes as she got dressed. The velvet basque was the color of a ripe persimmon. Tiny amber buttons marched from where the stand-up collar ended in a V, to the waist. The tafetta skirt was a deeper shade, drawn to the back with a velvet bow from which pleated ruffles cascaded down the back.

Addie spent more time than usual doing her hair, experimenting with a new style; swept up from her ears and held with tortoise-shell combs to a fall of curls in back. On impulse she took out her mother's opal jewelry. She held it, looking at it for a long moment, then after only a second's hesitation, she slipped in the earrings and fastened on the necklace. She then considered the effect in the mirror. Perfect!

When she went to see if Mrs. Amberly was ready, Addie's suspicions of Mrs. Amberly's envy of anyone younger or comelier were confirmed by the look of outrage on her employer's face. Obviously Mrs. Amberly felt it was not suitable for a "paid companion" to look so stylish.

But Addie refused to allow anything to spoil this evening for her. She deliberately complimented Mrs. Amberly on her own dress, a brilliant blue taffeta embroidered with black Brussels lace and jet beads. It had probably cost a fortune, although it would have been worn to better advantage by someone twenty years younger and forty pounds lighter.

For all her disparagement of the probable quality of the

evening's entertainment, Mrs. Amberly insisted on their going over from their cottage nearly an hour before the concert was scheduled to begin. That way they could choose the best seats. Even though embarrassed by her employer's pushiness Addie was glad that they did get seats in the front row.

Mrs. Amberly settled herself fussily. "I hope this isn't like some of the ghastly *musicale soirées* I've attended. Not that I expect much. I think she's probably third-rate. I never heard of her myself."

That fact was not much of a criterion by which to judge the artist, Addie thought, but not commenting on Mrs. Amberly's many observations had become one of Addie's skills.

However, when Della DeSecia entered, looking every inch a diva, no one could have failed to be impressed. She was a vision to behold. Gowned in apricot satin embroidered with crystal beads, the bodice draped to show off her white shoulders and rounded bosom. She held a fan edged in marabou. She glittered from the sparkling tiara nestled in the lustrous red-gold waves of her hair to the rhinestone butterflies that fluttered on her peach satin slippers. When she took her place in the curve of the piano the room hushed to awed silence.

As she began to sing in a clear, glorious voice, Addie felt tingles. The program was varied, beginning with a familiar soprano solo from Mozart's *Marriage of Figaro* and followed by the heartbreaking aria from Verdi's *Aida,* which brought tears to Addie's eyes. After a short intermission, she finished with some lighter selections, "leiders," lovely German love songs, and ended with a song from a popular light operetta.

The quiet that fell after the last bell-like note was sung broke into thunderous applause a moment later. Madame DeSecia took several bows and finally accepted the lovely bouquet of yellow roses Brook presented. Then people began to cluster around her with accolades and compliments. Mrs. Amberly was one of the first shoving her way forward to congratulate the singer. Addie let her go.

Still caught up in the music, which had temporarily lifted her out of the mundane, Addie drifted out into the lobby. She found a corner from where she could still see into the main lounge where a beaming Brook hovered over the singer, surrounded by her enthusiastic fans. Addie smiled to see him so happy at his successful achievement of his dream.

Suddenly something caught her attention. Addie drew in her breath. The towering figure of a man in the crowd. It was *he!* The man of her strange encounters! Seated as they were in the front of the room, she had not seen the rest of the audience taking seats behind. If he were among the invited guests, Brook must know him! Her heart began to thump excitedly. Perhaps Brook would introduce him to her during the postconcert reception, which Brook had promised would be as elaborate and elegant as anything given at the Palace Hotel in San Francisco.

A second glance brought the disconcerting fact that *he* was not alone. Standing next to him was a small, slender woman with masses of light, reddish hair, wearing a gray taffeta dress with a lace bertha collar. His wife? The possibility that he might be married had never occurred to her and caused an unexpected pang of dismay. How silly she had been, indulging in romantic daydreams about a stranger. Embarrassed by her own foolish fantasies, Addie panicked. She did not want to see him. Thinking only to escape she turned away and as she did bumped directly into Louis Montand.

"Careful, Miss Pride!" He regarded her quizzically. "Where were you going in such a hurry?"

"It was just a little stuffy," Addie improvised quickly. "I thought I'd get some fresh air."

"Come, then," Montand said, putting a strong hand under Addie's elbow. "I'll find us a nice, quiet spot near a window."

There was nothing Addie could do but accept his invitation. A quick glance informed her the concert crowd was beginning to flow out into the lobby, and she noticed that the alcove toward which they were heading was protected by a large potted palm. Placed just behind it was a small table and two chairs. Here Addie saw she would be concealed from the rest of the room.

Once they were seated, Louis remarked, "A penny for your thoughts, Miss Pride. I was observing you before I spoke to you, and you looked quite lost in another world—at least for a few minutes."

Addie's face grew warm and she wondered how long Montand had been watching her and what her expression might have revealed. She tried to keep her voice casual. "Oh, I think I was just still under the spell of the music. It was truly beautiful, wasn't it?"

"Yes, I suppose it was. Although I must admit music is not my forte. I'm sure I'm sadly lacking in true appreciation of it. Visual beauty attracts me more." His eyes made an appreciative sweep of her. "And to digress for a moment, may I say you are looking very beautiful this evening, Miss Pride."

Addie murmured her thanks. Then he continued. "Are you a student of music? Because if you are, I am certainly willing to learn, and if you'd care to give me your critique of tonight's performance perhaps I could be more appreciative."

"Oh, I'd never dare do that!"

"Come now, I imagine you've studied music to show such rapt interest. Do you play an instrument?"

"Like most Southern girls I was made to take piano lessons, so I play a little but not well at all."

Louis smiled at her indulgently. "I believe you are too modest about your talent. *All* your talents."

The lobby began to fill up with people, and the hum of conversation grew louder. Montand turned to look over his shoulder, then raised an eyebrow. "It amuses me how suddenly all these ranchers and farmers and storekeepers have become aficionados of opera. . . ."

Addie realized he was making fun of the townspeople now lionizing Madame DeSecia. She hated sarcastic comments. It was something she had to live with in her daily life with Mrs. Amberly. But she still hated it. Her father had always said sarcasm was the weapon of cowards. Feeling a stirring of dislike for Louis Montand, she looked at him. What was he really like under that veneer of sophistication?

The crowd began moving en masse into the card room where an extravagant buffet had been set up. A long table covered with a Battenburg-lace tablecloth, illuminated by tall white candles, held two large silver urns at both ends containing iced bottles of champagne; arranged down both sides were platters of sliced meats, salads, fruit, and elaborate desserts.

Apparently unconscious he had said anything Addie might not agree with nor approve of, Montand smiled ingratiatingly and asked, "Shall I get us some refreshment? A glass of wine?"

"I am thirsty. But I think I'd like some lemonade instead of wine."

Montand looked surprised but did not insist she change her request. "I'll be right back," he promised getting up.

After he left, Addie, hidden by the wide palm fronds, watched the panorama of the party. People were still pushing and circling around Madame DeSecia, whom Brook was trying to guide to a place where she could hold court as

70

well as sip some refreshing champagne. From the look on his face, Addie knew Brook was satisfied his goal had been accomplished. The evening was the brilliant success he had hoped. Next she glanced around the room to see if she could find the tall stranger and the woman again. But somehow they had merged into the crowd.

Soon Louis was back. He handed Addie her lemonade then sat down opposite her. He raised his glass of champagne in a toasting gesture. "To music and friendship and coincidence . . ."

Lifting hers, too, Addie took a sip. "That's a curious toast."

"Why so? It was impromptu, although I think appropriate for the moment. I enjoyed the music even though I confessed my ignorance of it; friendship because I hope ours will develop; and coincidence seemed altogether in keeping. Don't you agree, Miss Pride, that coincidence brought you and Madame DeSecia and me all to this small town that I don't think anyone ever heard of twenty-five years ago?" Louis smiled, his eyes narrowed. "I am more convinced than ever of what a large part chance plays in one's life. Sometimes the very things one looks upon as misfortune can be the very things that bring the most good fortune and happiness in life."

"Yes, that is sometimes true," Addie agreed.

"You see there was a series of unfortunate events in my early life—our parents died when I was only a little boy. Estelle was fifteen and at once took over my care. She has been almost like a mother to me ever since. And then as a child I was—delicate, suffering from various illnesses. So much so the doctors thought a change of climate might be advantageous to my health. That is how Estelle and I happened to come to California in the first place, seeking the most healthful place to live. And at last we came to the Napa Valley."

He took a long sip of his wine. "As you can see it was a very fortuitous decision of Estelle's, for here I became not only hale and hearty but we are—as they say—in the right place at the right time. We found wonderful land with good, producing vineyards. I foresee a prosperous future— all through no planning of our own. Now, do you understand why I believe in the unplanned, unexpected things in life?"

"For you. But I have known people who blame unforeseen circumstances for bringing them troubles and tribulations and—"

"Yes, but then we cannot blame anyone for our failures. Perhaps I should say I believe in such unpredictable causes to a limited degree. Sometimes we must recognize when life has brought us to a place of decision, and we then, using our knowledge, experience, and wisdom, make the right one."

Addie nodded. "Perhaps you are right."

"Take, for example, this property I own. I intend to make it the best known winery in California. I've been assured it is good, hardy stock, and I have been studying European methods of wine making." He leaned forward, eyes lighted with excitement. "I'll show some of these old-timers around here who think they have a corner on the market. I even have a name for it 'Chateau Montand.' Do you like it?"

"It sounds . . . very French."

Louis threw back his head and laughed. "It *is,* and you, my dear Miss Pride, are very tactful. That was the thing I noticed about you at our introduction. *Almost* the first thing." He paused. "I'm building a home on a beautiful hillside overlooking my vineyards. My sister Estelle is in San Francisco picking out some of the finishing details, drapery material, rugs. I've selected most of the furniture, but I felt it needed a woman's touch to complete the ambiance I want."

72

He looked at her over the rim of his wine glass, reflectively or was it appraisingly?

"I'd like very much to take you out to see the house as soon as it's finished."

There was no chance for Addie to reply to the invitation because just then Mrs. Amberly lumbered up.

"So here's where you've got to, I've been looking all over for you," she said crossly to Addie. Then she quickly altered her tone of voice. "Oh, Mr. Montand, I didn't see you. . . ."

He rose to his feet, bowed slightly. "You must blame me, Mrs. Amberly. I lured Miss Pride away from the crush of people. We were just enjoying a quiet chat, will you join us?"

Addie saw her employer undergo a painful decision. Addie guessed by this time of the evening, Mrs. Amberly's corset was biting cruelly into her layers of fat, her shoes killing her feet. Most certainly she could hardly wait to be in the privacy of her cottage where she could undress, soak her feet, and relax. On the other hand, Addie knew Mrs. Amberly was in awe of Louis Montand, and his invitation was a tempting detour from such relief.

As Mrs. Amberly hesitated, Montand suggested smoothly, "Perhaps the hour is too late? For a music lover like yourself, Mrs. Amberly, as delightful as the evening has been, you are probably emotionally exhausted. So may I escort you two ladies to your cottage?"

Addie could not help admire Montand's adroitness in managing to get out of an awkward half-hour's chat with Mrs. Amberly, a woman he clearly disdained.

Flattered, Mrs. Amberly took the arm he offered and, ignoring Addie, directed her conversation to him. "Mr. Stanton introduced me to Madame DeSecia—what a nice person—so thoughtful, Mr. Stanton, I mean. I thought she was a bit—well, stand-offish, if you know what I mean. And she can hardly speak English. . . ."

73

Inwardly Addie groaned. Didn't she realize that Della DeSecia *was* Italian, a star at some of the most renowned opera houses in Europe? The fact that this was her first American tour was written in the brochure Brook had had printed for this occasion. Evidently Mrs. Amberly had not read it.

Addie followed Montand's slow progress with Mrs. Amberly through the lobby. Although the crowd was beginning to thin, people were still gathered in small clusters chatting. At the front door, for some reason, Addie turned her head and saw—standing not five feet away—the tall stranger.

He was looking at her with an expression that startled her. Suddenly she knew she was blushing and why. Dazed, her heart hammering, Addie hurried out the door in the wake of Montand and Mrs. Amberly.

As they walked across the grounds she only half heard what Mrs. Amberly was rattling on about. At the cottage porch Montand said in his most gracious manner, "Good night, Mrs. Amberly, Miss Pride. It's been a pleasure. I hope when my sister returns from San Francisco we can have the pleasure of having you two ladies dine with us."

Addie saw Mrs. Amberly's mouth drop open in disbelief. She mumbled something incoherent, then glanced at Addie as if indignant that the invitation she had longed for from the Montands would include her *paid companion!* Inside the cottage Mrs. Amberly shambled off to her own room without so much as a good night to Addie.

As Addie went into her bedroom and shut the door, she felt suddenly let down. Something in the music tonight had struck a resounding chord deep within her. It brought back a memory from the past, one she had almost forgotten. When she was a little girl, maybe six years old, she had been awakened by the voices of her parents' departing guests and the sound of carriage wheels beneath her bed-

74

room window. She had slipped out of bed, run barefoot into the hall, leaned over the banister, and saw her parents dancing in the moonlight shining in from the open front door as her father hummed a waltz. She had watched as they circled slowly ending in an embrace that seemed to go on forever. Addie had tiptoed back to bed feeling somehow assured, safe in their love.

Her old longings for a love like she had seen in her parents, in Aunt Susan and Uncle Myles, even in Emily and Evan, swept over her in a deep wrenching loneliness. Would she ever find it?

Irrelevantly the old adage floated into her mind: "Journeys end in lovers meeting."

Was her journey to California to end in meeting her love? And who was it? Addie thought of the three men she had met since her arrival. Brook Stanton was the first. As interesting and fascinating as he was, Addie could not even consider him a possibility. Brook was a gambler, just like the man on the riverboat, and possibly every bit as dangerous. Louis Montand? He was undeniably attracted to her but—

Then the image of the tall stranger came. Could it be *he?*

Chapter 7

One evening, a few days after the concert, Addie was entering the lobby with Mrs. Amberly when Louis, who was standing at the reception desk with a tall, slender woman, saw them and raised his hand in greeting. After saying something to his companion, he came across the room toward them.

"Good evening, Mrs. Amberly, Miss Pride," Louis greeted them. "What a coincidence. I was just talking about you to my sister." He addressed them both, but it was on Addie his gaze lingered. "Estelle returned from San Francisco this afternoon, and we were just about to dine. Would you ladies care to join us?"

Mrs. Amberly blinked. She opened her mouth, then snapped it shut like a startled turtle. Was she undecided whether to accept the invitation?

Her employer could not have been unaware of Louis's attentiveness to Addie since the night of the Madame DeSecia's performance. Although *this* was the social opportunity Mrs. Amberly had long sought, Addie realized it galled her to receive it through her companion.

She glanced at her employer, watching Mrs. Amberly swallow this bitter pill.

"I realize this is short notice," Louis continued, "but after all, we are fellow guests here, and I say there is no need for formality in this casual atmosphere. Don't you agree, Mrs. Amberly?"

Mrs. Amberly's own eagerness to be seen at the Montands' table overcame the umbrage she *could* have manufactured at such a last-minute invitation.

"Well, if you're sure it won't be an intrusion—"

"Intrusion? Nonsense. It would be a pleasure," Louis reassured, cutting her protestation short. "Now come along, I'd like to introduce my sister."

While this little scene was taking place, Addie noticed Louis's sister, standing aloofly at some distance. She made no move to join them or to add her own to her brother's urgings for their company at dinner.

"Well, if you're *quite* sure," Mrs. Amberly dragged out the words as she glanced into the adjoining lounge. Puzzled, Addie followed her glance, then saw the Brunell sisters seated in there, craning their necks. She then guessed Mrs. Amberly's purpose in delaying. Mrs. Amberly wanted to make sure her card partners witnessed her being escorted by Mr. Montand over to his sister. Assured of that, she took Louis's arm. With some inner reluctance Addie took the other arm he offered.

Estelle Montand very much resembled her brother. Although he had told her she was fifteen years his senior, her brown hair, sweeping up from the same high forehead as his, was untouched by gray. She had the same sharply defined features in a pale olive-complexioned face. The marked difference between them was their eyes. While his were keenly alive, hers were moody and melancholy.

Everything about Miss Montand exhibited expensive taste. She was dressed in a tobacco-colored silk promenade dress trimmed with fluted ruffles, and carried a glossy brown alligator handbag; her pointed shoes were of cordovan leather. From between the reveres of her jacket rippled a jabot of ecru Brussels lace, fastened by a carnelian and gold brooch. Addie always noticed such details because her mother had been beautifully fashionable. Perhaps now that she could no longer afford fine clothing made Addie aware of them more.

"Estelle, may I present Mrs. Amberly, one of our fellow guests."

"So nice to meet you at last," gushed Mrs. Amberly.

"How do you do," replied Miss Montand with weary condescension.

"And this, Estelle, is Adelaide. Miss Adelaide Pride," Louis announced bringing Addie forward.

"Miss Pride." Estelle nodded. "So, you are real after all." She regarded Addie steadily for a long moment before extending her hand. It felt as dry as a leaf, and her fingers only lightly touched Addie's palm, then quickly withdrew. A smile briefly touched her thin lips, and she lifted an eyebrow. "Louis has waxed so rhapsodically about you, I began to believe you must be a figment of his overwrought imagination."

Addie felt the warmth rise into her cheeks under Miss Montand's gaze, and she knew she was blushing.

An awkward pause followed Estelle's comment. Louis was so busy gazing at Addie he lost the thread of conversation and missed his sister's implication. Addie was acutely conscious of Mrs. Amberly's stare.

Oblivious to both his sister's coolness and Mrs. Amberly's suspicious glare, Louis smiled serenely at Addie as if he had brought off some brilliant coup, "Well, shall we go over to the dining hall?"

Miss Montand's remark about Louis's talking about her made Addie uncomfortable. She was positive it was only at his insistence that she and Mrs. Amberly had been asked to join him and his sister. Perhaps Estelle had anticipated dining alone with her brother after being gone so many weeks.

At dinner Mrs. Amberly monopolized the conversation, trying to impress the Montands with long, boring tales of her European travels combined with name-dropping the famous hotels, mentioning some of the world-known celebrities and minor royalty who had been guests at the same time, broadly hinting that she had been acquainted with such personages. Certainly the Montands could see through this pitiful charade.

Didn't the woman have any sense at all? Didn't she know how she sounded? Didn't she realize the Montands would have a good laugh over her when they were alone?

During one of Mrs. Amberly's monologues Addie glimpsed a glint of undeniable scorn in Louis's eyes. Quickly, she lowered her eyes so that she would not have to meet his. She did not want to seem to be sharing in any way his silent mocking of her employer. What troubled her even more was what she saw in his eyes every time their glances met. It was something more than casual admiration, and it gave her pause. Did she want Louis Montand to be so attracted to her?

As the dinner progressed Addie became more and more aware of the subtle undercurrent of resentment beneath Miss Montand's icy politeness. She began to think the dinner would never end when something unexpected happened. Looking up from her untouched plate she saw Brook enter the dining room. With him were a couple. Immediately Addie felt her stomach tighten, her cheeks flame.

The man was the tall stranger who mysteriously intruded her daytime thoughts and invaded her dreams. On his arm was the same woman who had been with him at the concert!

With mixed emotions she saw Brook was approaching

79

their table bringing the couple with him. Addie clenched her hands, crushing the napkin on her lap.

With his usual cordiality, Brook greeted them. "Good evening, ladies and Mr. Montand. May I present Mrs. Freda Wegner and Mr. Rexford Lyon."

Addie's first reaction was relief. They weren't married after all. Her next reaction was to chide herself. What possible difference could it make to her? As Brook introduced each of them in turn, she was conscious that Mr. Lyon's gaze was as intense and unsettling as during their first encounter.

Carrying on his usual congenial conversation, Brook explained, "Mrs. Wegner and Mr. Lyon are both longtime residents of our beautiful area. Both are vintners. You have perhaps heard of Wegner Wineries and Lyon's Court?"

Addie chanced a second covert glance at the woman. She was perhaps thirty, very slender, looking small standing between the two men. She was not especially pretty. Her face was pale and lightly freckled, but her expression was alert and interested, her eyes keen and intelligent. She had a thin nose and a mouth that revealed . . . what? Addie wasn't sure. Perhaps that she had known sadness, suffering of some kind or physical pain. Possibly she was a widow since she was dressed in moderate mourning, a black dress trimmed with white ruching, stylish but not fashionable.

However, her smile was sweet and her voice low and pleasant when she spoke. "I hope you folks will enjoy your stay in the valley."

"Oh, the Montands plan to live here, Freda," Brook corrected her. "They've bought land—adjoining Lyon's, right, Rex? And they're building a magnificent house. Near completion now, isn't it, Louis?"

Louis shrugged. "As long as I keep behind those workers—who tend to loaf off, I'm afraid, if someone isn't riding herd on them every minute."

Addie saw Mrs. Wegner and Mr. Lyon exchange a knowing glance. She recalled what Brook had said about valley "old-timers" being cliquish, not too eager to have "outsiders" move into the valley. Were Mrs. Wegner and Lyon among those who resented the Montands buying up such a large amount of property and settling there?

But of course, nothing of such importance was discussed. A few more pleasantries were exchanged; then they left. Brook accompanied them across the room, seated them at a table opposite, in Addie's direct line of vision.

For the rest of the evening, Addie could not resist a few glances their way. She found herself distracted by their presence, curious about their relationship. Were they lovers or just friends? Or somehow related? Was Mrs. Wegner in mourning? If so, was it for a husband? Or a close relative? Although they seemed deeply involved in conversation, they did not seem to have the aura of romantic intimacy.

Addie did not have much chance to spend dwelling on the situation at the other table. She was too much aware of the tension she felt at her own table. Every time Louis addressed her, Mrs. Amberly darted her a sharp look. Louis made no effort to hide his interest in her. It was as if tonight, with her introduction to his sister, Louis felt free to express his attraction to her openly.

Addie had come to know her employer by now. She could almost read Mrs. Amberly's mind from the speculative glances she was casting at her. Was she debating whether or not to nip it in the bud or use Louis's interest to *her* own advantage?

Finally the meal ended and Miss Montand, pleading weariness from her trip, left them in the lobby to go to her room. Mrs. Amberly's bridge partners were waiting, and after thanking Louis profusely for dinner she departed to the card room.

"May I escort you to your cottage, Miss Pride?"

"No, thank you. I must stay until Mrs. Amberly has finished her game. She has some difficulty walking and needs assistance after sitting for so long."

A look of distaste passed like a shadow over Louis's face. He started to say something then changed his mind. "I meant what I said about wanting to take you out to Chateau Montand as soon as it is completed. The furniture and other things Estelle ordered this trip should be arriving soon, and when the interior painting is finished it will be ready to show and to move into. . . ." He paused significantly. "I *do* very much want *you* to see it."

Not knowing exactly how to respond to the emphasis in his words, Addie murmured something that she hoped was appropriate, and they said good night.

Later, alone in her room, Addie opened her journal. Maybe by writing down her mixed feelings she could sort them out. First the facts. Tonight she had learned her tall stranger was a native of Napa Valley, a rancher and vintner. This fourth encounter had left her even more confused. There was no doubt that something unexplainable had taken place between them on each occasion. But tonight he had been in the company of Freda Wegner. This was the second time *she* had seen them together. Were they more than close friends?

Feb. 14th

Well, at last, Mrs. A. has achieved her goal. She has met Miss Estelle Montand, *the sister!* It was as cool a meeting as one can possibly envision. I had the distinct impression that Miss Montand would rather the introduction had never taken place. I was a bit taken aback by the invitation to join them at dinner, which was all Louis's idea.

The most *unexpected* incident occurred after we were all seated. Brook escorted a couple into the dining hall, and when I saw who they were, I was quite startled. It was *my stranger.* Well, perhaps that is an exaggeration. It was the man I saw the day I arrived here. It all came back to me.

82

That feeling I had as I stepped off the train that he was there to meet me! Of course, it is all foolishness. But still, I had the exact same sensation tonight when we were introduced. His name is Rex Lyon.

Sitting at her desk, in the lamplight, Addie dipped her pen into the inkwell ready to continue writing. But she found it hard to go on. Pen poised above the pages her mind wandered hopelessly.

Then she began to think of Louis Montand. It was impossible to ignore his interest. Certainly he was charming, worldly, and sophisticated. However, his relationship with his sister was puzzling. Was it natural to be so deferential, so dependent on his sister's opinions, eager for her approval? Why had it been so important to him for Estelle to meet *her?*

In spite of any effort Mrs. Amberly might make to associate with Louis's sister, Addie felt sure Estelle would discourage any overtures of friendship. Also Addie sensed Estelle's disapproval of Louis's interest in her.

Addie put down her pen and closed her journal, her thoughts too disjointed to write more. Why should it matter at all what Estelle thinks? It was fairly apparent that her status of paid companion put Addie in a different social class than the Montands. *Why should I care?* she thought.

Estelle Montand? Aloof, cold, snobbish. Did Addie recognize those unlikable traits in Louis's sister because she herself had the same ones? Addie had to admit she often felt superior to others. Is that what she had seen in Estelle Montand that she disliked?

God help me, she thought, *if I am like that!* She knew she looked down on Mrs. Amberly, thought her lacking in social graces, mentally groaned at her murder of the King's English, her ignorance and malapropisms.

Addie flipped open the leather journal again and quickly

wrote in the date and printed boldly in block letters BEWARE OF PRIDE. PRIDE IS THE MOST DANGEROUS OF ALL FAULTS!

She undressed, put on her nightie, and picked up her Bible. The habit of reading a verse or two before going to sleep instilled early in her life still held. She knew the Scripture she needed tonight but she wasn't quite sure where to find it. Thumbing through the pages she came upon Obadiah. *Obadiah?* Addie stopped short. She stared at the chapter heading. Guiltily she realized she didn't even know such a book was in the Bible. It was short, only two pages.

Addie had been taught a rule of thumb in searching Scripture for guidance. That was to start reading until a certain line of a verse struck you or "quickened." If and when that happened, that was the particular lesson God was trying to teach you at that moment.

With this in mind Addie began to read. It took only a few minutes to read through the entire book of Obadiah. But two lines seemed to speak directly to her: "The pride of your heart has deceived you" and "As you have done, it shall be done to you."

Thoughtfully, Addie shut the book, blew out her lamp, and got into bed. She knew she often had a critical spirit, tended to make snap judgments about people—like her judgments about Estelle Montand and, yes, Mrs. Amberly. It was something she needed to guard against.

Lying there in the darkness, the verse she had first sought still eluded her, but the odd ones she had discovered in Obadiah kept echoing through her mind. That's what God wanted her to learn.

Addie's self-declared indifference to Estelle Montand's opinion and its effects on her, she soon discovered was wrong. Contrary to what she had thought, the arrival of Louis's sister *did* make a difference in Addie's life at Silver Springs.

After the night they dined with Montands things took an unexpected turn.

In the first place, Mrs. Amberly set out on a campaign to cultivate Estelle in ways that humiliated Addie. Mrs. Amberly seemed always on the lookout to waylay Estelle, corner her, trap her in a conversation or with an invitation. Mentally gritting her teeth, Addie had to stand by, dying by inches of embarrassment, while Mrs. Amberly, undaunted by Estelle's coldness, pursued her. If Miss Montand could not avoid her, Mrs. Amberly would summarily dismiss Addie, sending her away on a contrived errand—"Do see that the maid picks up my laundry, Miss Pride" or "Go to the post office, I need stamps" so that she could enjoy Miss Montand's forced company by herself.

It was doubly humiliating because it was obvious that Miss Montand could not endure Mrs. Amberly. Why could Mrs. Amberly not see that herself? Addie was terribly aware of unconcealed dislike in Estelle's eyes that included Addie as well as her employer.

Meanwhile, Louis Montand was not around the hotel as much as usual. He spent more and more time out at their property overseeing the finishing of the house. To her surprise Addie found she missed him. At least his company had helped pass the time during Mrs. Amberly's long evening card sessions. Louis was interesting, had many witty stories to tell about his travels and experiences. At least it was a welcome change from nightly being subjected to the overheard carping conversation of the bridge players.

Soon both Montands began to leave the hotel early in the morning to go out to their house, often not returning until dinnertime. It was usually in the evenings that Addie saw Louis in the dining hall. Of course, he was always with Estelle, and often they were accompanied by Milton Drew, their lawyer, or their architect, Leland Parks. But Louis always stopped at Mrs. Amberly's table to pay his respects.

85

One such evening, Louis told them he and Estelle would be leaving the hotel in a matter of days to move into their house although it was unfurnished except for the rooms they would be occupying.

At this Mrs. Amberly wagged a pudgy finger at him playfully. "Now, Mr. Montand, I hope you won't forget *us* once you're all settled in—for we shall miss *you* dreadfully here at the resort. You and your sister are such an asset to this place."

Addie clenched her jaw and moved the silver at her place nervously. How could Mrs. Amberly be so gauche? But Louis managed to handle Mrs. Amberly's obvious angling for an invitation and get a message to Addie as well.

"Certainly not, Mrs. Amberly. In a community this size I am sure we shall run into each other often." His eyes sought Addie's as he added, "I have no intention of allowing the pleasant acquaintances I've made here at Silver Springs to be neglected."

Later that evening Brook ambled into the card room where Addie was at her usual place waiting out Mrs. Amberly's card game. He pulled up a chair beside her. Leaning close he lowered his voice confidentially. "I couldn't help overhearing Louis Montand's reply to your dinner companion's *imploring* him not to forget his friends at Silver Springs once he moves to his grand new chateau!"

Addie knew Brook well enough to detect the half-teasing, half-serious note in his voice. She smiled but made no comment.

"He's quite taken with you, you know," Brook went on, regarding her closely, as if to see how she reacted to this statement.

"Oh?"

"Oh, yes, indeed. I'd say, quite taken." Brook still observed her shrewdly. "He's asked me all sorts of things about you. In a very gentlemanly way, of course. I told him

I only knew what I'd observed. That you were—apart from being beautiful—every inch a lady, with an impeccable character, and from a long line of blue bloods from one of the first families of Virginia."

Addie had to laugh. "Brook, you're incorrigible!"

"Why? What do you mean? Wasn't I right? You are an aristocrat of the first water, aren't you? Or have you come here under false pretenses?" He pretended to act very shocked.

"I suppose I could have and gotten away with it. California is a long way from Virginia." She smiled. "I guess anyone could make up any kind of background and no one would be the wiser."

"How true. And I imagine a good many people do just that. Who knows? Mr. Montand himself might be an impostor. As well as his very proper sister. Maybe they are both fugitives with a dark mysterious past, buying all that property and building this mansion on a hilltop with ill-gotten money. . . ." He paused. "What is it they say?—Nothing is as it seems, much is smoke and mirrors and magic." Then he laughed and got to his feet. "Who are *they,* anyhow? Everyone is always quoting *they* but no one seems to know who *they* are."

"Oh, Brook, what a treat you are! You always make me laugh."

"Good! Life is too serious. As *they* say—" He looked at her for a few seconds more. "Nevertheless, it is true, you know, Louis Montand has serious intentions toward you, Miss Pride. Mark my words, you'll have a proposal from him within a very few weeks if not sooner, or I'm greatly mistaken."

"You *are* mistaken, Brook," Addie said firmly, positive of her intuitive feeling that Louis's sister would have to approve of any choice of a bride Louis made and that Estelle did not approve of her.

"Wait and see if I am or not. If I were giving odds—"
Brook grinned.

"I don't believe in gambling," she cut in with pretend
primness.

"Then take a sure tip from an experienced gambler and
bet on it."

"You're impossible, Brook!" Addie shook her head, and
he sauntered off.

As it turned out it was Brook who provided Louis with the
opportunity to issue Addie a very special invitation. Since
the Montands had stayed at Silver Springs Hotel during the
eighteen months of construction of their house, he
announced he was giving them a farewell dinner party.

All the hotel guests were included, and to Addie's pleasure and pain, upon entering the dining room that
evening, she saw Rexford Lyon among the local invited
acquaintances of the Montands. She assumed it was
because now they would be neighbors, since the Montands'
property bordered Lyon's Court land. Her first pleasure at
seeing him was followed by dismay when she saw Freda
Wegner was also present.

Addie was angry at herself that the thought that they
might be more than friends caused her such dismay. He
was a stranger! What difference should whatever they were
to each other make to her?

However, the minute after she entered the dining hall
and he saw her, she was sure he had started over to her
when Louis, seeing her at the same time, intercepted and
came to her side.

"You're sitting beside me, at my right, in the place of
honor, at my request!" he told her, smiling. Taking her arm
he led her over to the large, exquisitely decorated table and
held the chair for her. As he took his place next to her, he

whispered, "I haven't had a minute alone with you for weeks—the dragonfly is always hovering."

Addie looked at him, startled, wondering if he meant Mrs. Amberly or his sister. Of course, he meant Mrs. Amberly. Louis and Estelle were singularly devoted. Only occasionally had she noticed the slightest suggestion of irritation on his part of something Estelle said or did.

To her surprise Brook escorted Freda Wegner over and seated her beside Addie. He leaned down between them. "I wanted you two to get to know each other. I have a hunch you could be great friends."

This could be an unexpected opportunity. By some tactful questioning Addie thought she would be able to find out just what Mrs. Wegner's and Rex Lyon's relationship was. However, there was not much chance for a personal exchange. The gentleman on Freda's right monopolized her throughout most of the meal while Louis did the same to Addie. Besides, as master of ceremonies, Brook demanded everyone's attention as he held forth with flowery speeches at intervals between courses, waxing loquaciously about the future of the valley, Calistoga in particular, and how wonderful it was to welcome new comers like the Montands who would add to its prosperity and the renown of the region.

Brook was an ebullient host, and the dinner party was his version of a Roman banquet. The food was superb; merriment and laughter were as plentiful as the champagne that flowed like proverbial water as frequent toasts were offered and drunk.

The round table at which they were seated provided accessibility to everyone and much cross talk was possible. As the evening progressed Louis, flushed and excited with the prospect of moving at last into his long-planned house, with a successful future almost assured, became more and more exhilarated.

In contrast, Addie became more and more remote. Louis, who had been verbally possessive at the beginning of the meal, became engaged in earnest discussion about the best kind of grape vines and methods of production with a local vintner on his left.

Seated at a some distance from Rex Lyon, Addie was careful to avoid looking directly at him. However, if she inadvertently glanced his way, he seemed to be gazing at her. It was as if they both were aware of something that neither of them understood.

After dessert—brandied peaches in meringue shells—the plates were carried away and coffee was brought in. Brook rose to his feet again and, tapping his fork on the crystal goblet for quiet, he made a closing speech.

By this time it was past midnight. After Brook's words, everyone began rising from their places, moving toward the lobby, and preparing to leave. Louis was finishing up a conversation with the man beside him when Freda touched Addie's arm.

"We didn't have a chance to get to know each other better, as Brook hoped we would, did we? Too much going on!" She gestured to the crowd. "But I would like very much for us to become friends. Would you be able to come visit some afternoon? I could send a buggy for you."

"How kind of you. Yes, I would enjoy that. I am free on Thursdays."

"Good, I'll send a note to confirm. Good night." Freda pressed Addie's hand and went to join Rex Lyon who stood at the door as if waiting for her.

Again Addie wondered about them. Rex had only nodded, acknowledging their previous introduction, but made no move toward her. Of course, Louis had been at her side all evening. Still, Addie felt oddly disappointed that he had not even come to speak to her.

Addie had no time to dwell on her feelings because Louis

leaned toward her, saying, "Estelle is tired and wants to leave, so I can't take you back to the cottage. I'll send a note. I want to bring you out to the house, want you to be our first guest. I want to have some time with you away from all these greedy-for-gossip eyes. I feel we are like gold-fish in a bowl here—," he made a wry face, "—especially with your *bodyguard* nearby."

He took her hand, held it. He might have continued holding it while looking meaningfully into her eyes if Estelle had not tapped him on the shoulder.

"Do let us go, Louis." Her voice was heavily laced with fatigue—or boredom? "It is very late, and I'm afraid I'm starting a migraine." Then added in a pained voice, "I'm *sure* Miss Pride will excuse you."

Chilled by Miss Montand's steely stare, Addie at once said, "Of course."

As the Montands left, Addie looked around just in time to see Rex Lyon and Freda go out the door. For some reason she felt ridiculously abandoned.

Chapter 8

*T*rue to her word Freda sent a note to Addie the day after the party to invite her to spend the day at the Wegner Ranch the following Thursday. Delighted, Addie immediately wrote back accepting the invitation.

A few days later, one evening just before her card game, Mrs. Amberly sent Addie back to the cottage for a pillow for her back. As Addie re-entered the lobby with the pillow, Brook came out of his office near the reception desk and motioned her over in a curiously secretive manner.

"What is it?" she asked curiously.

He looked mysteriously excited.

"My dear Miss Pride, or Addie, as you've now permitted me to address you." He spoke in a low tone of voice, and Addie felt instinctively he was up to something. "I hope I am not presuming on our friendship when I say I have always ascertained you to be a young woman of considerable courage, foresight, maybe even a little recklessness— or perhaps that is the wrong word. Certainly *adventurous*. Else why would you have vouchsafed to cross the country via the newly constructed railroad—alone—to accept, sight unseen, a position with an unknown employer and come to this valley hidden in the hills, about which you knew little or nothing?"

"Just what are you leading up to, Brook?" Addie asked warily, recognizing his persuasive methods in full force.

He put one hand to his heart, affected an innocent expression. "Up to something? Me? You think I'm about to make a preposterous proposal?"

"Perhaps," Addie said doubtfully.

Brook's eyes twinkled. "What makes you think so?"

"The grand inventory you're making of all my supposed virtues, which, I must say, you are grossly exaggerating."

"All right, I'll tell you straight out. I'm thinking of initiating a new treatment here, one that will not only be beneficial to my guests' health but may have amazing rejuvenating effects."

"Rejuvenating? Don't tell me you've discovered the Fountain of Youth right here in Calistoga?" Addie demanded in mock amazement.

"Well, perhaps not precisely. However, our mineral water *is* widely accepted as having positive health potential and restorative qualities. My idea will combine those benefits with an ancient Indian cleansing and purification ritual."

Addie put her head to one side and speared Brook with a suspicious look. "And what has this got to do with *me?* And my so-called adventurous spirit?"

Brook hesitated a split second, then said in a rush, "I want *you* to be the first to benefit from it."

Addie gasped, "You want *me* to be your guinea pig?"

"That's hardly the word for it."

"Well, I don't know what else you'd call it."

"I'm offering you a chance to be the first woman—the first non-Indian woman—to experience this treatment, to reap its myriad benefits."

"You're serious, aren't you?"

"Quite." He paused, watching for her reaction, then

continued. "I want you to tell me honestly what you think of it, whether you feel other women coming here would enjoy it, be happy about the results. If you agree, then I believe I'll have something to offer here at Silver Springs Resort that not even the most famous expensive resorts of Europe can offer people in search of health, renewed vigor, and beauty." He paused again. "Will you help me by taking the treatment?"

"What does it involve?"

"A mud bath. Now don't look shocked—," he cautioned her. "The baths are a mixture of the purest organic soil and volcanic ash and mineral springs water. The Indians of this valley came here for hundreds of years to bathe in the natural hot springs. The healing qualities are world renowned." He held up both hands as if to ward off any protest on Addie's part. "It will be absolutely private. The native Indian woman I've consulted will be there to assist you. She knows every phase of the routine. Addie, I promise you it will in no way cause you any embarrassment or discomfort. In fact, you'll feel absolutely marvelous."

Addie looked at Brook suspiciously.

"Trust me, Addie, I wouldn't suggest this if I weren't sure you'd enjoy and benefit from it."

"When will this great experiment take place?"

"Since it will be—at least, for the present—*our* secret, I suggest we plan it for the same time as Mrs. Amberly is having her treatment at the bathhouse. That will eliminate any questions on her part and any explanations on yours. You'll not be under any pressure and be able to relax and enjoy it."

"I don't know, Brook—"

"*Believe* me, Addie, you will *love* the results."

"I'll think about it—"

"What's to think about? I promise you a unique, pleasurable experience. Just say you will."

94

"Oh, Brook, can't it wait? I'm in a hurry, Mrs. Amberly's waiting for her pillow, and—"

"Please, Addie, I assure you, you will thank me for giving you the opportunity—"

"Oh, for pity's sake, Brook!" Exasperated, Addie laughed. "All *right!* I give in!"

"Great! Thank you. Tomorrow I'll come for you at the cottage and escort you myself," Brook said triumphantly and went out the front door, whistling.

Suddenly Addie had the feeling of being observed. Turning, she saw that Mrs. Amberly was standing in the archway of the card room. How long had she been there watching? Watching her with Brook. As usual, Brook had used wild gestures to make his point, talking with his hands as he tried to persuade her. She had probably been equally emphatic in arguing against it. How must the scene have looked? What kind of interpretation might Mrs. Amberly have put on their conversation? Addie could only guess.

"What kept you so long?" Mrs. Amberly scowled.

"I'm sorry," was Addie's only reply. Why should she explain when clearly Mrs. Amberly had seen that Brook had delayed her.

Mrs. Amberly grabbed the pillow and waddled ahead of Addie back to her waiting card partners without so much as a thank you.

Addie thought she had become used to her employer's surliness. Nonetheless, she still resented it. She hated the feeling of having to account for every action. She knew she had to accept she was Mrs. Amberly's employee and all that went with it. But she didn't have to like it.

Addie went into the card room and seated herself not far from the card players. She took out the needlepoint she brought along to pass the time on these interminable evenings. She felt upset. Not because she had agreed to

95

participate in Brook's experiment—although that might turn out to be a foolish mistake. It was her own ignominious situation that she chafed against.

Paid companions were not unlike the governesses Addie had observed growing up. Many Southern families sent their sons up north to be educated, but for their daughters they hired Northern governesses. Even as a young girl Addie was sensitive to their ambiguous position in the wealthy households in which they were employed. They were neither fish nor fowl. They took their meals with the family but were not treated as either relatives or guests. Mostly they were ignored. Even their influence in the schoolroom, where they should have received respect, was minimal. Southern parents, for the most part, considered their daughters' education of minor importance. A girl's future depended on making a good marriage, becoming the bride of someone in their class. *That* was her priority. Her attendance at a party or ball at a neighboring plantation *always* took precedence, even when it meant weeks of no lessons. This often left the poor young teacher wandering like a lost soul by herself in a deserted schoolroom or empty house. Governesses were never invited to accompany their charges to any of the parties or other events, nor were they ever included in the ones given at the home where they were employed. Addie had often looked at these women with pity, never dreaming that one day she would be in a similar position.

Recalling those days, Addie realized now these young women were probably of good family, perhaps even from backgrounds as privileged as her own, but fallen on hard times so that they were forced to earn their living. Certainly these Northern women were better educated than most of their Southern sisters. They probably had a wealth of ideas, interests, and intelligence to contribute to social occasions.

Yet they were pushed into the background for years—the best years of their lives.

How sad to be within sight and sound of pretty clothes, parties, music, dancing, and good times and not be allowed to enjoy them. They probably had been the same age as Addie was now, or perhaps even younger! After all, once you passed twenty-five you were on the brink of spinsterhood, and, if unmarried, a few years later you would be considered completely without hope!

Worse even than being relegated to the sidelines of social life would be—especially for someone as independent and proud as Addie—being obliged to be conciliatory, never expressing an opinion. Governesses must have lived under the constant fear of offending and being dismissed. That would have been a real threat if, like Addie, they might have had elderly parents or relatives dependent on part of their small salaries.

That was her own problem, the Sword of Damocles hanging over her own head. If she lost her job with Mrs. Amberly, it would mean the difference between the few comforts the money sent Aunt Susan and Uncle Myles provided or deprivation.

What a lot she was learning, understanding, now, if that was any consolation! Didn't Shakespeare write "sweet are the uses of adversity"? Perhaps this year would be richer for its very poverty than she could have predicted.

The next morning after Mrs. Amberly had gone for her regular treatment, grumbling as usual to one of the bathhouse attendants, Addie waited anxiously for Brook. He arrived almost immediately as though he had waited for the coast to be clear. He was in a jovial mood as he walked with her to the far end of the grounds where the last guest cottage was located, and there he left her.

"All right, Addie, everything's all set." He took her hand and raised it ceremoniously to his lips and smiled. "Enjoy!"

With some trepidation Addie went up to the cottage door and knocked. Almost immediately it was opened by a short bronze-skinned woman with straight dark hair drawn from a center part into a braid down her back.

"Good morning, Miss Pride. My name is Oona," she said in a pleasant, low voice. She smiled as she motioned Addie inside. The interior of the cottage was nearly empty. It was one of the most recently built ones, and it was not furnished like the others.

"If you will disrobe, miss," the woman suggested gently.

"Disrobe?" echoed Addie thinking perhaps she had better not. "Why?"

"For the treatment. For the mud bath." The woman parted plain white canvas curtains and revealed a tublike wooden structure filled with a dark gray mixture from which a vapor was rising causing herb-scented steam to fill the small room.

Addie swallowed. "I'm to get in *that?*"

The woman smiled, her teeth very white against her swarthy skin. "Oh, yes, miss. It's very nice," she assured her. "May I help you undress?"

Addie had half a notion to bolt out the door but then she remembered Brook's reassurances together with the fact that she was rather pleased he considered her progressive enough to try something as new and startling as this.

Shyly Addie let the woman unbutton her blouse and assist her out of her skirt and petticoats, chemise and pantaloons. She then wrapped Addie's hair in a soft cotton towel and showed her how to place herself into the tub. First to sit on the wooden ledge, then holding onto handles on either side, to swing her legs over. Slowly Addie felt herself sink into the warm, gritty, moist "mud," which was, the woman told her, a mixture of mineral water, volcanic

98

ash, and various natural herbs. The woman then packed it around and over her body from her neck to her toes. To Addie's absolute astonishment it felt wonderful.

There was a curved pillow cradling her neck and head, and Oona placed a folded cool cloth over her forehead and eyes, saying soothingly, "Now, just relax."

At first the weight of the warm mud seemed to press too heavily on her bare body. Gradually, however, Addie *did* lose all track of time and seemed to drift and float. She could almost feel all the knots of tension that had become a constant in her life—since becoming Mrs. Amberly's flunky—seep away in a kind of glorious euphoria.

"Time now to get out," Oona said just as Addie felt she was almost going to sleep.

Getting out was a bit harder than getting in had been, but with Oona's help Addie managed. The mud still clung to her body, and Oona led her over to a wooden stall where, with a hose, she freed her from most of it.

"Now, miss, you bathe." She opened a door into a rather Spartan bathroom and assisted her into a deep white porcelain tub filled with the bubbling mineral salts water. With a large sponge Oona scrubbed her back then handed the sponge to Addie for her to do the rest of the cleansing herself. This part of the treatment felt great too, stimulating and energizing. Maybe Brook actually *had* happened on an idea that would become a unique part of anyone's visit to the resort.

Oona soon reappeared and held out a huge towel for Addie to wrap herself in as she stepped out of the tub. "You like?" Oona asked hopefully.

"Very much."

"Now time to rest." Oona led her into another room where there was a small cot. She helped Addie stretch out, then she placed a light blanket over her, tucking it in on all sides, as one might tuck in an infant. Again a cool damp

99

cloth, wrung out in some sweet scented water, was placed across Addie's eyes and forehead. Then Oona left quietly, leaving Addie to sleep dreamlessly.

Addie wasn't sure how long she had been there when she felt Oona's gentle touch awakening her.

"Sorry, miss, but Mr. Stanton told me to have you back to your cottage by noon."

"Oh, my goodness! I can't believe I spent the whole morning like this!" Addie leaned up on both elbows, feeling a little dazed as Oona helped her into a sitting position.

"I help you dress," offered Oona, and Addie saw she had brought her clothes into the room.

Walking back across the grounds toward the cottage she was surprised to see a dark green one-horse carriage in front of her cottage. As she approached, Louis Montand got out and started toward her.

"I've been looking everywhere for you!" he said with a slight frown of annoyance. "I was afraid I'd missed you. I was just about to try driving up and down the streets of town searching for you."

"I was. . . .," Addie began, wondering how she could possibly explain where she had been or what she had been doing for the last hour.

Then she saw Brook striding toward her. As he came up to her his glance was roguish. "My, but don't you look especially radiant this morning, Miss Pride," he greeted her, grinning from ear to ear. "Indeed, I would say positively glowing, wouldn't you agree, Mr. Montand?"

"I would indeed," Louis said.

Addie could hardly keep from laughing, but she gave Brook a "You, rascal!" glance and murmured a discreet "Thank you."

"It must be the wonders of our climate here at the Silver Springs Resort—even the air has a certain quality!" Brook made a circular gesture with both hands as if embracing the universe. Then he looked at the carriage and let out a low whistle. "That's a splendid vehicle, Mr. Montand. New is it?"

"Just delivered to me yesterday," Louis said proudly running a hand possessively along the narrow strip of gold trim. "Rubber-rimmed wheels," he pointed to the bright yellow spoked wheels.

"It's certainly a fine-looking carriage. Haven't seen one like it in the valley," Brook said decisively. "Well, I must be off. Good day to you both." He nodded and walked away.

Louis turned back to Addie. "Miss Pride, I drove over this morning hoping I could entice you to drive out to the house with me? Have lunch?"

"I'm sorry, Mr. Montand. But I can't. I have only one day a week free, Thursdays."

"Tomorrow? Well then, we'll make it tomorrow. Shall we plan that tomorrow I'll come for you and we'll drive out to the house?"

"Again, I'm sorry. But I have already accepted an invitation for this Thursday."

An annoyed expression came over Louis's face. At first she thought he might demand to know with whom she had made plans. But his good manners prevented such a breach of etiquette.

"*Next* Thursday, then?" It was more a statement than a question. "I want so much for you to see the house—"

Over his shoulder Addie saw Mrs. Amberly and her bath-house attendant approaching. When she saw who was with Addie, Mrs. Amberly immediately quickened her step, waving her hand and calling, "Oh, Mr. Montand, hello! How nice to see you. I've been wondering about you and your sister—"

Louis stifled a groan, rolled his eyes before he turned to reply to Mrs. Amberly.

She was huffing and puffing as she came up to them. "So

what brings you over to Silver Springs from your lovely new home?" she asked coyly.

"To see if I could persuade your charming companion to take a drive with me," he said blandly.

Mrs. Amberly's hopeful look vanished as she realized the invitation did not include her. Her disappointment showed on her face. "Well she can't," she snapped. As Louis lifted his eyebrows, she must have realized how rude she had sounded because she quickly changed her tone of voice. "I'm afraid, Miss Pride will be very busy. I have a lot of correspondence for her to take care of for me this afternoon. Now, if you'll excuse me." She glared at Addie, then went past them onto the porch, leaning on the attendant's arm. The cottage door banged.

Addie dared not glance at Louis whom she sensed was amused at the woman's behavior. To avert his saying anything derogatory about her employer, Addie hastened to say, "Thank you anyway, it was most kind of you to ask."

"*Next* Thursday, then, please," Louis persisted.

Addie had some real reservations about encouraging Louis's attentions. But she was angry at the high-handed manner in which Mrs. Amberly had jumped in and refused Louis's invitation for her. Addie was furious, in fact. She may as well be a servant! Then she thought how it would annoy her employer if *she* got to see Chateau Montand first! On impulse, knowing hers was not the noblest of motives, Addie said, "Why, yes, that would be lovely." Later she worried that she had acted against her better judgment.

Louis looked enormously pleased which soothed her conscience a little. But not much.

After the noon meal, on the way out of the dining hall, Mrs. Amberly stopped to chat with someone and Brook followed Addie outside.

"Well?"

"Well what?" she asked innocently.

"You know very well what! How did the experiment go? Did you like it or what?"

Addie squinted her eyes, wrinkled her nose, and shook her head, "Ugh, awful!"

His face fell. He looked so startled, so taken aback that Addie could not contain herself. She burst out laughing. "I'm sorry, Brook! I was teasing! It was ... words fail me. You are right—it is a unique experience. Once women get over the initial shock of getting into that gooey mess, they're going to love it."

Brook flashed a triumphant smile. "I *knew* it. Now, I've got to build a special building just to house the tubs, the resting rooms, and then I have to train attendants—it will take time and money—lots of money." He frowned, "But that's usually not a problem. It's selling the idea to the right people." His grin broadened. "Thank you, Addie, you're a trump."

Addie watched him walk away, his hands in his pockets, whistling like a schoolboy. What other new idea was he dreaming up now?

Chapter 9

fter breakfast on Thursday morning Mrs. Amberly began to give Addie a list of errands she wanted done when Addie interrupted politely. "Excuse me, Mrs. Amberly, you must have forgotten this is my day off. I've been invited out to Mrs. Wegner's today for lunch. She will be coming for me in a few minutes. Maybe I can take care of these things tomorrow? Or if there is something urgent, perhaps we could send one of the hotel employees to town for you?"

Mrs. Amberly's mouth went slack. Her face creased with annoyance. "Seems like every time I want something done it's *your* day off."

"It is only one day a week, Mrs. Amberly. Thursday," Addie reminded her quietly.

"Humph," Mrs. Amberly, unappeased, grunted. "Where did you say you were going?"

Addie felt like retorting, "That's none of your business." But she controlled the urge and answered calmly, "To Freda Wegner's, Mrs. Amberly. You remember, the lady we met the evening we were having dinner with the Montands?"

"Oh, yes! Her! The widow woman who runs her own ranch and winery!" Mrs. Amberly sneered.

Addie stiffened at Mrs. Amberly's reaction. As though Freda ran a tavern or worse! She pressed her fingers together tightly, willing the inquisition to be over so she could be on her way.

Looking like she had taken a bite of a green apple, Mrs. Amberly pursed her lips and said, "I don't know whether I approve of your cultivating friendships on your own. You realize, *don't* you, that what *you* do, where you go, who you associate with reflects on *me*."

With effort Addie checked her rising indignation. What right did Mrs. Amberly think she had to talk to her this way? But she managed to keep her voice cool as she replied, "Even servants are free to go where they please and choose their own friends, Mrs. Amberly. And you need have no fear of my association with Mrs. Wegner reflecting badly on you. She is a respected citizen of this town, well-known to Mr. Stanton as well as Mr. Rexford Lyon, whom you also met the same evening. Besides they were both *invited* guests of the Montands to their farewell party."

This seemed to silence Mrs. Amberly momentarily although she still looked sullen.

"Now, if you'll excuse me, Mrs. Amberly, Mrs. Wegner is probably waiting for me." Addie turned to leave.

"Just a minute, young lady," Mrs. Amberly called her back. "Don't forget if I wasn't paying your expenses here you wouldn't even have the opportunity to meet people of the class of the Montands. . . ."

Literally biting her tongue Addie left the room. Outside in the hall she could still hear her employer muttering. Sending up a desperate plea for patience, Addie hurried to her own room to get her bonnet and shawl. By the time she was halfway across the grounds she saw Freda Wegner in a small "piano-box" buggy coming through the Silver Springs gate.

As they set out from town Addie noticed the countryside

105

just beginning to take on the look of spring. A pale green aura softened the bare branches of the trees on either side of the road leading to Freda's ranch, berry bushes showed their tiny white star blossoms. As they passed the hillsides of vineyards, Addie exclaimed, "It's so beautiful," pointing to the fields, golden with blossoming mustard plants.

"As well as good for the earth. The mustard will be plowed under, but it enriches the soil, giving it needed nutrients for the grapes."

Soon they turned off the main road onto a narrow winding one marked with a sign that said WEGNER WINERY. Freda's house, a yellow frame Victorian, was cradled in a wooded dell surrounded by oak and eucalyptus trees, behind it a vineyard planted in precise neat rows sloped down the hillside.

Freda reined the horse to a stop in front of the porch, trimmed with decorative white wooden lace. A smiling, swarthy man in work clothes, whom Freda addressed as "Rico," came from around the back to take the horse and small buggy to the barn and Freda invited Addie inside.

From the small entrance hall she led the way through sliding doors into a small but elegantly furnished parlor. Luxurious green ferns hung in the bow window and fresh flowers filled the room with scent and color.

"What a charming house."

"Thank you. I enjoy it myself. Since I don't have much company, that's so nice to hear." Freda gestured to one of two armchairs covered in flowered chintz. "Do sit down, Miss Pride."

"Please call me Addie—most of my friends do."

"Well, then, Addie you must call me Freda, because I'd like us to be friends. Would you like tea before lunch? Or perhaps a sherry?"

"Oh, tea would be fine."

"I hope that my asking if you'd have wine didn't shock

you? Here in the valley, it's very appropriate for a vintner to offer the fruit of her vine to guests. Of course, I'm still not used to my status." Freda shrugged. "You see, I'm the first and only woman vintner in the valley, probably in California, and it's something I never dreamed I'd be when I came here as a bride, believe me."

Freda walked over to the door and called down the hall. "Elena!" In a few minutes, a pretty, dark-haired girl with huge, black olive eyes, small gold hoops swinging from her ears, stuck her head in the parlor door.

"Please bring us some tea, Elena, and since it's such a lovely day, I think you could serve us lunch out on the side porch. Would you like that, Miss Pride—I mean, Addie?"

"Oh, yes, that would be delightful. I can't get over how warm it is here in March—like summer really."

"Good. Then we'll eat out there, Elena," Freda told the maid then seated herself. "As I was saying, running the vineyards and winery by myself was the last thing I ever imagined myself doing. We came here shortly after our marriage, mainly for Jason's health. The climate was recommended as beneficial, and we found it so. But Jason had a dream. He was the last of his family, you see. His father had recently died, and he had an inheritance. He wanted to put down roots of his own, something for the children we hoped to have. . . ." An expression of sadness moved across her thin face.

Freda halted as Elena entered with a tray. She smiled shyly at Addie and set it down on the low table in front of her mistress. After the girl left Freda poured the tea, saying, "So, we bought this ranch. We were told that some fine French vines were already planted on the land. Everyone who seemed to know told us that good root stock, such as we'd purchased was half the battle in the successful growing of wine grapes."

Freda handed Addie her cup, offered her cream and

107

sugar. "Of course, we were neophytes at the whole business, so we took everything at face value. In time we found that it also takes knowledge of the land, care, cultivation, and patience." She stirred sugar into her own cup and for a moment seemed thoughtful before going on.

"We had all the enthusiasm and excitement of youth, but Jason did not have the physical strength necessary for what we'd undertaken. He would be up at daybreak, work in the fields along with some of the Californios he hired to help. Eventually his health broke and he was very ill. I had to take over much of the overseeing of the vineyards and—" She gave a deep sigh "—I tried to keep Jason's spirits up; one of the side effects of tuberculosis is often depression."

"That must have been very hard," Addie commented gently.

"It wasn't easy but . . .," Freda paused, then continued matter-of-factly, "women are brought up to believe we cannot do certain things. It's etched on our inner selves from the time we are given a doll instead of the interesting set of building blocks our brothers receive. We're told over and over we can't calculate or decipher—in other words, not to even dare dream of all sorts of wonderful things, barred to us simply because of our sex.

"My husband, thank God, was not of that school. He didn't distrust or fear the fact I was intelligent. He gave me credit for good judgment, and he was not afraid to give me responsibility—when he was alive. I believe he trusted that if something happened to him, I'd carry on what he had envisioned here. . . ." She sighed. "Of course neither of us imagined it would come so soon."

Freda's mouth tightened visibly, and Addie did not press her further, sensing that further talk about Jason Wegner's death would be too painful. Freda paused. "Even after Jason died things would have been all right. We had had two years

108

of good grapes. The winery had the possibility of producing a superior vintage. Then—disaster struck! Phylloxera."

"Phylloxera?"

"A hideous blight on the vines. A voracious microscopic louse, usually hidden beneath the soil. It destroyed all our French grapevines. American rootstock is resistant because of years of exposure, but the European varieties were susceptible to it, and we had mostly the French kind." She took a last sip of tea, then set down her cup. "I don't know what I would have done without the help and support of friends. Especially Rex. Rexford Lyon. You met him the other evening at Silver Springs when we went there to dine."

At the mention of that name Addie's fingers tightened on the delicate handle of her teacup. Of course, Freda had no idea that there was no need to remind Addie who Rex Lyon was. Not a day had gone by since her arrival at the Calistoga depot that Addie had not thought of him. Perhaps now she'd find out exactly what his relationship to Freda Wegner was. She leaned forward half-dreading what Freda would say next.

"Even though Rex never wanted to come back to the valley, never wanted to be a vintner, he is very knowledgeable, very dedicated. A double family tragedy brought him back to run the vineyards and winery. Lyon's Court wines are famous throughout California. He took up the reins and has done a wonderful job." Freda paused, then said thoughtfully, "It's strange, isn't it? How sometimes Providence brings us to a place, into situations we would never have chosen on our own, but in the end, that place or situation turns out to be exactly what was supposed to happen?"

After a moment, Freda said thoughtfully, "I worry about Rex though. I don't think he's very happy."

Whatever else Freda was going to say about Rex was interrupted by Elena's coming to say lunch was ready.

109

On the porch during lunch the conversation turned to other subjects. Complimenting Freda on the delicious dessert of luscious strawberries piled on sponge cake covered with sweet whipped cream, Addie learned that growing flowers and fruit was one of Freda's many other interests.

"I love it here in the valley. Everything I enjoy is here in abundance," Freda said enthusiastically. "It's very different than the life I lived in the city before I was married." She told Addie that she had been the only child of an indulgent widowed father. She had been reared to marry well, to marry someone in her own set so that they could take their place in society. "But the best laid plans and all that," Freda sighed. "Jason's health was the reason we came here in the first place, and now I can't imagine living anywhere else. There's so much freedom. Especially for women. Can you see me wearing this any other place?" she laughed and got up to model what she was wearing. "See the skirt is divided so I can ride horseback astride instead of sidesaddle." She showed how the brown twill skirt was cleverly made. "It's wonderful for all the things I like to do—like squatting and kneeling when I'm gardening and of course horseback riding. I'll give you the pattern if you'd like."

The two young women found they had much else in common besides flowers, fruit, and fashion. They discovered a mutual love of reading, both novels and poetry, as well as an enjoyment of music. They were discussing their reactions to Madame DeSecia's concert when they saw a small one-horse trap coming up the winding road to the house.

"Why, it's Rex!" Freda got up, went to the porch railing, and waved. "How nice."

Addie clasped her hands tightly together, her heart tripping within her starched blouse. She closed her eyes for a second, trying to draw a long breath. When she opened them Rexford Lyon stood at the top of the porch steps.

"You remember Miss Pride, Rex; we met her with the Montands at Silver Springs hotel. I told you on the way home from their party that I was going to ask her out. . . ."

Addie did not hear what else Freda told him. She was too conscious of his slow smile, his eyes acknowledging her. It was almost as if he was saying, "Of course I know her. I feel as if I've always known her." In reality, she heard his deep, mellow voice say, "Yes, indeed, I remember. A pleasure to see you again, Miss Pride."

The words spoken in quiet courtesy fell on Addie like a caress. Oh, foolish, foolish girl! She felt as though she were swimming in deep water, trying desperately to reach shore. She felt as if she might drown. Get hold of yourself! Say something!

"Good afternoon, Mr. Lyon."

"Rex, you'll stay awhile?" Freda asked. "Have some coffee with us, won't you?"

"That would be fine, Freda, thank you." His eyes never left Addie.

"Good, I'll go make some fresh."

Freda immediately disappeared carrying the coffee pot, and Addie was left alone with Rex.

He lowered himself into one of the white wicker armchairs, settling himself more comfortably. He took off his wide-brimmed hat and put it under the chair. Addie was suddenly aware of everything about him: the high-bridged nose, the strength of his jaw, the curve of his mouth, the tawny streak of hair, the narrow white line on his forehead against his tanned face, probably made from wearing his hat out in the sun. She was even conscious of the combined scents of leather, sun-bleached cotton, and tobacco that emanated from him.

She felt nervous perspiration gathering in her palms.

111

Attempting to appear composed, she sat up straighter, wiping her hand surreptitiously on her skirt. With her hands demurely folded in her lap, Addie tried to catch one of the random thoughts floating through her head with which to start some sort of conversation.

Rex seemed utterly unaware of the internal havoc he was causing. In contrast he seemed completely at ease. It was he who broke the silence that had fallen at Freda's departure.

"So, Miss Pride, how do you like California by this time?"

"It is very different—at least different from where I came from, what I'm used to. But then, I have only twice been out of the state of Virginia, so I haven't much to compare it with. It is very impressive, very *big!* Almost overpowering—the trees, the hills!"

"And the people? Do you find them very different as well?"

She thought a moment, wondering how honest she should be. He was looking at her with those clear gray eyes as if he was really interested in hearing what she had to say. It gave her a welcome sense of freedom to be frank and not merely polite.

"Yes, I think so. Much more outspoken, direct. I'm afraid Southerners tend to be—well, careful not to reveal too much of themselves, to not always say exactly what they mean—especially to strangers. Westerners do not seem to have that same wariness, I guess you'd call it."

"Does that bother you?"

Addie considered that for a few seconds.

"It takes some getting used to. But I believe that's all to the good. To mature, a person should be exposed to other ways of thinking, acting. Otherwise you become narrow in your outlook. It's important to take people as they are. Not to put them through the filter of your own prejudices or the way you may have been taught things were, to find out for yourself. . . . Oh dear, I am going on."

"Not at all. I find it fascinating how someone coming from another part of the country sees things, sees *us*. You see, I was born here. I've never lived anywhere else. Never traveled outside California. I wanted to, meant to but . . ." He paused; then clasping his hands in front of him on his knees, he leaned toward her. "Please, go on."

"What I was trying to say is that I'm used to—you might call it a polite tip-toeing, not coming right to the point about anything." She laughed. "I don't know what my relatives would think of my dissecting them like this and particularly to a stranger."

"I hope not to be a stranger long, Miss Pride," he said earnestly. "I would like very much for us to be . . . friends."

The hesitation before the word "friends" caused an unexpected little flutter underneath Addie's heart. Then suddenly, Freda entered with a tray on which was the silver coffee server and cups. The conversation became general, with Freda and Rex discussing local matters.

Finally, Rex reached for his hat and stood. "I should be going and leave you ladies to your visit. I'm afraid I barged in uninvited and—"

"Not at all, Rex. You know you're always welcome here," Freda assured. "Besides I was going to drive Miss Pride back into town. She tells me she has to be back by four."

Rex fingered the brim of his hat. "May I . . .," he began, "perhaps, I could do the honor? And save you a trip, Freda. Since I was on my way into town anyway, I would be happy to take Miss Pride back to the hotel."

Freda looked askance at Addie who did not know where to look. Her heart had already jumped hopefully at Rex's suggestion.

"Is that all right with you, Addie?"

"If it isn't too much trouble—for Mr. Lyon, I mean."

"Not at all, a pleasure, Miss Pride."

The trip into town went all too fast although it seemed to Addie that Rex had slowed his horse as much as could be considered reasonable without walking him. The conversation was confined mostly to Rex pointing out the various vineyards along the way, telling Addie the names of the owners. Very conscious of the forced intimacy of the small buggy, Addie made only casual comments.

Addie felt both relief and regret when they reached Silver Springs. She still could hardly believe she had spent even this brief time with Rex Lyon.

"Thank you very much, Mr. Lyon," Addie said as he handed her down from the buggy.

"It was *my* pleasure, Miss Pride," he protested. His fingers closed around her hand, holding it tightly, as if he wanted to say something more. "I wonder if—would you like—may I . . .," he began.

Before he could finish, Addie saw Mrs. Amberly and the Brunell sisters come out onto the verandah of the main building. With them was Louis Montand. Their expressions were frankly curious when they saw Addie and Rex together.

Aware that she was being stared at, Addie withdrew her hand from Rex's while wondering if this scene would become tonight's topic at the card table. "Thank you again, Mr. Lyon."

Ignoring the group on the porch Rex asked, "Perhaps, I could call some afternoon?"

Rather breathlessly, Addie explained, "I'm not sure, Mr. Lyon. I'm rarely free to make plans. You see, I am employed as a companion and my time is really not my own—"

"Yes, I understand that. But surely—you have some time off. Some other Thursday?"

Even as Rex was speaking, out of the corner of her eye Addie saw Louis sauntering toward them. Before she could say another word he was within hearing distance.

114

"Good afternoon, Lyon," he spoke cordially to Rex, then turned to speak directly to Addie. "I hope I'm not intruding. But I've been waiting for you. Mrs. Amberly informed me you were visiting at the Wegner ranch. I was about to drive out there and escort you back to the hotel. I had to see you because I had something important to tell you."

Louis glanced at Rex as if to imply that this was going to be a private matter and the gentlemanly thing for Rex to do would be to leave. He paused, obviously waiting for Rex to do so.

Rex frowned slightly, but showed no irritation. He said to Addie, "Well, I must be off. It was a pleasure to be with you, Miss Pride. Have a pleasant evening." With a nod to both, he got back into his buggy and drove away, leaving Addie annoyed at Louis for interrupting. It had been a very unsatisfactory parting. She only hoped Rex would get in touch with her.

Louis's voice dragged her back to the present moment. Observing her closely, Louis said, "What I came to say, Addie, is that I'm sorry but I have to break our date for next Thursday. I have to go to San Francisco for a few days on business. I have to complete arrangements about hiring workers for our harvest. When I arrived here looking for you, Mrs. Amberly told me that Stanton had announced that tonight's dinner is going to be served early because there is going to be a magic lantern show for the guests, 'The Land of the Pharaohs.' It's supposed to be excellent, and Mrs. Amberly has kindly invited me to have dinner with you two. I hope that suits you?"

What else could Addie say but, "Of course."

He held out his arm. "Shall we join the others then?"

Having no alternative Addie took the arm Louis offered. She wished she had known before about the dinner hour being changed and the magic lantern show. It would have been a perfectly acceptable thing to invite Rex to stay for

115

it. It would have been a way of thanking him for bringing her into town. But Louis had cleverly finessed that.

As soon as Addie was seated at the dinner table, Mrs. Amberly said acidly, "I thought you spent the day with Mrs. Wegner. But I see you must have made other plans after you left this morning."

All the relaxed enjoyment of her day faded under Mrs. Amberly's caustic tongue. The rest of the dinner hour was a strain with Mrs. Amberly succeeding in monopolizing most of the conversation.

Later, while watching the magic lantern program, Addie allowed her mind to wander back over the afternoon at Freda's. Freda Wegner had all the qualities Addie admired: courage, determination, faith. She was what Aunt Susan would call a woman of character. Her aunt often remarked that how we deal with adversity defines who we really are. It was reassuring to see living proof that any challenge can be met with faith and belief in our God-given strength.

After the program, Louis walked her and Mrs. Amberly to the cottage, said good night, and left. Addie felt worn out. The evening had been tiring. It had been an effort to keep up the polite and mostly artificial conversation while pretending not to catch Louis's subtle innuendoes. His over-attentiveness made her uneasy. How could she discourage him when Mrs. Amberly was so obviously encouraging him—for her own reasons, of course. Still, as her employee, Addie could hardly avoid him if Mrs. Amberly made him so welcome.

She went to the window and looked out. Moonlight painted everything a luminous silver. The glass dome of the arboretum glistened like a giant jewel against the deep blue of the mountains in the background.

Old feelings of longing swept over her. In a few short years the age of thirty loomed ahead of her—the end of youth. Would it also be the end of possibly finding an enduring lifetime love?

She thought of Rex Lyon, remembered what Freda had told her about him. The family tragedies that had brought him back to the valley. That she thought he was unhappy. Why? she wondered. A broken romance? An impossible love affair? What was in his past?

How strange that their paths kept crossing. This time, not at a distance. They had sat together, talked, exchanged ideas, their hands had touched. Again she had experienced that eerie sense of recognition.

Addie sighed, closed the curtains, and got ready for bed.

Chapter 10

*A*ddie's personal tour of Chateau Montand was post-poned. From the prestigious San Francisco hotel where he was staying, Louis wrote a note saying that his business in the city would take longer than he had antici-pated and that his return to Calistoga would be delayed.

Within a few days she received another note. In it Addie thought she read some irritation between the lines. While he was away, without consulting him, Estelle had set the date of their housewarming party and invitations were already printed ready to be sent. Since many of the prepa-rations and arrangements still had to be completed, he would regretfully have to forgo the pleasure of seeing her until the night of the party. He would, with her permis-sion, come to escort her and Mrs. Amberly out to their housewarming.

A week later, when, as usual, she and Mrs. Amberly stopped in the lobby to check for mail before going to the dining hall for the noon meal, Addie's formal invitation was in her box. She opened the envelope, noted the date, then put it in her handbag. Mrs. Amberly finished a con-versation with one of the Brunell sisters, then asked the clerk for her mail. When *she* found *hers* in her box, her reaction was jubilant. She made a great show of displaying the handsomely engraved card to the Brunell sisters. From *their* reaction it was clear they had not been invited and they walked off in a huff.

Later when Addie and Mrs. Amberly were seated at their regular table in the dining hall, Mrs. Amberly placed the envelope prominently in front of her plate with a self-pleased smirk at having been singled out over most of the other Silver Springs guests.

"I don't suppose you could do my hair, could you?" she skewered Addie with a calculating look. "I doubt if there's a decent hairdresser in this size town. I'll have to check the livery stable see if I can rent a carriage; their house is quite a distance from town, you know."

"Louis said he would send his for us," Addie said quietly.

Mrs. Amberly's jaw dropped. "What do you mean—for *us?*"

"He enclosed a note in my invitation assuring me we had no need to worry about transportation—he plans to come in and escort us to the party."

Mrs. Amberly could not hide her chagrin that Addie had received such special treatment from people with whom *she* had tried so hard to promote a friendship. Making no attempt to conceal her pique she pouted for the rest of the meal refusing to speak. She would have been even more affronted had she known that the only reason *she* was included was to make sure Addie would come.

Her annoyance at the situation displayed itself in various ways almost up to the evening of the housewarming. Addie could do nothing right nor could anyone else. Nothing pleased, nothing suited, nothing satisfied. If Addie had not become used to such childish behavior, she would have been at the end of her rope. But she had learned it was best to ignore Mrs. Amberly's fits of temper and maintain her own composure. She refused to let a selfish old woman spoil her own anticipation of what promised to be an interesting evening.

Addie had to admit she was curious to see the Montands' mansion at last. She had certainly heard enough about it. From what she knew of Louis and observed of Estelle this party would certainly be an outstanding occasion.

It had been a long time since she had been to such an occasion, had a chance to dress up, and to look forward to an evening of music and dancing. It had been even longer since she had felt young and lighthearted.

Addie was glad now she'd given in to Aunt Susan's urging her to bring a party dress. "You just never know when you'll have an opportunity to wear it. Better be safe than sorry." It had been her wise advice. Against Addie's protest the dress had been packed in her trunk. Now a week before the Montands' housewarming, Addie took it out from the layers of tissue, shaking out the dried rose petals in which it had been packed, filling the room with the nostalgic scent of summer gardens.

The dress had a history of its own. It had been made for her to wear at the ball at Oakleigh to formally announce her engagement. But then the war had come, and within months Ran had been killed and the dress packed away unworn.

Addie examined it carefully. It was in perfect condition, still lovely—a rosy-gold satin with a net overskirt embroidered with gold thread, the rounded décolletage outlined with stiffened net ruffles edged with ecru lace.

Of course, she would not be wearing it with a hoop or layers of starched petticoats underneath as she would have in 1862. Nonetheless, the gown itself was so beautiful that perhaps no one would notice it was somewhat passé. Her mother's opals in their delicate gold filigree setting would be exactly right with the color of the dress. Excitedly she

120

put in the earrings and fastened the clasp of the necklace, then studied her reflection in the mirror.

Aunt Susan, bless her heart, had tucked in appropriate accessories as well: a small beaded evening bag, a lace and ivory fan, elbow-length kid gloves in their original box—never worn either. Addie smiled, feeling like Cinderella and that Aunt Susan was a veritable fairy godmother.

"I'll do you proud, Auntie!" Addie promised as she whirled around the room a few times holding out her skirt. "At least for one night I'll be Adelaide Pride again! Adelaide Pride of Oakleigh!"

She laughed at her own silliness but her happy mood lasted up until the night of the party when she donned her finery again.

Mrs. Amberly had somehow managed to find someone to "do" *her* hair and was closeted in her bedroom the whole afternoon. When she finally appeared, Addie had to employ rigid self-control not to betray her reaction to her employer's appearance. Mrs. Amberly looked like a walking jewelry counter. Her dress was ruby-red taffeta; her plump shoulders were bare except for a tulle stole. An elaborate coiffeur sparkled with brilliants and the rest of her shone with an array of diamonds, from a huge sunburst brooch on her breast to bracelets and rings.

Fortunately, Addie was not required to comment. It had taken Mrs. Amberly so long to assemble herself that it was already late when one of the hotel maids came running over to breathlessly tell them that the Montand carriage and driver had arrived and were waiting for them.

Brook, splendid in evening clothes, was standing outside the main building. He gave them a sweeping bow, complimenting them both extravagantly. But it was Addie on whom his gaze fixed. With a practiced eye he made a kind of inventory of her—not missing a detail—his approval apparent.

121

Mrs. Amberly was panting from hurrying and it took both Brook and the Montands' man to assist her into the barouche. Then Brook held out his hand to Addie, murmuring, "Absolutely beautiful, Miss Pride. If I'm not mistaken, tonight will determine Montand's decision—"

Addie sent a quick anxious glance toward Mrs. Amberly, hoping she had not heard this. But she was fanning herself from the exertion of getting settled and had not overheard.

"You look like a fairy princess," Brook said, his glance took in the fire opal necklace and earrings. "Are those the crown jewels?"

"They *are* heirlooms. They belonged to my mother."

"Perfect."

"Thank you, Mr. Stanton. I trust we'll see you later?"

"Indeed, yes. I wouldn't miss it." Brook's expression was enigmatic. What his real feelings were about coming to the Montands' party she could not guess. Did he feel the Montands were outdoing even *him* with this lavish affair?

"Save me a dance," he said as he waved them off.

The minute Rex entered the Montand house he saw Adelaide Pride. She was standing in the front hall talking to Louis. The glow from the glistening crystal prisms of the chandelier overhead sent dancing lights upon her dark hair. Her dress, a golden color of some filmy material shot with gold threads, reminded him of a sparkling champagne.

She looked so beautiful that momentarily he was stunned. It had almost physical impact, as if he had been thrown from his horse, his breath knocked out of him.

Rex had been undecided whether to come to this party tonight. He did not like Louis Montand. That was probably unfair because he did not really know the man. But he had heard some unsettling rumors that made him suspicious of Montand's motives for coming to the valley, taking over the Caldez ranch. But at the last minute he had decided to come, if just to avoid another solitary evening.

He had not been sure *she* would be here tonight. He had hoped she might be—had been almost afraid to hope—but was grateful for whatever had brought him here tonight. He took a few steps into the foyer, surveying the scene, then stood absolutely still.

At that very moment, as if drawn by some invisible cord, Addie turned her head and saw him. Instantly her heart turned over. She felt that same uncanny sense of recognition, leaving her again breathless and confused. Nervously, she unfurled her fan, trying to listen to what Louis was saying to her.

"I may have to devote myself to my guests tonight. Estelle has already warned me I must circulate, not spend too much time with one person more than another." He pressed her hand to indicate who that one might be, then continued, "Feelings in these provincial towns are easily hurt, she tells me. And I suppose she's right. People get offended, imagining slights where none were intended." He gave a little shrug. "Since we have to live here and there are people I may need—I must heed her admonitions." He smiled beseechingly. "I hope you understand?"

"Of course," Addie nodded, distracted, more aware that Rex was approaching than of what Louis was saying. And what did that matter to her anyway? The only thing that mattered was that Rex Lyon was standing in front of them waiting to speak. Addie felt almost dizzy.

"Good-evening, Montand," Rex said; then his glance moved to Addie, and he held out his hand. "Miss Pride, how very nice to see you again."

"Nice you could come, Lyon," Louis replied. "I was just telling Miss Pride my attention must be spread around among my guests this evening. It would be a favor to me if you would look after her until I can get away from receiving my new arrivals. The music for dancing has begun. Perhaps you could escort Miss Pride onto the dance floor?"

Rex looked down at Addie, thinking how lovely she was—those sherry-colored eyes, shadowed by dark, curving lashes—how luscious the glow of her skin, how sweet the tantalizing scent of her fragrance.

"I would be most happy to do so, if Miss Pride would do me the honor?" Rex assured him, his eyes brightening.

Behind her Addie heard a familiar high-pitched voice and turned her head to see Mrs. Amberly holding Louis's sister by the arm, her face pushed up into Estelle's, talking rapidly. Addie saw Estelle cast a look in Louis's direction. She assumed the Montands must have secret signals to use in awkward social situations because Louis immediately excused himself and went to his sister's rescue.

Left alone with Rex, Addie grew strangely calm.

"Would you care to dance?" he asked.

"Yes, indeed, thank you." Addie took his arm. Together they went across the hall to the drawing room where the furniture had been pushed against the wall, the rugs removed, and the floor highly polished for dancing.

A waltz was beginning to play. Rex led her out to join the gracefully spinning couples. He was a surprisingly good dancer Addie discovered. She had seen the way he rode a horse, seen his long-legged stride, his purposeful walk, but none of these had given a clue to his skill on the dance floor.

It had been so long since she had danced that Addie felt a little unsure of herself. At first she was too aware of Rex's hand on her waist, her hand in his. Then the music took over, and she fell in step with its rhythm. They circled the room several times, then reversed, all in perfect time with the three-quarter beat, gliding, whirling, as though they had danced together before in some other time, some other place. She felt as though it were a dream, floating on the rippling waves of the lighthearted music rising and swelling around her. For the first time in ages Addie allowed herself to be happy.

In the middle of a promenade Addie spotted Brook; he looked dashing and debonair as he stood in the archway of the hall. He must have just arrived for he was divesting himself of a white satin-lined cape. Seeing her, he smiled and gave her a little salute.

When the music ended they were at the end of the room near the bow windows, and Rex suggested, "Shall we catch our breath for a few minutes?"

"Oh, yes, let's," Addie agreed. They went over to one of the alcoves to sit on the velvet cushioned seat. Through the open window a cooling breeze brought in the fragrance of flowers.

Rex sat down beside her, looking at her so seriously and thoughtfully that Addie was compelled to ask, "Why are you staring at me so, Mr. Lyon? Is something wrong? Perhaps I have a fly on my nose or something?" She playfully brushed at an imaginary insect on the tip of her nose.

"Oh, no!" Rex said quickly. "I was just thinking how I nearly didn't come this evening and . . ." He hesitated for a long moment. "I just happened to think how many times that sort of thing has happened to me. Like the day I saw *you* for the first time—at the train depot. I hadn't planned to ride into town that day, either—"

"However, I'm very glad I *did* come." He made a sweeping motion with his hand. "This is quite a party, isn't it? I believe everyone in the valley is here, besides a few others I don't recognize."

"I understand Louis and Estelle invited friends from San Francisco, as well."

"Do you know them well—the Montands?" Rex asked.

"Well, they have been staying at Silver Springs for quite some time while this house was being completed. And you

125

know, my employer, Mrs. Amberly, stayed the winter so we have seen a great deal of them."

"It must seem dull to them after the life in the city, although Montand declares he wants to become a vintner." Rex shook his head. "Vineyards and winemaking are mostly family businesses here. That's how I happen to be here." He paused, frowning slightly. "I never intended to come back. I had planned to be a journalist, I had just started getting my feet wet, so to speak when . . ." an expression of infinite sadness passed over Rex's face ". . . my father died unexpectedly and my older brother was killed in an accident—and there was no one else to take over the business my great-great-grandfather had started."

"I know, I'm sorry. Freda told me something about it."

"It's a strange feeling to be the only one left in one's family."

"Yes, I quite understand. You see, I too am the only one left in *my* family," Addie surprised herself by confiding. "Two of my first cousins—boys I grew up with—were killed in the war, and both my parents are dead."

She realized Rex was the only person to whom she had told anything about her personal life since coming to California. His eyes softened, and he nodded as if no words were necessary to convey his sympathy. A brief silence fell between them, but it was not an uncomfortable one. Rather, it was an empathetic one; the unspoken acknowledgment of a mutual experience of loss seemed to bind them closer together.

After a moment, Rex asked, "Would you care for some refreshment? A glass of wine, perhaps?" He lifted one eyebrow and smiled. "Although, I can't vouch for its quality. I don't believe they're serving Lyon's Court vintage. And since Louis hasn't brought in his first crop yet or produced his estate bottled wine, it isn't Chateau Montand either." Rex leaned closer and said in an exaggerated whisper, "It's probably some inferior French champagne—" He shrugged. "But as they say, beggars can't be choosers!"

Addie laughed, delighted to see this unexpected side of Rex who had, before now, always seemed serious.

"What are you two finding so funny?" a voice asked and a smiling Louis stood before them.

Addie and Rex exchanged a conspiratorial look, silently agreeing Louis might not think a joke about his winery altogether humorous.

Not waiting for an answer Louis asked, "May I interrupt? I'd like to take this lovely lady on the dance floor and then in to supper."

Rex got to his feet slowly as though reluctant to surrender her to Louis. Addie stood up, feeling slightly dazed to have had her conversation with Rex so abruptly interrupted. But after all, Louis was their host. She could hardly refuse a dance.

"Did I tell you how absolutely beautiful you look tonight?" Louis asked as soon as they were dancing. "You know how a rare jewel looks in the right setting? That's how it is with you. Your sparkle, your delicacy, your grace is submerged in a place like the Silver Springs Hotel—it's not worthy of you, it does not do you justice. I can imagine the background you come from and how you fit there—that's why I wanted to see you *here*—in a setting I have created. I imagined you here. And it's just as I knew it would be—perfect."

Louis's dark eyes glowed with fiery sparks that seemed to burn into Addie. His intensity made her uneasy. The things he was saying. She looked at him warily. Of course, he was excited at the success of his party, probably overstimulated. Possibly he had drunk a great deal of champagne—responding to toasts of well-wishers as well as priding himself on the brilliant success of the party.

Louis's hand tightened on her waist as he swirled her

around to the romantic music of a Viennese waltz. "Tonight I have to share you—I don't really mind—it is very gratifying to see the envy in other men's eyes that *I'm* dancing with you! You do know you are the most attractive woman here, don't you?" He paused. "Of course, you don't. You're not the type of woman who is self-absorbed. You are different from most of the women I've met." Louis smiled. "Utterly charming. I find you absolutely fascinating. Even your name. Pride. It suits you somehow. Miss Adelaide Pride of Virginia."

Addie began to feel uncomfortable but did not know how to stop Louis. They circled the room again and then the music ended. Addie started to step away but Louis's hand on her waist prevented her.

"I'd like to ask you a great favor. I know we have not known each other very long, but I believe—at least, I *think*—we have become well-acquainted even in this short time. May I call you Addie? And, of course, *you* must call me Louis. After all, we're living in California now. And Californians, I've learned, do not stand on formality."

Addie was caught off guard. But before she could reply she caught sight of Estelle standing in the doorway, waving her fan to attract Louis's attention.

"I think your sister wants you."

"Ah, no!" Louis swore under his breath; then still holding on to Addie he walked over to where Estelle stood.

"Louis, it's time to announce supper. I hope you can relinquish him for a few minutes, Miss Pride?" She gave Addie a pinched smile, then took Louis by the arm as if to lead him away.

"I'll be with you in a minute, Estelle," he said rather brusquely. She looked annoyed but left and Louis turned to Addie.

"*We're* eating supper together. I'll just make the

128

announcement and be right back. Here, sit right down and I'll join you shortly."

Rex was nowhere in sight and had not mentioned supper, so Addie simply nodded and let him lead her over to a secluded corner to wait for him. A few minutes later he came carrying two plates filled with all sorts of delicacies: bay shrimp, creamed potatoes, fresh asparagus, and tiny hot rolls. Following him was one of the servants carrying a bottle of champagne and two glasses. After they ate, while the band tuned up for the last dance, Louis took it for granted that this would be his. Addie realized the evening was coming to an end and she had not had another dance or chance to talk again with Rex.

People began saying their good-byes, thanking their hosts and leaving. Louis settled Addie on a love seat in the small parlor adjoining the foyer to wait for him while he and Estelle saw off their departing guests. "I hope you aren't too tired, but I can't leave to take you and Mrs. Amberly back to Silver Springs until everyone else is gone."

"Of course, I understand. I'll be fine," Addie assured him.

Louis had hardly gone to join Estelle in the hall when Rex appeared at her side.

"I wanted to say how much I enjoyed being with you tonight, Miss Pride. You did say you were free on Thursdays, didn't you?"

"Yes—," she began but before either of them could say more, Mrs. Amberly came along, her face showing both annoyance and curiosity. Rex bowed and murmured good evening to her. She gave him a curt nod then turned to Addie.

"Go get my cape, I'm too tired to move," she said plunking herself down on the love seat.

Addie rose at once. She looked uncertainly at Rex, wondering if he was going to say anything else. But Mrs.

Amberly's presence seemed to have placed a pall on further conversation between them.

"Well, good night then, Miss Pride, Mrs. Amberly," he said, bowed again, and walked into the foyer.

"Well, don't just stand there," Mrs. Amberly said irritably, "I'm chilled. Hurry up."

Addie hurried off, half hoping Rex might still be in the hall and they would have another chance to speak. But to her disappointment, he was nowhere in sight. She noticed the last guest was saying good night to Louis and Estelle. By the time Addie emerged from the room off the hall where the ladies' wraps had been left, Louis was waiting. Mrs. Amberly's mood had undergone a miraculous transformation. She now appeared to be all smiles and compliments about the party to the Montands.

Within minutes they were heading back into town in Louis's smart barouche. At the cottage, while he bade Mrs. Amberly a courteous good night, Louis captured Addie's hand. To have withdrawn it would have been awkward, but it made her extremely uncomfortable. Finally Mrs. Amberly left them alone. Immediately Louis brought her hand up to his lips.

"Do you have any idea how proud you made me this evening, Miss Pride—Addie? You looked so lovely, and it delighted me to see you so happy."

His words set off an inner alarm in Addie's mind. Why on earth should Louis feel proud of her? She gave her hand a gentle tug, and after a second he released it. "It was a wonderful party. Thank you very much for everything. I must go in now."

"Yes, of course. But you never really answered the question I asked you earlier. Can we drop the *Mr. Montand?* I would like very much if you would call me Louis. . . ." He paused. "I think of *you* as Addie—and I think about you a great deal. . . . So may *I?*"

Addie hesitated. To use each other's Christian names was a step toward intimacy she was not sure she wanted to take with Louis Montand. But she could not really think of any reason to say no, without being rude. After all he had certainly shown her every courtesy and kindness. With some inner reluctance she said, "Why, yes, if you'd like to."

"I *would* like. Thank you, my dear. I'll be in touch. Don't forget I want you to come out to Chateau Montand when it is not crowded with people, so you can see it for yourself, see the beautiful home I've created."

He still made no move to leave. Feeling a little uneasy at his lingering, Addie moved toward the door. "Good night, Louis."

"Good night, Addie. I'll see you soon."

Inside her room Addie heard the carriage drive off, and she gave a sigh of relief. She hoped she had not given Louis Montand any false impressions, no reason for him to assume—whatever it was he was assuming about her.

But Addie didn't want to think any more about Louis Montand. She wanted to think about—other things. Tonight had been like being caught somewhere between the past and present, music, dancing, laughter. Addie felt as though she were on the brink of something wonderful. What was it? Were her feelings about Rex Lyon her own imagination or did they have any basis in reality?

Estelle Montand was waiting for Louis in the small parlor when he returned from taking Addie and Mrs. Amberly back to Silver Springs. She stiffened visibly when she heard him humming as he came in the house. She frowned.

"Ah, Estelle, you didn't need to stay up on my account!"

"I wanted to. I wanted to discuss our party. How do you think it went?"

"Splendidly, splendidly!" Rubbing his hands together in

obvious satisfaction, Louis asked, "Shall we have a nightcap while we share our comments?"

Not waiting for an answer he went over to the liquor cabinet and brought out a cut-glass decanter from which he poured two glasses. He handed one to his sister then sat down in one of the damask upholstered chairs opposite her. He raised his glass then took a sip.

"So, you delivered that dreadful woman back to the Springs." Estelle gave a little shudder. "I thought we were rid of her once we left the resort. Why on earth did you invite her?"

"Because, my dear Estelle, if I hadn't, I couldn't have invited the delightful Miss Pride. There was no alternative. And I decided not to deprive myself."

Estelle felt a quick little twinge of alarm. So her brother's interest in the charming Southern woman was still strong. At first she had thought it was simply infatuation. Darting a speculative glance at Louis, Estelle said carefully, "Of course, she *is* attractive."

"*Attractive?*" Louis sounded incredulous. "Why, she's downright stunning." A smile played around his mouth as if he were contemplating an image of her. "She is also intelligent, charming, and completely captivating.

Estelle tried to keep her tone casual. "Well, of course, I didn't have a chance to get to know her while we were staying at the Springs. I was too busy trying to avoid that terrible woman whose secretary or companion she is—"

"Well, you'll *have* the opportunity very soon, Estelle. I want to have her out as soon as possible. I want her to see everything—the house, the gardens, the grounds, the winery—*really* see it, not like it was tonight, filled with people, but as it might be—as a home."

Estelle had a sickening sensation. So things had gone *that* far! At least as far as Louis was concerned. And that woman probably saw him as a "good catch," someone to rescue her from her menial position. *Well, we shall see about that!* The question was, was it too late for *her* to do anything about it? Perhaps not. But to her brother she said mildly, "Yes, that's a nice idea, Louis. Perhaps in a week or so when we're more settled."

Perhaps all she needed was a little time.

Chapter 11

he day following the Montands' housewarming party, Mrs. Amberly was out of sorts. Her feet were swollen from squeezing them into too-tight, fashionably pointed shoes the night before, and she had indigestion from indulging in the bay shrimp and salmon mousse, the chocolate eclairs and chilled champagne at the lavish buffet. She stayed in bed most of the morning, and in the afternoon she sent Addie into town to buy her some patent medicine and some peptic pills at the pharmacy.

The next day she had recovered sufficiently to give Addie a new shopping list, which now included her favorite confection—caramel covered walnuts. That afternoon while Mrs. Amberly was napping, Addie walked back into Calistoga to take care of another number of errands.

It was a springlike day. Addie was glad to be out in it and away from the strident demands of her employer for a few hours of freedom. She decided to enjoy it. As long as she was in town, she decided to go to the library and select more reading material. Books were Addie's sometime alternative to needlepoint to offset the boredom of the long evenings while Mrs. Amberly played cards. If she didn't occupy herself somehow, Addie found herself inadvertently

134

listening to the shallow conversation, inconsequential comments, and trivial gossip of the players. It amazed her that these people, affluent enough to come to this luxury resort, had so little to absorb and interest them. The place reverberated with undercurrents. Casual remarks were sometimes misconstrued, resulting in feuds when guests magnified small slights into insults so that some of the guests did not speak to each other and others took sides in the most ridiculous way.

Of course, Mrs. Amberly was in the middle of most of it. She relished hearing both sides of any battle, relaying what had been said, fueling the flames, so that some unintentional action would be blown into a full-fledged war.

Addie managed to stay clear. She never let herself be drawn into any discussion of the other guests by Mrs. Amberly. Her reticence threw her employer into sullen sulks, but she eventually gave up trying to bring Addie into the conflicts.

Well, she wasn't going to worry about any of what went on at the hotel, Addie decided, not today. It was a beautiful day, the kind of day when one should only think happy thoughts. It was the kind of day when anything could happen.

"Miss Pride!"

Startled, Addie turned in the direction of the voice calling her name and saw Rex Lyon waving to her from across the street. Grinning broadly, he whipped off his hat. In a minute he was crossing toward her. He was a little out of breath when he reached her.

"Hello! This is a bit of luck. I was just thinking about you. . . ."

She had to laugh. He was so boyishly candid. No proper greeting, no polished manners, just direct.

"I mean, I was trying to think how to . . . well, I was planning to send you a note. I didn't want to just come by the hotel. I might not have picked the right time—a good time for you, with your job and all—" He stopped abruptly, then asked, "Are you in a hurry? Could you have a glass of cider or some ice cream—at the candy shop down the street?"

"As a matter of fact, I was headed that way. I have to get some caramels for Mrs. Amberly." She almost giggled as she added, "She's feeling a little under the weather."

"The very thing. Caramels will do the trick," Rex responded straight-faced.

They both laughed and they walked down the sidewalk together.

At the drug store Addie purchased a pound of caramels while Rex got them glasses of chilled apple juice, and they sat down at one of the small, round marble-topped tables.

"I really enjoyed the other night," he began looking at her with steady gray eyes. "At the Montands' party. You know I almost didn't go. Or did I tell you that?" he smiled a little sheepishly. "I said a lot of things the other night. I can't remember talking so much. Not for a long time at least." Then abruptly he asked, "Do you ride?"

"Yes," Addie answered. "But I haven't ridden for quite awhile; there wasn't the opportunity. . . ." Her voice trailed off. She could have told him more, explained that they had horses at Oakleigh; then the war came and the horses were needed. Actually, her father had volunteered them for the Confederate Army. How could she tell Rex all this? How could she tell how bitterly she had wept when her beautiful little mare Phaedra was led away? Oh, she wanted to be patriotic, but it was hard. After all, she had been hardly more than a child—at sixteen, heartbreak, whatever the cause, is still heartbreak.

Rex did not seem to notice her hesitation. He waited and when she did not go on, he said, "The reason I ask is because I've just found out some friends of mine are here in the area. The man, Rob Baird, is someone I knew when

I lived in Monterey, down the coast. We both worked on a newspaper there and then again in Oakland before I came back to the valley two years ago. . . ." He paused, frowning, as if the background of the friendship was too long and complicated to get into at the moment. "Anyway, he hasn't been too well, getting over a bout with pleurisy I understand, and he's come up here for the milder climate—actually he and his wife are camping out in the hills above town, and I'd very much like you to meet them."

Addie raised her eyebrows. How very odd. Camping out? What did that mean? Every day she seemed to hear something new and startling about western ways.

"I can bring you one of my horses. I know just the one and we could take a picnic." He looked at Addie with a kind of mischievous twinkle in his eyes. "It might be a welcome change from all the formality of the Silver Springs dining room. What do you say? How about next Thursday?"

Addie took a few seconds to decide. It was an unusual invitation. But she lately had developed a taste for new experiences. Her curiosity was aroused by Rex's description of his nonconformist friends. Why not?

"Yes, I'd like to—very much."

They finished their drinks, and Addie suddenly became conscious of the time. She consulted her watch pinned to her jacket. "I have to go," she said, gathering her small packages and standing up. "Mrs. Amberly will be waking up from her nap soon and expect me to be there."

They walked out of the shop into the afternoon sunshine.

"I'm glad about Thursday," Rex said. "It's all set then?"

"Yes, I'm looking forward to it," she told him knowing how much she was.

"Well, good-bye."

"Until Thursday."

He seemed not to want to be the first to turn away so

137

Addie finally said good-bye again and started walking up the street toward the hotel, knowing that Rex was probably watching her. At the same moment she became aware of two figures across the street. The Misses Brunell! *They* quickly turned their heads as if window-shopping at the millinery store. But Addie was sure they had seen her and Rex Lyon come out of the pharmacy, stand talking together. She was just as sure they would report it to Mrs. Amberly.

She didn't care. Addie lifted her chin defiantly. She was entitled to a life of her own—even if it was only on Thursdays.

She walked on, but her steps slowed as she got closer to Silver Springs. It *was* strange that she and Rex had run into each other today. Sitting opposite him in that little sundries shop had seemed so natural. They had talked as easily as if they had known each other a long time. Even the other night at the Montands' party, their conversation had not been the light exchange most social ones usually are. They had told each other important things about their lives. It was as if it was important to find out as much as possible about each other as quickly as possible. And that day at Freda Wegner's, he had asked her *real* questions about how she felt and thought. He had treated her like an intelligent woman whose opinions were worth listening to, as if he had actually wanted to get to know her as a person.

Was it all her imagination? She hardly knew him. Was she being foolish? How could she tell whether he was what she imagined? Maybe it was just an infatuation, a physical attraction—the way his hair fell on his forehead, the impatient way he had of brushing it back, the humorous mouth, the strength of his jaw.

In sight of Silver Springs gate, Addie stopped suddenly. Standing under the shade of a large oak tree, she was almost overcome with a longing for a love that had no beginning and no end. All her life she had been waiting for someone to come into it who would accept her as she was, know her, love her, look at her the way Rex Lyon had looked at her today.

Addie drew a long shaky breath. Today in his eyes, Addie thought she had seen what she'd been searching for all her life.

As he rode back from town, Rex Lyon's mood was elated. The chance encounter with Adelaide Pride had lifted his spirits enormously. Since the day of her arrival in Calistoga when he had happened to be at the train station and he had felt that strange stirring in his heart, she had lingered hauntingly in his mind. He could not rid himself of that uncanny sense of having known her somewhere before. Until the other night at Montand's, there had only been two other brief meetings. To run into her this afternoon when he had not even planned to come into town seemed just luck. Or was it Divine coincidence? His mother had always told him, "Nothing happens by chance." Now, Rex was becoming a believer.

Today they had talked at length and he had drummed up the nerve to ask her to go with him to see his friends Rob and Nan Baird. For the first time in a long while a curious ripple of anticipation coursed through him; next Thursday seemed a long time off.

At the sign LYON'S COURT, Rex turned his horse into a lane lined with majestic eucalyptus trees standing like sentinels on both sides of the road leading up to a turreted stone building. The house his French great-grandfather had built in this California hillside was modeled on a chateau in his village in France. The rays of the late afternoon sun glazed the diamond-paned windows with a lustrous gold and gave the native stones a silver patina.

He brought his horse to an abrupt halt when he reached

the arched porte cochere, and dismounted, hailing the dark-eyed lad who ran out from under the shade of the oak tree near the driveway. The boy greeted him, "Evenin', *Señor*."

"Howdy, Pedro. Take Roi to the barn and see that he gets a rubdown and some oats. Then tell your mama I'm home."

"*Si, Señor*," the boy nodded, rubbing the horse's nose affectionately.

Pedro's mother was the housekeeper and cook, and her husband oversaw the vineyard workers. The Hernandez family were Californios, descendants of the first Spanish settlers who had come here long before the Gold Rush in '49, before the vineyards even. As a girl Maria had worked for Rex's mother and had stayed on after her death to keep house for him.

Rex went up the stone steps and into the house. For a moment the old loneliness welled up inside him. A man should come home in the evening to a fire burning, lights shining, a woman's soft voice, a welcoming kiss, the sound of children's laughter. Not to this . . . emptiness. However, almost immediately Rex seemed to hear the words "not for long" echo in his mind. Was it his imagination or some internal assurance? He felt an odd hope that it might be true.

He walked into the library, the fading sunlight slanted through high, curved windows, and then was lost in the high-raftered ceiling of the large, rectangular room. Rex lifted the cap of a cut-glass decanter on the refectory table and poured himself a glass of cabernet, instinctively holding it up to the light as if to test the clarity of its jewel-like ruby color. Then he lowered his six-foot frame into a deep, worn leather chair, stretching his long legs out in front of him.

His eyes roamed the magnificent room restlessly. Family

140

portraits in heavy, ornate frames hung on the walls. Rex's ancestors came from the wine-growing regions of France, a family of wealth and influence, producers of a famous Tokay wine. His great-great-grandfather, Gerard Deleon, had been a young boy of fifteen when the French Revolution swept its ruthless path across his country.

Although of noble birth, the young man's sympathies were with the peasants. At an early age he had been disturbed by the plight of the poor. He had often seen coachmen of the aristocrats whip an innocent peasant by the side of the road, and he was disgusted. He despised the merciless brutality rampant at the time. At first, he had seen the Revolution as the hope of the peasants, the class who had no rights, no dignity, no future.

But the reign of terror swung close to home and his own family's name was listed with those sentenced to the guillotine. Helped by English friends, the family escaped to England, bringing only the clothes on their backs and a small quantity of some of their choicest grapevines from the family's vineyard.

They had believed the Revolution would be short-lived and that they could soon return to their native land. But it soon became clear that it would be a long time before they could safely return. Gradually, over the years, in gratitude to their English benefactors, the Deleons became Anglicized. They changed their name to Lyon, their religion to the Church of England; their manners and attitudes soon became those of the country of their refuge.

Gerard decided to go to the new world of America to seek his fortune. He had heard much of the fabulous West Coast as the "promised land" of America. So he traveled across the country on the Santa Fe trail to San Diego, then on up the coast to San Francisco and into the Napa Valley. There he was able to buy land, plant his vines, and establish a vineyard.

By 1857 Lyon's Court Wineries were famous throughout California as producing some of the finest wines, comparable to those of France. Gerard settled down, married, raised a family, and prospered. Since that promising beginning, an unfortunate series of tragedies had occurred—the untimely deaths of Rex's father and older brother—and only Rex was left to carry on the splendid legacy his forebears had worked so hard to acquire.

He put down his half-finished glass and went over to the long windows overlooking the sloping hills down to the vineyards. In the afterglow of sunset, Rex's thoughts returned to Addie and the unexpected chain of events that had brought him back to the valley and to meet her.

After his mother died when Rex was fourteen, he was sent away to boarding school in Sacramento where his talent for writing was first recognized and encouraged. As the younger son he had not been expected to follow his father and older brother into the family's wine-producing business. So he had been allowed to follow his ambitions for a literary career.

He had loved the life of a journalist. He worked on newspapers in several California towns, mingling with other young men with the same goals. He became part of a small circle of writers in the towns where he had lived: Monterey, Oakland, and then San Francisco. Then had come the shocking news of his brother's fatal accident. Riding in the vineyards, Philip was caught in a sudden lightning storm, his horse had become frightened, reared, and thrown him, killing him instantly. While the family was still reeling from this shock came another shattering tragedy. Their father died from a heart attack. Rex, home for the funeral, had no alternative but to take over the ranch and the winery.

He had deeply resented giving up his career to take up the reins of a business in which he had no real interest. Now, however, he saw that there might be some unknown reason for everything that had happened, and how he had chanced to be here when Adelaide Pride arrived in Calistoga.

His first sight of her at the train station was etched indelibly on his mind. Even though it had been a few brief minutes he had memorized everything about her. The graceful figure dressed in black, the delicate lift of her chin, the glimpse of rich, dark hair swept up from her slender neck under the little black bonnet. He recalled how she had turned toward him and he saw her lovely eyes—clear, sherry-colored eyes. Then for an unforgettable instant they had looked at each other and something indescribable, yet very real, had passed between them.

Rex ran an impatient hand through his tousled hair. Was he mad? Was it only his own longing that persuaded him to think that? Still, he was sure she had felt something, too, although she quickly turned her head away.

For weeks he had thought about her, wondered who she was, what she was doing in Calistoga, was she a widow, married, single? Then the night he and Freda went to have dinner at Silver Springs, they were introduced. This was followed by indecision of how he could get to know her.

Now, everything seemed to be falling in place. At least, he was getting a chance. What the future held, who could say?

Addie's Journal:

March 16
I haven't written in a long time, but must record something extraordinary that happened today. A chance encounter with Rex Lyon in town resulted in an invitation to go riding with him, up into the hills, to meet some friends! I am overly excited, I'm sure. But we had a wonderful conversation, a real meeting of minds—

PART 3

SILVERADO SPRING

Chapter 12

Thursday morning Addie awoke with a sense of excitement. She got out of bed and hurried over to the window to check the weather. The sun was already out; the sky a cloudless blue. A perfect day for a ride up into the hills to meet Rex's friends.

She hummed as she washed and got dressed. Instead of pinning up her hair, she brushed it back, braided it, and fastened it with a slide at the nape of her neck. She put on the divided skirt of sturdy blue cotton she had made from Freda's easy pattern; with it she wore a light blue shirtwaist, over this she slipped on a biscuit brown saxon-cloth jacket. Lastly she pulled on her leather riding boots, which some instinct had prompted her to pack.

Making a final check in the mirror she could not help compare her present outfit to the elegant riding habit she had worn in Virginia before the war. That one had been ordered from a prestigious New York ladies' tailor and cut to her exact measurements. It was made of dark blue fine English wool with a superbly fitted jacket and sweeping skirt. With it she had worn a plush derby, veil, her hair clubbed into a velvet snood.

Ah, well, that had been in another lifetime. This was

now, in California, Addie shrugged, realizing that, for the first time, she wasn't looking back with regret; she was looking forward with anticipation.

Since the day promised to be warm, before leaving the cottage she grabbed up a wide-brimmed straw hat to take along in case the sun got too hot. As she crossed the grounds, she saw Rex just coming up to the main building on his horse and with another one on a lead.

Seeing her, he waved. "Good morning!"

"Good morning," Addie said, coming alongside the cinnamon-colored mare, putting out her hand tentatively to pat the sleek neck. "What a beauty! Did you bring her for me?"

"Yes, this is Gracia. She belonged to my mother. She's a lady's mount, very sweet."

Addie felt complimented that he would bring this horse for her to ride even before he had ever seen her on horseback or known how she could handle a horse. No, it was as if he *had* known. Again she felt that bond between them.

Rex helped her mount and handed her the reins. Addie leaned forward and stroked the silky mane. Then he swung up onto his own horse and led the way out of the resort grounds, then at the gates eased into a canter. Addie followed, intuitively sure that curious eyes were watching. For once Mrs. Amberly had not asked her about her plans that day. Addie felt positive the Brunell sisters had told her about seeing her with Rex in town. But today Addie was determined to leave behind her at the hotel all worries about what people thought or said.

At the end of town, they turned off the road onto a narrower one, hardly more than a bridle path leading up into the hills. The terrain was rough and rocky, so their progress was slow. But this gave Addie a chance to notice everything. The woods on either side were dense with tall eucalyptus and madrone; the ghostly, gray lichen-covered oak trees and redwoods towered lordly over all.

Eventually they came to a clearing where a meandering stream trickled over brown, sun-flecked rocks. Here Rex suggested they stop for a while to let their horses drink and take a rest after the arduous climb.

He took out a suede-sheathed flask of water from his saddlebags, poured some into a small silver cup, and handed it to Addie to drink. The water was cool and refreshing to her dry mouth and throat. They didn't talk, but Addie did not feel awkward about it. It just seemed natural that they both quietly enjoyed the short rest in the shady glen.

After a while they remounted and started climbing the narrow, rocky trail hollowed out by thousands of horseback travelers before them. Gradually it widened and they rode side by side. They passed the stagecoach station and a tavern, and began a steeper climb into the hills.

"It isn't much farther now to where the Bairds are staying."

"Tell me a little about these friends of yours. I accepted your invitation to visit them without receiving a real invitation from them. I do hope they're expecting us? Or at least that they know you're bringing me?"

"Of course, you're invited. When I saw Rob he said come any time. I rode up here the other day to tell them about you . . . well, that we would both be coming."

By the puzzled look on Rex's face, Addie realized he considered her question absurd, as if the protocol and social amenities she had been brought up to believe necessary were unimportant in the West. There *was* a kind of openhanded, openhearted, open-door generosity of spirit that did not stand on ceremony.

"Well, what do you want to know about them . . . the Bairds?"

"Oh, just . . . things . . . so I can get more of an idea what to expect."

Rex chuckled softly. "There's really no way to explain Rob. He's unique, like no one I've ever met before or after. We worked on the same newspaper in Monterey; that's where I met Nan too. She and her family were staying there, and Rob had just arrived from Scotland. Did I mention he's a Scotsman?"

Addie shook her head. "And what did he come to California for?"

"To find Nan. To persuade her to marry him." Another pause. "You see they met in France, at some artists' colony where Nan was spending the winter. They fell in love there and . . ." Rex paused again, then said, "Actually, they are on their honeymoon—"

Addie checked her horse, turned slightly in her saddle, looking at Rex. "On their *honeymoon?*" Addie gasped. "Then, should we be visiting them like this? I mean, aren't honeymoons supposed to be rather private affairs?"

"Well, *her* son is with them," Rex answered matter-of-factly, keeping his eyes steadily upon her, watching her reaction.

"Her *son?*"

"Yes, he's a capital little fellow—about eleven."

"But, Rex . . ." Addie frowned as though puzzled. "Oh, I see, she's a widow."

"Not exactly. She divorced her husband to marry Rob."

This time Addie could not conceal her astonishment. She gave a sharp pull on Gracia's reins, twisted around in her saddle to face Rex.

"*Divorced!* Why didn't you tell me?"

"Would it have made a difference?"

Addie thought a full minute. In her experience divorce was the kind of thing never spoken of, or if it was, in whispers. There was always a sense of shame or scandal about

150

it. A tragedy for the woman even if she were not at fault. Unjust, unfair as that seemed, that's just the way it was. A divorced woman was not even received in the society in which Addie had grown up, much less *visited* and on her *second* honeymoon!

"Answer me, Addie, what difference does it make?" Rex asked. "The Bairds are the same people I told you about. Wonderful human beings. That hasn't changed. Does it make a difference to you?"

Addie could not think of anything to say. She felt troubled. She had never been faced with this situation before.

"What is it, Addie? Don't tell me you have some kind of bias against my friends without even meeting them?" Rex chided gently. "Weren't you telling me—just the other day—that you thought in order to mature one had to grow out of narrow ways of thinking, overcome built-in prejudice, presuppositions about people, and look at each person with an open mind?"

Addie felt her face get warm. "I hate having my own words quoted back to me."

"Well?" Rex raised his eyebrows. "*Isn't* that what you said? Or don't you really believe what you said?"

"Of course," she snapped. "I only meant—well, I guess I was surprised."

"Come on, Addie, don't tell me I've been mistaken in you."

She hated explaining what seemed too obvious. Surely Rex must know that back east, people took an entirely different view of divorce. But Rex's searching gaze was relentless and seemed to demand an answer. She looked down at her leather-gloved hands, twisting the reins, before she began speaking in a low voice: "You have to admit divorce isn't very common, and it isn't considered—that is, not in most places—acceptable."

"All marriages may not be made in heaven, Addie," Rex

151

said quietly. "I think if you knew the circumstances, you'd understand." He waited a few seconds, then said, "If you feel the least bit uncomfortable, Addie . . ." He let the implication dangle.

The very air seemed still. It was suddenly so quiet between them that the buzz of insects in the tall grass and the wind brushing through the evergreens on the hillside even sounded loud.

"No. Of course not. Let's go on."

Addie picked up her reins again, flicking them against the mare's neck and they started up the path again. They rode on a little further in silence until Rex broke it. "You won't be sorry you came, Addie, I know, when you meet them. Rob is a whimsical, warm, generous fellow and Nan—she's different, very creative, vivacious—well, I know you'll like them." Rex reached over placed his hand over hers, saying softly, "I wanted *them* to meet *you*, Addie—I wouldn't have put you in any kind of embarrassing situation if I hadn't been sure you'd be great friends."

She turned and met his intent gaze, struck by how important this was to Rex. In that moment, she also knew it was important to whatever relationship they were destined to have. It only took a second more for her to realize that made it important to *her*.

A little farther on the trail Rex turned in his saddle and pointed down the hill to a clearing where Addie could see a weathered shed, hardly more than a lean-to. "Here we are."

"That's *it?*" she gasped. "*That's* where they're staying?"

Rex grinned, "I told you they are an unusual couple, didn't I? Come on."

The "honeymoon cottage" convinced her the situation she was coming into was stranger than she could have imagined. What kind of woman would agree to spending her honeymoon in such rugged accommodations?

The horses made their way down the precipitous path; the rolling stones under their hooves made it a jolting downward trek. Addie leaned back in her saddle, holding her breath. Before they reached the bottom they heard the sound of a dog barking. When they came in sight of a slant-roofed, dilapidated gray-frame building, a rusty, scruffy-coated dog, looking like a cross between a spaniel and setter, was out on the platform loudly announcing their arrival. Almost at the same moment a man's figure—so tall and thin he looked almost like a shadow against the sunlight—stepped out from the door of what looked like an abandoned miner's shack.

He waved both hands like a windmill and bounded down off the ledge toward them, scrambling down the pebbly path, sliding and slipping as he came. He hailed Rex with a shouted, "Hello, old fellow!"

Rex dismounted. In a few long strides he clasped Rob Baird's outstretched hand and shook it heartily. Their greeting was that of two long-lost brothers. After a few slaps on the shoulders and much laughter, Rex came back over to Addie, took hold of her horse's bridle, and held up his hand to help her down.

"Addie, I want you to meet one of my best friends, Robert Baird. Rob, Miss Adelaide Pride."

Baird made a courtly bow. "Miss Pride, delighted! Welcome to our domain." He raised his head, rolling his eyes mischievously. "Now come to meet the queen of all you survey, my gypsy wife." He gestured to the door of the shack where a small, stocky woman, in an ankle-length denim skirt and striped shirtwaist, stood hands on hips, observing them.

"Hello!" she called. "Glad you could make it. Couldn't have asked for a better day."

The three of them walked toward the shack and Addie got a better look at Rob Baird's bride.

153

Nan Baird had a strong, interesting face framed by masses of curly dark hair done up quite untidily and tied with a rather frazzled ribbon. Her complexion was tawny, her arms, under the rolled-up sleeves of her blouse, sunburned. She had a pert nose and laughing brown eyes. Her smile was spontaneous and genuinely friendly. But it was her eyes that gave her face a special beauty; their warm brown pierced you with their genuine interest and depth.

"Been picking berries," she told them as they came up to the makeshift shelter, wiggling her blue-stained fingers as if to prove it. "But look what bounty!" she declared, holding up a bucket filled to the brim with glistening blue-black berries.

Rob was all Rex had described: tall, lanky, thin-to-gauntness. His lean, high-cheekboned face was pale in contrast to his wife's tan, and Addie remembered Rex saying he had recently been ill. He wore his hair long, curling around his scrawny neck, and his drooping mustache was scraggly. But in spite of his spectral appearance, his handshake was firm, his voice strong and rich with a Scottish accent.

Lowell, the boy, was a fine-looking, sturdy child with tousled maple-colored hair, sun-streaked from the days in the glorious sun of the hills. He was outgoing without being cheeky. He had beautiful manners, which made Addie concede that even though his mother and new father might live in an unorthodox way, he was as well-behaved and attractive a child as many a parlor mother's pride.

Addie soon saw the truth of what Rex had told her about the Bairds. They obviously adored each other. They were totally unself-conscious about displaying their affection. It wasn't embarrassing to others because it was so natural. Rob's running dialogue with Rex was frequently punctuated with questions to Nan. When he needed confirmation of a date of an event or replenishment of his faulty memory of a name or a place, he'd ask Nan, "Was it not, love?" or "Correct me if I'm wrong, darlin' mine." He always listened intently to any comment she made, and his remarks were sprinkled with direct address to her as "gypsy," evidently an endearing nickname prompted by her Romany looks.

Addie had never before been exposed to such open and easy communication between married people. Her own parents, whom she was sure dearly loved one another, used formal terms of address with each other as did most of her adult relatives. Her mother called her father "Mr. Pride," and her father always called her by the name he used during courtship, "Miss Lovina." It had never seemed odd to Addie. But now, seeing the Bairds made her a bit wistful, a bit envious and longing to know that same kind of sweet intimacy someday herself.

When Rob announced he was famished, Nan immediately declared it was time to eat. His eyes followed her as she moved around briskly, setting up a dining table by placing a wide wooden plank across two large flat stones.

Rex unpacked the wicker baskets he had brought on his horse, two bottles of Lyon's Court best vintage, a half ham, cheese, oranges. Nan produced a loaf of bread she had miraculously managed to bake on their homemade grill oven, and happily declared it all "a feast fit for a king—or a poet." She looked fondly at her husband.

From bits and pieces dropped casually as the three "talked shop," Addie found out that Rob was widely published in Britain, his articles printed in the prestigious periodical *Cornhill*. Although Rob was self-effacing, Nan would not let him get away with false modesty. Apparently Nan thought her husband a brilliant writer.

The conversation was as sparkling as the wine Rex had brought, bright with literary references, plays on words, teasing banter in which Addie surprised herself by joining

155

in, even making some quips herself or retorting to some playful jest or conundrum posed by Rob. He seemed to have an endless supply of stories and kept them spellbound with hilarious incidents of his many traveling adventures. He had come across the country on an emigrant train that should have been the death of such an emaciated physical specimen as he. But it was his indomitable spirit and out- rageous sense of humor that had not only kept him alive but alert to the characters who had shared his car, to all the nuances involved in such a journey.

"As a matter of fact, I've just about completed the first draft for a book on the subject!" he laughed. "It should pro- vide me with enough cash so I never have to use that par- ticular mode of transportation again!"

Nan brought out a delicious cobbler that she had also whipped up while Rob was showing Addie and Rex their "kingdom."

There was such a holiday atmosphere about the day that Addie soon fell under the spell of her two unusual hosts and found herself relaxing in a way that was new to her. In fact, perhaps, for the first time since she had come to Cal- ifornia, she felt completely carefree.

"Now, both Lowell and Rob must take a *siesta*," Nan declared as she started gathering up the remains of their picnic. When both the gentlemen named began to protest, Nan said firmly, "No arguments!" Her tone was severe. With hands on her hips she regarded them both. "Rob, you *know* you're here to recover your health, and Lowell, if you want to stay up late by our campfire and hear the rest of the story Rob started last night . . . well, you know what you must do!"

Rob threw out both thin hands in a helpless gesture, say- ing to Addie and Rex, "You see who rules with an iron hand?" He unfolded his lanky frame and pointed up the hill. "Rex, if you want Miss Pride to see the most beautiful view in the world just take her up a ways; there's a peak—not a difficult climb, my dear—," he said to Addie, "but well worth the trouble."

Rex looked askance at Addie who nodded. "Yes, I'd like that, but first I'm going to help Nan."

Nan did not turn down the offer but said over her shoulder to the men, "It won't take long."

Addie followed Nan down a little path to a creek where Nan bunched up her skirts, stooped down, and began expertly scrubbing the few tin plates with sand, then rinsing them in the water that rushed and gurgled over rocks. She cast a look in Addie's direction, then went back to her chore saying, "So what do you think of us, Miss Pride? I suspect a motley crew?"

"Not at all. A happy band."

"I suppose most folks would think we were a bit daft, as the Scots say. But it's done Rob a world of good to be up here in all this clean, pure air, the sunshine." She sat back on her heels and faced Addie. "You know they've given Rob only a year to live?"

"Oh, no! I'm sorry."

"Of course, I'm not going to let him die," Nan said fiercely. "You know people told me I was a fool to marry him. That I'd be a widow before six months. He was that sick when he got to California," she sighed. "But I knew if I'd marry him, he would live. And what choice did I have? I loved him."

Addie said nothing. She had been an eyewitness to the evidence of such love.

Nan placed her hands on her back arching it. "How much has Rex told you about us?"

"Not too much, except that he's very fond of you both."

"Yes, Rex is one of the staunch ones. You can depend on Rex." She gave Addie a long look. "I was married before, you see, to a philanderer, a gambler. Nothing worse than not being able to trust someone. We were separated when I met Rob. I'd taken my children and gone to Europe. I'm an artist and we went to the south of France. I thought our love was impossible, so I returned to America, tried to make my marriage work again. But it was no use. Even the Bible says adultery is a cause for divorce, you know. I left him again and moved to Monterey. Then Rob wrote that he was coming." Nan started piling up the plates. "He was in real bad shape after the horrible trip. I nursed him back, but the doctors . . . well, what do doctors know, when it comes to that?

"Anyway, my husband agreed to give me my freedom. But I would have to file for the decree myself. Desertion was easy enough to prove. I had to sell a painting to pay the lawyer who got my divorce—one of my favorite ones too," she laughed. "But it was worth it. You can see what a prize I got. And he's going to get well, *really* well. We're going to find the perfect year-round climate for his health, and we'll—as they say—live happily ever after."

She smiled confidently then got to her feet. "Come on, let's go. These are finished, and I have to go round up my boys, see they follow my orders. And you and Rex want to go up the mountain."

Rob and Rex were talking in quiet voices when the women came back to the shack.

"Ready?" Rex asked, handing Addie her straw hat.

"Here, you'll be thirsty when you reach the top," Nan said and tossed them each an orange.

Tucking the orange in the pocket of her jacket, Addie followed as Rex led the way out of the small enclosed campground over the rubble of stones and onto a winding upward path.

It was a quiet, still afternoon, the sun warm on their backs as Addie and Rex climbed slowly up to a hillside above the "mountain castle," stopping every so often to look down on that little settlement. At the top was a lovely plateau. Large rocks bounded a cleared space surrounded by dwarf manzanita and madrone. In the cracks and crevices of the heaped-up rocks, hardy wildflowers struggled to bloom, adding unexpected color and scent to the unusual beauty.

Addie sighed a peaceful sort of sigh. She had never felt so tranquil in all the time she had been in California. Shielding her eyes with her hand she looked out over the ledge and saw, as Rob had predicted, a magnificent view of the entire valley. She glanced over at Rex who was leaning his back against a boulder; his eyes were squinted, almost closed. She wondered if he were drowsing.

Addie turned back to the view, unaware that under his half-shut eyelids Rex was observing her, finding her profile much more enchanting to contemplate than the view.

Rex watched as Addie took the orange from her pocket, turned it over in her palm once or twice, then began to peel it. Her broad-brimmed hat had fallen back, hanging by its ribbon around her neck and the sunlight sent sparkles through her dark hair.

In that moment he realized he had fallen in love with her, with this lovely woman who had appeared in his life, out of some dream, here in Calistoga, where he had not wanted to return. "God works in mysterious ways" passed through his mind like a confirmation.

Suddenly a fierce longing to tell her what was in his heart gripped him. But he knew it was too soon. To make such a declaration after so short an acquaintance would frighten someone like Addie, gently reared, not long from the strict social protocols of the East, especially the South. He must bide his time, give her time to get to know him, to know the life of the valley she would have to learn to live if—if—

He wanted so much to share everything with her, his

159

hopes, his dreams, his accomplishments, as well as his failures and disappointments. He wanted to share his life with her. That's why he had wanted to bring her up here to meet the Bairds, to see him through their friendship. He said her name over and over to himself—Adelaide, Adelaide, my love, my *wife!* The word touched him with a deep sweetness. There was a sense of inevitability about it. Why else had she come from half a world away, across the plains, across the country—to this place and time in both their lives?

As if his thoughts had somehow reached her, Addie turned and smiled at him, and his heart lurched. It had to happen. It had to be. He was determined it would be.

"I like your friends," she said.

"I'm glad. I hoped you would." He smiled back at her. "I was fairly sure you would—being the discerning person you are."

She laughed softly, tipped her head to one side. "What gives you the idea I'm discerning?"

"I could tell—"

"But you hardly know me."

"That's true, not as well as I want to." Rex paused. "I'd like to know everything about you, Addie. So, tell me," he urged. "I'd like to know about you, your childhood, your home, and family."

"Well, there's not that much to tell, really. When I try to think of how it was before the war, it's hard to remember. One tends to romanticize the past, especially a past that is irrevocably gone—forever." She looked wistful. "The war changed everything for us, you see."

"The war all seemed to be happening so far from here—a long way away. We didn't seem to be part of it. California had its own problems at the time—I was working as a reporter covering the gold mines in the northern territory while it was going on."

160

"You should be glad you were." She shook her head. "And it was all such a terrible waste—of men and lives—young women left widows, children orphans, families destroyed—all so needlessly. And what did it really accomplish?"

"Freedom?" Rex's question was gentle. "For the black slaves."

"Yes, perhaps. But also years of bitterness and unforgiveness on both sides," Addie replied. "I know my father was concerned about what would happen to the slaves—after it was all over. He was afraid it would take at least a generation until the country would really be one nation again."

Addie felt her old sadness as she remembered her father. He had been a man of wisdom, vision, and compassion. If he had lived he might have helped bring healing.

They fell silent, each pondering the other's words. Addie considered Rex's comment to her question of what the war had actually accomplished. Freedom, for the black slaves. But in a strange way it had also brought her freedom, she thought with some surprise. For all its devastation, deprivation, destruction, pain, and loss, she had gained a freedom she would never have dreamed of before the war. If the war had not happened, she certainly would never have come to California! Unconsciously she turned and looked at Rex. She thought, *And I would never have met Rex Lyon.*

"Tell me what it was like for you when you were a little girl."

Addie's expression grew thoughtful. "I guess you'd say my childhood was ideal. I had loving parents, doting grandparents, uncles, aunts who cared for me, cousins to play with, parties to go to. But I always felt that . . ." She halted.

"What did you feel? Go on, Addie, tell me."

"Well, it'll probably sound strange, but it was as if I was always waiting for my *real life* to begin, as if there were

161

something missing, that I hadn't found yet." She felt his eyes upon her and she laughed a little self-consciously. "Oh, my, that *does* sound fanciful, doesn't it?" She reached for her hat, straightened it on her head and tied the ribbons.

"I guess we'd better get started back," Rex said reluctantly. He rose, then held out his hand to pull her to her feet. Looking about her, she sighed.

"It's so beautiful here."

"We'll come back another time," Rex promised.

Addie's heart lifted, happy that Rex said *they would* come back, that there would be other days spent together like this.

The sun sent long shadows on the hillside as they left the Bairds' idyllic kingdom hidden away in the hills. Addie could not remember when she had wanted so much to see a day last longer.

Finally they said their good-byes to the Bairds and started down the rocky, winding trail back to town. It was all over too soon, Addie thought. Evening was coming on by the time they reached Calistoga and approached Silver Springs. A sense of melancholy overtook Addie the closer they got to the resort. They walked their horses through Silver Springs gate and dismounted in front of the main building. Rex tethered both horses to the hitching post. Overhead the sky had turned a lavender gray. Tiny pinpricks of stars were beginning to show, and a thumbnail moon shone palely through the trees.

No one was in sight. It was after six, and Addie knew all the guests were in the dining hall. She was glad. She didn't want to see anyone, have anyone break the spell of this lovely day. As they strolled across the grounds toward her cottage, Rex's hand brushed hers, then took it, held it tight. She did not withdraw it. Instead her fingers interlaced with his. She felt the roughness of his palm against her own, the

162

pulse of his wrist beating against hers. When they reached the cottage, Addie slowly relinquished Rex's hand.

"It was a wonderful day, Rex."

He stepped up on the porch beside her. His nearness made her breathless and she dared not move or turn. But then he touched her gently, turning her toward him. "I wish this day could go on forever," Rex said. Addie drew in a deep breath and as she did, he raised her chin with his finger, and for a moment all their unspoken feelings trembled between them.

Then she was in his arms, her face upturned, and he leaned down to kiss her. When it ended, Rex said quietly, "I've been wanting to do that all day. Maybe even longer. Since that first day—Addie. I don't know how to say this—except that now, I think I know why I came back to the valley—"

"Don't!" she said gently, placing her fingers on his mouth. "It's . . . too soon, it's . . . We must get to know each other—give ourselves time."

For some reason Juliet's words to Romeo from the world's most famous romance came into her mind. This was all happening too quickly, too suddenly "like summer lightning."

Slowly Rex let her go, holding her at arm's length.

"Yes, of course, you're right. I won't say any more. For now—"

She felt his fingers press her upper arms and understood how much it was taking him to control his emotion. She shivered slightly.

"I better go in. Good night, Rex."

"May I?" he asked softly leaning down to kiss her again.

"Good night," she said breathlessly and hurried into the cottage, down the hall to her room.

Shutting the door behind her, she leaned against it for a minute, pressing her hands against her breast, feeling her racing heart. She closed her eyes savoring what had just happened, the strength of Rex's embrace, the warmth of his lips on hers.

When she opened her eyes they fell upon the picture of Ran. Were those clear eyes accusing her of faithlessness? Had she in the space of one afternoon forgotten him, what he had meant to her, what they had meant to each other? Had she betrayed him by what she felt for Rex Lyon?

She crossed the room, picked up the framed photograph, studied the face of the man—the boy, really, only twenty when this picture was taken. That was before Ran had gone to war or known its madness or paid its ultimate cost. It was a handsome face, the eyes looking out at the world with hope and confident expectation that life was good and fair and decent. It was a kind face, a gentle one in which she saw no rebuke.

They had been so very young. *Oh, Ran,* she thought, *we never even got a chance to find out who either of us really was—or could become.* If he had come back—but he hadn't and there was no use trying to imagine what would have happened.

Still holding his picture, Addie knew looking at Ran was looking backward, to a time and place, a way of life, that could never come back. Ten years had passed. She was a different person than the girl this young soldier had left when he had ridden away to battle. If he had lived Ran would be different, too, from the man she remembered.

It was time to put the past to rest, to allow new thoughts and ideas and a new self emerge. Carefully wrapping the portrait of Ran in tissue paper, she pulled out her trunk from underneath the bed, opened it, and placed the picture at the bottom.

As she closed the lid she thought of the Scripture verse that Aunt Susan often quoted: Philippians 3:13, "Forgetting those things which are behind and reaching forward to those things which are ahead—" Addie knew she should be thinking about the future. What was her future? Was it here in California? And was Rex Lyon a part of that future?

It was hard to trust her own judgment about Rex. She wished Emily were here to confide in, advise her as she had all the years they were growing up together, sharing secrets.

Unconsciously, Addie put her fingers to her lips, tracing their outline, thrilling again to Rex's kiss. Was what she had felt real? Or had she been swept away by a dream of her own making?

The next morning while Mrs. Amberly was over at the bathhouse Addie took one of her favorite Jane Austen novels and went outside. The weather was spring-like and warm. It would be pleasant to sit on one of the iron-lace benches near the arboretum to read. However, her mind kept drifting from the page to the picnic yesterday. Thoughts of Rex distracted her.

She felt sure he had been about to tell her he loved her before she stopped him. How would she have responded if he had? She wasn't sure, she didn't know. Addie knew he had awakened something in her she had never experienced.

She had had plenty of beaux back in Virginia. But even Ran had not drawn the kind of response from her she felt with Rex Lyon. The more she saw of him, the more she wanted to know, to discover. It was more than his rugged good looks, his outward attractiveness. She knew, somehow, there were layers to him yet to unfold if only she got to know him better. She felt instinctively if that happened—

"Daydreaming, Miss Pride?" Brook's teasing voice made her jump. His shadow fell over the unread page and she looked up into his laughing face. "Lost in reverie? You seemed to be. You have a dazed look in your eyes! Aha! A certain glow—can I guess what gives you that special glow this morning?"

Addie put a finger in her book to mark the page, closed it and gave Brook a mildly reproachful look. "Aren't you ever serious?"

"But I *am* serious. You *do* look especially radiant. Could riding off on horseback with a handsome rancher yesterday have something to do with it?" he asked, all wide-eyed innocence.

"We had a lovely time," she answered primly. "We took a picnic and visited some friends of his."

"Aha! I can guess who they were. Rob Baird and his wife? Correct?"

"Yes, how did you know?"

"They stayed here for a week when they first came from San Francisco. In that cottage over there, as a matter of fact." Brook pointed to the first one in the row. "That is until they moved to a more private, if rustic place—seeking more solitude. They're on their honeymoon, or did you know?"

"Yes, Rex told me."

Brook paused for a moment. "Do you know the circumstances?"

"Yes, if you mean what I think."

"Well!" Brook sounded both surprised and pleased. "I'm very impressed, Miss Pride. Gratified. You have fulfilled my estimation of you. That you are able to see beyond the circumstances that some would not. In fact, some would even condemn."

"To be honest, at first I was a little shocked. But after Rex explained what they had been through, I couldn't help but admire—even envy—them for having such a great love and faith in each other."

"Love endureth all things," Brook quoted, giving her a speculative look. "Would it shock you to know I am somewhat in the same circumstances?"

Addie turned a startled face toward him.

166

"You mean—you're—?"

"Not divorced. An early marriage—annulled. My fault entirely. Of course, I was too young. We were both too young. Childhood sweethearts. Everyone paired us off early, expected us to ... even though I was way too unsettled to have ever gotten married in the first place. I always had this reckless, adventurous streak, I guess you'd call it. I wanted to come West, had 'gold fever' like so many did— and my child bride wouldn't come with me. Wouldn't even come join me after I sent her the money." He shrugged. "We were together less than a few weeks and never—well, I don't blame her. By the time I got the papers saying she had the marriage annulled, charging me with desertion, I had already made my first fortune!" He paused, sighed, shrugged. "I'm not proud of any of this, you know. All I can say is that when I came to California, I changed, or it changed me. I'm not the man—or rather the boy—I was then." He stopped abruptly, gave Addie a rueful grin, saying, "Then you would forgive my dark past?" Brook seemed suddenly serious as though it really mattered to him.

"Of course. My father used to say 'to understand all is to forgive all.'"

"Well and wisely put. All that's over and done with, and I believe we should put the past behind us—move on to the next horizon!"

"Of course, I believe that," Addie agreed. "That's what I'm trying to do too."

"Good! And if you're really looking into the future, Addie, you couldn't find a better man than Rexford Lyon," Brook said emphatically. "I applaud him on *his* good taste, as well."

Addie felt warmth rising into her cheeks at this.

"Well, I must be off," Brook said with a sigh. "Must get back to the books, my ledgers. I've been working on my monthly accounts, trying to make both ends meet. A hopeless task, keeping one jump ahead of the sheriff so to speak." He laughed, started away, then turned back. "What are you reading?"

Addie held up the book so he could read the title.

"*Pride and Prejudice.* That's a provocative title. Is it interesting?"

"Yes, it's a good story, but there's a lot of wisdom in it too."

"Such as?"

"The foolish foibles of society, the pretenses people go to great lengths to maintain—in other words, pride and prejudice."

Brook nodded, then quoted, "Pride, the never failing vice of fools."

"And yet there is some pride that is understandable, isn't there?" Addie asked thoughtfully. "Family pride, for instance. I was brought up on that. Being always careful not to do anything to bring dishonor on it."

"I seriously doubt *you* would ever do anything other than heap glory on your family name," Brook declared. "Well, I really must get back. Good day to you. Keep happy, Addie." He strode back toward the main building.

After Brook left her, Addie mused over their conversation. Brook was certainly a man of many facets. On one hand, he seemed always to be in high spirits, confident, assured. No one would ever guess there was a brooding side, a past he regretted, hopes unfulfilled, love lost.

Addie opened her book but somehow she could not concentrate on it. Her thoughts turned again to yesterday, to Rex. The ride up into the hills, the slanting sun shining through the leaves, the smell of sun-warmed grass and of orange—a day to remember always, a day that shone bright with sunshine against the shadows of what lay ahead.

Chapter 13

*T*aking up her chores as companion to Mrs. Amberly seemed more tedious than ever after the day with Rex and the picnic with the Bairds. That day Addie had caught a glimpse of something new—that life could be joyous and interesting even if it was different, and that happiness was possible in many unexpected ways if it was shared with someone you loved.

In spite of all the Bairds had been through—separation, sickness, sorrow—they had not let it embitter them. They had known disappointment, delays, difficulties of all kinds, the ostracism of society because of Nan's divorce, and who knows what else. They valued each other and what they had found together. It had made Addie see everything in a different light.

Only a few months ago, life had seemed leaden; now it had endless possibilities. How much she had learned, changed, and grown since setting out for California.

More and more she was beginning to believe there had been a purpose behind it all. One that was becoming more and more clear. Rexford Lyon. Was he the real reason she had come?

Thoughts of Rex Lyon were the last she had at night, the

first that entered her mind in the morning. What they had talked about, what they had shared, especially the memory of the kiss lingered.

But the weekend passed without any word from him. On Monday she thought there might be a note suggesting plans for them to spend the following Thursday together. But there was nothing, and Addie felt a slight uneasiness of doubt. Perhaps she had imagined a meaning where none existed? Had his kiss really meant Rex felt something deep and tender and passionate for her? Or had it been only her imagination?

Tuesday morning the desk clerk told her there was mail for her in her box. In happy anticipation she tore open the envelope. But instead of the note she hoped for from Rex, to her disappointment it was from Louis Montand. He asked if he could call for her Thursday morning before noon and bring her out to the new house for lunch with him and Estelle?

Addie debated. Should she wait another day to see if Rex came by or sent a note? Maybe she was expecting too much, being too sensitive. After all he was a busy rancher with a vineyard to oversee, a business to run. He had told her his days went from sunup to sundown. She would rather think he was working too hard to get away than that she had mistaken his interest in her.

For a moment, she held Louis's note. Then with a sigh of resignation she decided to accept that it would be better than spending her day off at the resort. If she remained here most certainly Mrs. Amberly would find some excuse to give her a chore or an errand to run. It would be safer to be gone. After all, Louis was amusing and it would be a distraction from her own nagging worries and useless wondering about Rex Lyon.

April 1

April Fool's Day! I write this because I'm beginning to believe I am the biggest fool imaginable.

Almost a week has passed and not a single word from Rex. I don't understand. Could I have been completely wrong about him? I close my eyes and see the way he looked at me, feel his kiss upon my lips, the warmth of my response—Fool!

Fool to get my hopes up, fool to dream that the "secret desire of my heart"—to love and be loved—was on the brink of happening.

On Thursday morning she chose her outfit carefully, knowing it would come under Estelle's severe scrutiny. The thought of Louis's sister almost took all the pleasure out of her day off, but it was too late now to back out. A glance out the cottage window told her Louis had already arrived. He was standing beside his shiny black phaeton, talking to Brook.

Both men's eyes registered approval as she joined them. Her fawn faille suit was one of Aunt Susan's remodeled creations, but the material was fine and her refurbished accessories were also stylish.

"You look charming as usual, Miss Pride."

"And I believe her stay in our beautiful clime has brought fresh roses to her cheeks and a sparkle to her eyes," commented Brook with a wicked twinkle in his own. His slow wink behind Louis's back reminded Addie of her secret "experimental treatment."

Addie returned the look with a reproving glance while maintaining her air of propriety for Louis's benefit. What an incorrigible tease Brook was!

Louis assisted Addie into the smart carriage, climbed into the driver's seat beside her, then picked up the reigns as Brook waved them off. As they started off at a trot, Louis remarked, "You may have noticed I called you "Miss Pride""

171

instead of Addie as you've given me permission to do. That was for Stanton's benefit. No use setting Silver Springs tongues wagging—at least *not yet!*" He glanced at her with a sly smile.

Louis must not have thought it necessary to wait for her to confirm the remark. Smiling confidently he turned onto Lincoln Road and started toward the center of town.

"I hope you won't mind, Addie, but I have to make a brief stop at the train station before we set out for home. I would have done so before coming to pick you up, but the train was late, and I didn't want to keep you waiting. It won't take but a few minutes. My overseer should be there to receive a shipment. I just want to check with him."

He pulled the buggy into the shade of a leafy oak near the train depot and placed a buggy brick to brake the wheels before crossing the street to the depot.

Addie watched him go, thinking how immaculately dressed and well-groomed Louis always was. Somehow he did not seem at all suited to the life of ranching or owning a vineyard. Addie had noticed how casually clothed other ranchers were when they came into town. Many frequented the gentlemen's lounge at the hotel, and they all had a certain look about them—a rugged, outdoorsy "western" style—like Rex Lyon.

At the thought of Rex, Addie felt a twinge of resentment. She was more disappointed than she cared to admit that he had made no effort to see her since the day of the picnic with the Bairds. Could he actually be *so* busy that he didn't have time even to send a note?

As she sat there waiting, Addie glanced idly about her. Her attention was drawn to what seemed to be an animated conversation—an argument?—between Louis and a shorter man in workman's clothes standing at the end of the platform of the train station.

Her eyes followed to where the man was pointing and

she gave an unconscious gasp. She saw a group of twenty or more men squatting on the ground near an open box-car still on the tracks. They were dressed in faded blue jackets, their bare feet were in sandals, their black hair was pulled back into long braids hanging down their backs. Why, they were *Chinese!*

Other than the glimpses she had had of the cook at Silver Springs, Addie had never seen Chinese, except in pictures in books—pictures mostly of plump mandarins or empresses adorned with jeweled, embroidered costumes, long curved fingernails and tiny bound feet, round faces painted white with shining black almond-shaped eyes. These men were not at all like that. There faces were gaunt, sallow, and they looked pitifully thin.

For some reason Addie felt a sick churning in her stomach. A terrible memory flashed into her mind. Once when she was a very little girl she had been in Richmond with her father, riding in a carriage over to visit relatives. They had passed a wagon in which some black men were huddled. As they went by, Addie had seen the same blank, hopeless stare on their faces that she saw now in these Oriental men. Later, much later, she had learned those men were on their way to the slave market.

Involuntarily, Addie shuddered. She blinked as if to erase her memory. Even though she had been brought up in Virginia, her parents had both hated the system of slavery and thought it should be abolished. Her father had been a lawyer, not a planter like her grandfather Pride. Although they spent summers and holidays at Oakleigh, in the winter she and her parents lived in town. Except for Renie, Addie's nurse when she was a tiny child, the only servants they had were Essie, the cook, and Lily, a maid. Thomas, the butler, also served as coachman and her father's valet. Addie had never thought of them as slaves. They were just adults who were black, friends, part of her life. All had eventually been freed.

As she grew older, her father talked to her sometimes about more serious matters. He had been vehement in his denunciation of slavery. "It's a horrible institution. The sooner abolished, the better for the South. It corrupts as much as it demeans human dignity, and has a demoralizing effect on everyone it touches."

Addie remembered that as she could not turn her gaze away from that pitiful group of Chinese. What were *they* doing here in this pleasant little California town?

"Well, now, we can be on our way," Louis said briskly as he got back into the buggy. "Sorry to keep you waiting."

"Who are those men, Louis?"

"Chinese I hired to work in my vineyards. Just came up from San Francisco. I've had some building the limestone cooling caves. Good workers. Hard workers, much better than some of these locals who don't even put in a day's work—" Louis's mouth tightened. "But let's not talk about *that*." He turned and smiled at Addie. "I don't even want to think of labor problems or work today. Today is to enjoy!"

Addie had many questions she wanted to ask about the Chinese workers. They looked sick and undernourished. How could they possibly outwork the well-fed, hardy Californios she had seen in the fields around Calistoga? But obviously Louis had no intention of discussing it.

The countryside out to the Montands' place was beautiful. The winding road was flanked on either side by trees, and acre upon acre of vineyards on the hillside golden with mustard blossoms.

At length, they turned into a lane that led steeply up a hillside. At its crest a large white house gleamed in the sunlight. They entered by a crushed stone drive with yards of manicured lawn on either side edged with flowering

174

bushes. As they got closer to the house Addie noticed a formal garden with circular flower beds.

"What lovely grounds, Louis. It was dark the night of the housewarming party so I didn't see them."

"That's all Estelle's province," Louis replied expansively. "I have no feel for flowers."

He pulled on the reins, and they stopped before the rococo Victorian house, circled with balconies, a deep verandah shadowed by elaborate fretwork. Between the porch posts all along the front were large hanging baskets of pink fuchsias and purple lobelia.

To Addie the three-storied structure looked austere, unwelcoming. Perhaps it was the dark-painted closed shutters on the long windows all across the front that gave that impression.

When Estelle came out to greet them, she was cordial and gracious if cool. But then again, Addie tried to remind herself that Bostonians could not be expected to have the warm effusiveness of Southern hostesses. Addie tried to put aside the feeling that Louis's sister was not all that glad to see her.

"Good day, Miss Montand. What a lovely place you have," Addie said sincerely, holding out her hand, which Louis's sister did not seem to see.

"So much still to be done, I'm afraid," Estelle said with a show of ennui. Then she turned to her brother, saying, "Louis, Manuel wants to talk to you. He's waiting for you. I think it's about—," she checked herself, "He said it was important."

"Excuse me, my dear," Louis said and went back down the porch steps over to where a man stood under the shade of a large oak tree nearby.

"Come along inside," Estelle said to Addie.

Addie tried to forget her initial snub, and giving Estelle the benefit of the doubt that she had not seen her extended hand and had not simply ignored it, she followed her into the house.

As Estelle led her inside, she explained the dimness of the interior saying she had learned it was necessary to close the shutters against the heat of the day in order to keep the house comfortably cool. The spacious entrance hall was paneled, as was its wide stairway in glowing redwood.

The parlor was, although elegant in every respect, almost overmuch. There were scalloped valances about the floor-length windows draped in brocade satin and curtained with starched lace. The furniture was heavy carved mahogany upholstered in emerald velvet. A richly flow-ered carpet covered the floor up to the marble hearth in front of the white marble fireplace over which hung a gloomy landscape framed in ornate gold.

It seemed ironic to Addie that with the abundance of real flowers growing in the yard an arrangement of artificial wax flowers under domed glass was placed on a polished table in the center of the room.

"Louis has excellent taste and is very particular," Estelle said as she moved over to the windows, fidgeted with the tassels, adjusted the tiebacks.

Estelle darted a quick glance her way, as if to see if she was sufficiently impressed. Although her statement seemed to beg some response, Addie could not think of any to make. She had been brought up in a gracious home with the understated elegance of fine English furniture, most of it brought over early in the eighteenth century by her Pride ancestors. She was a little at a loss of how to react to such ostentation.

"Louis told me he wanted you to see the whole house, so we'll indulge him." Estelle spoke with affection not untinged with condescension, a tone she often used in regard to her brother. Estelle moved toward the hall out to the broad staircase. "So, come along, we'll go upstairs."

176

Addie followed Estelle up the steps, noting the flocked wallpaper, the crystal prisms on the globed gaslights at the landing and at the top. As an invited guest, she had never before been asked to inspect the premises. Evidently complying with Louis's request, Estelle was doing the honors with some reluctance.

Addie remembered how Louis's conversations had been sprinkled with insinuating remarks—hinting at some point in time when his mansion was finished, when he was settled on his own estate, of some decision he would make. With even more discomfort Addie recalled Brook's predictions regarding Louis's intentions. With each step she took Addie's apprehension increased.

Estelle proceeded down the thickly carpeted hall, then opened a door at the end. Her voice jerked Addie back from her random thoughts. "This is the master suite. Go in, look around," Estelle urged, stepping back to let Addie enter.

Almost hesitant, Addie walked in and looked around at the lavishly decorated bedroom. Pink cabbage roses bloomed on the wallpaper, matching pink satin draperies hung at the bow window, pink marble tops were on all the surfaces of the dark wood furniture, a mirrored bureau and tables. An enormous, ornately carved bed draped in pink satin dominated the room.

"Louis ordered all *this* furniture himself. It's Philippine mahogany, hand carved by Spanish artisans. The marble is from Italy," Estelle said as she crossed the plush, flowered carpet and opened another door. "Here is the bathroom," she said triumphantly, gesturing with a flourish into what appeared to be a giant seashell. The walls and floor were pink marble. A huge porcelain tub stood on a polished wooden dais. Sculptured gold taps and faucet on a pedestaled wash basin rose like a huge opening flower, thick bath towels monogrammed with an embroidered M hung on a scrolled rack nearby.

Addie *was* impressed. Who wouldn't have been? Certainly no expense had been spared in the completion of Louis's house. To live here with his sister? Or alone? Certainly he had something else in mind with all these luxurious accommodations.

"Louis said you would be staying for luncheon?" Estelle hesitated as if expecting—hoping?—Addie would correct her. Addie felt puzzled.

"Why, yes, at least that is what I understood," Addie replied. Surely Estelle must know that Louis had invited her for lunch. It was hard to believe his sister would be so gauche as to ask such a question, unless . . . Then Addie recalled something she had heard her Aunt Susan say: *A lady is never rude unless intentionally.* Was Estelle *intentionally* trying to make her unwelcome?

"Well, then, I must go consult with our cook." Estelle spoke as if she must avert a culinary crisis. "In the meantime, please feel free to use the facilities to freshen up before we dine. Louis is with his overseer and may be some time coming in." With that Estelle swept out of the room.

Addie moved over to one of the long windows, parted the lace undercurtain, and looked out. Morning sun drenched the lawn—and the vineyards and the hills beyond—with golden light, and for a moment Addie felt a wave of nostalgia for the Virginia countryside. Suddenly she was back at Oakleigh and she felt the tug of homesickness for those other more familiar fields, trees, and views.

She turned back into the room with its ornate furnishings with a sense of loss and disorientation. All at once she felt stifled for air and hurried out of the overdecorated room. At the door she paused in brief confusion trying to recall which way to turn to the stairs. Then seeing the large brooding landscape she had noticed at the top of the landing, she hurried along the hallway and down the stairway.

The front door stood open, and Addie went out onto the

verandah in search of Louis. Standing on the edge of the porch steps she saw him at the far end of the lawn in an intense conversation with a man dressed in workman's clothes. As they spoke the other man punctuated his speech with hand gestures. Was this the Californio Louis said he had "inherited" along with his purchase of the land? Whatever they were talking about appeared important, to do with the vineyards. Addie did not want to interrupt. She turned her attention to the lovely gardens, the circular flower beds filled with blooming plants of all colors, the gravel paths that wound through the Italian statuary and birdbaths artistically placed at intervals. At the end, where the terraced lawn sloped down into the vineyards, stood an elaborate latticed gazebo.

Just then Louis turned as if to walk away from the discussion. Seeing Addie, he raised one hand to wave and started walking toward her. As he came within hearing distance he asked eagerly, "So, did Estelle give you the grand tour?"

"Yes, and it is very impressive indeed."

Looking pleased, Louis took the verandah steps two at a time and stood smiling down at Addie. He took her hand and drew it through his arm. "Well, then perhaps I should show you around the grounds a little. There are extensive orchards as well as the vineyards."

Just then Estelle came out the front door, and Addie said, "Louis is just going to show me your lovely garden, which he tells me is your creation."

"A garden is constant work. There is always much more to be done and our gardener is very slow—" her mouth tightened, "—very stubborn, set in his ways. I give directions but . . ." Estelle shrugged indifferently. Then without thanking Addie for the compliment she spoke directly to Louis, "Don't forget Father Paul is coming for lunch, and Milton should be here soon."

"Of course, I remember, Estelle." There was a tiny hint of irritation in Louis's voice. As they started down the verandah steps he explained, "She has invited Father Paul Bernard whom we knew from Saint Helena before we came to Calistoga and our lawyer, Milton Drew, to join us."

Addie thought of the little scene earlier when Estelle had seemed unsure whether she was going to stay for lunch. Did she really *not* know? Or was that an act? If so, why?

"I'm so glad you were able to come today, Addie. To see all this." He gestured broadly as they began strolling through the garden. "It's all turning out just the way I planned. I've been eager to share it with you."

They walked around the gazebo where the graveled paths formed a circle. Addie paused at a pansy bed filled with large purple, yellow, and lavender flowers. Leaning down to touch a velvety petal delicately with one finger, she said, "Everything is picture perfect, Louis."

"I'm glad you find it so, Addie. Next we'll go down to the orchards," Louis said. "If I weren't so determined on becoming the premier vintner in the valley, I think I would cultivate more fruit trees," Louis remarked. "But wine is becoming increasingly popular in America. Cultivating wine grapes will be a lucrative crop. Growers and vintners are bound to have increased prestige. I mean to show all these naysayers that you don't have to be born into a wine-making family to succeed. In fact, eventually, I will have my own dynasty to pass on to my children and grandchildren."

Addie was conscious of the emphasis he put on the words, *children and grandchildren.* She felt him looking at her with special significance but she pretended to be admiring some calla lilies and did not meet his gaze.

They left the garden and turned down a path that led into the bordering orchard planted with precise rows of fruit trees. Louis stopped to point out a peach tree with its greenish yellow globes that would soon ripen into luscious fruit. As Louis examined the leaves of one branch, Addie heard a rustling sound and saw movement at the end of the lane in which they stood. She squinted through the heavy foliage and was sure she saw several blue-coated figures huddled behind some trees at the end. She tugged Louis's sleeve, "Louis, are there people working here? I thought I saw some . . ."

He turned around, a deep frown creasing his forehead. "Where? Oh, yes, those are the workers I employed to build more cooling caves when my first harvest of grapes is ready. . . ."

Suddenly Addie remembered the Chinese coolies she had seen at the railroad station. "What are they doing here, Louis, and why are they hiding?"

"Hiding?" Louis seemed annoyed at the question. "They're not hiding. Most of them speak no English, so they're shy of strangers. Keep to themselves. They sleep out here in the orchard. Cook the strange food they like to eat. But they're hard workers, and I shall put them to good use come harvest time." He patted Addie's hand, which he had drawn through his arm again. "It's nothing for you to concern yourself about, my dear. Come along, our guests will be arriving soon, and I don't want Estelle to be cross with us if we're late for what I presume is a perfectly planned luncheon."

Somehow his answer did not satisfy Addie. Instinctively she felt there was something wrong, something furtive about the explanation. But realizing Louis did not want to discuss it further, she did not pursue it further.

As they walked back toward the house they saw a rickety black buggy coming up the drive.

"Ah, Estelle's good pastor right on time," Louis said with a touch of sarcasm, pulling out his gold watch and

181

consulting it. "He doesn't want to miss what will most surely be his best meal of the week."

The priest was old, his face wrinkled and brown as a nut, but his eyes were bright and shiny as black shoe buttons.

"Welcome, Father. May I present our guest Miss Adelaide Pride. Addie, Father Paul Bernard."

"A pleasure, Miss Pride. I beg your pardon for my appearance," the old man said, brushing great puffs of dust from his shabby cassock and worn boots. "I made some pastoral visits on my way here since I don't get over here from Saint Helena as much as I would like. Many of the places were off the beaten track."

"No apology necessary, Padre," Louis said jovially while giving Addie a wink behind the priest's back.

Addie felt a prick of distaste that Louis would make fun of this obviously nice, sincere minister. It struck her as arrogant and insensitive. But she had no more time to think about it as he was escorting her up the steps into the house where Estelle was entertaining her other guest, Milton Drew.

The three of them went inside where they found Estelle seated in the parlor already conversing with Milton Drew. Introductions were made and the men shook hands.

"Now, shall we all enjoy a friendly libation? Which shall it be a glass of Zinfandel or a sherry?" Louis asked.

Orders were taken and Louis poured the requested wine into tulip shaped crystal glasses already set out on one of the heavily carved tables. While Louis was so occupied, Mr. Drew, a balding man with a pale, jowly face turned to his host. "Your overseer, Manuel stopped me just now, Louis, complained bitterly of your plan to replace local workers with the Chinese you brought in to extend the limestone cooling caves. He is upset, you know. It's never been done here before. It could cause you a great deal of trouble."

"Milton, I realize you have lived in the valley a long

time. You were instrumental in getting me this property and negotiating the terms, and I am most grateful for your expertise in doing so. But I draw the line at being told by you or anybody else, for that matter, most of all by a Californio *overseer,* whom I can hire to work for me!"

Addie saw the muscle in Louis's cheek twitch and could tell he was extremely angry. But when he turned around to hand the filled glasses of wine to each guest, his expression was bland, his smile pleasant, his demeanor cordial. "Now, let's forget about all these unpleasant things and enjoy ourselves," he suggested and lifted his glass in a toasting gesture.

Addie accepted the delicate glass that Louis handed her; then he gave her an indulgent smile as if they two shared a special secret. The thought of the huddled Chinese coolies flashed into Addie's mind, somehow connecting them with the slave market memory of her childhood. Feeling slightly sick, she set down her glass untasted. She knew she didn't want to share anything special or secret with Louis.

Underneath his pleasant-mannered suavity, Louis was as hard as a diamond, calculating and caring little for the feelings of others. She had been appalled at the way he had put down his lawyer, a guest in his home, in front of his other guests, in such a dismissing way. She realized that what she had taken for self-confidence was actually arrogance.

Addie glanced at Estelle, wondering if Louis's sister had been at all dismayed by her brother's behavior. But Estelle had simply asked Father Bernard a question, turning to a less controversial topic. The half-hour that followed was as smooth as silk, although to Addie, the conversation seemed stiffly polite and artificial. Finally the muted sound of a gong echoed from the hall. Estelle stood up and announced they should go in to lunch. Although the dining room was large, high-ceilinged, and opened out onto the verandah that wrapped around the house, it seemed overcrowded. The walls were hung with too many heavily framed gloomy landscapes of the Hudson River school, a huge, carved sideboard took up one side of the room, and the windows along the other side of the room were draped and swagged in maroon velvet. It seemed a shame on such a beautiful spring day that the sunshine was blocked out by drawn lace curtains. Addie felt suffocated by the cumulative effect.

The table was elaborately appointed. There was a plethora of silverware at each place. A centerpiece of twin silver peacocks with sweeping tails on either side of the silver epergne was piled with dripping grapes, purple plums, polished golden apples.

The meal, although elegantly served, was a bit too highly seasoned and sauced for Addie's taste. She could manage to eat only a little for politeness's sake. With the conversation flowing around her, Addie's mind drifted. The lavish lifestyle of Louis and his sister was overwhelming. Luxury had once been an accepted part of her own life, something that her family and others of their class were used to, but it had not seemed so overpowering as the Montands'.

Since the war Addie had not known anyone who could afford to live as they had formerly. Of course, there were despised carpetbaggers, who had come to the defeated South, taken over the big houses, flaunted their wealth. But no one Addie knew associated with them—that is except Cousin Matthew, she thought ruefully, remembering it was *he* who was responsible for her coming to California.

"Addie, my dear?" Louis's voice, slightly puzzled, broke into her wandering thoughts. "Estelle was asking if you are quite finished? We are going to have our coffee in the drawing room."

"Oh, yes, sorry ... .," Addie said looking down at the unsliced pear on her dessert plate.

184

Louis came around behind her chair to assist her. As they went into the drawing room together he asked in a low voice, "Are you quite all right? You looked—pensive somehow."

She shook her head. "I'm fine, really."

But her day off had not had the restorative effect Addie had hoped. In fact, by the time Louis drove her back to Silver Springs she felt oddly depressed.

They drew up at the main building, and as Louis helped her out he asked solicitously, "Is there anything wrong, Addie? You were very quiet on the way into town."

"Oh, nothing, I assure you. A slight headache. Nothing more. I'm sorry if I seemed uncongenial."

"Perhaps you found the company today dull?" he persisted, frowning. "I wish Estelle had not included Father Bernard and Milton. I'd wanted our lunch *en famille*. I did not know they were coming until—" He broke off. "Next time we'll plan something livelier, more interesting."

Addie did not really want to make any future plans with Louis. Today she had seen a side of him she did not like, a side she had not really been aware of before now. Their walks and talks while he was still a guest at the hotel had been a pleasant enough distraction, but she did not want to encourage any greater intimacy. She was anxious for him to be gone.

"Thank you, Louis. It was very kind of Estelle, a lovely luncheon."

"Good afternoon then, Addie, I'll be in touch."

Seemingly reassured he mounted back into the carriage and drove away.

Addie hurried into the lobby. She wanted to check her mailbox, hopeful there might be a note from Rex. How different her last day off had been spent with *him*. With Rex she had felt at ease, not tense as she had at times today out at the Chateau Montand. She recalled how quickly she had

185

dismissed Brook's assertion that Louis's intentions were serious. Marriage had never been mentioned, yet there had been a subtle change in his attitude toward her today, a kind of possessiveness that alarmed her. Addie was sure there would be a series of tests any prospective bride of Louis's would have to pass. Estelle's approval, of course, would be first, and she did not think *she* would ever get that, did not even want it! Addie shuddered, imagining a life under Estelle's critical supervision.

She checked her mailbox. Still nothing from Rex. Her disappointment was assuaged a little when she saw there was a letter from her aunt Susan. Seeing the familiar spidery handwriting, Addie felt a sudden stab of homesickness. She realized how starved she was for news of home and family. She waited until she reached the privacy of her room to read it, then she tore open the envelope hungrily.

Addie raced through the three thin pages of closely written script. Her aunt wrote just the way she talked. Addie could almost hear her softly accented voice telling of incidents about people she knew, recounting the small events that made up her daily life. It might have seemed like trivia to most, but to Addie it was food and drink.

When she came to the last paragraph tears blurred the lines her aunt had written, "We miss you, dear girl, and California seems a long way away."

Addie let the letter fall into her lap and she stared blankly into her room full of shadows as daylight was fast fading. California *was* a long way away. It was miles and worlds away. The people were different; life here—the way people talked and thought and acted—was infinitely different. Her aunt's letter had brought back so poignantly everything Addie had left that her heart felt almost bruised.

Now, Addie realized what had happened to her during the luncheon at the Montands, why she had found herself so detached from the company, the conversation. It came

186

to Addie that the war and all it had meant to the South, to her family, to herself had only been a distant drumbeat here in California. She had glanced around the table, from face to face, knowing they understood nothing of what she had been through. Through all the violence, the battles, the men who had fought and been killed, this valley had slumbered peacefully, moving from season to season. The war that had cut like a saber swath through Virginia had left the people here untouched. She felt empty and infinitely lonely.

Memory is mysterious. It is like a mansion with many doors, each opening and leading down several corridors, into halls and hidden rooms and even dark closets you may not want opened. Addie thought she had put away her memories of the past, of Ran, of what might have been. Perhaps she had been mistaken. Maybe she imagined that she had seen in Rex Lyon's eyes, felt in his kiss her own deep longing for love, her hope that such a love was possible.

She folded the pages of Aunt Susan's letter and put them back in the envelope. She felt depressed. She did not even feel like writing in her journal. She felt as though she were standing on a precipice over a great yawning void of loneliness, of empty days, maybe even of years, stretching ahead.

Probably she was just tired. The day with Louis and his sister had been a strain. She would have liked a reviving cup of hot tea but didn't feel like going over to the dining hall to get it. She certainly wasn't up to an interrogation by Mrs. Amberly for details about the Chateau Montand. So she would do without.

Addie washed her face, braided her hair, put on her nightgown, and climbed wearily into bed. She fell asleep quickly, slept heavily, but the impressions of her day colored her dreams. The plush draperies, the flocked wallpaper, the velvet upholstery of the Montands' house seemed to close in upon her, clinging to her smotheringly. Distorted images of Estelle and Louis, and lurking in the background the shadowy figures of the Chinese in the orchard, were all seen as if through the cloudy murkiness of a crystal ball.

She woke suddenly, heart pounding, and pushed away the blanket and quilt. She struggled into a sitting position. Perspiration beaded her face, her damp nightgown clung to her; she was shaking. Gasping for air, she told herself it was only a nightmare. But it was a long time before she could fall asleep again.

Chapter 14

The next morning and the two that followed, Addie woke up with the feeling she was plowing through quicksand. Mrs. Amberly seemed more difficult than ever. The necessity of being polite during the forced companionship of the day was bad enough. But biting her tongue, clenching her teeth through the long evenings while she listened to the shallow, pointless conversation at the card table, the gossip rife with rumors passed on with malicious relish—all this was even worse.

Addie was honest enough to admit it was her own inner frustration that made it all seem especially irritating. With each day that passed with no word from Rex, Addie grew more puzzled. Why had he stayed away? Why had he not sent her a note? Was there any explanation? When she thought of those kisses exchanged on the shadowy cottage porch, her cheeks burned. Had she taken too much for granted? Rex had not seemed like a man to play with a woman's affection. What could possibly be the reason?

In contrast, the day after she had been to the Montands', a bouquet and a note had been delivered from Louis. He had written in his flowing script:

Yesterday was one of the most enjoyable days I have spent since coming to California. Without a doubt it was being with you that made it so. I hope we'll spend many such lovely days together at Chateau Montand. Seeing you there made my vision of my home perfect.
Devotedly, Louis

Addie tore the note up. She was glad Mrs. Amberly had been at the bathhouse having her treatment when the note and flowers had come. Addie did not want to satisfy her employer's avaricious curiosity. After her first chagrin at Louis's interest in Addie, Mrs. Amberly began to regard it as a possible path to gain access to Estelle.

Addie did not want to be interrogated—especially about Louis, concerning whom she had more and more troubling questions. Under his suavity, his pleasant manners, there was something unlikable. He had a rapier wit that edged perilously close to cruelty. He had a need to feel superior to others, and in order to maintain that he must make others look inferior. He was often sarcastic—and there was something else she had seen yesterday. When Mr. Drew was expressing some doubt as to the wisdom of hiring Chinese workers, Louis had ruthlessly cut him short with the same kind of contemptuous disdain Addie had seen in Estelle. Two of a kind, birds of a feather—all the old adages seemed appropriate when applied to the Montands.

Louis's note made her vaguely apprehensive. Addie decided she must definitely not encourage him.

Wistfully Addie thought how she would have welcomed Rex Lyon actively courting her. Why could *he* not have sent flowers and such words after *their* day together? Try as she might not to mind, it really hurt.

That afternoon, during Mrs. Amberly's nap time, Addie caught up on some personal chores, some mending, repairing a hem that had come loose, putting a new lace collar on a dress. But her thoughts spun endlessly on the question to which she could not find an answer. Why had Rex Lyon so suddenly dropped out of her life? Was it his work? Or was it his will?

That evening as she and Mrs. Amberly entered the dining hall, to Addie's dismay the first person she saw was Louis. He was dining with Milton Drew. As soon as she and Mrs. Amberly were shown to their usual table, Louis came over.

Immediately Mrs. Amberly went into her act assuming the saccharine tone she always used when speaking to him. "Well, well, Mr. Montand, how lovely to see you. Miss Pride has told me *so* much about your beautiful home, I'm *languishing* for a glimpse of it myself!"

At this Addie flushed with embarrassment. What an outlandish fib! Even under her employer's relentless questioning, Addie had hardly said a word about Chateau Montand. Knowing the sly ridicule with which Louis regarded Mrs. Amberly, Addie refused to meet his mocking eyes and nervously rearranged the silverware at her plate.

Mrs. Amberly obliviously bumbled on. "So, Mr. Montand, what brings you into town this evening?"

"Business, not pleasure, I'm afraid. A meeting to settle some legal details with my lawyer," Louis replied smoothly. His gaze, however, rested on Addie even as he addressed Mrs. Amberly. "But when we're finished, perhaps I'll stop by the card room later and see who's winning."

Mrs. Amberly shook her head coquettishly. "You know what they say, Mr. Montand: lucky at cards unlucky at love!"

"But I'm sure, Madam, *you* have had the good fortune to be lucky at *both*," Louis teased, looking directly at Addie.

After Louis went back to his table, Mrs. Amberly lapsed into her usual complaints about the food and her fellow guests. When they finished they went into the card room. Addie settled herself with her needlepoint for another endless evening. She positioned herself at some distance from

191

the table where Mrs. Amberly sat with her cronies. She tried to turn a deaf ear to their chatter, concentrating on the design on the pillowcover she was making to send to Aunt Susan. But even as she plied her needle steadily, her thoughts were of Rex Lyon. Why had she not heard from him? Addie considered all possible reasons why, making up excuses for him, imagining how he'd explain it when she saw him. And when would that be?

She knew it was futile to guess. But she couldn't help herself. Rex Lyon filled her with hope, answered that longing in her heart. There must be some explanation. From that first unforgettable moment on the day she arrived, she had felt *something*—and now, after getting to know him, she discovered other qualities about him—his integrity, his intelligence, his gentleness—that appealed to her. What could be keeping him away?

The evening moved with creeping tempo. Addie willed herself not to sneak too many glances at the clock over the reception desk in the lobby nor look at her little gold watch pinned to her bodice. She knew she could not leave until Mrs. Amberly's game was finished, and her employer was insatiable at cards, especially if she was winning.

About an hour into the evening, Mrs. Amberly's acerbic voice penetrated Addie's boredom, jolting her to attention.

"It's said the widow Wegner's mortgaged to the hilt. Her husband was no businessman and left a mountain of debts. They say *he* died under *very* mysterious circumstances."

Her employer was talking about *Freda!* Where on earth had Mrs. Amberly picked up this piece of outrageous gossip? Addie seethed. She longed to rush to the defense of her friend. Helpless rage at her position trembled through Addie.

"Of course, nothing was proven—this being the small town it is—they all protect one another. *But . . .*" Mrs. Amberly paused significantly. ". . . I've had it on *very good authority* that she's used up all her credit, and the bank won't extend her another loan. Several ranchers are waiting until the bank forecloses so they can pick up the land at a low price—which tells *me just* how *loyal* friends *really* are when it comes to a good deal!" Here she gave another dramatic pause. "*But* she has another trick up her sleeve—I'm told . . ."

The Misses Brunell and Mrs. Cranby leaned forward like three scrawny buzzards to pick over the kill.

"To *remarry!*" Mrs. Amberly announced triumphantly. "A rich husband would solve her problems, right?"

She turned, jerking her head to where Louis and Milton Drew could be seen conferring in the adjoining lounge.

"I understand the widow Wegner has set her cap for *him.*" She raised her voice slightly. "With his wealth and class he'd certainly be a catch—especially for a penniless woman."

Addie checked the urge to contradict her suppositions about Freda and Louis. What would Mrs. Amberly think if she knew the truth—that Louis's interest lay closer at hand. Addie smiled ruefully. Perhaps, if there were no Rexford Lyon, even *she* might—*no,* of course not. She would have to be desperate indeed to consider marrying Louis Montand.

"What are you smiling about?" a voice asked and she looked up startled to see Louis standing in front of her. "It must be something pleasant. I could hope you might be thinking of me."

He drew up a chair and angled it so that when he sat down beside her his back would be to the nearby card table and none of the players would be able to overhear what he said.

To avoid answering his question, Addie asked, "Did your business meeting go well?"

Louis frowned slightly. "Ah, well, some small problems—these locals . . ." he started to say something more, but

193

changed his mind. Instead he smilea. "When shall we plan another afternoon together or an evening?"

Before Addie could reply, over Louis's shoulder she saw a tall familiar figure enter the lobby. Then Rex was at the archway, scanning the card room as if looking for someone. Addie's first happy surprise at seeing him was followed by excruciating embarrassment. She almost raised her hand in a greeting when she saw him cross the room toward them. Louis half-turned and followed the direction she was looking. When he saw Rex he stood up.

The four heads at the card table swiveled curiously. As Rex came closer, Addie saw his expression. Anger had turned his gray eyes to burning steel. Suddenly she felt unreasonably frightened.

Rex acknowledged her with a brief nod then spoke directly to Louis in a hard, tight voice, "I have to talk to you, Montand."

Louis lifted an eyebrow. "Now?"

"Yes, *now*. It's important."

"If you insist." Louis shrugged indifferently. "But surely this is not the time nor the place, Lyon."

"I agree. Shall we go into the Gentlemen's Lounge?"

Louis turned to Addie and in a tone that implied annoyance asked, "Will you excuse us, my dear? This should not take long." Then to Rex, "Let's go and be done with it."

Without a glance at Addie, Rex spun around and led the way out, his boots loud on the polished floor. Louis followed more slowly.

Addie froze, every muscle in her body strained. What were the two men going to discuss? Why was Rex so angry? Just then she heard Mrs. Amberly declare, "I always thought there was bad blood between those two. I felt there was going to be an explosion in *that* quarter soon, mark my words. What's their trouble? Land. In California that's what any kind of battle seems to be about. Montand can

194

outbid, outspend Rex Lyon, and he's known for getting what he wants. And he wants the widow's property—I don't think he's willing to *marry* for it, but he *is* willing to pay a high price for it—higher than any of the ranchers around here can scrape up. Especially Lyon. I understand his family's fortune was all turned into the land, no cash. And the widow wants out—she's tired of the drudgery and lonely—although it's said she has plenty of company—when she wants it."

Addie was almost too upset at the moment to pay attention to Mrs. Amberly's ugly gossip. Then suddenly the bone of rumor Mrs. Amberly had thrown for the others to gnaw on came through to her. Could Mrs. Amberly have for once heard something *true?* Addie's hands clutched the canvas-backed needlepoint so tight that the needle jabbed into her finger. She gave a little gasp and looked down to see a small spot of blood rising at its tip.

What *really* was going on between the two men? She *had* to find out.

The card players were too preoccupied with their game and gossip to notice as Addie slipped out of the room. She crossed the lobby and stood concealed by one of the fluted pillars. From behind the swinging louvered doors of the Gentlemen's Lounge she heard raised voices.

"You're hiring Chinese?" Rex's was intense.

"Yes, if that's any concern of yours," Louis replied coldly.

"You're darn right it concerns me. Just as it will the other ranchers. Anything that happens in this valley concerns us all. I'd like to know why you're importing cheap labor when we have plenty of willing workers right here—people who were born in this valley, live here, support their families by working the vineyards, Californios who love the land, take pride in their work, have worked for vintners for years with loyalty and—"

"One Chinaman can work twice as long and three times

195

as hard as any Californio you've got in your vineyards, Lyon. It's a free country. You're free to save money yourself any way you can. Don't tell me how to conduct my business. You run your ranch the way you see fit, and I'll do the same. I'm just trying to make an honest profit on my investment."

"At the expense of the rest of us? At the expense of those poor devils brought here like cattle in boxcars? I was at the station just after they arrived. I saw the conditions in which they traveled seventy miles in the heat of the day—no light, no air, no water—" his voice became heavy with contempt, "—no thanks to you, it's a wonder they didn't die en route. Now, I hear you have them sleeping out in your orchards."

"They're used to a lot worse in their own country—"

"I guess you think the Chinese are less than human. The lowest form of humanity, right? They swarm over to this country like rats. They're only peasants in their own country, why should you care if they're treated decently? Or what conditions they live under after they get here? Just so you get twelve or sixteen hours a day of work out of them."

"I think you've said quite enough, Lyon. I warn you, don't go too far." Louis's voice dropped, attempting a lighter tone. "Come now, let's have a drink together like two reasonable fellows who happen to disagree."

"Drink with *you?* No thanks."

Before Addie could move, she heard the creak of the doors of the Gentlemen's Lounge being pushed open. She shrank back against the post, flinching at the sight of the ironlike expression on Rex's face as he stalked across the lobby. As the slam of the front door of the hotel reverberated, Addie discovered she was trembling.

PART 4

VALLEY OF THE HEART

Chapter 15

*A*ddie did not sleep well that night. Louis's soothing assurance that it had all been 'a little disagreement' between the two men—nothing she should worry "her pretty head about"—failed to satisfy Addie. She did not tell Louis how much she had overheard, since that would place her in the awkward position of being an eavesdropper. But when she tried tactfully to find out the real reason, Louis became irritated. He told her he had to be off to Chateau Montand, that Estelle would worry if he was too late.

What bothered Addie more was Rex's coldness toward her. She had seemed to be included in his animosity toward Louis. What could possibly have happened to change his attitude so drastically?

She was awake at dawn, her head aching, her eyes heavy from lack of sleep. Maybe some fresh air, a walk would clear her head. She got up, dressed, and went out into the cool gray morning.

The image of Rex's angry unsmiling face lingered in her mind. The way he had looked at her last night was so different from what she had seen in his eyes before. Or had she imagined it all? After all, she scarcely knew him—one day together was all they had really had. One magical day. Hardly enough on which to build a dream. And yet . . .

Head down, Addie trudged on, heartsore. She had just turned in the gates of Silver Springs when a familiar voice jerked her out of her melancholy reverie. "Whoa there, Miss Pride! Hold on!" She turned to see Brook striding purposefully toward her. "Addie!" he smiled as he came alongside her. "What are you doing out so early on this gloomy morning?"

"Escaping!" Addie tried not to look guilty even though she felt sure Brook knew how difficult Mrs. Amberly was.

"I understand." He gave her a solemn wink. "'One hour of thoughtful solitude may nerve the heart for days of conflict, girding up its armor to meet the most insidious foe,' eh?"

"I'm not sure I recognize that," she said as they fell into step and started walking again.

"Percival, a rather obscure philosopher. I like to collect that kind of quotation, then I can spring them once in a while when it's appropriate, and my friends think I'm erudite."

Addie laughed. "Well, *I'd* think that anyway, Brook. I'm convinced you are very clever indeed." They walked along a little farther. "Now, I'll ask you the same question you asked me. What are you doing out and about so early?"

"Well, I'm going out of town for a few days—to San Francisco first. I need to talk to some of my investors, explain my plans for the race track and other expansions I have in mind." He glanced at her smiling. "In other words you might say I'm going prospecting for gold!"

"You don't look dressed for it!" As usual Brook was impeccably dressed.

He acted surprised. "Don't you know the secret of borrowing lots of money? You have to look like you don't need it!"

"Well, you *don't*. You look as though you owned the world," she told him, surveying his superbly cut coat, snowy linen shirt, silk cravat.

Brook swung his gold-headed cane and his expression became serious. "Well, let's hope the men I'm going to see will agree that Calistoga *can* become the *Saratoga* of the West. If we're going to draw the racing crowd we've got to have thoroughbred horses, attract the top jockeys. It will mean a sizable investment. But well worth it, if I can just convince them." He frowned for a minute. "Let's just hope these men will be willing to part with a great deal of cash—otherwise . . ." He let his thought fade away like the morning mist; then he smiled down at her. "Wish me luck?"

"Of course, I do. Although Silver Springs seems almost perfect just the way it is—if you didn't do another thing—"

"Ah, but then you don't have my dreams."

"Dreams," she repeated thoughtfully. "I guess, maybe—I've seen too many dreams dissolve."

"Don't give up dreaming, Addie. That's fatal. Remember, 'A man's reach must exceed his grasp'—or else, as the poet says, 'what's a heaven for?'"

"Browning. I got that one right, didn't I?" Addie smiled. "I didn't know you also knew poetry."

"But then, dear Addie, there are many things you don't know about me."

"Perhaps in time . . ."

"Time. There is never enough of it, is there? But maybe, if you *did* you'd be disappointed—disillusioned—" He broke off abruptly. "Well, I must be off."

"Will you be gone long?"

"I can't be sure. It depends." He smiled enigmatically. "To quote Will Shakespeare, 'As good luck would have it'—what success I have in my endeavor."

"I'll miss you anyway, however long. The Springs is never the same when you're away."

Something curious softened Brook's glance. "And I shall miss you, Addie." Then he gave the brim of his hat a flick, bowed, and nonchalantly said, "*Adios. Hasta luega,*" and walked quickly away in the direction of the main building.

Addie watched him go regretfully. She had been tempted to tell Brook about the quarrel she had overheard between Rex and Louis, and ask him if he could guess what it was about. Brook was discreet, but he knew the town well, the undercurrents as well as the rumors and the facts. However, she did not have a chance because Brook had seemed very distracted as though he had other things on his mind today than valley conflicts.

What an enigma Brook was. She had never met anyone like him. Outgoing, congenial as he was, there was much about him that remained mysterious. A few times he had let her see a part of him he mostly kept hidden. Ambitious, creative, impulsive, he had made no secret of his goal of bringing Calistoga prosperity and fame, and becoming a millionaire before he was thirty—whatever that took. This Addie found fascinating.

She sighed. As mercurial as he was, Addie knew she would miss him. His presence around the resort was certainly energizing and gave the humdrum days a needed spark.

However, this time Brook returned as suddenly as he had departed. Going to check her mail one morning a few days later, Addie was surprised to see him behind the reception desk in the lobby.

"Brook, I didn't know you were back! How was the mining? Successful?" she asked teasingly.

He looked blank for a few seconds as if he didn't know what she meant. Then he must have recalled their conversation, and his face broke into a smile—a rueful one. "Not quite as successful as I'd hoped. But as they say, 'thar's gold in them thar hills'—*other* hills. I've still got my plans, just have to dig in another spot."

But there was something in the way Brook spoke that made Addie wonder.

In the next few days the weather turned changeable; there were days of drizzling rain and days of brilliant sunshine. On some afternoons, fog began drifting over the land, moving with eerie swiftness, its misty veil giving a sense of isolation and beauty to the valley.

The damp spring weather had an adverse effect on Mrs. Amberly's rheumatism, and she complained loud and often about how little good the treatments were doing her. Even when the rain stopped and there were several mild days in a row, the sky remained sullen with low-lying clouds, and Mrs. Amberly became vocally irritable, talked of leaving. Then one of the other guests, an elderly lady Addie quite liked for her dignity and aloofness, suggested that she might try a few days in the lake country at the geyser resorts. The air was said to be drier and the weather a little sunnier. Mrs. Amberly began to talk of joining the group of guests from the hotel who were going to make the trip to Lakeport.

At breakfast she told Addie to make inquiries about arrangements. When Addie left the dining hall and started toward the main building she nearly collided with Brook. He was walking toward her, his head down as if in deep thought. He seemed startled when she spoke to him. "Brook?"

For a second he almost seemed to be trying to place her. Then he smiled and held out his hands to her. "Addie! Sorry! I was woolgathering."

"I was hoping to see you before we left," she said.

"Left?" he seemed puzzled.

"Maybe Mrs. Amberly didn't mention it to you, but she's planning to go up to Lakeport to the geysers for a few days.

She's heard it's warmer, less damp up there—" Addie halted, mid-sentence. Brook seemed so distracted. Obviously he had something more important on his mind than hearing about Mrs. Amberly's plans.

"What? I'm sorry, Addie, I guess I'm a little preoccupied today."

"Thinking about racetracks and thoroughbreds?" she teased.

Again he seemed to draw a blank for a minute before giving a short laugh. "Oh, yes, right! Racetracks and thoroughbreds." He paused then said, "I may have to go away again for a few days."

"Oh, are you planning another *gold mining* expedition?"

"Well, maybe, I guess you could call it that." Brook reached for her hands and held them in his. "Good-bye, Addie, in case I don't see you before I leave." He gave her a smile, more tender than his usual roguish one. "You're a very special lady, you know. I wish—" he halted and resumed his teasing way, "—but then you know what they say about wishes—if they were horses, beggars would ride? My wishes tend to run to thoroughbreds—very, very expensive thoroughbreds."

Brook held both of her hands a little longer, then gave them a gentle squeeze before releasing them. "Good-bye, my dear Miss Pride."

Addie watched him walk away with his self-confident stride; then quite suddenly the swirling mist rising up from the ground seemed to encircle then blot him from her sight. For a moment Addie felt an icy shiver course down her spine. A premonition of some sort? Of danger? No, of course not. It was just that it had been a strange sensation seeing Brook disappear like that into the fog.

The arrangements to go on the morning stage up to Lakeport and the geyser resort were made. In a flurry of packing and last-minute decisions of what to take, Mrs. Amberly belatedly remembered she would need cash for the trip, so she sent Addie to the bank before it closed for the day. Addie dropped everything else she was doing and rushed off to town. Just as she reached the bank door, it opened. Rex Lyon was coming out.

Both halted. Blood rushed hotly into Addie's face. The day of the picnic with all its romantic promise, the days of diminishing hope that followed, her disappointment and sense of hurt seemed to culminate in this unexpected encounter.

For a moment they both seemed locked in an embarassing inability to speak. For what was there to say? Neither could pass because the other was blocking the way. Speechless, Addie nonetheless searched Rex's face for a clue as to what he might be feeling. But his eyes regarding her steadily revealed nothing, and his expression told her even less.

But behind that steadfast gaze Addie thought she saw some reproach, disappointment. In her? Why? It was *he* who had failed to pursue what had seemed to begin that day of the picnic. She still did not understand what could have happened to change things. But her pride prohibited the question for which her heart begged an answer. Imprisoned by convention, her smile became fixed.

An eternity seemed to pass in the space of a few moments.

He removed his hat, "Good afternoon, Miss Pride."

"Mr. Lyon." Her voice sounded unnaturally hoarse over the tightness of her throat.

She stood there in anxious uncertainty until he spoke again. "Maybe, you'd be interested to know ..." He hesitated, then went on, "Since I saw you, my friends, the Bairds, have had some misfortune. Nan, Mrs. Baird, and the boy, Lowell, both developed diphtheria. I had to help

Rob move them down from the hills, find them a place to stay in town where they could have medical attention and recuperate."

"I'm sorry to hear that." Addie's natural sympathy for the Bairds was countered by her questioning of Rex's motives. Was he telling her this just an excuse? Sick friends or not, if he had wanted to, he could have come by or at least sent a note of explanation. But her years of drilling in social graces compelled her to say, "I hope—are they—how are they getting along now?"

"Yes, much better, steadily improving. In fact, they will be leaving at the end of next week to go to San Francisco and then back east to take a ship to Scotland. Rob wants his family to meet Nan and Lowell."

Addie managed to say something she hoped was suitable. Standing here was becoming increasingly uncomfortable. "If you'll excuse me . . ." She moved to go past him. "I must get to the teller before the bank closes; we are leaving tomorrow on a trip to the geysers, and Mrs. Amberly needs cash."

"Of course." He immediately stepped aside.

In spite of herself, Addie hesitated a few seconds, to see if—hoping that Rex might say something more. But he simply stood there waiting for her to go into the bank. In a surge of wounded pride, Addie swept past him. As she did she heard him say in a low tone of voice, "I wish you every happiness . . ."

At the cashier's cage, heart racing, his words suddenly came back to her, before she actually *heard* what he had said. What did he mean? "I wish you every happiness?" That was the cliché people used when congratulating someone on an upcoming felicitous event—like an engagement or marriage. Involuntarily Addie turned her head to see if Rex was still there. But he was gone.

"May I help you?" came the cashier's impatient voice.

"Oh, yes." Addie turned back, flustered. Tugging her gloves off hands clammy with nervous perspiration, she quickly thrust Mrs. Amberly's cheque through the window for cashing. Distracted by Rex's puzzling remark, she stepped away from the counter. "Miss! Your money!" The clerk's sharp voice bolted her back from her trance.

Addie gathered up the stack of bills and left the bank still baffled by the upsetting encounter with Rex and his enigmatic words.

The next morning was overcast. After breakfast the Silver Springs contingent going to Lakeport assembled outside the main building to wait for Henessey's Stage Line's big six-horse passenger wagon. There was much good-natured complaining about the fog drifting grayly around the verandah posts. Joking remarks about hoping the driver could see his way out of the fog up to the sunnier hills were greeted with laughter.

Addie tried to join the merriment that surrounded her. But her heart was still heavy from yesterday's jolting meeting with Rex. She had relived the incident a dozen times. Accusing herself of stupidity, over and over she thought of things she could have said, how she might have handled it better. But finally she had to admit she had been too much in shock.

She vacillated from frustration to indignation. It was *his* fault it had been so awkward. *He* was the one who should have apologized, made some excuse, given some explanation for not contacting her. Oh, the shame of it! Every time she thought of it she died of humiliation all over again.

In spite of everything that had happened, in her secret heart Addie blamed herself. She had allowed herself to believe that what had taken place between them was special. If it was anyone's fault, it was hers for being such a fool.

Forget it! Forget him! But the old adage was true: Easier

said than done. She had let her heart rule her head. She did not know how long it would take her to get over it.

As she was giving herself all this advice, to her surprise she saw Louis's phaeton, drawn by his high-stepping horse, come through the gate. After parking the vehicle he jumped out and came over to her.

"I've come to see you off," he told her jauntily, then handed her a small basket of grapes nestled in glossy leaves. "Compliments of Estelle."

Addie doubted the gift *was* his sister's idea, and she had to credit Louis himself for the thoughtful gesture. Still feeling she must, she forced an appropriate response. Addie replied, "How kind of her. Please give her my thanks."

A murmur of approval came from the ladies gathered on the porch observing the little tableau. "What a gentleman," "How nice," "*She* should be flattered."

Louis did not miss the consensus of approval, and smiled benignly.

"I hope you have a delightful time but I shall miss you, Addie," he said, looking at her significantly.

Addie was aware that Louis always did the *right* thing, the socially correct thing. It was as inborn as the Boston accent. Maybe there were worse things than being a "proper gentleman." She could not help, though, thinking of Rex's spontaneity, his openness, his "California" naturalness. That seemed a great deal more sincere.

Before her thoughts could slip further along this dangerous line, someone shouted, "Here it comes!"

They all turned to see the big, brightly painted red and yellow stage pulled by three matched pairs of powerfully built horses come through the Silver Springs gate and pull up in front. Buck Henessey, the driver, well-known for his expertise on the mountain roads, climbed down. He was a large, barrel-chested man, with a ruddy complexion, bright blue eyes, and a bushy mustard-colored mustache, which

208

twirled up at either end giving him the look of a roguish pirate. He lifted his pearl-gray Stetson to the group and greeted them jovially, "Good morning, folks! You all are in for the time of your life! So, now, if you'll jest git on board, we'll git goin'."

Since the stage was open, everyone had donned canvas dusters and swathed themselves in protective veiling. To all the many questions asked him, from queries as to the weather, the roads, the accommodations when they reached the geysers, Mr. Henessey gave the same hearty assurance, "Finest kind!"

Because she was the youngest of the travelers and because it seemed proper, Addie volunteered to sit up front beside the driver. It suited her fine since seated up there she would not have to sit by Mrs. Amberly on the twenty-mile trip. As she settled herself Henessey assured her that in that seat she'd get the "finest kind" of view.

Shortly after they left town the day began to clear. They started up the torturous mountain roads. Some of the curves were so short that the lead horses were out of sight on one side as the stage was rounding the other. The sharper the curves the louder the gasps and small cries coming from those in the seats behind. Addie realized they were probably suppressing screams and clutching each other as they swerved around the serpentine road.

Addie too might have been really terrified if Brook had not sung the praises of Henessey. He was the best stage driver around, he had assured her. Sitting beside him on the high driver's seat, Addie was impressed by his dexterity. Even so Addie gripped the hand bars several times and held her breath.

But Buck was a master at what he did; the reins were firm in his grip, his shouts sometimes punctuated by an occasional twirl of his whip, which echoed through the mountain pass like the crack of a pistol shot.

The view of the valley was breathtaking from this height as they ascended the steep grade, and Addie was kept amused by Buck's commentary as they made their way up the narrow road. At one point, he pointed with his whip to an immense, conelike peak that rose sharply up against the now cloud free sky. "That there's Lover's Leap," he told her. "Legend tells that a young Indian couple fell in love with each other but were from different tribes, and their folks wouldn't agree to them marrying, so they come up here— on a moonlit night so the story goes—" here Buck gave her a broad wink, "—and took a flying leap off'n that rock." He chuckled. "That's the valley's own kinda Romeo and Juliet tale, ain't it?" and he roared with laughter.

By noon they reached Lakeport where they were to stay at the inn for two full days. Henessey was to return for them on his way back to Calistoga from Santa Rosa. After the long trip, everyone was eager to try the famous geyser soda springs. The air was crystal clear and dry, the weather mild and delightful.

Addie knew the change of scene should lift her spirits, and scolded herself because it didn't. The memory of the embarrassing incident with Rex in front of the bank blunted her enjoyment. She kept mentally kicking herself for her awkward handling of the situation.

By the second day she did succeed in taking advantage of the exhilirating air and the mild weather. She was also allowed unusual freedom from Mrs. Amberly's carping. Her employer seemed to have found nothing to complain about and was socializing with the new people she met at the Lakeport Inn. Left on her own, Addie tried to enjoy her delightful surroundings and forget Rex Lyon. She managed the first but found the second impossible. He seemed to have lodged himself permanently in her mind—and heart. The question of his changed attitude toward her remained a mystery.

210

The two days passed pleasantly enough and many of the Silver Springs exiles were loath to leave the high, dry climate for the valley, where the damp, foggy weather possibly persisted. Buck Henessey paced, smoking one of his long cigars, waiting while his erstwhile passengers caused countless delays. By the time all the baskets, boxes, and valises had been stowed and lashed securely, it was late when they got started down the mountain.

Since on the return trip Henessey had a helper sitting beside him on the front seat, Addie had taken a seat with the others in the coach. The sight of the man with a shotgun had momentarily alarmed her until Henessey explained the man was an employee of Union Express in Santa Rosa who required it because they were carrying a cash box containing the miners' payroll, a standard precaution, he told her calmly.

All the passengers seemed quieter on the return trip than they had on the way up to the geysers. Two days of the hot spring treatments, long walks, hearty food, and nightly square dances had taken their toll. Heads were nodding and conversation faded away after they were on the road a few miles.

Mrs. Amberly had soon fallen asleep, and Addie stared at the scenery. Lulled by the rocking motion of the stage, she was in a half-dreamy state. She still couldn't seem to keep her thoughts from wandering back to Rex Lyon. Why did something nag at her, keep her from accepting the obvious fact he did not want to continue their relationship? It was just that it didn't make sense. He had told her she was discerning, hadn't he? Well, there was something strange about his sudden turnaround. Something had happened. What, she couldn't guess. Why hadn't she been bold enough to ask him if she had done anything to offend him? Of course, that would have been out of the question. Yet—there had been something—even that day, in the

211

awkwardness of that meeting—something in his eyes, his expression that made her wonder—and that strange thing he had said—"I wish you every happiness." What had that meant? It was as if he never expected to see her again. Bewildered, Addie shook her head.

As they came up the other side of the mountain, Lovers Leap came into view. It brought the legend Buck had told her about to Addie's mind. Would lovers *really* do anything to be together, no matter how misguided? Or were stories like *Romeo and Juliet, Tristan and Isolde,* and all the romantic classics just that—figments of the imagination of some author or dramatist?

Then she thought of Rob and Nan Baird. They were certainly a *real* love story. Thinking of the Bairds, of course, made her think about Rex again. What was it Freda said about him? That he was the most honest person she had ever known. If that were true, how could he have said all the things he had said to her and mean them, and suddenly not call or send a message, a note of explanation for his silence?

Addie remembered what else Freda had said: "Love is always a risk. You open yourself up to hurt, betrayal, and loss." Freda had known her husband had a history of tuberculosis when she married him, that he might die young. She had taken a chance that with her love and care he would recover. He didn't. But perhaps he was given a few years more of life because of her love. Freda said it had all been worth it. Those few perfect, happy years together had been worth what came after—the pain, the sorrow, the loneliness.

Nan Baird felt the same way about Rob. Love was worth the cost, that when you really love someone, you gave yourself, relinquished that inner you, it was worth it. Addie thought of the legend of Lover's Leap. When you put your life and happiness into the hands of someone else—it was a kind of jumping into the unknown. Maybe, some things in life are worth risking everything for and maybe love was one of those.

Or was that just romantic dreaming? Maybe it only made sense when the person you love, loved you in return. She hadn't asked for this heartache. She hadn't wanted to fall in love. It had just happened.

The stage slowed as they started up a steep incline, a precipitous section, steep cliffs and only manzanita and brush to hide the drop to the river far below on one side and on the other side the dense woods. Outside, the day seemed to darken. Addie leaned back, steadying herself against the lurching vehicle as they moved steadily up the mountain.

Then quite suddenly they jolted to a stop. Addie heard shouts, the whinnying of the horses. She sat up straight, clutching the seat handles. The stage rocked precariously, as if the horses were rearing and backing up. Mrs. Amberly, aroused from her slumber and struggling to sit upright, bonnet askew, narrow eyes wide open, grumbled sleepily, "What's happened, what's going on?"

"I don't know. Perhaps a fallen tree's blocked the way."

But before the words were out of Addie's mouth, there was the sharp report of gunshots. She started up from her seat, leaned out, and saw something that turned her blood to ice. A group of three or four masked men on horseback had blocked the stage; their upraised shotguns were pointed directly at Buck.

Addie's heart froze. Every nerve in her body tingled. Even as her conscious mind registered what was happening, another part of her refused to absorb its reality. The cries of the other passengers pierced the air. A loud voice declaring, "This is a holdup, folks!" brought it all to immediate understanding. A stagecoach robbery! The kind she had read and heard about in stories about the "Wild West" was happening right here before her eyes! Her stomach dropped

213

sickeningly, then knotted. She tried to speak but her throat tightened as though she were being strangled. She could neither swallow nor speak. She could hardly breathe.

"All right, Buck, don't try any funny business. Get down, nice and easy—hands above your head, that's right. Nobody'll get hurt if you just do what we say."

The way the man was talking so familiarly to Henessey was almost as if he knew him. Had he known Buck would be driving this stage? Had he and his men been lying in wait at this point to ambush the stagecoach?

This man was on the horse in front. He was evidently the leader. He was wearing a long buff-colored canvas duster, which covered him from neck to the tops of his boots. His face was masked by a triangular blue bandanna, the brim of his wide-brimmed, brown slouch hat shadowed his eyes.

He pulled a long-handled pistol from his belt, and waving it toward the man beside Buck, he ordered one of his men, "Relieve that gentleman of his shotgun." To Henessey he said, "Now, Buck, I don't mean you no harm, so if you'll just hand over the cash box, everything will be just dandy and you all can go on your way." The man had a pronounced drawl, almost as though he were imitating a Southerner or a Texan.

"This is foolishness," growled Henessey. "You're taking' an awful risk. This here fellow is deputized a U.S. Marshal from over Santa Rosa, you'll be in big trouble if you—"

"Don't want to argue, Buck. Don't you worry about us; just do as we say and there won't be no trouble."

In a few minutes, one of the men had climbed up and unbuckled the steel cash box from under the driver's seat and carried it down.

"What about the passengers, Boss?" one of the masked men asked him.

"What about them?"

214

"Cash, jewelry?"

The man nodded almost indifferently, turned in his saddle, then motioning with his gun ordered, "Get them out and line 'em up."

Until now, the passengers had been too frightened to say anything. But as the man, waving his shotgun as though it were a palmetto fan, ordered them out, there were whimperings, moans, and mutterings as one by one people climbed down from the high wagon and stood huddled together against the side of the coach.

"Keep your eye on these two," the leader said sharply to the men still on their horses, indicating Henessey and the deputy. Then he dismounted and sauntered over to where the passengers stood trembling.

"Sorry, ladies and gentlemen, to inconvenience you like this—if you ladies'll just hand over all that pretty jewelry and the gentlemen their wallets and watches, and if you've got a tie pin, that'll be fine. Then we'll be on our way and no one the worse for it."

He gave one of the men a chamois drawstring bag and gestured for him to take it around to each passenger to fill with their valuables.

"This is an outrage!" spluttered Mrs. Amberly who had gone ashen. But as the bag was thrust at her by the man pointing the gun, her fat fingers fumbled at the diamond brooch at the neck of her blouse.

One of the men passengers started to protest, but when the man's gun waved in his direction, he subsided into a terrified silence, unhooked his gold watch chain, and handed it over without another word.

"Those rings too, Madam, if you please," the man continued. "And the earrings as well."

The clinking together of jewels inside the bag was the only sound as one by one the women nervously dropped cameos, pocket watches, ropes of gold chains, strings of

215

crystal beads, pearls, and rings of all kinds into the bulging leather pouch.

Addie's hand trembled as she unfastened the chain from around her neck, with the locket containing her parents' pictures. She held it for a second before relinquishing it, then she slipped out the garnet earrings, undid the cameo brooch. Lastly she drew out the narrow velvet box containing the opals she carried in her handbag and added it to the rest of the loot. The bag now heavy and lumpy, bulged with its horde.

"Thank you kindly, one and all. Be assured your treasures will be used for a good cause," the bandit said politely. He chuckled, drew the leather thongs closing the bag, and backed away from the carriage. He made a slight bow and tipped his hat.

At that gesture, something clicked in Addie's head—it came and went like the flip of a goldfish's tail before she could grasp it. Yet the something—of what she wasn't quite sure—hovered like a hummingbird on the edge of her mind. She tried to catch it, but it slipped away before she could even name what it was that occurred to her.

Then it was over. The horsemen rode away, vanishing into the thick woods. Everyone remained absolutely still until the sound of their horses' hoofbeats on the pine-needled path thudded away. The woods seemed to echo with silence. A collective sigh followed. They were safe. No one had been killed, no one hurt in any way. Then pandemonium broke loose. Everyone began to talk at once, loud voices, interrupting each other as the mixed reactions of fear, relief, and excitement reached a fever pitch. It was bedlam for several furious minutes. Calls for smelling salts mingled with cries of rage, anger, indignation, much of it directed against the driver and the guard. Recriminations, threats, declarations of revenge, demands for retribution, and wails of distress over valuable lost property filled the air.

Addie did not join in with the others. After all, her jewelry had nothing but sentimental value. Hers had no precious stones, no priceless diamonds. She felt a sadness for what had been taken. But they were only symbols of what she had already lost.

Once the immediate danger was past, Mrs. Amberly's howls of rage gained volume and vehemence. Addie winced at the woman's insulting condemnation of the driver for his lack of protection of his passengers during the robbery. She must not have noticed the gun pointed at Henessey's heart the whole time. She included the Union Express clerk in her recriminations, even though the poor man had been reduced to a quivering mass of jelly by the entire episode. His protestations that it would have meant his very life had he resisted did not seem to convince her. The tirade continued unabated.

Gradually Addie simply withdrew into her own confusing thoughts. An indefinable notion kept nagging at her, that there had been something vaguely familiar about the highwayman. Even as Addie told herself it *must* be her imagination, she could not erase the impression.

Finally the coach plodded into Calistoga and pulled to a stop at the sweep of the drive in front of the hotel. When the uniformed employees came out to assist the passengers, they were assailed by the story of the robbery. A whole new cacophony of attacks began, heaping blame on the driver. Henessey finally drove off in fury, leaving the hotel staff to deal with its guests.

Mrs. Amberly's voice could be heard above the rest as she stormed into the lobby demanding to see Brook. When told he was out of town, she stamped her foot in rage and ordered the cowed desk clerk to send at once for the sheriff.

Of the seven passengers, each had a different version of

the robbery story to tell the sheriff, who arrived soon after having been informed of it by Henessey. Listening to the others, Addie began to wonder if she had even been there, the tales grew so tall in the telling. The robbers loomed much larger, bolder, more threatening to life and limb than they had been in reality. Actually it had seemed to her they were a rather orderly bunch, following the low-keyed orders of their leader. But even descriptions of him were so disparate, Addie began to doubt her own impression. But when it came her turn, Addie tried to relay as factual a picture of the bizarre event as she could and even surprised herself that she had remembered it all so clearly.

However, the sheriff was a canny fellow. "Well, now, I'm mighty sorry you folks had to go through such a bad time, and I'm pretty sure I got the picture now. I can't promise anything, but we think we've got a pretty good clue as to who these men are. They've pulled some fifteen or twenty robberies over the past two years. They're well-planned, and they usually happen about the same way—"

"I hope, sheriff, you are going to apprehend these vicious criminals!" Mrs. Amberly interrupted.

"We are certainly goin' to do our best, Ma'am."

"I had some very valuable pieces of jewelry stolen, you know—," she began, ready to repeat her story again. But the sheriff was moving toward the door, nodding his head.

"Yes, Ma'am, my deputy has a description of everything that was taken. We'll let you know as soon as we have any more information. Now, thank you ladies and gentlemen, for your cooperation." The sheriff tipped his broad-beamed felt hat and left, followed by his deputy.

It wasn't until later that night, after Addie, with the assistance of the hotel maid, had helped a still furious Mrs. Amberly to bed, that she had a chance to be alone, to sort out her own reaction to the episode. She felt exhausted but was too wound up to sleep. She had always wondered how she would react to danger. Many times during the war she had wished she were a man so she could do more than stay behind when so many she cared about were on the front lines fighting the invaders of her beloved homeland. The young men she knew never talked about fear. She had grown up believing bravery was the highest and noblest attribute one could attain—to face danger and death and not be afraid.

Now, she had learned that you can be both afraid *and* brave. At least, she had not become hysterical or disgraced herself. Although her throat was dry from fear and her heart banging so fast and hard she thought it might explode during the robbery, she had not fainted, collapsed, nor made a spectacle of herself.

Addie recalled how she had repeated the Scripture, "'Thou, O Lord, shall be my shield" during the robbery. It sprung into her mind from the realms of her childhood when as a self-willed, stubborn little girl she had been sent to her room and made to memorize a verse. Addie smiled, remembering that was the only kind of punishment her gentle mother had ever inflicted. Its reward had been a supernatural calm throughout the frightening ordeal.

As frightening as the experience was, it was not only that that made her strangely restless, unable to relax. She couldn't get hold of the fleeting impression she had about the leader of the band of robbers. It kept eluding her. What exactly was it?

First, he had not fit her idea of an outlaw. For instance, there was a theatrical air about him. Almost as if he had been playing a part. And his politeness as he conducted the crime—even if it had a certain mockery in it. He had an air of unquestioned authority that the other men recognized and obeyed. Then there was his voice—had she been mistaken or had she heard it somewhere before? Or one like it? Not a decided accent but there was a slight drawl to it.

Unable to put her troubled thoughts in any kind of order, Addie prepared for bed. After a while she fell asleep, but her slumber was shallow, interrupted by startled reawakenings and confused dreams.

The following afternoon, a very concerned Louis arrived at the cottage. The news of the stagecoach robbery had spread rapidly, even to the outlying areas, and he had ridden into town at once to see if Addie was all right.

"It must have been a terrifying experience," he said solicitously, taking both of her hands in his.

"Actually not as much as one would think, Louis. It was very strange; after the first few minutes, I felt very calm. The leader was so—I know this will sound incredible—but he was so polite, even while he was stealing from us—so gentlemanly—"

Louis frowned. "Then you've heard?"

"Heard what?"

"I stopped at the sheriff's office before coming over here. I wanted to get the story directly from him of just exactly what had happened. I assumed you women had become hysterical and may have been unable to give all the details of the incident, but I thought the driver would have given a straight report and that the sheriff could then tell me exactly what had taken place."

Addie had to suppress her annoyance at Louis's assumption that she, along with the other women passengers, had become *hysterical*.

"And what did the sheriff tell you then, Louis?" She tried to keep from sounding sarcastic, but it annoyed her for Louis to be so condescending.

"Do they know who the robbers were?"

"You say the leader acted *gentlemanly*, right? Well, they suspect the man who robbed your stage was none other

220

than the famous, or I should say the notorious Gentleman Jim. He's been the perpetrator of many successful stagecoach robberies. He seems to have it down to a science—knows when and where to attack—usually he goes for a stage carrying a payroll or the claim payoff of mines, or a bank's supply. He's gotten away with it. A real rascal." Louis shook his head. "But always described as *gentlemanly*."

Addie recalled her own reaction to the masked leader. He had been almost gallant in his manner. Still, something in her memory caught her attention, but Louis was speaking and she lost track of what she was trying to grasp.

"You've had a severe shock. It would be good for you to come out to the house, be our guest for a few days. Estelle agrees with me."

Addie was startled at this. Privately she wondered how long it had taken Louis to persuade his sister to accept what must have been his idea.

"That's very kind of you, Louis, and of Estelle too. But I couldn't possibly come. I have to stay with Mrs. Amberly. She was very upset by all this, and I'm sure she would be most indignant if I went away. She would feel as if I had deserted her when she needed me most."

Louis frowned but finally conceded that this might happen. "Tomorrow is your regular day off anyway, isn't it? I'll come for you early, and we'll take a drive. It will get your mind off all this."

Chapter 16

*O*f course, the robbery was the topic of everyone's conversation that evening and even the following morning at breakfast. Those hotel guests who had not gone on the fateful trip to Lakeport crowded around the ones who had and wanted the story retold. Nothing delighted the tellers more. They were basking in the reflected glory of their experience. As one witty old gentleman commented to Addie, "They'll dine out on this for months—maybe even *years!*"

Addie could not help agreeing with him. Mrs. Amberly was milking the episode for all it was worth. She held court, and each retelling was more embellished with details Addie could not remember. No pistol had even been held to anyone's head, least of all *hers*. Even the driver and his aide were treated with courtesy. But Addie held her tongue. If anyone asked her for her version, she was brief and factual. This seemed dull in comparison to what the others who had shared the experience were saying. Eventually she was not asked for her story anymore.

There was no one Addie could really talk to about it. She wished Brook were back. She knew he would listen. He would help her sort through her fragmented impressions of the robbery, perhaps recall some clue that would aid the sheriff in identifying the robbers.

It was a relief when Louis came to take her for a drive. She was tired of the constant talk of the robbery and hearing the exaggerations that grew larger with every successive telling. As they left Silver Springs Addie lapsed into a reflective silence. They had driven quite awhile before Louis asked, "Why so quiet, Addie?"

"I'm sorry, Louis, I didn't mean to be rude."

"Not rude at all, my dear. It's understandable. You've been through a terrible ordeal; it's bound to have an effect." He reached over and took her hand. "I wish I could help some way."

Louis guided the buggy over to the side of the road, reined his horse, then leaned toward Addie. "I wish I could protect you from anything unpleasant. Take care of you, always. Does that surprise you, Addie?"

Addie drew back a little. "I don't think I—"

"Addie, don't you know? Haven't you guessed what I feel? That I am—*very* fond of you? I haven't said it in so many words. I know you're under contract to stay with Mrs. Amberly until the end of the year. And also I wanted to have my own plans settled, the house completed, the winery under way before . . ."

Addie controlled an involuntary shiver. She didn't think she wanted to hear the rest of what Louis was going to say.

"I've been looking for someone with your qualities for a long time. Almost as soon as I met you I *knew*—I couldn't wait to tell Estelle, to have her meet you . . ." Louis's hand tightened on hers. "Addie, I have so much to offer you— *want* to offer you."

"Oh, Louis, don't—"

"Why not, Addie? It's true. Maybe, you don't love me now—not yet, but you do care for me a little, don't you? You must. I think we get on very well together. You would

223

enjoy having a home like ours, a position in the community, wouldn't you? You were born to it. I know you would be a grace to my home, be an asset in every way. And I'd try very hard to make you happy."

"Oh, Louis, I'm sure you would. But I—I just haven't thought—"

"If I should marry—*when* I marry, my wife would be mistress of Chateau Montand. Estelle plans to travel extensively in the next few years. She has spent her life caring for me, but once I am happily settled, she would pursue her own interests."

Addie understood what he was implying. In case a sister-in-law in residence would present an obstacle to her, Louis wanted her to know that would not be the case.

"I don't have to have an answer right away—," Louis continued. "Just consider what it would mean to both of us. Think of what it could be like—all your problems, your financial worries, the future—all taken care of for you. That's what I want to do. Please, Addie, think about it, won't you?"

Addie moistened her dry lips with the tip of her tongue and took a long breath. "Yes, of course, Louis. I will. I can't promise you anything but—yes, I can do that."

Seemingly satisfied, Louis picked up the reins again, and they continued to drive. He didn't force her into conversation and try as she might, Addie could think of little to say. Louis's proposal had pulled her wandering thoughts back into the present, to decisions that would soon have to be made about the rest of her life.

Much of what Louis said was true. What he was offering was, actually, an escape. Hadn't she been praying for a way out? Addie knew after she had fulfilled her year's contract with Mrs. Amberly she still had to find a way to earn a living. But how? She wasn't any better prepared than she had been a year ago. She assumed she would go back to Virginia. What then, she had no idea.

Now Louis was giving her a choice. But a marriage without the passion and romance like the Bairds had? To give that up would be giving up a cherished lifelong dream.

But perhaps, after all, life wasn't a love story. The hopes she had allowed herself to have about Rex Lyon had vanished, been crushed. Maybe she should consider a marriage of mutual respect, security, and companionship. Addie knew many such marriages had turned out to be good.

But in her heart of hearts she *knew* she could not settle for that.

After a while Louis suggested he take her back to Silver Springs so she could rest.

Before Louis left her at the main building, he said, "You'll feel better after a good night's sleep. I'll stop by again tomorrow to see you. Estelle told me to be sure and tell you that after the flurry dies down, she insists you come out to the house. She wants very much to get to know you better."

Addie wondered if Estelle knew he was going to propose to her today.

"I don't want to press you, my dear. But I shall be very busy when my first crop is ready to harvest—so I would like to know as soon as you feel you can give me an answer."

"Louis I—"

"No matter, my dear, don't fret yourself," he said quickly. "We have plenty of time to make plans."

"You are very kind, Louis."

She watched him ride away. Louis *was* kind, thoughtful. But marriage? She would have to feel something much stronger for him to seriously consider that.

Glancing at the verandah she saw Mrs. Amberly sitting in one of the rocking chairs, surrounded by a small group. Probably holding forth to those who had not heard the adventure or perhaps were listening to it again. Since Mrs. Amberly's back was to her, Addie saw no reason to make her presence known. It was still her day off, her free day, and she was going to enjoy her freedom as long as possible.

Besides, her head ached. The drive with Louis had not refreshed or relaxed her. In fact, after Louis's proposal, she felt even more tense. Maybe, if she lay down for a while it might help. She would soak a handkerchief with cologne and place it on her throbbing temples.

In her cottage bedroom, when Addie opened her bureau drawer to get one out, she saw, to her surprise, one of Brook's monogrammed handkerchiefs among her own. She remembered that one day when they were out walking, a cinder had blown into her eye, and he had taken his out of his pocket and lent it to her. She had washed and ironed it then forgotten to return it to him. Since his larger one would make a better size headache band, she decided to use his, then give it back later.

Dear Brook! She wished he were back from the city. She missed him. If he were here she knew she could confide Louis's proposal to him. She could trust him to be honest, to help her decide what was the best thing to do.

She poured water into her washbowl, added a few splashes of cologne, then dipped Brook's handkerchief into it. Soaking it thoroughly, then wringing it out, she folded it into an oblong. She lay down on her bed and pressed the fine linen cloth over her forehead and closed her eyes.

It took a long time for her to quiet her jumbled mind. So many questions to which she could not find answers. She longed for some simple solution to the turmoil churning inside her.

Addie stirred. How much later, she wasn't sure. She felt stiff and fuzzy-headed, almost as if she had taken a sleeping powder. But her headache seemed to be gone. She removed the cloth from her eyes, dry now but still fragrant from her violet cologne. Opening her eyes to darkness, she realized evening had come. She must have fallen asleep. Slowly she sat up. The bedroom felt hot and airless. She got out of bed. Fumbling for the matches she lit the lamp on the bedside table, then went to fold back the shutters, open the window.

A pale moon shed a milky sheen over the hotel grounds. It must be very late. There were no lights on in the main building.

It was then she saw something move outside the cottage. A shadowy figure standing under the palm tree at the end of the path. Or was it her imagination? Addie leaned on the sill and peered out. There was no breeze stirring, nothing moved. *Was* someone standing there? Instinctively she shrank back, afraid the light in the room behind her might have silhouetted her in the window frame making her visible to anyone lurking about.

Who *was* out there? A prowler? Burglars? An involuntary shiver passed through her. She pressed her arms tight against her body, cupping her elbows in her palms, and waited until the shuddering stopped. She had not yet recovered fully from the experience of the robbery. That's what made her so fearful, so easily frightened.

She looked again. Maybe it had been one of the hotel guests, restless, sleepless, out for a stroll on this moonlit night. Back to the window, she cautiously pulled aside the curtain and looked out again. A cloud moved across the moon momentarily blocking her view. When it passed, the place under the palm was empty. Slowly Addie let out her breath. It must have been a shadow, a trick of the moonlight.

Meantime the wind had risen slightly, blowing some refreshing cool air into the room. She still felt tired, unrested. She would get undressed, get into bed properly.

Now that her headache was gone, perhaps she could sleep well.

Addie awakened suddenly, as if someone had shaken her. Gray light slithered through the slotted bands of the shutters. She sat up in bed, looking around, feeling as if there was something she should remember, something she should do.

She fell back against the pillows. Why did she feel so depressed? She'd had a troubling dream. Was it the dream that had bolted her so abruptly into wakefulness? She tried to recall it but couldn't. It had seemed so real. But now the details were blurred, confusing—events, people all so mixed up, she couldn't piece it together.

Lying there a minute longer she felt strangely disturbed. Something was different. Something out of place. Things were not quite the way they were last night when she had blown out her lamp.

Her gaze traveled the room to where she had draped her clothes over a chair the night before, too tired to hang them up, then to the window from where she thought she had seen someone outside. Had she opened the shutters? Left the curtains drawn? She couldn't remember.

Then she saw an envelope propped against the bureau mirror. Where had that come from? How had it gotten there? Had one of the maids slipped in and placed it there while Addie was still asleep?

Addie threw back the covers, got up, and went over to the bureau. Her name was written on the front of the envelope. Reaching to pick it up she saw a small suede bag behind it. She set the envelope aside. Her hands fumbled as she undid the leather drawstrings, opening it. When she saw what was inside, she gasped. She put her hand in and slowly drew out . . . her small gold watch, the cameo

228

brooch, the garnet earrings, and, lastly, the narrow velvet box containing her mother's opal necklace and earring set!

Her heart thudded. She took up the envelope again, ran her fingernail under the flap, and opened it. She took out the letter inside and unfolded it. She had only seen that handwriting once, but now she recognized it. Suddenly her knees felt weak. She backed up to the bed, sat down on the edge, and began to read.

My dear Addie,

By the time you read this I will be far away, because I cannot come back. I have to go on—there are too many bridges I've burned behind me. My debts have mounted; even my tested methods of getting cash, when all else fails, have not been able to meet the amount I now need. Not enough to cover my enormous debts. Many would say I took too many risks, expanded too quickly. Now, I have to admit, they were mostly right. I have to relinquish the dreams I had for Calistoga and Silver Springs Resort.

I had no idea you would be on that stage. I would never have taken your jewelry except I didn't want to single you out from the rest of the passengers and so align you with me in any way.

At least Gentleman Jim is enough of one to return your family heirlooms.

In many ways I wish that our paths had crossed earlier in my life—but even when you were coming of age, I had already misspent my youth!

Believe me, I will always be glad for meeting you and coming to know you. I want you to know how much I valued your friendship and often wished it might be more. I never told you I loved you, but now that it cannot hurt either of us, I can. I don't claim to know much about love except that the only kind of love that lasts is unrequited love. So, I shall love you always.

I suspect your love lies elsewhere and with a more worthy man; I hope you will make the choice that will bring you great happiness in your life.

229

You have touched my life with sweetness and goodness,
a radiance I can only admire and perhaps even envy—

When Addie finished reading, her hands holding the letter began to shake. *Gentleman Jim? Brook was Gentleman Jim!*

She never knew how long she sat there, stunned, holding the letter. Finally Addie stood up and began to dress. Her fingers moved numbly, fastening buttons, doing up her hair. She picked up her watch and smiled wanly to see that it was set and ticking—how like Brook to do that! The tiny hands pointed to a little past six in the morning. Mechanically she pinned her watch to her bodice.

The dining hall opened for breakfast at six for early risers. She decided to slip out of the cottage and go there to get some coffee. She threw a shawl over her shoulders, inched the door open, and went out. Brooding clouds hung in the clay-colored sky. Addie shuddered. What was she to do with what she knew?

In the dining hall, huddled at a corner table, she drank two cups of black coffee, hoping it would bring clarity to a mind muddled by disbelief. Addie was torn by her contradictory feelings. Half of her mind told her that Brook *was* Gentleman Jim; the other part argued it was impossible. She longed desperately for it *not* to be true. Little by little things began to add up: his wild spending, elaborate parties, his long absences. Finally she stopped denying the terrible truth.

Whom should she tell? Should she go to the sheriff? How would she explain her returned jewelry? Had the jewelry of any of the others been returned? When the waiter came to refill her cup, she waved him away. She must keep her nerve, be calm, be careful.

The dining room began to fill up with other hotel guests. With a start Addie realized an hour had gone by. She must get back to the cottage. Mrs. Amberly would be up by now, ready for her "logger" breakfast, impatient for Addie's arm

230

to lean on as she made her way stiffly over to the dining hall. Hastily Addie rose and left. She was hurrying across the grounds when she heard Mrs. Amberly's shriek. Startled, she picked up her skirt and ran the rest of the way, dashed up the cottage steps and into the house.

Mrs. Amberly was standing in the hallway. When she saw Addie, her face turned a purplish-red, her eyes were bulging, her mouth hung open. One of the hotel maids stood by looking scared out of her wits.

Addie's first reaction was horror. Her eyes darted toward her open bedroom door. Addie felt her face get hot. Her cheeks burned, but her tone was ice cold. "What's going on? What were you doing in *my* room?"

"Don't take that tone with me, young lady," Mrs. Amberly said spitefully. "I don't think you'll be so high and mighty once the sheriff gets here. How do you account for *this*, pray tell?" Mrs. Amberly advanced toward Addie threateningly, shaking the jewelry bag left on Addie's bureau.

"Whatever the reason, Mrs. Amberly, you had no right to go into my room."

"I had every right to," Mrs. Amberly said savagely. "I waited and waited for you to come to help me get over for my breakfast, and when you didn't, I thought you might have overslept or something, so I knocked and knocked. When you didn't open the door, I thought you might be sick, so I *did!*" Mrs. Amberly lost all visible control. Her voice rose to a pitch. "And that's when I found *these!* How do you explain *this*, Miss Pride?"

Addie struggled for control, to keep her voice steady. "That happens to be *my* jewelry."

Mrs. Amberly's lips curled back in a snarl. "This is *stolen* property! And if you claim it's yours, you're no better than a thief—an accomplice to a gang of highway bandits!" she snarled with a venom that caused Addie to draw back.

By now Mrs. Amberly's voice was so loud that other guests, coming from their cottages and passing by on their way to the dining hall for breakfast, had stopped to see what all the ruckus was about.

As upset and angered as she was, Addie made two quick decisions. She would not try to defend herself. The woman was too far gone. And she would not betray Brook.

His note was safely hidden in the pocket of her skirt. However unjustified her action of invading Addie's privacy was, Mrs. Amberly's discovery had made disclosure on Addie's part unnecessary. Addie could protest ignorance of how the jewelry had gotten into her room. That much *was* the truth. How or when she had no idea. Was it Brook, or had he paid one of the employees to do it? Could it have been put there yesterday even when she was gone during the afternoon? Had she been too distracted over Louis's proposal to notice it? Or had someone with a key to the cottages slipped in silently while she slept and put the bag and note in her room?

She wouldn't lie. She would simply tell the facts as she knew them. But she would not volunteer any information. The jewelry had simply been returned. When or how, she did not know. She had no explanation.

Behind her she heard the rumble of murmuring among the people now crowding around the cottage. Then she became aware of shuffling behind her. She turned to see Louis pushing his way through to reach her. With him was the sheriff.

While Mrs. Amberly continued to shout accusations at her, the sheriff, accompanied by Louis, closed the front door upon the curious crowd and requested Addie and Mrs. Amberly to go with him into the cottage's small parlor. Here the tall, ruggedly built sheriff silenced Mrs. Amberly by saying, "Please, Ma'am, just hold your fire. Let's just have the facts," he said firmly. He listened patiently while Mrs. Amberly spouted off her furious charges. Without making any comment, he then halted her with a raised hand and turned to Addie. "Now, you, Miss Pride, please."

Louis stood behind Addie's chair as she recounted how she had found the jewelry that had been taken in the stagecoach robbery. During her account, although guiltily conscious of the note in her pocket, she did not mention it. Addie's father had been a lawyer, and Uncle Myles still practiced in a small, musty office where hardly any clients ever came, so Addie was somewhat familiar with the law. She realized that legally she could be charged with concealing evidence. But most of what Brook had written was personal. She could not turn it over to be read and misinterpreted by hostile eyes.

While pulling at his handlebar mustache, the sheriff kept his steely gaze upon her as he listened to her explanation. His expressionless face would have done justice to a poker player. It gave Addie no indication of his reaction, whether he believed her or not. When she finished he got to his feet and said, "I see no reason to suspect Miss Pride here with anything—collusion, conspiracy, or any of the things you've accused her of. This Gentleman Jim is known to be unpredictable and also known to have an eye for a pretty lady—as we can all see Miss Pride is. It's just like him to do something unexpected, like returning her jewelry—as some kind of compliment." The sheriff shook his head. "Nobody's yet figured out the fellow."

As he moved toward the door he spoke directly to Mrs. Amberly. "I know you're upset, Ma'am, but I assure you, we're going to bring this gang to justice. We're forming a posse, and we'll be searching the hills around here where they may be hiding out. Gentleman Jim's band—seems to have inside information. This coming Friday the vineyard's payroll comes through. They may be waiting to rob it. We

233

have plans underway to trap the fellow, but, of course, I can't go into detail." His hand on the doorknob now, he turned for a final say. "Don't fret, ladies, we'll round him up and soon."

Dead silence followed the sheriff's departure. It seemed the session had left even Mrs. Amberly speechless. Her face had gone slack. She pushed herself up out of her chair. Her mouth worked like one of those comic rubber dolls children squeeze to change their expressions as though she wanted to say something more to Addie.

Perhaps to avoid another possible diatribe from Mrs. Amberly, Louis stepped over to the door and opened it for her. After giving Addie a scathing look, she left the room without a word. Addie listened tensely to her employer's shuffling footsteps go down the hall; then she heard the sullen slam of her bedroom door.

After a moment Addie stood up, hands clenched, heart thundering with rage. The anger she had suppressed before rushed up in her now. She looked at Louis expectantly. Why? For some possible explanation of why he had not risen to her defense. The woman to whom he had proposed marriage was accused of being an accomplice to a stagecoach robbery, and he said nothing! It seemed unnatural, to say the least. Did he have some reason? She waited, but when nothing happened she demanded, "Why didn't you *say* something, *do* something? You heard what she said about me!"

Louis met her outraged look with some surprise. "What could I say? The woman's upset; that's all." He shrugged. "A real tempest in a teapot, my dear Addie. It will all blow over—"

"But she accused me of being a *thief*, an *accomplice* to a *stagecoach robbery!* Don't you *care?*"

"Don't worry. No one would possibly believe her."

For a long minute, Addie stared at him in disbelief. What

kind of man was he? Then suddenly she felt drained. She passed a hand across her forehead, swaying a little. "You'll have to excuse me, Louis, I'm not feeling very well. I can't go out with you today. Give my apology to Estelle."

With that Addie swept past him, out the parlor door and started down the hall.

"Addie, wait." He followed her. She paused outside her bedroom door. Louis's voice was apologetic. "My dear, please. Of course, I understand. Do rest. I know you're distraught, but it will pass—all of this—you'll see."

"Good-bye, Louis," she said stiffly.

"Addie—" He started to say something more, then, as though thinking better of it, finished lamely, "I—I'll stop by tomorrow."

Addie did not reply. She just went in her bedroom and shut the door. Once she was alone, Addie felt the weight of her secret press down upon her. Was Brook hiding somewhere in the hills, as the sheriff suspected? Would he then be hunted down by men with rifles like a wild animal or a fugitive? But wasn't *that* exactly what Brook was—a criminal? Robbing stagecoaches? Addie shook her head, it was so hard to comprehend. The dapper, elegant, fastidious Brook Stanton—with his immaculate linen, gold cuff links, and silk cravats—a common thief? Had he been so desperate for money? Or had it been some kind of crazy aberration of his personality? Acting out in reality some childish fantasy like children playing bandits or pirates?

Addie took out the note again and sat down on the edge of the bed to reread it. What she read between the lines was even more confusing than the words themselves. To think Brook had fallen in love with her but had been afraid to speak because of the double life he was leading! It was incredible.

Addie crumpled up the note. Perhaps she should destroy

235

it? But would that incriminate her further if it became known that there *was* a note with the jewelry? Oh, dear God, give me light! If ever she needed wisdom it was *now*. What was the *right* thing to do?

Feeling frantic, she paced the small room, literally wringing her hands, torn by her contradictory feelings. Those vague suspicions that had puzzled her during the robbery seemed to be validated by the note.

Addie longed desperately for it *not* to be true. The Brook *she* knew seemed such an unlikely stagecoach robber. From the way the yellow journals and Wild West "penny dreadfuls" pictured stagecoach robbers, they were vicious outlaws, ruffians, bandits of the lowest kind, preying on helpless passengers—women and children. For the Brook who had impressed her with his fine clothes, his good manners, his quixotic personality, his familiarity with poetry and literature—surely *he* could not be the leader of a band of stagecoach robbers.

Yet the very same traits attributed to the notorious Gentleman Jim could also fit Brook Stanton: flamboyant, dashing, risk-taking, a gambler.

Wearily, Addie sat down on her bed and leaned back against the pillows. She felt drained. Her brain was confused she could not even think anymore. Disjointed, inarticulate prayers sprang into her mind, but she could not even finish them. What should she do? What was going to happen? She felt overwhelmed. She wished she could go to sleep and wake up to find it had all been a nightmare!

Addie awoke with a jerk. She thought she had only lain down for a few minutes, but in spite of everything she had fallen asleep. But it had been an uneasy sleep, and she felt hot, fuzzy-headed, and unrested. She sat up, her pins had slipped out, and her loosened hair was tumbling down over her shoulders. Pushing it back with both hands she got stiffly to her feet.

She had just sloshed her face with water and was patting it dry when a tap came at her door.

"Yes, who is it?" she called.

"The maid, miss; you have a caller."

"I don't want to see anyone."

There was a pause, a murmur of voices, then another gentle rap.

"Addie, it's Freda, please let me in."

Addie hurried to the door, opened it and the two friends embraced.

"Oh, Freda, I'm glad you've come. You don't know—," began Addie, feeling a rush of tears stinging her eyes.

"I know. I heard. It's all over town," Freda said quietly, coming into the room and shutting the door.

Addie almost said, "About Brook?" but stopped before the words slipped out. She asked, "About *me?*"

"You? Well, about the stagecoach being robbed. It must have been dreadful."

Quickly Addie gathered her scrambled thoughts. Of course, Freda didn't have any idea about the returned jewelry.

"Yes, it was pretty frightening," she answered. "Excuse how I look; somehow I fell asleep and ..." she picked up her brush and ran it through her hair several times.

"Are you all right, Addie?"

Addie finished twisting her hair up into a knot and secured it with tortoise shell pins. Then she turned around and gave a bitter little laugh. "Except that I'm under suspicion."

Freda's brows drew together. "Under *suspicion?* What do you mean? For what?"

"Maybe you haven't heard yet. But you will soon enough. I know small towns have active gossip mills. Especially something *this* juicy." She paused, turned around from the mirror, and faced Freda. "My employer has accused me of being an accomplice to the stagecoach robbers."

"*You,* an *accomplice?*" Freda gasped. "How could she? Why?"

"Because, you see, my jewelry taken during the robbery has been returned."

"What? How was it returned?"

"Mysteriously. I'm not sure just how or when. It's left quite a cloud over my reputation." Addie shrugged. "But I think as much as anything else, Mrs. Amberly is furious because *her* jewelry was much more valuable than anything of mine. Mine was mostly of sentimental value, things belonging to my mother."

"And that leads to the assumption that the robbers *knew* that?"

Addie nodded, then sighed, "How else can it be explained?"

"Oh, Addie, that's terrible *and* ridiculous. *That* woman! I disliked her on sight." Freda shuddered. "There was something about her—I sensed right away—you know how it is with some people? You get a feeling—and I certainly got it that night we were introduced."

"Well, it doesn't matter, I suppose. Since *I* know the truth." Addie hesitated. She wondered if she should confide in Freda? Tell her about the note, about Brook?

But before she could decide, Freda said, "Listen, Addie, I know you must be under a great deal of stress, but I came because—there's someone else who wants to see you, and he did not want to come by himself—afraid he might cause gossip."

"What do you mean? Who?"

"Rex. Rex Lyon," she answered quietly.

At the name Addie's chest tightened as if she could not draw a deep breath. She was still holding her hairbrush, but now she put it down, rearranged the toilette articles on

238

the top of the bureau, lining them up in a row, trying to steady herself.

"He asked me to see if it was all right. He was afraid Louis Montand might object . . ."

Puzzled, Addie turned toward Freda and asked, "But why should Louis object?"

Freda only gave her a strange look and hurried on, "That doesn't matter now, but will you see him? He seems to think you might not—but I must tell you, Addie, I've rarely seen a man so worried. Particularly Rex, who never seems to get upset."

Addie hesitated. She thought of their last awkward encounter at the bank before she had left on the ill-fated trip to Lakeport. She remembered the stilted conversation and his strange comment. It had been weeks since he had tried to see or contact her. Why did he come now and want to see her?

Freda put her hand on Addie's arm. "Do see him, Addie. He's waiting on the other side of the arboretum. Won't you go out there? Hear what he has to say?"

Addie turned away from Freda's searching gaze, afraid her own hurt, her longing, and her feelings for Rex might show in her face. Didn't Freda know Rex had made no move to see her since the day of the picnic with the Bairds? Should she tell Freda how she felt, why she didn't want to see Rex?

She walked over to the window, pushed aside the curtain, and looked out in the direction of the arboretum. As she stood there she saw the sheriff and his deputy ride up to the front of the hotel, dismount, and stride into the building. A minute later Louis come out of the main building, out on the verandah, then hurry down the steps and come marching toward the cottage.

Addie turned around and said to Freda, "I'm sorry, Freda, but it's too late. The sheriff just came, and Louis is coming this way. Something important must have happened."

239

When Addie opened the door, Louis was there. "The sheriff has an announcement to make, and he wants us all to assemble in the main building," he said.

"Shall I come with you, Addie?" Freda asked anxiously.

Addie stretched out her hand to her, but Louis shook his head. "I'm sorry, Mrs. Wegner, but this meeting is only for Silver Springs guests, I'm afraid. I'm sure you'll learn about it eventually." His face was grim.

Addie threw her friend a bewildered glance, but Louis's hand was firmly under her elbow and he was leading her out of the cottage.

"What is it, Louis?" Addie asked as they started across the grounds.

"You'll hear soon enough. Come along, Addie."

The room was crowded, buzzing with the sound of voices, probably all swapping rumors, exchanging conjectures as to what they had been called together for. Addie saw Mrs. Amberly wedged in between Harriet and Elouise Brunell. Mrs. Amberly glared at Addie as she came in on Louis's arm.

The sheriff stepped to the front, clasped his hands behind his back, and cleared his throat. "First of all, I may as well tell you we've had some reports that a man fitting Gentleman Jim's description was seen around here the last day or so. Some folks thought they recognized him. During the night he left a horse at the livery stable that's been identified as being like the one he was riding at the time of the stage robbery." The sheriff smiled ironically. "He took a fresh horse and left a bundle of paper bills to pay for it, something Gentleman Jim would be likely to do."

The hum of voices reacting to this statement rose dramatically. A flurry of questions peppered the air. "Any trace of the other outlaws?" "The members of his gang?" "Any trace of the payroll money?" "Have any of the stolen goods been found?"

240

The sheriff held up both hands. "Just a minute folks! Just a durn minute. I'll get to that. Gimme time."

The mumbling died down and the sheriff stood there, his head down as though either waiting for the room to quiet or uncertain as to whether he should disclose anything further. Finally he raised his head and looked directly into the crowd. "Now, this next will probably shock you folks, but you have a right to know...."

Again he paused. Everyone sat forward on the edge of their seats, eager to be shocked. The sheriff glanced over at Louis, and Louis's hand tightened on Addie's. "Since Mr. Montand already knows this, the way news travels in this town, you'll hear it one way or another, so it might as well come from me. We think we can identify *who* Gentleman Jim really is."

There were immediate cries of surprise, exclamations of curiosity, demands to know. The sheriff had to hold up his hands for silence again until the uproar faded.

"Based on some conclusive evidence, we believe Gentleman Jim is the owner of Silver Springs—Brook Stanton."

At this Mrs. Amberly let out an indignant gasp and staggered up onto her feet, "What did I tell you?" she looked at the Brunell sisters for confirmation. Then pointing her finger at Addie, she sputtered, "Didn't I say *she* knew the outlaw, the man that so brutally robbed all of us! All of us but *her!* Why was *her* jewelry returned and none of the rest of ours? She must have known about it all the time. Didn't I say there was something mighty suspicious about her being so insistent on having her Thursdays every week? Probably went off with *him.* Told him we'd be on that stage! She knows how valuable *my* jewelry is!" Mrs. Amberly shook her fist at Addie. "Why you, you—thief—"

"Now, just a minute, Ma'am," the sheriff's voice lashed across the room like a whip cutting short the sputtering

241

words. "Don't go accusing anyone. We've seen before how Gentleman Jim operates—he don't need no accomplice."

The Brunell sisters were tugging at Mrs. Amberly, embarrassed, trying to get her to sit down.

"Now, just keep calm, everybody," the sheriff went on. "I understand how you all must feel about this. But I guarantee you *this* time Gentleman Jim won't get away. We've been keepin' track of him, and every time we've got closer to nabbing him. We know he can't be far from here. He didn't know it, but the horse he took has a weak leg. Tends to go lame when he's ridden too hard. We'll bring him in, for sure, and we'll get as many of your belongings back as possible. His mistake was taking the payroll cash box from a United States deputy. We've got a warrant for his arrest, and I mean to serve it to him—personal."

People began to talk among themselves. The noise level in the room soared steadily as everyone mingled, merging into small groups, discussing the startling new facts, and swapping opinions.

In the confusion, Louis took Addie's arm and managed to maneuver their way through the lobby, out the front door. Even her relief in not having to keep Brook's identity secret any longer did not take away the sting of Mrs. Amberly's accusations. Mrs. Amberly had publicly humiliated her, and Addie was shaking with fury.

On the verandah she pulled away from Louis and turned to him. "Did you hear what she said *this* time?"

"Oh, Addie, the woman was hysterical. Anyone could see that. No one paid any attention to her."

His nonchalance infuriated Addie even more. She looked at Louis, every hair in place, unruffled, detached, regarding her with a kind of indulgence. All at once something struck her. An appalling idea. Something she saw in Louis's eyes. Doubt? Did he possibly think some of what Mrs. Amberly said was true? Struggling to keep her voice even, she confronted him. "Surely you don't believe what she's saying about me?"

"It doesn't matter, my dear Adelaide. I told you she was out of control," he said placatingly. "Of course, it was obvious to everyone at the hotel that Brook was infatuated with you, but that isn't the point. The rumors will die down, it will all soon be forgotten. I'm sure she won't stay here long now that she knows about Brook. I wouldn't be a bit surprised if she'll leave to go back east as soon as possible."

"And spread all sorts of lies about me? You can be sure she'll inform her nephew who will tell my cousin and destroy my good name and reputation so that my relatives will have to bear the shame!" Addie started to pace the room, then stopped, whirled around, "Don't you *care* that she publicly vilified me?"

Louis made a dismissing gesture with his hand. "Napa Valley is a small, remote place, the people hopelessly provincial. Who could possibly give a fig about what happens here?"

Addie looked at him aghast. Had he no deep feelings, no passion? The woman he had asked to be his wife had been accused in front of dozens of people of being an accomplice in a stagecoach robbery, of aiding and abetting a criminal, and he brushed it off with as little concern as if he were flicking away an annoying insect.

"Louis! You don't understand at all, do you? That I've been accused of being an accomplice to a stagecoach robbery, that I'm a *thief!*—" and here Addie's voice became cold as steel. "Surely, *you* wouldn't want to marry a woman under that kind of suspicion—I know Estelle would not want me as a sister-in-law." Scornfully she added, "In the *South*, a *gentleman* would demand satisfaction!"

Louis raised his eyebrows. "You would have *me* challenge *Mrs. Amberly* to a duel?" He gave a short sardonic laugh. "My dear, Addie—Mrs. Amberly is hardly a worthy adversary—she's nothing, a nobody, a vulgar *nouveau riche* woman. Her ridiculous ranting scarcely would call for such a violent response."

Addie continued to stare. Her heart thundering, hands clenched, every nerve in her body seemed to vibrate. Although she felt physically shaky, her brain was sharp. In the last few weeks she had struggled with uncertainty, but now everything was clear. Louis was not the kind of man she could ever respect, much less *love*—no, nor trust, nor depend on. She might have been speaking another language for he had not seemed to comprehend a word she said nor understand an emotion she had expressed. It had all left him unmoved. It was suddenly as clear as glass. There was no place in her heart for him and no place in his life for her.

She turned away from him. The thought that she had ever considered, no matter how briefly, accepting Louis's proposal sickened her. A man she could neither trust nor respect? She felt disgusted. She had to get away, be by herself. She started down the verandah steps.

"*You,* Miss Pride! You! Wait, just you wait, young lady. I'm not done with you!" Mrs. Amberly shouted from behind her.

Addie turned to see the woman burst out the hotel door, her body propelled faster than Addie had ever seen her move, waving both arms threateningly. Her beady little eyes, narrowed even further in her fleshy cheeks, made her look for all the world like one of those grotesque faces carved on wooden Swiss tobacco holders people brought home from Europe as souvenirs. Her mouth gaped open, little beads of saliva sprayed out as she spat out her words.

"Have you no shame? Carrying on with that man—that *outlaw*—right under my very nose—while I was footing the bill for the roof over your head, every bite of food you put in your mouth! And to think I paid you to steal from me!"

Addie's hand gripped the porch railing, her whole body rigid.

Teetering on the top step, Mrs. Amberly's mouth twisted viciously. "You think you fooled everyone with your soft Southern ways, your hoity-toity superior air, your honey-coated manners. Well, not *me*, you didn't! Not for a minute, young lady. I seen through you right from the first." In her anger Mrs. Amberly had lost any pretense of gentility.

Addie glanced at Louis to see if *now* he would defend her against this venomous attack. But he had backed away from the sight of Mrs. Amberly's huge, hulking figure, almost as if he were afraid of her.

All the while Mrs. Amberly's voice rose higher and higher into a screech, Addie recalled the countless times under Mrs. Amberly's verbal abuse she had contained her true feelings, held herself in check, because she knew if she ever let go there would be no turning back. Always the thought of Aunt Susan and Uncle Myles had restrained her. Now Mrs. Amberly had gone too far. All the incidents of injustice, the petty slurs, her meanness and sarcasm marched through Addie's mind turning her once half-pitying contempt for the woman into loathing.

Addie walked back up the steps and stood directly in front of her accuser. "You are a liar, Mrs. Amberly, not only about what you are saying about me, accusing me of, but you lie about almost everything. I've been with you day in and day out these last months, and I've seen your lying ways. From cheating at cards, oh, yes, you've even bragged about it—to never tipping the maids here for all the extra services they give you. Talk about stealing, what about all the money you've won from your so-called friends? You lie all the time, Mrs. Amberly, about your travels, the people you know—all lies. Well, I don't have to take it anymore.

245

I don't have to listen to your lies. I certainly don't have to listen to your lies about *me!*"

"Addie," Louis gasped and grabbed her arm, but she shook it off.

"Don't touch me." She ran down the steps, picked up her skirt, and ran across the yard and over toward the cottage.

Addie closed her bedroom door and stood there a full minute trying to get control of herself. Her lungs felt as if they might burst, and each breath dragged from deep inside was painful. Across the room she caught sight of her reflection in the bureau mirror and was shocked by her pallor, the wild look in her eyes. She flung herself on the bed, feeling weak and sick. Surely she had just been through the two worst hours of her life.

She did not know how long it was before she heard the front door of the cottage open, then voices, Mrs. Amberly's and one of the hotel maid's, the shuffling sound of Mrs. Amberly's feet along the hallway. Addie sat up, bracing herself. Then the banging on her door came, bam, bam, bam.

"You listen here, Miss Pride. Don't think you're gettin' away with anything. You're dismissed. Do you hear *that?* Pack your things. I want you out of here. I don't want to see you again. Never, you understand? Not after the way you talked to me, the way you've behaved!"

Impulsively, Addie walked over to the door and yanked it open. In startled surprise, Mrs. Amberly stumbled backwards, her arm still raised, hand doubled as if to continue knocking.

"You can save your breath, Mrs. Amberly, I was going to quit anyway. I couldn't stand working for someone like you any longer." With that Addie closed the door in Mrs. Amberly's shocked face.

But a moment later her rasping voice came again so loud she must have been pressing her mouth against the keyhole.

"You—you! Listen! Don't think I'm paying you a penny

of this month's salary—not a red cent! And don't think you'll get any references from me, either! Did you hear *that*—Miss Pride!"

Addie covered her ears to shut out the sound of that spiteful voice, the ugliness of whatever else she was saying. Finally it stopped. Then she heard the muffled footsteps as Mrs. Amberly went down the hall and slammed her bedroom door.

Addie drew a long breath. Ridiculously she felt like laughing, but instead she cried. She realized she must be on the edge of hysteria. Curiously enough, her strongest emotion was relief. It was as though someone had thrown open the prison gates and she was free! Free of that old harpy, her demands, her miserly ways.

Yet even as that thought took hold, Addie knew she had burned all her bridges behind her. She had told off Mrs. Amberly and rejected Louis. All in the space of a few impulsive moments she had thrown away her job, her chance at a wealthy marriage. Now, she had nothing. Quickly she corrected that—she still had her pride. But even that was in tatters! After Mrs. Amberly's public castigation, what was it worth? People thought whatever they wanted to think.

Even though she'd had her moment of self-justification, of pride, in doing so she had thrown away everything else. What did she do now? The uncertainty of her life at the moment seemed unbearable. Reality began to set in; she had no job, no place to stay, nowhere to go! Most of all, she would no longer be able to send the small monthly amount to help Aunt Susan and Uncle Myles. In one reckless gesture of independence she had beggared herself as well. She was sure Mrs. Amberly would carry out her threat—she would not pay her another "red cent"—certainly there would be no severance pay, no return train ticket. Addie was stranded, penniless, except for the tiny bit of money she had been able to squirrel away.

247

She did not want to spend another night under the roof, nor eat another meal Mrs. Amberly had paid for, she would have to wait until morning to make arrangements to leave. And there were hours and hours of the night to get through.

It started to rain. She heard the staccato patter of raindrops on the tin roof. She went to stand at the window peering out into the night. Was Brook out there somewhere in the rainswept dark, alone, desperate, hunted? Addie felt almost as alone and desperate.

Addie prayed for clear direction. It came in the name Freda. What Freda had said that afternoon. "If you need *anything*, if there's anything I can do, any way I can help, please let me know."

Going to Freda meant sacrificing her pride, asking for help. After all, she had known Freda only a matter of months, weeks really since they had become friends. Addie's pride held for another few minutes. She had prayed for guidance, hadn't she? She had to believe she had received it. Trust and obey. The title of the old hymn sang itself into her mind.

In another moment Addie threw a few things into her valise, flung her cloak around her, slipped quietly into the hall, then out the front door.

It was raining hard. As she stood on the little porch the wind whipped her cape around her and blew her hair stingingly into her eyes. She reached for the hood, pulled it up over her head, and tightened the drawstrings under her chin. Then, bending her head, she started walking fast in the direction of town. There she would go to the livery stable and hire a horse or a buggy to ride out to Freda's ranch. She hoped she remembered the way.

Chapter 17

*A*ddie had not remembered the way into town being so long. The wind-driven rain pelted her relentlessly as she struggled through the dark. Frantically she searched her memory to remember where the livery stable was located. After two wrong turns, she saw its wooden sign swinging wildly back and forth in the wind, and she hurried toward it. There was no light and no one anywhere about. She banged on the door with both her hands, calling hello at the top of her voice. Finally she heard the creak of the stable door and saw a lantern held up in front of a sleepy groom's face.

"Hey, what's all the racket for?" he asked grumpily. "We're closed, been closed since seven."

"I'm sorry, but I'm in urgent need of a horse and buggy. I must get out to the Wegner ranch tonight."

He shook his head. "Well, now, Miss, the boss ain't here, and I got no small buggy fit for a lady to handle, and all the fresh horses went with the sheriff and his posse. Sorry."

Addie's heart sank. She could not go back to the Springs. She must get out to Freda's some way. "Could you drive me? I'll pay you, of course," she offered even as she mentally counted her small amount of cash.

The boy shook his head. "No, Ma'am. The boss'd have my hide if I left the stable and horses unattended." He backed away and started to slide the door shut again.

"Wait!" Addie pleaded in sudden panic. Making another desperate decision she asked, "Have you a horse I could ride?"

The groom hesitated, "Well, there's old Sal, but she'd be a handful if I got her out on a night like this. I mean she's gentle enough but old—"

"That would do fine. I'll take her. How much?"

"—haven't got a sidesaddle—"

"That doesn't matter. I can ride a regular one," Addie assured him, grateful for the denim skirt cut from Freda's pattern she was wearing.

The boy still sounded hesitant. "I dunno what the boss would say—"

"Look, I'll pay you extra for your trouble," she offered rashly.

"Well—" the word was dragged out as if he were mentally considering a nice sum for his own pocket, then he said, "—all right."

A few minutes later he led out the nodding mare. Addie stepped up on the mounting block and slid one foot into a stirrup. Gripping the pommel she settled herself securely in the unaccustomed saddle, wedging the small valise behind.

"Sure you're all right, Miss?" the groom asked, doubt strong in his voice.

"Yes, fine," she said, sounding much more convinced than she felt. "Thanks. I'll bring Sal back tomorrow." She clutched the reins, gave the horse a gentle kick in the sides to urge her forward. Resentful of being roused out of a warm stall where she was comfortably settled for the night, old Sal shook her head indignantly, and not until the groom slapped her flanks did she move.

250

Once out into the drizzle and on the road Sal gradually started into a bumpy trot. The rain continued steadily, soaking through Addie's lightweight cloak. Her hood slipped back with the motion of the horse. Her hands were too busy holding the reins taut to attempt to cover her head again. Soon her hair was wet, streaming down her face and plastered against her forehead.

Clinging to the pommel, the reins twisted around her cold hands, Addie felt desperate. Between clenched, chattering teeth, she prayed using for a prayer the only thing she could remember at the moment, the words of the hymn "Lead, Kindly Light." Sal tugged stubbornly against the reins, tossing her head to show her distaste at being ridden in this wild, dark night on an unfamiliar road.

Addie squinted into each side road they passed, trying to recall just where the one leading to Freda's was. At last, in the distance she thought she dimly saw lights. She pulled sharply on the reins. With effort she turned the still recalcitrant Sal into the winding road she was pretty sure led to the Wegner ranch.

Through sheets of rain she spotted the outline of the house. By the time she awkwardly dismounted, every muscle stiff and aching, Addie was completely drenched and exhausted. Looping Sal's reins about the small iron hitching post, she stumbled up the steps of the porch. She leaned against the door frame and twisted the metal doorbell. After a few minutes, through the glass oval of the front door she saw a wavering light, as if someone carrying a lamp was approaching. When the door opened Addie nearly fell into Freda's arms.

With a startled exclamation Freda drew Addie into the house, calling to Elena as she did. "Ring the farm bell for Rico to come up to the house, take Miss Pride's horse to the barn, and rub her down and give her some oats." As a wide-

251

eyed Elena scurried off to do her mistress's bidding, Freda led Addie into the kitchen.

"You're shivering. We'll have to get those wet clothes off you quick," she said briskly. "You can do it in here by the stove. There's no one here but Elena and me."

Shuddering with the cold seeping into every pore Addie proceeded to drag off the soaking garments.

"Here, put this blanket around you. I'll get some water heated for your feet and to make some tea."

Still shaking but now swathed in a cozy blanket, Addie sat in a rocker pulled close to the stove. She gratefully accepted the steaming mug Freda handed her. Cupping it with both hands, she sipped it slowly. Gradually the hot liquid took off the edge of chill, and warmth began to spread through her.

Freda knelt on the floor in front of Addie and with Elena's help tugged off Addie's boots and pulled off her stockings, then gently placed her numb feet into a pan of steaming water.

Freda's sympathy showed in her expressive eyes as Addie poured out the whole story of what had taken place at Silver Springs since Freda's visit.

"So, that's how it is," she sighed. "I'm sorry, Freda. It's really inexcusable for me to come here without warning like this—imposing upon you this way. I had nowhere else to go, no one else to turn to. I don't mean to sound like a poor homeless waif, but—"

"But that's *exactly* what you are!" Freda cut in, finishing for her. Then they both began to laugh, although Addie's laughter was close to tears.

"Now, look here," Freda said firmly, "I don't want to hear another word about imposing from you. You are more than welcome no matter the circumstances. I get very lonely out here night after night all by myself. I love having company. Even unexpected company, or maybe I should say *especially*

252

unexpected company! You know what the Bible says don't you? 'Be not hesitant to entertain strangers, for thereby some have entertained angels unaware.' Hebrews 13:2. That's chapter and verse even though I may not have quoted it just right."

"Thank you, Freda, you're very kind."

"My goodness, no need for thanks. We're friends, aren't we? That's what friends are for. All right, now, the best thing is for you to get a good night's sleep. Everything will look better in the morning. Although I detest people who quote adages, I know from experience, that life always seems 'darkest before the dawn.' So, let me show you the guest room."

She took Addie upstairs, to the room where Elena had already turned down the bed.

"First thing tomorrow we'll send word to the hotel for your clothes and other belongings to be packed and delivered out here," Freda said firmly.

Addie could just imagine a red-faced, furious Mrs. A. standing over Letty, the hotel maid, as she packed, watching to see nothing that was not strictly Addie's got put in by mistake or intent. She was too weary to protest. Tomorrow would be time enough to make plans, to decide what she should do next.

She looked around Freda's guest room with gratitude and pleasure and a little nostalgia. It reminded her somewhat of her own girlhood bedroom at Oakleigh with its spool bed, candlewick coverlet, ruffled curtains. For a moment the memories were sweet yet tinged with melancholy.

Addie thought sleep might be impossible given all she'd been through. But almost as soon as she slipped between the lavender-scented sheets, she went blissfully to sleep.

When dawn lighted the room, Addie awoke, unable at first to place where she was. Slowly the events of the day

253

before—the showdown with Mrs. Amberly, the confrontation with Louis, her flight from the Silver Springs cottage in the driving rain—all came back to her. She lay there for a moment, turning each over in her mind, testing her emotions. In spite of knowing that today would require much of her, she felt surprisingly calm. She had several important decisions to make. With God's help, she would make the right ones.

She got out of bed, went to the window, and knelt there looking out at the vineyards. What should she do now? Where could she go—without money, without any references. Surely Mrs. Amberly would keep her word and deprive her of any sort of recommendation. The old anger and resentment knotted Addie's stomach as her hands gripped the windowsill. Mrs. Amberly's had been no idle threat.

She could not stay indefinitely at Freda's but she needed a few days at least to review her options and try to make some plans. The only thing she could do was to discuss her situation honestly with Freda. She had put herself in the position of asking for help. Much as this hurt her pride, she had to do it.

The house seemed very quiet. Addie opened the bedroom door and peered into the hallway. Outside were her boots, cleaned and polished. Next to them were her clothes, dried and pressed, folded over a chair.

Addie dressed quickly and went downstairs in search of Freda. The front of the house was empty, no one about. Then she heard a voice singing. Was it coming from the kitchen? She ventured along the hall where she remembered going last night. Elena turned from the stove and greeted her with a smile. *"Buenos dias, Señorita."* She told Addie that Freda was down in the vineyards and would be back shortly. "She goes early, sometimes even before the men are in the field." Elena shook her head. "The señora

254

sent Rico into town to take back the horse to the livery stable and to deliver a note to the hotel to send out your belongings. Señora Wegner said I was to fix you a good hot breakfast when you woke up. I'm just taking my bread out of the oven now."

Elena set a place for her at the round oak table by the windows that overlooked the rolling hills. After a huge breakfast of cured ham, fried eggs, fresh warm bread, apricot jam, and delicious hot coffee, Addie felt more able to face the day ahead.

So many things to think about. How could she get back to Virginia? Cousin Matthew, who had been instrumental in getting her the job with Mrs. Amberly, was the *last* person Addie felt like asking to borrow money from, but he was the *only* relative she knew who had any. Addie's pride would not let her even consider that. *Pride, always that.* Sometimes that was more a vice than a virtue. In the meantime, she had to remain at Freda's until she could think of some way to earn enough herself.

Addie went back upstairs to the guest bedroom. Her Bible lay on the bedside table where she had unpacked it from her small valise. When she saw it she thought if there had ever been a time for her to seek guidance, *this* was it. She knew she should pray. How often in times of crisis had Addie seen her mother on her knees in prayer, an open Bible in front of her? And Aunt Susan whose strong faith had seen her through a war that had robbed her of sons, fortune, future.

The Psalms had always been Addie's favorite part of the Bible, maybe because most were written by David: emotional, impulsive, *proud*—someone she could identify with. She flipped through the pages to Psalm 46: "God is our refuge and strength, a very present help in trouble—" She squeezed her eyes tight and tried to pray.

But the scene with Mrs. Amberly was all that came into

255

her mind. She kept seeing that malicious face, hearing those vicious slanders, those stinging insults. Addie felt righteous anger well up hotly within her. How dare that woman accuse her of such things? Addie felt herself tremble with fury.

And Louis! Her original impression of him had been right! Again it made her skin crawl to think she had, even for a moment, considered his proposal! She could never marry someone she could not respect. He had stood by, not lifting a finger to defend her, while she was being verbally attacked by Mrs. Amberly. Worse still, in the lobby, in front of *everyone*, he had remained silent.

"Crisis always reveals character," Addie's father used to say. This time it had proved more than true. For all his wealth, education, and sophistication, Louis Montand was weak, not worthy of respect.

How different everything would be if he had been. If she could have depended on him, if he had really shown his loyalty and love, she would not be facing this bleak future. If he had been someone like Rex Lyon. . . . She put her face in her hands. She hadn't meant to think of *him*.

Abruptly, Addie got up off her knees. It was no use. She was in no mood to pray. Her heart was too full of vengeful thoughts. The only Scripture she could think of was, "The heart is deceitful above all things, and desperately wicked. Who can know it?" The trouble was Addie knew her heart too well. It was proud and rebellious.

She closed the Bible regretfully just as there was a knock at the bedroom door.

"There's someone to see you, Miss Pride," Elena's voice called through the door.

Probably someone from the hotel bringing her things, perhaps wanting her to sign for them. Whatever it was, she would have to deal with it. She hurried down the steps.

There was no one waiting in the hall so she started into

the parlor. She slid back the panel door and saw a man standing in front of the fireplace. At the sound of the door opening, he turned. She caught her breath and stared at him,

Rex too was speechless. She looked so beautiful—wide-eyed, lips parted with surprise. All he had come to say departed from his mind, leaving him without words. He looked at her long and steadily.

"Why, Mr. Lyon," Addie faltered, immediately conscious of her appearance. She had rushed downstairs thinking it was probably a hotel employee or maybe Rico with some malicious message from her former employer. She had not bothered to look in the mirror. Instinctively her hands went to her hair, patting the coiled twist at the nape of her neck, tucking a stray curl back of her ear.

Rex cleared his throat. "Addie ... I ... I wanted you to know how sorry I am about all that's happened ... to offer whatever help I could—if you need—I mean Freda says ..." He stopped midsentence as if he felt he might have said too much.

"Thank you," Addie murmured, wondering if Freda had sent for him.

"I came to the hotel the other day to see you but—"

"Yes, I know. Freda told me. It was kind of you, but we were called into a meeting. The sheriff wanted to give us a progress report on ..." All at once the chilling information about Brook struck her with full force and her voice wavered. "They think they know who is responsible for the stagecoach robbery, and for some of the others over the past year and a half."

"Yes, I heard," he said quietly. "I'm sorry. He was your friend, wasn't he?"

"Yes, that's what makes it all the more awful." Addie felt tears rush to her eyes. She tried to blink them back. "I still can hardly believe it." She groped in her pocket for a hand-

257

kerchief, and as she did, she felt the edges of Brook's note still there. She thought of what he'd written and was overcome. She sat down on the nearest chair helpless to stop her tears.

In a moment, Rex was on his knees beside her, his arm went around her. She leaned against his shoulder sobbing. He held her, letting her weep. At length, she realized what she was doing and she drew back, wiping her eyes and nose.

"Oh, my goodness, look at me! I'm sorry. It's just that all of this has been such a shock."

"It's all right, Addie. I understand."

Rex got to his feet and moved back over to the fireplace. He stood there, his elbow resting on the mantelpiece, allowing her to compose herself.

"I'm so embarrassed," she said dabbing at her eyes.

"Don't be, Addie. It's only natural after what you've been through."

She sniffled and wondered what she should do now. She had broken all rules of etiquette and propriety in the presence of the man who had until now distanced himself from her and all that concerned her, the man who had been the cause of some sleepless nights and recent heartache, the man whom she had treated with haughtiness the last time they met. Where was her pride now? Shattered like everything else.

"If you know everything about Brook, I suppose you also know that *I* am suspected of being his accomplice because only *my* jewelry was returned!"

He nodded.

"Then you probably know I disgraced myself behaving like a harridan in public toward my employer." She smiled weakly and corrected, "My *former* employer, I should say. I'm dismissed. Not that I care."

"So, what are you going to do?" Rex asked.

At this question the consequences of her rashness hit again.

"I don't know."

The words, stated baldly, hung there between them. Rex looked at her so steadily Addie felt absorbed by his demanding gaze.

"Are you going to marry Louis Montand?"

"No! Of course not. What makes you think that?"

She saw Rex struggle for a minute, then he said, "May I speak very frankly?"

"Of course."

"Please don't be offended by what I'm going to say."

"Why should I be offended?"

"What I'm about to say may seem inappropriate at this particular time. But . . . the fact is, I love you, Addie. I have loved you since the first moment I saw you. I would have told you that day in the mountains, the day we spent with the Bairds, but I was afraid it was too soon, that I would put you off. I thought we would have time . . . so that you would get to know me, that I could somehow prove my love. . . ." He came toward her, reached for her hands, captured and held them. "I longed to tell you. Even the very next day I wrote you—poured out my heart on paper—how I felt, what I hoped, what I dreamed for *us*."

"I never got it," she stammered.

"I never sent it. I tore it up. I thought it was too sentimental, that you might think it silly. After all, I'm a grown man not a schoolboy. I started out to Silver Springs to see you, planned to tell you—I don't know how many times after the day of the picnic. Then I turned around and came back. I've never felt this way before and I didn't know exactly how to handle all that I was feeling." He smiled ruefully. "I guess I *was* acting like a lovesick boy. Anyway, that next Thursday I got courage up enough to come and I was told—your employer took great pleasure in telling

259

me—that you had driven out with Montand. She implied that you were engaged."

Addie's eyes widened, recalling Mrs. Amberly's ambiguity about Louis's interest in her.

"Then, that same week I found out about Montand's hiring Chinese coolies, importing them into the valley in boxcars. I was furious. So inhumane. I was determined to confront Montand. That very night I rode out to his place, but they told me he was in town, at Silver Springs. Do you remember the night I came to the hotel?"

"Yes, it was awful. I was frightened."

"I know you must have wondered at my behavior. But I was so angry I could not trust myself." Rex paused. "Remember he suggested we talk in the Gentlemen's Lounge? That's when he told me he did not want to have any discussion in front of you—his *fiancée!* He said that since you would be living at his home, he did not want you upset. After your year's contract with Mrs. Amberly was over you two were to be married."

"That's not true!"

"I believed him. What else could I do?" He added scornfully, "A *gentleman's* word. After that, I did not feel I had the right to see you again."

Addie searched his face. Of course, he was telling the truth. It was like Mrs. Amberly to play the spoiler, and it was like Louis to make a possibility into a fact. There was no disputing the honesty in Rex's eyes. Addie's heart melted to see something else in Rex's eyes. He loved her! That too was the truth.

Suddenly it seemed so right that Rex should love her—there was something so beautiful and natural about it—and that she in turn should return that love. All the misunderstanding, the hurt, the sadness she had felt at what she thought lost had now faded. Now she understood.

"I'm sorry. It's all been a mistake."

Rex took both her hands and drew her up out of the chair, close to him, placed her arms around his waist, saying, "Well, it's over. Now you know I love you, Addie. I've loved you from the first day I saw you—remember at the depot the day you came in on the train?"

"Yes." It had been impossible to forget.

"Will you marry me, Addie?"

"*Marry* you?"

"Yes. Will you?"

She searched his eager face, the eyes beseeching hers. Was this *truly* love she felt, or was it gratitude? What Rex was offering was a chance out of all her pressing difficulties. She wanted to be sure, *had* to be sure. Rexford Lyon was a man of honor and integrity with whom there could be no falsehood. Could she be sure of her own heart?

"Addie? You do care for me, too, don't you?"

"Oh, yes, but I don't want you to marry me just to—rescue me."

He threw back his head and laughed. "*Rescue* you? No, you are the one who'll rescue me from loneliness, emptiness, from terrible despair. Oh, Addie, I love you so very much. I want to spend the rest of my life loving you, trying to make you happy—please give me a chance to do that."

Then he leaned his head down, brushed her lips with his and began kissing her slowly with infinite tenderness. Although Addie was considered tall for a woman, she had to raise herself on tip-toe so he could kiss her again. This time the kiss was deep, lingering. Her response had a spontaneity Rex found incredibly sweet.

When his lips finally left hers, she was breathless, slightly dizzy. He steadied her, smiling down at her, happiness transforming his face. He was about to say something when they both heard voices in the hall: Freda's raised in questioning, Elena's softer tones replying. They broke apart, and Rex moved over to the bow window and looked out. Addie automatically smoothed her hair. Her hand moved to her collar, straightening it, as Freda entered the room. "Ah, there you two are! Rex, I saw your horse as I came up from the vineyards. I'm so glad to see you. We must talk, make some decisions about what Addie is to do. I've asked Elena to bring coffee."

Addie's hands nervously made small pleats in her skirt. She hoped Freda would not guess what she had almost walked in upon. Addie glanced over at Rex wondering if he would say anything. But he turned to Freda showing no outward sign of what had just taken place between them.

"I have told Addie she must stay here until she makes further plans. She has left Mrs. Amberly's employ." Freda tactfully omitted the fact that she had been summarily dismissed. "I don't want her to leave the valley just when we have become friends. So we shall try to find some way for her to stay here. At least for a while."

Addie held her breath wondering if now Rex would blurt what *he* wanted Addie to do. If he had been about to, he was delayed by Elena's entrance with a tray on which were coffee service, cups, and a plate of honey and walnut squares. The next few minutes were occupied with Freda filling cups, passing them around, and offering the cakes.

Addie realized Rex was allowing her the privilege of confiding his proposal to Freda or not. But how could she? She had not given him an answer except her kiss. She needed time to search her own heart, her motives.

"For the time, I think Addie should remain with me," Freda said. "Things must be chaotic at Silver Springs with Stanton out of town—*and* under suspicion of being Gentleman Jim. I still can hardly believe it's true."

Addie made no answer. Knowing Brook's note to her was all the evidence anyone would need to prove whether or not he *was* the stagecoach robber. Still she could not turn it over to the authorities. Didn't they already have all the proof they seemed to consider necessary to arrest him?

Rex did not add any suggestion nor offer any solution to Addie's dilemma. She knew he was waiting for her to say something. Finally he set down his cup and stood up. "I must be going, ladies," he said. "I'd be pleased if you would come and dine with me tomorrow evening." He glanced at Addie. "Since Miss Pride has never been to Lyon's Court, Freda, I'd like very much to show it to her."

"What a splendid idea!" Freda said enthusiastically. "Addie could ride over early, and you could show her around, then I could join you both later for dinner."

Addie realized she was in the presence of two strong-minded people used to taking charge—something, that at the moment, *she* seemed unable to do. So it was arranged that the following afternoon Rex would ride over and escort Addie to Lyon's Court.

After Rex had ridden off, Freda turned to Addie. "What a fine man he is. If you only knew what a personal sacrifice it was for him to give up his own dreams and come back to the valley and take over his family's ranch, the vineyards, and winery. I've never known a more honest man than Rexford Lyon."

She gave Addie a knowing look that made her wonder just how much Freda knew or suspected. Had Rex ever confided to his friend the feelings he had just confessed to *her?* The new happiness that filled her tempted Addie to confide in Freda. But something else made her want to keep it to herself a little longer.

Freda said, "I think Fiddle, my own mare, would be perfect for you to ride tomorrow. Do you have something you can wear? No, that's right, your things haven't been sent out yet from the hotel." Freda frowned. "I wonder if that old harpy is responsible for that? Well, never mind you can borrow one of my riding skirts."

Freda bustled away to talk to Elena and see about some household matters, and Addie went back upstairs to the guest room. She needed time alone to think. Rex's explanation of his apparent loss of interest in her—followed by his proposal—both excited and bewildered her.

She felt riled at Louis's arrogant assertion that they were engaged. And Mrs. Amberly's insinuations. Of course what else could she expect of someone who found it easier to lie than tell the truth?

But could she trust her own emotions in this matter? She knew Rex had awakened a physical response that was like a flame within her. But she needed to examine one thing: was this enough? Feelings could alter, passion could fade, was there enough there between them to make for a love that would endure? Was there strength, honesty, compassion and mutual goals to last a lifetime? Or was what Rex offered just the rescue she had hoped for, prayed for?

The next day Addie's trunk had still not arrived from Silver Springs. Incensed, Freda sent Manuel in to town to find out why Addie's request had not been complied with. Addie began to give some credence to Freda's suspicion that Mrs. Amberly was behind the delay. But since this was the evening she and Freda were dining at Lyon's Court, she put aside that troubling thought for the moment. The prospect that she might have to once again confront Mrs. Amberly was not at all appealing.

Rex was coming in the early afternoon for Addie, and Freda would join them later for dinner. Addie knew he wanted to show the vineyards, his land, the house, because he wanted her one day to live there. The thought both thrilled her and frightened her a little. Now that all she had longed for, dreamed of, was within her reach, all sorts of doubts and uncertainties assailed her.

Waiting downstairs for him to arrive, she felt a fluttering

in the pit of her stomach. She went frequently to the front door to look down the road and checked her appearance in the hall mirror several times. She had borrowed one of Freda's riding skirts and a patterned blouse with "leg-o-mutton" sleeves and a Byron collar. She took one of several wide-brimmed felt "cowpuncher's" hats hanging on the hat tree by the door to shield her from the sun.

But the minute Rex came into sight, she felt an unmistakable heart-soaring joy. Maybe *this* really was it!

Rex had brought Gracia, his mother's horse, again for her to ride, and as he helped Addie mount and placed the reins gently into her hands, she felt again the special significance of it. She hardly dared meet his eyes, almost afraid of what she would see there, or perhaps that *he* would read what must be shining in her own.

They rode side by side down the road lined with towering cypress trees and came at last to the tall, scrolled iron gate with its arched sign: LYON'S COURT. They passed through it and up a winding drive under a canopy made by the crossed branches of the oaks. Rounding a bend, Addie had her first glimpse of Rex's ancestral home. It was a castle-like structure with turrets built of gray stone, but the afternoon sun upon it cast its light, tinting it bronze and giving the latticed windows a jewel-like brilliance.

Addie felt Rex's glance as if he were watching her reaction, waiting for her response.

"It's beautiful," she murmured. But it was so much more. It was breathtaking. It looked like a castle that might have been literally moved from a jutting cliff overlooking the Rhine River of Germany, or taken from a lush valley of France's own grape-growing area. Actually, that was probably more accurate. Rex's family, he had told her, were originally French, and after emigrating to England then coming to American they had anglicized their name from Deleon to Lyon.

265

"First, I'll show you the orchards and vineyards, the aging cellars—give you a tour of the entire place, explain the whole process so you can get some idea of what it is all about. Then we'll come back here—sit on the terrace, watch the sunset." He paused. "Would you like that?"

"Yes, very much."

Addie took in everything. She listened carefully to everything Rex explained and pointed out to her. She wanted to see it through his eyes, to understand his family's heritage, to appreciate its prestige. Lyon's Court was one of the most highly regarded vineyards in the valley, producing the finest wine grapes.

She admired the fact that although it had not been his desire to do so, Rex had honorably taken up the standard from his fallen brother. He was committed to carrying on the tradition his ancestors began. Implied was the hope that she would share it with him, unspoken was the feeling that unless she did, it would be an almost unbearable burden.

As the afternoon shadows lengthened, they rode back to the house. In front of the house Rex dismounted, came around, and lifted Addie down, his hands circling her waist lingering for a moment. As if summoned by some silent cue, a smiling stable boy appeared and, catching the reins of both horses Rex tossed to him, took their horses to the barn.

"Shall we go inside?" Rex asked, holding out his hand to Addie. She gave hers to him and they went up the shallow stone steps together.

As they approached the massive oak door Addie halted to study the stone coat of arms above it. A shield divided into four sections, on two of which were sculptured lunging lions, on the other two clusters of grapes, and on the curved bar across the top were the French words which she could translate to read, "ABOVE ALL HONOR, FAMILY, TRUTH."

"Quite a lot to live up to," Rex remarked ruefully.

"Somehow, I feel you do," she answered quietly.

"Thank you. I try."

For a breathless moment they stood looking into each other's eyes. It only lasted a few seconds, but it seemed to say more than words possibly could.

Then Rex opened the door with its brass lion's head knocker, pushed it back, and turned to Addie with a hint of mischief in his smile.

"I would like to carry you over the threshold. But perhaps I am too optimistic? Am I? Have you thought of what I asked you yesterday?"

"Of course, I've thought of little else," she answered truthfully. "But there is much to be considered, discussed before any such—"

"Don't tell me you want a contract?"

"No contracts! I've had my fill of contracts," she held up both hands in horror.

He pushed the door open wider so she could pass through. "Then I must use my best persuasive abilities. 'Come, let us reason together,'" he said, gesturing her to enter.

"Are you trying to impress me by quoting Scripture?"

"Whatever it takes," he smiled.

He led her through the high-ceilinged foyer, through the library, and out onto the terrace that overlooked the acres of vineyards. It was still warm and the air was soft.

"It's so warm and the evening promises to be mild, I thought we could dine out here."

On the terrace a table had been set with an embroidered cloth, a bowl of flowers, candles in glass hurricane lamps, and handsome silver. Crystal goblets gleamed in the rays of the slanting sun. A bottle of wine was chilling in a chased silver bucket.

"Yes, that would be lovely." Addie said moving over to the balustrade and looking out at the magnificent view.

The sun was beginning to set; orange, purple, pink ribbons streaked the clouds hovering above the hills.

Watching her, Rex thought how this light gave Addie's face a special radiance; a kind of golden glow touched her skin and the dark cloud of her hair. His throat constricted. Not only was the woman he loved beautiful, she had wit, courage, and honesty. Did he dare hope?

His hands shook a little as he lifted the chilled bottle from its nest of ice. "Let's have a glass of Lyon's Court's best?" He filled two glasses holding a sparkling rose wine. He raised his glass first, then touching the rim of hers, they each took a sip. "To us!"

His eyes caressed her. "I love you, Addie," he said quietly. "Please say you've decided to marry me."

"Oh, if it were only that simple," she sighed, shaking her head.

"It *can* be. All you have to do is say yes."

He set down his glass and came over to her. She allowed herself to be drawn into his arms. She leaned against him, a feeling of warmth, comfort, and safety swept over her. She knew if she surrendered to it, she would no longer be able to think rationally. Instead she would be lost, drowned in this new, exquisite ecstasy.

"No, Rex, wait, we mustn't." Trying to still her seesawing heart, she pushed him gently away.

"Oh, Addie, why do you keep denying what we both know and feel?" he demanded. "Something happened to me the moment I saw you—and it happened to you too, I know. Why won't you admit what we both sensed from the very beginning?"

"Because—because, it doesn't make sense. It isn't *real* and I don't think you make a decision as important as marriage on feelings."

"Don't be afraid of feelings, Addie; they are more *real* than anything else. I know I love you. . . ."

He moved to take her in his arms again, and this time she did not resist.

Later that night, back at Freda's, Addie found sleep out of the question. Why, *why* was it so hard for her to give Rex the answer he wanted so much?

Did she think she didn't deserve what he was offering? Was it too much like an escape? Was it because she knew there was unfinished business for her to settle? Things she must do herself? Was it *pride* holding her back from accepting his protection, the security of his love, the prestige of his name?

She had always been told pride was her "besetting sin," and she had been warned that it would always cause her the most grief, the most trouble, get her into the worst situations.

Suddenly she saw the truth about herself. Addie realized she had exhibited some of the worst, most despicable traits of pride in her relation to Mrs. Amberly. There was no question that she had looked down on her, disdained her, considered herself superior. The fact that these were under the surface, and no one else knew about them, was no excuse. Until now, she had never admitted it even to herself.

What would Rex think if *he* could look into her heart and see what lay hidden there? She shuddered to think. Of all character qualities, he valued honesty most. Honesty in himself and others.

She remembered when she had tried to search the Scriptures for guidance and come across David's anguished cry in Psalms: "Search me, O God, and know my heart. Try me and know my anxieties and if there is any wickedness in me, lead me in the way I should go." But it was another verse that had seemed to speak more directly to her: "The

269

heart is deceitful above all things and desperately wicked: Who can know it?"

It became very clear to Addie that God was answering her through David's own plea. He had shown her "the wickedness" within. He was leading her "in the way" she should go. If she were ever to know peace or happiness with Rex, be able to accept what he was offering as God's will for her future, there was something she had to do.

Chapter 18

*T*he following morning Addie awakened to a sensation of purpose. She could see from the bedroom window a day of sunlight and blue sky, fields golden with mustard, the vines already heavy with grapes. Spring had come to the valley at last, just as happiness had come to her after the long winter.

Freda was already up and gone when Addie came downstairs. Elena told her the señora had taken the small buggy to attend to some business at another ranch but had left word that if Addie wanted to go anywhere, Rico would saddle Fiddle for her.

Addie wrote a short note to Freda, telling her where she was going and that she should be back by noon. She dressed quickly, and when Rico brought Freda's gentle mare around the front of the house, Addie mounted and started down the lane onto the road.

All the way into town Addie had to keep bolstering her resolve. Everything in her rebelled against what she knew she had been directed to do. She could not leave the conflict with Mrs. Amberly unresolved.

Running away had not solved anything. It might even have galvanized peoples' opinions, strengthened the suspicions planted against her. She knew Rex was more than willing to fight her battles for her, shield her from gossip and slander, provide her the security of his name, prestige, and position in the community. But that would be cowardly. It would still leave things unsettled. To salvage her pride she must do this herself.

It seemed a contradiction that to save her pride she had to humble herself this way. Addie argued with her conscience. Didn't she have the right to hold on to her righteous anger? Mrs. Amberly had treated her dreadfully. Wasn't Addie justified to exact her "pound of flesh" from her? She had not been paid her last month's salary—wasn't she due that? She wasn't asking "a red cent" more.

It was not a matter of money. It was a matter of pride. In all sorts of ways during the time Addie had worked for her, Mrs. Amberly had consisténtly stepped upon Addie's pride. It was her reputation, tarnished by Mrs. Amberly's accusations, that Addie wanted to restore.

Pride in who you were was only part of it. Louis had probably been right about one thing. Perhaps Mrs. Amberly's tirade would soon be forgotten, perhaps nobody cared. What *was* important were the other things—character, integrity, tolerance—that gave a person worth. Addie had clung to her pride, in her family name, her background, what it stood for throughout it all.

What had been lacking in her attitude toward her employer were compassion, understanding—forgiveness. Mrs. Amberly couldn't help *who* she was. How and why she had become that way made no difference. All she had was money. In everything else that really counted, she was a pauper.

Addie knew now that while she had shown her employer courtesy in public, in private she had held her in contempt. Her opinion of her employer had been unkind, critical, and unforgiving. The unforgiveness rooted itself in her heart and was festering there. It was spoiling her newfound happiness. Addie knew it had to be taken care of. How could she expect God to bless her new life when there were things of which she was ashamed in her old one?

Addie thought of her father. In his law practice he had often run into dishonesty, ingratitude, betrayal—clients who revoked sworn statements, witnesses who promised to testify then disappeared. Although he had met all the inconsistencies of humankind, Addied never saw him angry or vindictive or condemning. She had often heard him speak tolerantly about the very people who had let him down. One of his favorite sayings had been, "He who cannot forgive breaks the bridge over which he may one day need to pass himself."

Closer to town Addie reminded herself of the passage she had read this morning before she left Freda's. To be truthful, she had picked up her Bible as a matter of habit. However, when she turned to Matthew and read verse 24 in chapter 5: "Be reconciled with your adversary quickly," it seemed prophetic.

Ironically, now that she had the guidance she had prayed for, she did not want to follow it. In the time it had taken her to ride into town, the focus of her coming had shifted. At the gates of Silver Springs, she was strongly inclined to turn the horse around, but there was no turning back now. It had become a matter of pride to live up to her own highest ideal.

The grounds looked deserted. No guests strolled around the arboretum, going to and from the bathhouses. There were no gardeners about, clipping hedges or raking; no sign of the usual activity. A strange pall hung over the place. Where was everybody? Addie hitched Fiddle to the fence in front of the main building, then went determinedly up the steps. As she entered the lobby the clerk at the reception desk looked up.

"Miss Pride!" The desk clerk recognized her immediately.

273

Although many of the hotel's women guests were possibly more beautiful, more fashionably dressed, he had always thought Adelaide Pride far more attractive and interesting looking. She had a kind of understated elegance about her.

"It's good to see you, Miss Pride!"

"Good morning, Michael," Addie replied, hoping her nervousness did not show. "I've come to get my trunk and other belongings. Could I have one of the boys help me load them?"

His face flushed and he looked embarrassed.

"I'm sorry, Miss Pride. There's no one left to help. You see, with Mr. Stanton gone—well, they weren't paid and . . ." He lifted his shoulders. "I'm only staying on because the sheriff—well, as you can see," he gestured to the empty lobby, "most of the guests have left too, or are leaving. . . ." He shook his head. "What can I say?"

"Is Mrs. Amberly still here?"

"Yes, but—" his face got redder "—about your things, Miss Pride. We got your note, and we would have sent out your trunk, but Mrs. Amberly locked her cottage and said not one thing could be taken out because . . ." He stopped in an agony of embarrassment.

"I see." Addie tried to absorb this bit of unforeseen information. After a moment she asked, "Where is Mrs. Amberly now?"

The clerk leaned forward and lowered his voice. "I believe she's in the card room with some of the other ladies."

"Thank you. I'll attend to it myself then."

Addie unconsciously squared her shoulders. There was no alternative. She would have to confront Mrs. Amberly in public, something she dreaded to do. For a moment, she stood perfectly still smoothing each finger of her gloves, gathering her courage, knowing Michael was watching her curiously. Then she took a deep breath and started across the lobby toward the card room.

Harriet Brunell saw her first. Seated at the card table facing the lobby, she looked up from her cards just as Addie stepped into the archway. Her mouth made a silent O, and she darted a quick glance at Mrs. Amberly, whose back was to the door.

A kind of hush fell on the room as others became aware of Addie standing in the doorway. Addie knew she must have been the target of much gossip, speculation. The sudden quiet, followed by a collective murmur rippling through the room, the squeak of chairs as heads turned for a better look—all this must have alerted Mrs. Amberly. Slowly she shifted her chair, stiffly turned, and saw Addie.

As Addie approached she felt every eye upon her. All card playing stopped. Every ear strained so as not to miss a single word of the expected confrontation.

Mrs. Amberly's face twisted in a sneer. "So you've come crawling back?"

"Not at all, Mrs. Amberly. I came to collect my things. But I understand you have not allowed anyone to get them from my room and send them to me."

"Certainly not!" retorted Mrs. Amberly, giving her head a little toss. She glanced around the table to be sure she had the attention of the avid spectators, then said loudly, "Not until I'd personally inspected them, made *sure* you were not taking anything that did not belong to you!"

Addie felt a quiver of rage at this insult. She willed herself not to give in to it. With supreme effort she ignored the implication and spoke evenly. "Now that you have assured yourself of that, may I have the keys to the cottage so that I can have my trunk and other belongings removed?" Addie held out her gloved hand palm up.

Mrs. Amberly looked both startled and uncertain. Perhaps she had expected to create another scene, bait Addie

275

into an angry denial or rebuttal. Addie's composure seemed to rattle her.

While Addie stood there waiting, Mrs. Amberly pulled her beaded, fringed handbag from beside her on the chair and fumbled in it until she pulled out the ring of keys. She clutched them as if still not quite ready to hand them over, as if she were trying to think of something more to say.

"Thank you, Mrs. Amberly," Addie prompted.

Mrs. Amberly fidgeted. "So, you didn't come to get your job back—"

"No, Mrs. Amberly. We both know that would be impossible." Her hand was still outstretched. Finally Mrs. Amberly detached one of the keys and grudgingly dropped it into Addie's cupped hand.

Her fingers closed around the key clutching it so tightly its edges bit into her gloved palms. She remained standing there, knowing she still had to say what she had come to say. As she looked at the woman's smirking face, the hate-filled eyes, pride gripped Addie's throat as if to choke off the words. This woman did not deserve her humbling herself. Why should she give her such satisfaction?

But something else, something stronger than pride hardened in Addie, giving her the strength to finish it once and for all. She forced the words out over her aching throat, her dry mouth.

"Just one thing more, Mrs. Amberly, I want to tell you that . . ." she swallowed, ". . . that, I forgive you for the things you said about me, the way you treated me."

Mrs. Amberly's face collapsed into a doughy mass. Then it reassembled itself into a reddish-purple mask of indignation. "*What* did you say? *You* forgive *me? Forgive?*"

Addie realized she would have to say the rest quickly and leave fast before Mrs. Amberly had an apoplectic fit.

"Yes, Mrs. Amberly. I do." Her voice was steady. "I also

276

ask you to forgive me for failing to be the kind of companion you thought I'd be. That's all."

With that Addie spun around and, head held high, walked out of the card room. As she came through the card room into the lobby she saw the desk clerk hunched outside the door. He'd been eavesdropping. He clapped his hands silently in a gesture of congratulations, winked. Addie simply held up the key triumphantly, pointed out the door in the direction of the cottage, and they both marched out of the hotel together.

Within minutes her trunk was loaded onto a cart and trundled over to the main building. The desk clerk told her he would put it on the hotel's wagon and deliver it to the Wegner ranch that afternoon.

Addie thanked him, remounted Fiddle, and was on her way. Just outside the gate she began to laugh. The fantastic scene with Mrs. Amberly replayed itself in her mind as though she had watched it on a stage. Riding through town she tried to suppress the laughter—not too successfully—that kept bubbling up inside. On the road heading out to the countryside, her laughter started all over. Tears streamed down her cheeks, and she could not stop laughing. Addie had always had a sense of the ludicrous, often finding things funny when humor was not necessarily appropriate. But there were so many things in this experience that were both heartening and amusing.

At least she had done what she set out to do and had done it without malice. What she most *prided* herself on—in the best sense of that word—was that although she certainly had provocation to wither Mrs. Amberly with sarcasm, to use the most blistering words to validate herself, she had resisted that temptation. *That* was something of which she could legitimately be proud.

Again she felt the laughter come, and she let herself laugh. She was truly *free* now, no longer bound by resentment, animosity, or revenge. Giving forgiveness had a wonderful bonus to it—freedom!

Addie clicked Fiddle's reins and eased her into a canter. She couldn't wait to share it all with Freda. And of course with Rex.

She was about a quarter mile from the Wegner ranch when she saw a buggy drawn by a high-stepping horse coming down the road from the other direction. She soon recognized it as Louis's smart phaeton. In it were Louis and Estelle. At the same time he saw her but did not recognize her until they were almost alongside. Then he shouted, "Whoa!" and pulled to a stop.

Addie felt an urge to ride by without speaking, then thought better of it. She reined Fiddle to a walk then halted.

Louis's expression was a mixture of irritation and worry. "Addie! Where have you been? No one at Silver Springs knew and—"

Addie regarded him coolly, she saw Estelle's face tighten anxiously.

"Where have you been?" he repeated. "I've been frantic." Then, "Where are you going?"

"That no longer need concern you, Louis." Addie answered then picked up her reins again.

"Addie!" Louis protested, "We must talk."

"There is nothing for us to talk about, Louis. Once there might have been a chance that we could have found something together. But you—well, let's say we both failed to be what the other one needed or wanted. I forgive you for that as I hope you'll forgive me."

Louis's face underwent a rapid series of changes. Shock, disbelief. Regret? Addie did not pause to see what came next. She gave Fiddle a nudge with her heels, flicked the reins, and started off.

"No! Addie, wait!" Louis called after her.

"Let her go, Louis, she isn't worth—" Estelle cut it.

"Oh, be quiet, Estelle, will you? Just for once, be quiet," Addie heard Louis say curtly.

Their raised arguing voices followed her as she cantered down the road. She felt herself smiling, then laughing out loud. The wind blew her hat back, tore at the ribbon holding her hair, and she let it stream down behind her like the horse's mane as they raced away. Addie had never felt so free in her life.

At last she turned into the road leading up to Freda's house. At the turn of the lane she saw a tall, familiar figure standing at the bottom of the steps, talking with Freda on the porch. It was Rex! Addie's heart lifted joyously.

As she trotted up, he came toward her, put his hand on Fiddle's neck. "Is everything all right? Did you have any trouble getting your things? Why didn't you tell me what you planned to do? I would have been more than glad to go in, get them for you—"

"Thank you, I know you would have, but this was something I had to do myself."

In that brief exchange, Addie's heart knew what Rex was really saying was that his strength, his protection, his love, and his life were hers for the asking.

Rex took hold of Fiddle's reins and helped Addie down out of her saddle. Standing in front of him, she put her hands on his shoulders and looked up into the face regarding her with tender concern. She reached up and touched his cheek with the back of her hand and whispered, "Yes, Rex. The answer is yes."

"Oh, Addie, Addie," he murmured, drawing her into his arms. She felt his body tremble as he held her close.

Nothing more was said, nothing else was necessary. In that moment of surrender Addie knew there would be time later to explore the depths of their passion, to fulfill each other's dreams. There would be a whole lifetime together.

Epilogue
HEART'S HARVEST

*N*apa Valley shimmered in the golden haze of early autumn as Adelaide rode her tawny mare from Calistoga on a late September afternoon. On either side of the eucalyptus-lined road stretched vineyards harvested of their bounty, but not yet pruned nor stripped of their leaves. Their glossy leaves now turned rich colors of cabernet, claret, peridot, and amethyst glistened like stained glass in the sunshine.

Addie, graceful and elegant in her russet velvet riding habit, was deep in thought. She was returning from the post office after sending the monthly check to her aunt and uncle. Its amount was greatly augmented by Rex's generosity, and they would never want for anything again. There among her mail she had found a much-traveled postcard bearing a South American postmark. Although unsigned, in a handwriting she recognized was an enigmatic scribble.

> Riddle of destiny, who can show?
> What thy short visit meant or know
> What thy errand here below?

Brook, Addie sighed. Who else could have written her such an obscure verse. Much had happened since his mysterious disappearance. Gentleman Jim had never been caught or brought to justice. In time, the stagecoach robberies had stopped, but no trace of the members of the gang or clues to what became of the "loot" had ever turned up. Brook seemed to have simply vanished. Now this. Addie tried to remember the good things about him and hoped he had mended his ways and was not just pursuing some other doomed enterprise.

Only a few weeks after the hold-up in which the identity of Gentleman Jim was alleged to be Brook Stanton, Silver Springs, the main building, and some of the cottages, were ravaged by a terrible fire that swept so rapidly through the resort that little could be saved. There was talk of arson but nothing could be proved. It stood there as a blackened reminder of all Brook's amibition, his extravagant dreams, and in the end, their destruction, all in ashes.

Addie's life, too, had changed drastically since then. Emily's inscription in the journal she had given her had proved prophetic. Her journey to California had, indeed, ended in "lovers meeting." She and Rex were married in June, the time of year when valley vintners could take their ease before the hectic harvest season began in August. Freda insisted on giving their wedding in her garden. It was in full bloom and the ceremony was a beautiful affair. At least, so Addie had been told. To be truthful, Addie was so dazed with happiness, even now she found it hard to remember the details of that day. Afterwards, she and Rex left by steamer for a honeymoon in San Francisco, and returned to make their home at Lyon's Court.

The last few months had been so busy, Addie hardly saw her new husband as Rex was involved in every aspect of the grape harvesting: overseeing the workers so that the grapes were picked at their peak, then the packing and shipping of Lyon's Court grapes to markets and restaurants throughout California; the selection of grapes that would be kept for their own crushing, which would then be stored in oaken casks in cooling caves for fermenting and later bottled into wine under their prestigious estate label.

It was with a special smile that Rex showed Addie the label he had designed for a new variety they were experimenting to produce to be known as Lyon's Pride.

Addie knew she had been blessed far beyond her expectations in her husband. The love and devotion she had seen in her family and friends, had envied and longed for herself, was now hers. Surely her "cup runneth over."

At the end of the summer, the Montands had held a huge celebration, the Blessing of the Grapes festival, followed by a lavish outdoor party on the grounds of Chateau Montand. Father Bernard had officiated at the ceremony, and guests from San Francisco and as far away as San Diego came for the gala event. Of course, Addie and Rex had not been invited.

There were recent rumors that the Montands were leaving the valley, that their property was secretly for sale. Since Louis had imported the Chinese workers, he was resented and not very well liked by the "old-timers." Although other vintners accepted his hospitality, attended his parties, he was never really considered "one of them."

Addie turned her horse into the driveway leading up to Lyon's Court. As always at the first glimpse of the magnificent stone house at the top, she experienced a thrill. She still found it hard to believe that this was now her home, hers and Rex's and—one day—their children's.

Reaching the crest of the hill, Addie halted, turned in her saddle to look out over the vineyards.

How beautiful this valley was. In its way, every bit as lovely as the Virginia countryside. Her heart filled with contentment, happiness. Her lifetime longing for enduring love had come to her at last.

They say home is where the heart is. Napa Valley was now her home, Addie realized with love and pride. This was where her heart was.